Acclaim for *Ladies' Night*

"Dee Zee has done a magnificent job by sharing the tales of a bachelor's life—as an erotic dancer and playa. The fascinating story takes readers on an exciting journey that feels surreal that it places you directly into his fictional world of madness.... He takes it where no other author dares to go."

--**Halle B.**, CA

"Dee Zee is a clever storyteller, with impressive ability to paint a colorful scene with words, no matter how much of a perv he might be."

--**Stacy P.**, Co

"Each page of Ladies' Night will win you over."

--**Cathy S.**, NJ

"Ladies' Night would resonate well with both men and women."

--**Jasmine G.**, TX

"This book is most definitely gonna be the next blockbuster masterpiece ... and you can bet your dirty draws on it, too. I'm gonna have it on DVD before it hits the movie theaters. So holla at a nigga!"

--**Carlton P. (DaShawn's cousin)**, FL

"I don't like the fact that I am referred to as the neighborhood hoe and quite frankly I do not want you to use my name in any way in this book of yours.... So by all means, I would appreciate it [if you] can replace my name with another name."

--**Amanda M** (Dee Zee's former girlfriend), FL

"Dee Zee has what it takes to be a creative writer.... Ladies' Night grabs you quickly and becomes impossible to put down."

--**Marilyn W.**, GA

"Ladies' Night is one helluva book.... I found it in the trash can."

--**Ricky B. (the neighborhood crack-head)**, FL

"This is a must read book."

--**Jennifer R.**, NY

Advanced Acclaim for *Casanova*

"Dee Zee's novel has the right ingredients in it to ensure his readers to embrace the humanity of the characters in Casanova. His characters love, cry, laugh, and experience the same turmoil of our daily lives. I loved it."

--**Diana R.**, CA

"Casanova is absolutely tantalizing and spellbinding novel…. Dee Zee has done an excellent job. I give it two thumbs up."

--**Nicki M.**, NY

"Stunning … panty-wetting … a beautiful read."

--**Isabell D.**, FL

"Dee Zee has delivered a hit."

--**Larry B.**, OK

"A must-read book for emotion, drama, and sex."

--**Monica S.**, WA

"Casanova is a compelling page-turner, once you start reading it, you can't put it down…. So grab your butter popcorn and a dildo."

--**Wanda S.**, TX

"One word: Boredom…. I was not impressed. Not at all."

--**Stephen C.**, NY

"There is no way you can put Casanova down once you have started."

--**Shirley B.**, FL

"Wow! It was mind-blowing. I was literally swept away. Dee Zee knows how to entertain hot cougars, like myself…. I want him."

--**Betty W.**, CA

"Bullshit! That's how I would rate this book, with a middle finger pointing directly at him."

--**Betty B.** (Dee Zee's former mother-in-law), FL

Ladies' Night

Decorous' Books, Florida

Published by Decorous' Books

A division of Decorous Circle, Inc.
Naples, Florida

Ladies' Night is a work of fiction. The names, characters, places, and incidents are either the product of the author's imagination, and any resemblance to actual person, living or dead, business establishments, events, or locales is entirely coincidental.

No part of this publication may be reproduced or transmitted in any form or by any mean, electronic or mechanical, including photocopy, recording or any other information storage and retrieval system, without prior permission in writing from the publisher.

The Publisher does not have any control over or does not assume any responsibility for the author's or third-parties' Website or their content.

First Edition
ISBN-13: 978-0-692-59228-1
ISBN-10: 0692592288

For information regarding special discount for bulk purchases, please contact Decorous Circle Special Sales Department online at: **www.decorous-circle.com**

For Mom

Decorous' Books present

Ladies' Night

Attention all readers!

Please see provided casting info for Ladies' Night on page 532, if you are inspired to become an up and coming actor, actress, or vocalist.

Dee Zee

You could play any role in this fictional work, and the people from Decorous' films and production knew that. That's why they chose you and sent their best director for this project.

You had your makeup and costume on, standing behind the bar.

The other cast were all set and ready to go as well.

The director looked at you, smiled, and then took her seat. Then she requested, "Music, please!"

The deejay threw on the remake of "Ladies' Night" by Lil' Kim.

After a brief moment, the director looked at the knuckle-head in front of you and told him, "You need to get serious and stop playing over there."

"I'm sorry," he said, then cut back at you.

Then the director shouted:

"Lights!"

"Cameras!"

"Action!"

"I don't give a fuck what y'all say about that ugly bitch over there!" Andrew shouted so Kevin and I could hear him over the loud music inside the club. "Because that hoe got some good pussy!"

"For real?" I kept my eyes on Jamie—some Dominican chick from up north who Andrew was talking about—while preparing one of my customers a mixed drink.

"Hell, yeah!" he replied, cutting his eyes back to me. "And her mouth feels even better!"

"Word?!" Kevin stopped drinking his cognac.

"Hell, yeah!" Andrew smiled.

"Here you go!" I passed my customer his drink. "Your Nasty Bitch on the Beach."

He gave me a ten dollar bill and walked away.

I twisted back to my homeboys, Andrew and Kevin, each of whom were enjoying themselves at the club tonight. But they weren't actually a bartender like me though. So let me put it in perspective: They were both male strippers.

"And just to let you know something," I wanted to tell Andrew how I felt about that oral sex mess, "that shit sounds gay as hell. Because nothing could ever feel better than a piece of pussy!"

"So you say!" Kevin cut in, jokingly. "Because I see you never got your dick sucked by Andrew's mom before?"

Andrew punched him in the chest. "I told you about playing that momma shit with me already, my nigga!"

"The truth hurts, huh?" Kevin laughed at him, rubbing his chest.

Andrew then threw him in a headlock.

"Alright! Alright!" Kevin broke free, laughing. "You got that. But the next time when your mom wanna sneak over to the crib and wanna suck a nigga up again, I'm just gonna hit her off for the ass instead—"

Andrew went for his neck again, playing.

"I want the Long and ... Strong."

I turned toward the intoxicated voice.

It was a drunk middle-aged woman standing beside Kevin. She looked to be in her late-forties. Maybe early fifties. I wasn't sure. She had a slender build with a coffee brown skin complexion. She wasn't all that attractive to me, but she was still doable. She leaned in close.

"I'm sorry." She had the audacity to smile after belching in my face.

"That's all right." I lied to her. "What's that you wanted again?"

"I would like to have one Long and—" she started, then twisted toward Kevin because he had palmed her ass. "A Long and Strong," she said to Kevin instead. Then she stuck her index finder inside her mouth, slowly bobbing her head over it while giving him the indication that she could work wonders on something else.

"That's what I'm talking about." Kevin stretched a smile across his face, grabbing hold of his dick through his pants. "I have your Long and Strong right here. Why don't you put your mouth down here and try to take a sip of it."

"Oh, really?" She rested her hand directly on top of his. "I just gotta see about—"

I cut in: "Ma'am, here you go! Your drink, Long and Strong. Ten dollars, please."

She gave me a twenty dollar bill and said, "Keep the change, cutie", before she staggered away with her drink in her hand.

We all laughed.

"I have your Long and Strong right here," I mocked Kevin.

Andrew played along, too: He smiled with one of those mischievous, perverted smiles and leaned toward Kevin's shoulder and said, "Oh, really, Big Boy." Then he reached down and squeezed Kevin's manhood.

Kevin slapped Andrew's hand away. "What's your fucking problem?! You need to chill out with that shit. You gay-ass nigga!"

Andrew laughed it off and took two snapping bites right before his face, mimicking that drunk lady's action.

"Yo, that shit ain't even funny, my nigga!" Kevin tried to joke between a fake chuckles yet being serious. "Because that shit was gay as fuck! And when you do shit like that, it only makes me think—" He froze and glanced over at me, then to him again. "Better yet," he went on to say to Andrew, "that shit only make us think that your punk-ass is a muthafucking fag for real, my nigga! So you needa stop playing like that, you fucking faggot!"

I laughed at both of them. "I don't know how y'all could even be doing this shit!"

Kevin took his attention off of Andrew and looked at me. "This shit ain't anything to it," he said as if he knew exactly what I was talking about. Then he looked into the thick crowd of people and added, "All you have to do is give these bitches what they want…. Tease them a bit and get paid for it." He gave Andrew a high five, then twisted back to me. "So don't hate the game because your hoe doesn't allow you to get some extra money on the side."

"So you think," I began to admit, "but I will never do this shit!"

"Never say never, my nigga," Andrew cut in, wanting to throw his two cents in, "because that's the same shit I used to say before I started dancing."

"DASHAWN!"

I twisted to the right to see who had shouted my name. And it was none other than my girlfriend, Jessica, fighting her way through the crowd, walking toward me. When she arrived at my bartending post, I managed to say, "Hey, sweetie—" before she cut me off.

"We needa talk!"

"What's the matter? Is everything all right?"

She kept silent for a few seconds before she stumbled with, "Yeah…. No! I mean—"

"Oh, hi, Jessica," Kevin intervened, trying to be sarcastic about it. "I didn't even see you standing there."

She looked at him as if he was an idiot, then turned back to me. "Now, DaShawn! We need to talk!" She shot back at Kevin, then to her left side at Andrew, and then back at me. "In private!"

Don't get it twisted: Jessica used to be good friends with Kevin and Andrew, but it wasn't until recently—no more than about three weeks earlier, if I remember correctly—that she started to feel different about their friendship. Now she considered them both to be wanna-be gigolos; especially Andrew whom she hated more for some reason. But from what she had told me the week before, she regarded him as a typical lowlife bastard (in her own words), without wanting to go any further into it. I could only respect her wishes.

Kevin wasn't upset, but I could see that he was bothered by Jessica's attitude when he told me he would catch up with me "later on" —based on how he described her— "when it's gone."

"Your mother!" Jessica snapped at him. "You punk bitch!"

He laughed at her.

I stepped in: "Jessica! Are you all right?"

She turned to me; Kevin and Andrew walked away.

Then I went on to tell Jessica, "Just give me a minute until another bartender can take over my cash register."

"Oh, so you can't stop what you're doing to hear what the fuck I have to tell you?!"

I kept quiet: I refused to answer that.

And just when she started going off on me now, two females walked up to the bar counter and asked for, "Two Comfortable Screws please!"

Perfect timing.

"Jessica, give me a second." I stepped aside to prepare those females drinks.

Needless to say, Jessica didn't like that at all. As soon as I handed those females their drinks, Jessica started tripping again, saying something like, "I'm fucking tired of this ..." and the rest of her words were carried away with the loud music inside the club.

"What'd you say?!"

"I said that I'm fucking pregnant!" she shouted, then stared at me, probably trying to read the expression off my face. But there was nothing there. Not a thing. Why? Because I was trying to read the expression off her face too, wondering whether she was playing a trick on me or not. But from the look of it, she wasn't. She seemed dead serious. And that was when it felt like my stepfather had punched me in the chest—one of the last things I remembered about that sucker before he walked out on my mom—caving it straight in.

Fatherhood, I thought. That was something I didn't anticipate on.

"What the hell are you talking about?" I asked. "How you got pregnant? I thought you said you were on the pills?!"

There was a pause.

I was kind of confused here. I even tried to think it out thoroughly, but nothing logically popped up in my mind. I took a deep breath. Think. But still, there was nothing. I finally gave up after a few more seconds and said something foolish.

"How the fuck this happened?"

She shot me with a wry look, then mocked me: "How the fuck I got pregnant? Are you that fucking stupid? I'm pregnant by you, since you're the only muthafucker who's sticking his dick inside of me!"

I'm like, whoa, if she put it like that. "What are you gonna do?" I shot her a quick recommendation. "Get rid of it, right?"

"What the hell do you mean by what I'm gonna do about it?" she asked. Then, since I kept quiet, she went on to add, "Well, I know one thing for sure ..."

I was all ears.

"I can't get myself pregnant, which only means that you played a part in this! So don't you mean, what are we gonna do about this?"

"But, you sure that I'm the father, right?"

In a split second I realized that I had just asked her. I can honestly say that one really slipped out of my mouth by accident. It did. I felt like an idiot. I knew I messed up this time when I saw one of her eyebrows making a frustrated arch, while she was looking dead at me. It was sort of like that stare in which that WWE wrestler, The Rock, would give to his opponent when someone tried him in the ring. And I just wondered what kept her from reaching over the bar counter and slapping me across the face.

"I'm sorry." I felt like those were the right words to say to her before she did something stupid, since she glanced at that empty Heineken bottle in front of us. "I swear, I didn't mean that."

She rolled her eyes at me and walked away, cutting and weaving through the crowd while heading toward the exit.

"JESSICA!" I yelled out, knowing that it would be impossible for her to hear me over the loud music inside the club. So I chased after her instead, leaving my cash register unattended.

Damn!

She exited the club and disappeared into the heavy crowd outside in the parking lot. I tried to spot her but she was nowhere in sight. I gave up after a while and went back inside the nightclub to finish up my work.

At the end of my shift I couldn't stop thinking about the event that had transpired with Jessica. The whole thing. I felt discombobulated. Trapped. I shared my thoughts with Kevin and Andrew, looking for some sort of reasonable feedback, as to what I should do about Jessica's situation.

You're not going to believe this, though: Kevin didn't show any kind of concern. I wasn't surprised by that; neither should you. He seemed to be pleased in a way to hear that Jessica had run out of the nightclub with her feelings hurt. Because according to him—get this—we could hang out like we used to before she came into the picture.

Andrew on the other hand saw things from another angle. He seemed a bit concerned about Jessica, I guess, due to the nature of the relationship I had with her in which he asked me, "If you don't mind, you should let me talk to her for you."

"Nah, that's all right."

After all was said and done, Kevin and Andrew tried to cheer me up by inviting me to hang out with them over some nymphomaniac's house who they had met in the club earlier. But I declined their offer. I had Jessica on my mind.

When I got home, I made several attempts to contact Jessica by phone, but she didn't answer. The answering machine kept picking up on me. I left a few messages on it, hoping that she would call me back. But she never did.

Now days had gone by, and still there wasn't a response from her. I had no other choice but give her some space to cool down a bit. Hopefully, in time, she'll come back to her senses, I thought. But in the meantime, I decided to visit Aunt Enid for some advice.

When I arrived at her home, I was feeling really confused. But my confusion faded away when I saw about eight kids—maybe nine of them—running through the house playing hide-and-seek, just how I used to play when I was about their age. I enjoyed the quick flashback I caught before I entered into the living room and saw Aunt Enid sitting on the couch, near the window, bottle-feeding a young infant.

Before I go any further with this, let me give you the 4-1-1 on my auntie first. You see, Auntie Enid operated a day care center from her home. Having her whole life surrounded by people who looked up to her as their own mother, she was beloved in the neighborhood. In a way, I thought she was as good as Mother Teresa, because my auntie looked out for so many needy people and gave to those who needed her help; and never did a hungry person come to her home for food and was sent away with an empty stomach. Although she was childless, she raised a lot of children as if they were her very own; that's including myself as well. And I loved her for that. I gave her a kiss. "How's everything?"

"Just fine." She switched the little infant from one arm to the other. "And yourself?"

"Yeah, I'm doing all right."

"And Carlton and James?"

"Yeah," I hesitated a bit. "They're doing all right too."

"Is there something on your mind?" She seemed a bit worried. "I can see something is bothering you. What's the matter?"

I slowly shook my head, not knowing where to begin.

"You can tell me. What is it?"

So, since she gave me the go-ahead, I took a short moment to put my thoughts together in which my memories brought me back to the last conversation I had with Jessica a couple of days earlier. It flashed through my mind. The club scene. Jessica's light-brown skin complexion. The Apple Bottom jeans she wore. Her glossy lips. Those slanted eyes of hers and, of course—let me keep it real here—that facial expression she shot me that night: A disdained, mean look that could kill. A look that I would probably remember for the rest of my life. But only if I could have said something different that night, or at least, could have been a little supportive to her about that whole ordeal, I would not be feeling so dismantled right now. I felt like some shit! And I do mean that literally. The memory stuck in my mind. I didn't know if I could ever forgive myself for that. What could I say? I loved—

"DaShawn!" Aunt Enid said, interrupting my reverie and bringing me back to the reality. "Are you sure you're okay?"

"Huh?"

"I said, are you sure you're okay?"

"Yeah …" I stammered. "Of course. It's just that I heard some news and I guess I'm gonna need your advice on it."

"So what is it?"

"Well, remember my girlfriend I told you about a few weeks ago?" I waited for some sort of sign from her to see if she knew who I was talking about, but since she had that impassive look on her face, I added: "Jessica, Auntie."

"Oh, yeah, that's right. Why? What about her?"

"She's pregnant." I then took a seat beside her.

I guess Aunt Enid figured I wasn't pleased about Jessica's pregnancy, because she asked me to explain everything to her.

And I did. I started from the beginning when I first met Jessica, all the way up until she dropped the bomb on me about her pregnancy inside the nightclub.

Aunt Enid fell into a deep silence as though she was thinking about it thoroughly. After what seemed like a lifetime within that short moment, she said, "Honey, please pay close attention to what I have to say to you. And you can do whatever you feel; whatever you feel is best for you. Remember it's your life."

I nodded.

And she continued: "An abortion is outta the question for me. So if you're looking for some type of support there, I'm the wrong person to seek that sort of advice from. That's a decision you would have to make on your own and live with for the rest of your life. But lemme say this, too: You gotta understand that unborn child didn't ask to come into this world to be slaughtered by you or some insane doctor either. So whether it was prearranged, casual, or just one of those heat-of-the-moment things y'all had while practicing unprotected sex with each other, that's something you two have to live with … whether you want this child in your life or not."

My countenance dropped.

"I remember when your mother passed away when you were barely eleven years old." She paused for a few seconds. Then went on to add, "You were such an adorable young man. And when I learned that the State wanted to take you away and put you in one of those foster homes, I just couldn't allow them to do that to you. So I claimed custody over you, even though I didn't have a clue as to being a parent. And the Good Lord knows that I'm not lying to you. Now just look at you now ..." her voice trailed into silence. Then she added with a smile on her face, "You were the best thing that could have happened to me. You changed my life for the better. And if it weren't for you, I probably wouldn't be running this day care right now." She stopped for a quick moment, looking toward the doorway. "I've done told y'all to stop running through the house like that!" she shouted at a few children who were chasing after someone. "Go outside and play!"

"So," I brought her back to our conversation, "what do you think I should do?"

She shrugged her heavy shoulders about the same time she gestured her head to the side as if she didn't know. "You just gotta do the right thing, baby. Because I know you will."

Something clicked inside my head and then a smile grew on my face.

I'm gonna be a daddy, I thought,

I leaned over and kissed her on the cheek just before I ran out of the living room, heading toward the front door.

Seconds later, I heard Aunt Enid shout: "Out of all people, you should know better than anybody else ..." and the rest of what she said faded away as I ran out of the house.

This shit didn't make any sense to me.

I stood outside Jessica's apartment, ringing the doorbell but there was no answer. So I tried it again and again, and still no answer. Just when I was about to give up after the twentieth ring and leave, the door swung open.

I almost ran when I saw a black man, who seemed to be particularly irritated about something, stepping out of the apartment with a large box in his hands. Then I got my senses back. I stood still.

"Was that you ringing this damned bell like that?!" this gorilla-looking chump had the nerve to ask me with an attitude.

I'm like, Whatever, dawg. He could huff and puff all he wanted to. I ignored his question because I had a few questions of my own to ask him first. Like, for starters, Who the hell are you? Or better yet, What the fuck are you doing in my girl's crib without your shirt on? But being that this guy seemed upset already—and not to mention HUGE. Yes, HUGE, with all capital letters—I decided to take it down a notch or two. I wasn't stupid. I was like a buck seventy-five. A little too thin to win in my weight class.

"That's my fault," I said, while trying to look over his shoulders inside the apartment just in case my girl was in some sort of trouble in there. Like tied up or something, after being raped by this muthafucker. "But I'm looking for my girlfriend who lives here."

"Who? Jessica Anderson?"

"Yeah." I tried to stay cool, cutting back to his stolid eyes.

"She's gone."

"Do you know when she's coming back?"

"She ain't." He then headed to his pickup truck with that box in his hands. "She doesn't live here anymore."

"What?" I didn't give him time to reply before I added: "What do you mean by that? She left?"

"Yup!" He laid the box on the tailgate of his truck.

"Do you know where she moved to?"

"Now how in the hell I'm gonna know where she moved to? And even if I did know, I wouldn't be telling you a damn thing anyway." He paused for a split second, then headed back to the apartment, blowing hot steam under his breath as if I could hear him: "Ringing this bell like a muthafucking asshole. And now he wanna ask me where she moved to...."

I headed toward my Buick Regal with my countenance down, feeling lost.

"All I know," he said to grab my attention, "she wanted her month security back, and said that she was leaving town."

I twisted around. I heard him loud and clear. I tried to raise my eyebrows like a man, but my face wouldn't allow me to. I felt relieved that he shared it with me. But in a way, I wished he hadn't. I didn't even thank him. I wanted to, but I couldn't. I guess I didn't have the strength for it. I just walked away, feeling disappointed because Jessica didn't even give me a chance to apologize to her.

Now that's messed up.

But that didn't stop me from wanting to chase after her, though. Because later on that night when I got home, I made extraordinary attempts to find her whereabouts. I called just about everybody I know who was acquainted with her, hoping they can help me locate her. I even went so far as to contact some dudes from Fort Lauderdale that I know she used to mess around with back in the day. But like me, they were all clueless. They didn't know anything. And to top it off, even her best friend Tracy didn't have a clue as to where Jessica had gone to. And I believed Tracy too, because she wouldn't lie to me.

And how I know she wouldn't lie to me?

Let me just put it like this: when she was a freshman in college, I used to visit her a lot off campus before Jessica and I got serious.

Which, it's easy to say, she wouldn't lie to me because I have something over her head.

And the key word here is "head". And plenty of it.

It was weird though: It was like Jessica had fallen off the face of the earth. She was nowhere to be found.

So I gave up. Or so I thought. I just laid on my king-size bed and fixed my eyes on the ceiling fan. And for some odd reason, it felt like I was going under some sort of trance while watching those fan-blades go around in circles. I became lost in my thoughts. I began to wonder where Kevin and Andrew were at too, because they were nowhere to be found either.

And that was when it dawned on me. I remembered something my mother had told me just before she passed away: "You came into this world by yourself, so don't be afraid to be by yourself. Because just before you realize it toward the end, you'll notice that you made it thus far by yourself."

Maybe it was just me who had a hard time understanding that bullshit and facing reality, because the thought of me being alone gave me the heebie-jeebies.

My phone rang.

I wiped my eyes, then picked the phone up on the fifth ring.

"Hello."

It was Kevin.

EIGHT YEARS LATER

If you love someone, set her free.
If she comes back, it was meant to be;
If she stays away, so let it be.

For some unexplained reason I stopped at a particular apartment door that drew my attention. I knocked. But no one answered. I knocked some more. And still no answer. Then, all of a sudden, the door ajar on its own.

"Hello!" I stuck my head inside the apartment. "Is anybody home?" I paused to scan the room. Then I came up with a quick one: "You left your door open!"

There was no response, but I could hear a female's voice somewhere inside the apartment. It sounded familiar to me. But it can't be, I thought.

"Jessica!" I stepped inside the apartment. "Is that you?!"

No response.

I looked to the corner of the living room and saw a few suitcases lying on the floor. I followed the soft melody, pulling me around that first bend on my left. And with one more step toward the kitchen doorway—Oh, my god—I saw Jessica standing right there in front of the stove.

Yes, my Jessica. She was beautiful as ever, singing her favorite song, "Anytime" by Brian McKnight.

"Jessica?"

She twisted around, looking surprised with an apron on, cooking fried fish.

"Why did you leave me like that?"

She didn't respond. She stood there, staring at me with a smile on her face.

"But I thought you loved me?"

She finally broke her silence: "I do love you."

I smiled back. I took a moment to get a good look at her. She took her apron off. She looked just like I remembered her: extremely beautiful and sexy. She was most definitely a dime piece from a scale from 1 to 10. Her exquisite body seemed like it was chiseled to that perfection that all men dream about. She had the whole shebang: thick thighs, toned legs, firm breasts, and, of course, her invigorating feature. And sure enough, it seemed like she hadn't aged a bit from the last time I saw her. I swear.

"I'm sorry—" I began to say, compelled to apologize for what I had said to her a few years ago inside the club, but she cut me off when she placed her finger over my lips.

"I know you are. You don't have to apologize, boo." Then she removed her finger.

"Jessica." I paused when she reached in to kiss me. I felt a heavy burden off my chest. I wanted to hold her in my arms, but I decided to take it slow. "We have much to talk about."

"I know."

Then, out of the blue, I heard knocking sounds coming from the corner of the room. Although I felt like I had not control over my body, I still looked over there and immediately felt a warm sensation that showered me with a feeling that I had never felt before. I saw a little boy sitting in the corner—in an Indian position with one leg folded over the other leg—banging some sort of red truck on the kitchen floor. He looked to be about five, or maybe six years old, but I wasn't sure.

My tongue broke free because I was dying to know: "Is he my son?" I cut back to her.

"What do you think?"

Without another word, I twisted back to him. I watched the little youngster. He kept his eyes on me, too, while banging his toy truck on the floor. I smiled; he smiled back.

Daaaamn.... I have a son, I thought.

The banging became louder if not more clearer. Then the weirdest thing happened to me: I lost my vision within a split second when I woke up from my sleep. Somebody was heavily rapping on my bedroom door.

I got up to go answer the door, while trying to get rid of my enervating thoughts.

It was Kevin. "What the fuck you got the door locked for?" He scanned the room. "It ain't like you have a muthafucking' hoe up in here with you."

"Like that woulda made a difference to you." I took a seat on the edge of the bed. "Because either way you look at it, you were still gonna beat on my door whether I had a girl up in here or not."

He sucked his teeth and walked over to my dresser cabinet. He pulled the dresser drawer open.

"Yo," I slid my pant on. "I had this crazy dream a moment ago."

"Man, I don't wanna hear about that shit! You just needa get dressed before we be late again." He snatched one of my underwear out of the dresser draw. "I needa borrow this."

"My favorite speedo?"

"Yeah."

"Are you retarded?" I got up and reached for my shirt. "How many times do I have to tell you, no, before you could understand that?"

He ignored me and walked out of the room with my red underwear.

About ten minutes later, I strolled into the family room where I found Kevin playing a battle match against my cousin Carlton in a game of Mortal Combat.

Carlton started complaining the moment Kevin's action figure started whipping on his: "You can't be doing that shit!"

You see, Carlton is my cousin from my father's side of the family. He stands about six feet and appears to be in good shape.

He wore blue jeans and Timbs on the regular. His eyes stayed on bloodshot-red from all the marijuana he smoked, since he was about fourteen years old—if I could remember correctly. So, in a way, I guess he was a true thug. He didn't have a life of his own like normal folks because he had a silly notion that some mysterious god had placed him here on earth to enjoy the comfortable lifestyle with fat blunts and thick shawties to please him in every way he wants.

"C'mon, Kev!" I threw on my baseball cap. "Let's get outta here."

"Hold up. Give me a second." Then within a moment he started laughing. "That's what I'm talking about," he said to no one in general. "Punish his ass!"

Carlton shut off the video game, trying to save himself from the humiliation.

"My nigga," Kevin started laughing, while getting up from the couch, telling Carlton, "you needa pick your game up because you play like some shit!"

"Nigga, fuck you!"

Kevin laughed at him some more, and we left the house before Carlton started acting stupid again.

I jumped in the passenger seat of Kevin's SUV. "So where my shit at?"

"It's in my bag."

I twisted to the backseat and grabbed his duffle bag. I pulled the zipper across and smiled when I saw Kimnaisha's flicks.

"Yo," I cut back to Kevin. "There are four pictures missing out of the stack."

"Which ones?"

"The ones she took up there in Mississippi with her legs spread open."

"Oh, those." He looked at me, then went back to the windshield. "I sold them."

When Kevin and I arrived at Club Mansion, the front entrance had a rack of females trying to get inside. I saw Robin, Crystal, and big butt Monique near the front of the line, smiling at me, as we walked pass them. We entered the club and headed straight for the dressing room; even in there was packed.

It was all about the green paper tonight.

"That's about enough!" I had to snatch my baby oil from Kevin's hand. "You're killing my shit!"

"That cheap shit! It ain't like I can't buy my oil. You pretty ass nigga!"

"Well, you need to start buying your own oil then so you don't have to be using my cheap shit anymore." I squirted some oil in my hand and started rubbing it over my body.

"Yellow ass nigga," he mumbled under his breath while throwing his vest on, looking at me. "You think you're all that."

I laughed at him and twisted to my left where a few of my friends were getting dressed too. "Yo, Butterfinger!"

"Yeah, what's up?"

"This black muthafucker right here just told me that I think I'm all that! Should I remind this fool again?"

"Hell, yeah!" he laughed. "Give it to him raw!"

I twisted back to Kevin. "You silly ass nigga, I don't think I'm all that: I know that I'm all that! I have what the ladies want." I smiled, showing him my best side. Then added: "So hate and hate on, baby. Because there are a lot more haters where you come from."

"You sound like a fag."

"Your father."

"Yours."

"Your whole family tree, with you in the middle of it, sissy."

I sat down to put the baby oil back in my duffle bag, waiting on his retort, but he didn't shoot one back at me. I looked at him to see what the holdup was and noticed that he was distracted by some heated tension that just resonated between two other dancers, Mikey and Viagra, who were verbally humiliating one another.

It was pure entertainment for some.

It seemed as though several people in the dressing room were enjoying the war of words, acting like little instigators on the schoolyard play ground with their "Whews" and "Ahhs", as if they were hoping for something to kick off between them. Being that Mikey was a white guy—one of the coolest guys in our clique—the other chump, Viagra, was criticizing him because of Mikey's milky skin complexion. So it seemed. Or perhaps it was only a front because I think Viagra was just hating on Mikey for some other reason: like Mikey's popularity among the ladies, using his skin color as an excuse.

"So why don't you do us all a favor," Viagra went on to say to Mikey, "and take your white ass to another nightclub and dance."

"I can't do that because I think I'm falling for you in those cute thongs you had on yesterday. But if I'm not mistaken, it looked like the same ones I had bought your girl the other week when I met up with her at the hotel. I hope you don't mind but she wanted me to bang her brains out for her since, as she puts it, you weren't doing a good job at it. And to be honest with you, she wasn't all that impressive in bed either."

A few people in the room laughed. I did too: to show support for my homeboy.

Then Viagra snapped on us: "I don't know why y'all laughing with this fuck-ass cracka for! Because it won't be long before they take over our shit!" He took a quick breather. Then cut back to Mikey: "First, your white folks stole us from Africa against our will, forcing us into slavery; then after slavery, y'all found a way to snatch us away from our Black sisters by sending our brothers to prison for x-amount of years, making Black sisters vulnerable and dependent on y'all for comfort while making them y'all little Black bitches on the side. And now you wanna come up in here in our muthafucking' club to humiliate us, by dancing beside us like you're cool. Nah, cracka, you ain't cool at all. At least with me that is, because I know your kind."

Everybody who was laughing at the time, including myself, had stopped. Not because of what Viagra had said, but rather, because we saw he was getting in his feelings while approaching Mikey.

It didn't look good.

Mikey stood his ground, and they both started sizing each other up as if they were about to get into a fistfight.

Kevin was the first one to jump up; then me. But Mikey quickly held his hand out towards us to indicate that he had it under control.

"First of all," Mikey began to tell Viagra, "you were born right here in America. And just to let you know a little something: it was your ancestors in Africa who sold their own people off to the Europeans by throwing them into slavery. Somehow your African ancestors believed it was a come up for them. Which I would like to add, it's no different from what your Black brothers are doing right now in their own neighborhoods, exploiting and selling crack cocaine to their own Black people for their own little come up, too.

"So don't get it twisted, because the same Black brothers who you were referring about a short moment ago, some of them not only destroying their communities with drugs but they are exploiting their own sisters as sex objects. Taking advantage of Black sisters' weakness because they are, your sisters, trying to find love and security in Black brothers. And yes, some of these same Black brothers who you are defending before me, who would then, in turn, pimped their own sisters to their homeboys or put them out to work on the streets: Like Biscayne Boulevard for your Black brothers own little pathetic come up too. So before you start pointing a finger at someone, just start with some of your homeboys first. Because they are the real ones who are hindering your people from succeeding in life, not me.

"And from the look of things, I don't see anybody holding you down from doing what you wanna do for your Black folks. If anything, it's your own lack of motivation to move forward because you're so stuck on that racism shit! And it was because of reasons like these is why I supported Obama on his first term in office, because he wanted to bridge the gap on this racial division between our races, so we can be stronger as a nation. But the more I think about it, it's like you and others of alike opinions wanna keep that racism alive, dwelling on the past to find an excuse for y'all failures in life when y'all give up y'all selves."

"Yeah, right." Viagra disagreed. "But I bet you won't put your life on that?"

"For real, though," Mikey said, ignoring his comment. "I just think you need to learn how to forgive and forget about what my ancestors might have done upon your people back in the day; and move on with your own life. Because if you don't, you will never see a brighter future for yourself in this country or for your generation to come."

"Well, you need to tell your Jewish people that same shit then and let's see if they can forget about what the Nazis have done to them too. Because, for real" —he tried to mock Mikey with a little bass in his tone, bouncing his head on every word— "I don't wanna hear your bullshit!"

Mikey slowly shook his head, giving him a piercing yet disdained look before he jumped to another topic. "And if you really wanna keep it real, just think about this then: Stop treating your Black sisters like bitches and hoes. And just maybe then they might stop seeing other people outside of their race" —he dangled two fingers on each side of himself to indicate quotation marks— "like this Jewish cracka here. And maybe they'd see something in you other than a brotha treating his Black queen like a BET bitch in the rap videos."

That one had to hurt.

Viagra sucked his teeth and sat down. "I don't wanna hear that fuck-shit, cracka! Just make sure you stay outta my may."

The room grew quiet.

Then one of our homeboys, Butt-Naked, walked over to Mikey, throwing his arm around his shoulders, and said, "Little Bro, fuck all this shit! I don't know why you just don't go ahead and tell these fools the truth that you're my little brother. Don't be ashamed of that shit! Tell them!" He turned Mikey toward us and said: "Ay, y'all! I wanna let y'all know something! And y'all better take heed to this shit too, because I don't wanna fuck one of y'all up over some bullshit! So y'all better leave him alone, for real. And that's real talk."

We all knew he sent that symbolic message out to Viagra.

The room grew quiet again.

Then Freaky Red shouted between a laugh to bring humor back inside the room: "Nigga! Your black ass ain't his brother!"

"Yeah, I am." Butt-Naked seemed like he wanted to laugh back with him. "We came from the same mother and father. But it's just that our mom gave him a little more milk than she gave me. Can't you see? Our dicks are about the same size." He then flipped his flaccid muscle out of his underwear and look down at it. "See!"

We all started laughing—everybody but Viagra—when Butt-Naked tried to snatch Mikey's underwear down to display his dick too.

"Stop that bullshit!" Mikey pushed Butt-Naked's hand away, laughing.

"Just show them your shit!" He laughed along with him. "And stop being scared. These niggas in here don't believe me that you have an eight inch albino python down there."

"You're a sick bastard!"

"Hey, Goldie!"

I turned toward the doorway to see who called me. It was the club manager, and it seemed like he was a little ticked off about something.

"Yeah, what's up?"

"Yeah, what's up?" he tried to mock me. "You needa get your yellow ass out there and go to work! You're up next!"

I stood up, threw my cowboy hat on, and headed for the door. And as soon as I stepped out of the room, I heard somebody shout behind me, "Oh my God! There he goes!"

"Heeeeeere's" the club deejay dragged a bit, while playing a bootie shaking music in the background before he announced me as "Goldie Lox!"

I hopped onto the dance platform as if I were riding a wild horse in a rodeo, hopping from one leg to the other, straight into the center of a screaming crowd. Then the sound of the music stopped for a brief moment, and so did my equitation motion. I stood still, my adrenaline racing. Then, on that following second, a loud sound-effect explosion screamed through the speakers—as planned—and another of Miami's bootie music started back up again: "If You Happy and You Know It," by the sound of the beat. I was like that. I popped my hips for a short moment before I started gyrating them in a rough circular motion.

The crowd got excited. They were loving it. Women of all ages were extending their hands out, feeling on my body parts. Which, of course, I didn't mind.

Then out of all people, I picked this one heavyset broad who wore a purple knee-high skirt from out of the crowd to help me out with my performance. I swear, she looked identical to that big broad Precious in that movie. But check it, though: before she mounted the platform, the club bouncers had to literally push everybody aside to allow her to go up on the stage with me. And once she got up there, I ground up against her. Very close.

"Oh, yes!" She had the nerve to lean toward my face and tried to kiss me.

That was a no-no in my book.

So before she could lay her lips on mine, I turned her around to position her from the back. She slouched over a bit, her hands on her thighs, holding herself up. You should have seen her. She started backing that ass up on me.

"Shake it for me!" I told her. "And show me whatcha working with!"

"Oh, yes! Give it to me!"

I ground against her again, but this time with a pumping motion. I acted as if I were actually fucking her from the back, slapping her hips a couple of times with the tempo. Right on the beat. I was acting a fool out there.

"I want you to fuck me!" she begged. "Right here, right now!"

I laughed when she pulled her panties down from her legs and tossed them aside. I slapped her ass cheek when she bent over even further for me this time, exposing herself. She had a meaty pussy. I ran my hand across it, then popped a finger in her; then two fingers. I started pumping them inside her, trying to give her a quick climax.

She dropped on all fours, daring me: "Stick your dick inside me right now! I want it!"

I smiled. Any other time I would have accepted her offer. But this time, I had to take a few steps back when I saw two bouncers approaching the stage area for her. They escorted her off the platform. That didn't stop me from continuing though. I kept dancing for the rest of the crowd. Within a matter of seconds, an older woman, who must have been in her mid-sixties, wiped the sweat off my forehead with a handkerchief.

Thanks!

I knew the perfect gesture of appreciation for her good deed. I snatched the hanky from her hand, stuck it inside my G-string to wipe the sweat off my balls, and gave the rag back to her.

She became excited. She blanketed her nose with the handkerchief, then rubbed it all over her face. I laughed at her. Her wig was sliding off. She turned around to the crowd, showed the handkerchief to them, then waved it in the air.

Someone snatched it away from her.

Later on that night I was back inside the dressing room with Kevin and a few of our homeys, getting dressed.

Speaking for myself, I had a good night. I made enough money—about eleven hundred dollars—to be pleased with and the club wasn't even closed yet. From the look of things, Kevin had a good night too. And to tell the truth, we were exhausted from dancing for nearly four hours straight. That was the only reason why we called it quits for the night.

I grabbed my duffle bag and cut back to Kevin. "You wanna go grab something to eat at IHOP?"

"Yeah, I don't mind."

Butt-Naked and Mikey decided to come along.

About an hour later we were seated at our usual table near the back wall, bullshitting around.

"So check it," Mikey said, kicking off with a typical question that is normally asked among the fellows. "If you were granted the gift to start a Garden of Eden all over again, who would y'all choose to be your Eve to help you lay the foundation of mankind?"

"Shit, that's easy!" Kevin smiled. "I would have to choose Trina."

"Euw!" I disapproved.

He twisted to me. "What the hell you're euwing about?"

"Her."

"What about her?"

"Nothing really. But I wouldn't pick her to start our foundation off with."

"Speak for yourself, because have you seen how thick that hoe looks?" He paused. Then went on to add: "I could fuck the hell out of her day and night; and stay satisfied for the rest of my life."

I shook my head.

"So, who would you pick then?" Mikey asked me.

"Who?"

Kevin jumped in: "Yeah, who?"

"I don't know. But I would have to probably say, Amy Holmes."

"Euw!"

I knew Kevin was going to say that.

"But whose that anyway?" he asked.

"That's that cute Republican strategist from CNN. She's smart as hell!"

"A white chick?"

"Nah. She's Black."

"Well, I still don't know who you're talking about, so she doesn't count."

"That's not my fault, stupid-ass. You just needa watch CNN to see who she is then."

"Well, whether I watch CNN to see who she is or not, it still ain't gonna be enough anyway. Because she has to shake her ass inside of King of Diamonds' so I can see what I'm gonna be working with." He turned to Butt-Naked. "I'm the one who was granted the gift, not her. That's why I can pick any hoe I want. They come in dime a dozen."

"You got that right." Butt-Naked bumped knuckles with him.

About fifteen minutes later while we were just about finished eating our blueberry pancakes, Kevin suddenly sprung at attention. "My nigga, look at them over there."

"Who?" Mikey asked, his eyes scanning the restaurant.

"Them over there." Kevin tilted his head in the direction toward the front entrance. "Don't look. They're coming our way."

We all pretended we did not notice the waitress ushering three females to a nearby table.

If I had to take a wild guess, I would have to assume they were from South America or from one of those Caribbean Islands because they all had that golden skin complexion with long curly hair.

They were most definitely beautiful, especially that cute one on the far right who was strutting with that sexy ass swagger. She had an ass like the size of Kim Kardashian's before the pregnancy. It was about yay big.

Kevin was the first one to leap from his seat, but Butt-Naked grabbed his arm. "Waita second!"

"For what?"

"Because I'm not ready yet."

"Do you think I give a fuck if you're ready or not?"

I faked a cough.

Kevin and Butt-Naked stopped arguing and looked at me. I barely twisted my head in the females' direction, trying not to be obvious about it.

Kevin twisted to the left and saw them looking directly at our table. He shot them an embarrassing smile and sat back in his seat.

They sort of waved back with ogle smiles.

Now we all got anxious to visit their table, a lot more than before.

Kevin leaped from his seat again, but immediately sat back down. "Hold up."

We all sat back in our seats.

"What happened?" Mikey asked him.

"It's three of them over there, but there's four of us over here. That means somebody needs to stay back and take the bullet."

"Shiiit," Butt-Naked dragged, "not me."

"Me neither," I followed his lead. "I'm not staying behind."

But before Mikey could get his words out, Kevin cut him off with a great suggestion: "Let's draw some straws, and the shortest straw stay behind." He then gave all of us a stolid look. "Do y'all'' agree?"

After a slight hesitation, we all nodded.

We started from my left with Butt-Naked and went in a clockwise direction. He didn't argue about why he had to go first, but then again he did show a sign of nervousness when he quickly snatched a straw out of Kevin's hand. He passed. It was a long one.

Damn!

Now Mikey was next up in line to pick a straw. He tried to analyze the tip of the straws contemplating on which one of them to go for.

"My nigga," Butt-Naked began to snap on him, "just pick a fucking straw! You're killing me here."

"See, I didn't even say anything to you when you had to pick yours."

"Because you didn't have to: I just picked any one of them to get it over with."

Mikey sucked his teeth and reached for a straw from Kevin's hand. I guess he wanted to get it over with too. He probably didn't care anymore whether he made it or not. So who could blame—

Shit!

And just his luck, that son-of-bitch picked the right one. He got excited.

Kevin looked at me; I looked back at him.

"Homey," he said. "It's down to just you and me now. We're the only ones left. And you know what that means? One of us gotta stay behind." Then he seemed to be taking his own words into consideration.

As I reached for a straw out of Kevin's hand, he dropped both of them on the table and leaped from his seat.

"I'd seen them first," he began to tell me, "and I'll be damned if I have to be the one who has to stay behind and allow y'all to have all the fun." He ran away from me, with Butt-Naked and Mikey, to the females' table before I could contest his default.

But he got that.

I took it as a loss and stayed back for one reason only: I would never be classified as a cock-blocker. Never that. It wasn't a part of my genetic makeup. I'm considered a true playa to the game—not a hater—and that was my main reason why I stayed at the table, periodically watching Kevin and them putting their phony game down on those females.

Then, about ten minutes later, I heard a slight commotion a few tables away, on the other side of me.

"Oh, my God!" said a young lady, who looked to be in her late twenties, or possibly her early thirties, pointing her finger at the floor for the waitress to see. "It was right here." She scanned the room for a possible suspect. "I had all my important information in there."

"But, ma'am," the waitress said, with a suspicious tone as if she didn't believe her. "I'm sorry about your purse, but you still have to pay your bill."

"I'm going to pay the damned bill! But I need to know where my purse went!"

I got up from my table when I saw their argument escalating to a near fistfight. I walked over there and got between them, facing the waitress first. "How much is her bill?"

"Five dollars and seventy cents," the waitress told me in a heated tone, looking at her nonpaying customer as if she wanted to be the first one to throw a punch. "They're always coming here making up excuses so they don't have to pay their bills."

Her customer tried to argue: "You don't even know me—"

"Chill out, ma'am," I cut her off, while pulling money out of my pocket. I twisted back to the waitress. "Here's a fifty. That should cover both of our bills. And whatever is left over, you can have it as a tip. All right?"

The waitress rolled her eyes at her customer and walked away from us.

I cut back this cutie.

"I don't need you to pay my bill," she had the audacity to tell me with a solid, brisk tone. "I don't need any help from you."

I gave her that you-have-to-be-kidding-me stare. And it seemed like she realized what she had just said to me because she cut her eyes to the floor to hide her chagrin. She then strode away, heading for the exit.

That's more like it.

I walked over to my homeys. "Are y'all ready to bounce?"

"Now?" Kevin responded first since the both of us had driven there in the same vehicle together.

"Yeah, I wanna head home."

"Why don't you go ahead and order something else to eat; and chill out for a little while longer, my nigger."

"Man, just gimme your keys and catch a ride with them if you're not ready to go yet!"

But before Kevin could reply, Butt-Naked cut in and told him, "Go ahead and give him your keys so he can go somewhere."

One of the females at the table lifted her hand about halfway up and greeted me with a soft hello.

I didn't have any interest in her, or anyone of them at this point. So for the sake of it, I shot her a specious smile, then cut my eyes back to Kevin.

He snatched the keys out of his pocket and held them out to me. "Alright then, I'll get up with you later when I come over to pick my shit up."

"Yeah, whatever." I exited the restaurant.

And to my surprise, I saw the same female, the one who was arguing with the waitress inside of IHOP, standing by the telephone booth. She was by herself, looking vulnerable as an easy prey. The first thing that came to mind—besides some Ted Bundy copycat shit!—was whether she was going to be okay or not. She seemed stranded out there all alone. But before I could ask her if she needed some sort of assistance—maybe a lift somewhere or something—she rolled her eyes at me.

Then I saw a black Nissan Sentra pulled up in front of her, with dark tinted windows.

Have fun.

This didn't make any damn sense!

As soon as I stepped inside the house I heard the television volume blasting from the other room. I walked straight to the family room and found Uncle James sleeping on the couch with his pants open, snoring away.

I looked at the fool box and noticed there was a sex video playing. Bootylicious; Dat Bitch Can Take It. It was one of my favorite fuck flicks on DVD. And from the look of things, it seems like it was one of Uncle James' favorite videos too.

You see, Uncle James was fifty-nine years old and he looked every bit of it. Even though he had been a heavy drinker since god-knows-how-long-that-might-have-been, he didn't consider himself an alcoholic, although everybody else thought otherwise. But I guess his real downfall in life, besides his excessive drinking, was when he was married to a good woman by the name of Esther; in which their six years of marriage ended badly.

It was sad, though, because I really liked Esther as my aunt. I did, really. But after she had one big quarrel with Uncle James about his drinking problem three years ago, she finally gave up and threw in the towel: she sold their home behind his back and filed for a divorce. Within a month's time, he was left homeless when the buyers, a pair of newlyweds, wanted to move into their first home together.

Who could blame them?

When Uncle James was forced out of the house by the authorities, he gave the bridegroom a word of advice before he got kicked out: "Don't ever trust a woman who doesn't drink alcohol with you. She'll rob you blind."

I found that to be nonsense, so you could only imagine how the bridegroom felt.

The last time we heard anything about Aunt Esther's whereabouts, she was living somewhere in the Caribbean Islands with a young stud who was beating her back out for her.

A twenty-three year old youngster, with a lot of stamina.

Now that was messed up, with all that ass Aunt Ester had back there, she could have easily asked me to tap it for her once in a while to keep her content. She would have enjoyed it. Or at least I know that I would have.

What? We weren't blood related. So, you can say what you wanna say.

I reached for the remote control on the cocktail table to click the TV off. But then I froze. I noticed the bottle of lotion sitting right beside the remote control. My curiosity arose. I cut back to Uncle James, then to his pants. I thought of the oddest possible reasons to justify as to why his pants zipper was down, but then it dawned on me.

I turned toward the TV, then to the lotion again; and afterward back to Uncle James. "You dirty muthafucker," I murmured to myself, feeling disgusted.

He rolled over on his side.

I grabbed the remote control and noticed a nearby pillow which was lying at the end of the couch. I grabbed that shit, too!

When I hit the off button on the gizmo, the TV shut off, and the whole room went pitch black.

I swear, I swung that pillow with all my might.

"Ow! What the fuck's going on?!" Uncle James leaped up. "Who did that shit?! I'm trying to sleep over here! You fucking asshole!" He paused. Then said, "I know it was you, Carlton!"

I snuck out of the family room.

Uncle James was sleeping on the couch, slightly moaning out "Mmm's" and "Aaah's" as if he were actually copulating with someone. But the truth was, he wasn't. He was off in some sort of cloud nine. Or whatever the hell you wanna call a wet dream.

And the only thing that spoiled the moment for him was when someone started knocking on the front door. Then seconds later, the doorbell rang.

He rolled over on his side, doing his best to ignore the chiming sound in his ears. But within seconds, the pounding came back on the door and that lasted for about three minutes straight.

Lo and behold, that did it.

Uncle James fought one of his eyelids open and looked at the clock on the wall. It was a half past eight in the morning. He got up from the couch and started staggering toward the door, putting his thoughts together.

"This shit better be important," he muttered. "Because if it ain't, I'm gonna have to kick somebody's—"

"Psst!"

Uncle James looked to his right side.

It was Carlton. "Don't answer it," he told him. "It's the po-po!"

"The, who?"

"The po-po. The fucking police." Carlton then ran into the other room with a small bag of marijuana in his hand.

Uncle James opened the door anyway.

It was the sheriff's deputy.

"How can I help, Officer?"

"Are you Mr. Powell?" the deputy asked. "Mr. DaShawn Powell, sir?"

"No, I'm not. But why?"

"Does Mr. Powell live here at this residence?"

"Yeah. But why do you ask?"

"May I please speak with him, sir?"

"But what seems to be the problem, Officer?"

"I can't discuss that with you."

That did it: Uncle James shook his head. "Well, if it's like that then, I can't help you either. Go find him yourself."

"Excuse me?"

"You heard what I said. I can't help you either. The two of us can play this game all day, if you like. Because if you don't tell me why you're looking for my nephew, I'm not telling you anything. Not a damn thing!"

From a short distance away, Carlton listened to the deputy and Uncle James going at it. He stashed his weed.

"Sir, I'm only asking you a simple question," the deputy proceeded with a little force in his tone. "Can you tell me where I can find Mr. Powell?"

"God dammit! It seems like you're hard-of-hearing! I have just said I'm not telling you a damned thing! I know my rights. I'm a goddamn citizen in this country! So go find him yourself!"

The deputy had a discontented look on his face.

"Better yet!" Uncle James went on to say. "Why are you still standing here at my door? Do you have a search warrant? I know my damned rights! Now get the hell off my front porch!"

Carlton walked up. "Are you looking for DaShawn Powell?"

"Yes. Are you Mr. Powell?"

"Nah, the person you're looking for isn't home right now. But when he gets back from California, I'll let him know that the po-po was over here looking for him."

"The, who?"

"I mean, I'll tell him that a police officer came over here looking for him."

"Oh. Well, let me ask you something?"

"Yeah, go ahead."

"Are you his brother, or a close relative of his?"

"Yeah, he's my cousin."

"That's good then." The deputy said, showing a sign of relief. "Well, if that's the case, do you mind signing this summons for him? It's just a simple verification that I delivered this subpoena to this address, to a relative of Mr. Powell."

Carlton hesitated for a few seconds. "Sure, why not. I can do that for you." He drew near to the deputy to sign the release form.

But the deputy immediately smelt something odd yet familiar to him. As he took a good whiff around Carlton, he asked him, "Were you smoking any illegal drugs?" He paused for a brief moment, looking directly into Carlton's droopy-eyes. Then added, "Like, perhaps, marijuana?"

"Nah, I don't mess with that type of stuff." He stepped back. "I'm a Christian."

"Oh, you are, huh? So why are your eyes looking like that?"

"I don't know. Probably because my allergies are acting up again."

"It's not even allergy season." The deputy looked at Uncle James, then back at Carlton, then shook his head. "Uh, forget about it. I didn't come here for that. Just sign right here."

"Right here?"

"Yeah."

Carlton signed the release form; the deputy then gave him the summons and left the house.

Carlton and Uncle James hid behind the curtains, peeking through the window until the deputy drove away. From there, they both took off running down the hallway, yelling on one accord.

"Yo, DaShawn!"

"**DaShawn! Get up**, get up! Get yo' ass up, boy! I know you hear me talking to you!"

I thought I was dreaming at first until I felt a slap across my face that woke me up from my sleep. "What the hell's your problem?!" I quickly moved my head away from Uncle James, while putting my thoughts in order, seeing Carlton on the other side of him. "And how you two get in here?"

Carlton cut in: "The po-po was here looking for you."

"For what?"

"I don't know! But he gave me this shit to give to you."

I immediately got up and read the envelope. "Family Court," I whispered to myself.

Hearing this, Carlton and Uncle James clustered close to me, trying to get a look at the envelope, too.

I jolted my shoulders a bit. I wanted some space. They got back a little, and I looked at the Family Court's logo again. I was struck silent until I managed to mumble out, "What the hell they want with me?" I looked at Carlton, then back to the envelope. "This must be a mistake." But I opened it anyway.

In short, the summons required me to be at the Family court in three weeks for a hearing concerning—out of all things—a child I had no knowledge of.

A child?

Oh, hell nah! Obviously, this is an error that could be easily corrected, I thought. Because, for one, I don't have a child.

"Why don't you call Aunt Enid and see what she has to say about this?"

That was a good idea. I took Carlton's advice and gave her a call; she answered the phone on the third ring. "Auntie, it's me."

"Hi, baby." It sounded like she was washing dishes in the background. "How's everything?"

"It's alright. But hey, I need a favor from you."

"Sure, what is it?"

"Well, I received a summons from the Family Court a few minutes ago" —I looked at Carlton, then to the envelope again— "and I'm gonna need your help to look into it for me."

"The Family Court?"

"Yeah,"

"So, why are they contacting you?"

"I don't know. But it's regarding a child, I think."

"A child?" her voice changed to something much stronger. "I thought I had told you about not messing with those girls you be meeting at those strip clubs. I raised you better than—"

"Nah, Auntie," I cut her off before she blew it out of proportion. "This must be a mistake, I haven't been sleeping around like that. Especially unprotected. I'm not stupid."

Silence took over the phone for a brief moment, then she asked, "What's the case number on that summons? I'll make a few calls to find out what this is all about."

I gave her the case number.

She hung up on me without saying good-bye.

Later on that evening, Kevin and I were in Dade Land Mall, shopping at this new urban sport store for outfits. Kevin snatched up two fitted shirts off the clothes rack.

"Which one do you think I should buy?"

"None of them." I tried to keep it real with him. "Those colors don't fit you."

"This color is me right here." He held the green shirt up to his chest. "Ain't it?"

"I hope you don't believe that shit!"

"Hating ass nigga. I don't know why I even asked you for anyway." He cut his eyes from me, sweeping the area. "Excuse me, beautiful," he called to this skinny-looking female who was browsing through a clothes rack not far from where we were standing. She looked at him and he continued: "May I ask you for your advice on something?" He glanced at me, then went back to her. "Since we have haters all around us."

She nodded her head. "Sure, what can I help you with?"

"It's just that I'm a little confused about something here."

"With, what?"

He looked at the two shirts in his hand, then back at her. "I don't know which shirt I should buy. The cream or the green one?" He paused. Then added: "But I know a cutie like yourself can help me out on the right choice, though."

"Uhhh, I don't know. They both look about the same to me."

"Well, let me see if I can help you choose the right one then." He pulled his shirt off exposing his muscular chest before he tried on the green shirt first. It snuggled his chest a bit tight. You could still see the ripples and muscles from his abs. He looked like a young Tyrese Gibson, trying on an Incredible Hulk costume.

At first, it seemed like she wanted to turn her head away from him, but I guess she couldn't fight the temptation when he started making his chest bounce for her.

I stepped off, shaking my head when she smiled.

And it was about that same time when my cell phone began to ring: I answered it.

It was Aunt Enid.

"Honey, listen to me carefully," Aunt Enid cautioned. "When can you come over here to see me?"

"Why? What's the matter?" I paused. Then proceeded again: "Is there something wrong?"

"No. It's about the summons I looked up for you."

"So what'd they say?" I asked, hoping that she would come out with it. "Is everything all right?"

"Oh, sure. It's just...," she stammered. Then said, "I'd rather not discuss it over the phone with you."

And there was no doubt in my mind it sounded serious. I was suspicious about the severity of what she wanted to share with me in person. But then that train of thought derailed when Kevin walked up beside me, talking on his cell phone.

"Hold on for a second," he told somebody through the receiver; then turned his attention to me. "Yo, Shawn, I have these Brazilian mommies on the phone with me and they wanna know if we wanna link up with them tomorrow night?"

I didn't verbally respond but I did one of those things with my eyebrows: didn't know who he was talking about.

So he added: "Those shawties from IHOP the other night...."

"Yeah." I felt lost, but still nodded my head for the sake of getting out of that conversation with him. "Whatever. I don't care."

Kevin put the receiver back to his mouth. "Yeah, he's down with it. But just make sure it's that same shawty who was sitting beside you in the yellow sun dress.... Yeah, that one because I don't wanna hear his shit if you bring someone else who looks ugly as hell." Then he laughed about something that was probably said back to him by the person on the phone. He walked away continuing with his conversation.

"Hello," Aunt Enid said through her phone line. "Are you still there?"

"Yeah, I'm here. Now where were we again?"

"When can you come over here because we need to talk before Monday afternoon?"

Monday afternoon?

Something sounded fishy here. "Well, I'm supposed to work tonight. But if it's that important, I'll come over there instead." I paused to see what she would say about that. But she didn't. Then I asked, "Auntie, is there something you needa tell me?"

There was another pause. Then she broke her silence with a wary but a straightforward tone, "Jessica had a child, and they have you listed as the biological father. That's why you were notified."

"By who?" I wanted to make sure I heard that correctly. "Say that again for me."

"Jessica ... Anderson."

"Jessica Anderson?"

"Yeah."

"So what's she trying to do: throw me on some sorta child support?"

Aunt Enid sighed. Then after a short break she said, "No. Not exactly. But I'd rather discuss it with you when you come over here later."

"That's crazy! You're joking right?"

"No."

I kept quiet.

Then she added: "I'm serious."

"Well, I'll be there in a little bit. I'm not going to work tonight then."

"No. Just do this instead: Go to work tonight and stop by my house tomorrow afternoon when I get back from church.... Come by about one o'clock. Okay? And I'll explain everything to you."

"All right." I still felt confused. But at least tomorrow I would find out what the hell she wanted to tell me about Jessica.

When Kevin and I left the mall, I sat in the passenger seat of the SUV while he drove. I sat quietly. My mind wasn't there. It was somewhere else. And who knows where, because I didn't give a damn. I stared out the side window, lost in my thoughts.

"My nigga!" Kevin broke my concentration. "What's going on?"

I looked at him.

"Ever since we left the mall you haven't said a word to me. What happened? I did something fucked up again?"

"Nah, it's nothing. It's just that Auntie said something to me that messed my head up."

"Like what? You needa start going to church with her?"

"Nah, something worse: she said Jessica had a baby and had me listed down as the father."

"Goddamn, my nigga." He glanced over at me. "Now that's some fuck shit! But who's that though?"

"Who's who?"

"That hoe Jessica?"

I should not have had to answer that. I shot him a wry look instead.

Kevin turned back to the windshield to check how he was driving, but then quickly twisted back to me. "Oh, hell nah!"

I started bobbing my head without saying a word.

"You're fucking lying?" He sorta doubted me. But I guess that cleared up when he saw the expression on my face. He tried to cheer me up, adding, "But that ain't shit though, my nigga. I've been hearing shit like that about me all the time, from all sort of bitches who be trying to throw their kids on me too." He gave me a weird look, raising his eyebrows, then relaxing them. "So don't even sweat that shit. It'll blow over your head before the sun goes down."

That bothered me. "So, it is true?"

"Is what's true?"

"If you have kids out there, running about?"

"Damn, my nigga, you sound stupid! How the hell I'm supposed to know if that's true or not when I'd just told you that I don't believe half of the shit these bitches be saying about me?"

"So what do you believe then?"

"What I believe in?" He looked at me, then to his driving again.

"Yeah."

"I believe when we go to work tonight," he started with a smile, then looked at me, "I'm gonna get some pussy. That's what I believe in. And I'm still gonna get paid for dicking those hoes down tonight." He laughed, then turned his eyes back to the road.

What an idiot, I thought. "You just better be careful before you end up like Andrew."

The SUV swerved a little.

"C'mon, my nigga!" Kevin protested, spooked. He kept his left hand on the steering wheel and with the other hand he quickly cross-blessed himself by touching his forehead, chest, then shoulder to shoulder; then got serious. "Why in the hell would you jinx me like that?"

I laughed at him. "You're a superstitious bitch!"

"Man, fuck you! That's why that baby's yours. Now how you like that for being superstitious?"

I didn't like it at all.

It was a little after eleven o'clock at night, and a few Southern Baptist Church members had just ended their yearly convention in the Holiday Inn's reception room. Four of the church elders—one married couple and two older ladies—entered the elevator, went up to the fifth floor, and headed toward their rooms.

"Okay, Sister Betty," the elderly man said, with his wife at his side. "We'll see y'all in the morning."

"Lord willing, we'll see you tomorrow morning."

As they were about to depart to their own room, the hotel suite right across from them—Room 512—suddenly burst open and nearly frightened the life out of them. With a blast of music, three females ran out into the hallway and ran up the corridor, wearing transparent lingerie and screaming playfully.

At the sound of those female's shrill cries, the elderly man shove his wife into their hotel room and slammed the door behind them to avoid any mishaps. But that wasn't the case for those other two elders, whose names were Ms. Betty Brady and Mary Singlebee. They stood there, looking appalled.

Within seconds, Kevin dashed into the hallway, wearing only a lime colored speedo underwear, yelling, "Y'all wanna fucking play, right?!" He chased after the three females, then quickly catching up to them. "I got something for y'all asses to play with!" He caught one of them. Jasmine. The high yellow chick. She was an albino with thick legs. "Your ass is mine now!"

From a distance, Ms. Betty saw Kevin manhandle that young lady, throwing her over his shoulder as if she was a rag doll. "Oh, my Lord!" she exclaimed with one hand in the air, then jerked her upper body with a loud shout. "In the name of Jesus! Help me!"

As Kevin headed back to his room with Jasmine on his shoulder, the two other females were playing on his back like two horny nuns breaking free from the Vatican.

"Excuse me, young man!" Ms. Betty stopped Kevin just before he ducked back into his room.

"Yeah," he sort of looked down at the wizened face old lady who appears to be in her late sixties, "what's up, granny?" He let Jasmine go and she ran back into the room with the other two females.

"Granny, huh?" Ms. Betty mocked, taking a few seconds to compose herself before she put him in check. "Did your mother ever teach you any manners when you're in public places?"

"Nah, not really. Why?"

"I can only imagine so," she said in a way meant to belittle him. "But unfortunately, this is not your ghetto hood, so to say. It's a hotel where common, decent people like myself and others who can come here for a comfortable rest, and not to be bothered by heathens like yourself, running through the hall, half naked."

"Oh, yeah!" Kevin palmed his dick over his speedo and said, "Bitch, here's your muthafucking' heathen right here!"

"How dare you?!" Ms. Betty turned her head from him with disgust and strode toward her room. "C'mon, Sister Mary!"

"You fuck-ass hoe!" Kevin added before he walked back into his room.

Ms. Betty opened her room door and realized that she was standing there by herself. "Sister Mary! I'm waiting on you!"

"Oh, I'm sorry," she said, breaking loose from her trance.

Ms. Betty held the door open for Sister Mary and said, "He won't hear the last of this," before slamming the door behind them.

The bachelorette party was off the chain; it was one of my best ones ever.

The females who attended the party—in Room 512—were having a ball, playfully yelling out together, "Fifty ... eight! Fifty ... nine! ... Sixty! ... Sixty ... one!" in unison, all around Kevin while he seemed to be relaxed on the couch, with his arms stretched out wide on top of the back rest. And when they all shouted, "Sixty-two!" on one accord, another female from out of the blue, I believe her name was Michelle if I stand correctly, lift her head up from Kevin's lap because she had just finished sucking him off.

And I would be damned! I lost the bet. She did it under a hundred strokes.

When she got off her knees and stood up, she turned toward me, then to her friends with Kevin's gooey nut drooling from her mouth.

They cheered her drunk ass on.

I still couldn't believe.

She had the audacity to say, "I told y'all bitches, I'm like that!" She spat Kevin's semen on the floor, then twisted back to me. "So pay up, nigga!"

I was astonished.

They all laughed at me. This shawty was wild as hell. I shot her a fifty dollar bill.

And it was about this same time we heard someone rapping on our hotel door. Jasmine and Nikki ran to answer it while Kevin and I kept entertaining the other seven females in the room with us.

"You know," this one Amazon broad, with biceps bigger than mine, began to say, while fondling my Johnson in her hand, "I could make you explode just under fifty strokes."

I almost laughed at this chick who stood about three inches taller than me. "How?"

She flopped my thick sausage out of my underwear, got on her knees, and crouched a bit.

I shut my eyes when my dick grew strong in her mouth.

"Yes, how can I help you?" Jasmine asked an elderly man, Ms. Betty, and Sister Mary at the door.

The elderly man who had salt and pepper hair was the first one to speak. "Miss Baker?"

"No, that's my friend, Hellen," Jasmine corrected. "Is she expecting y'all?"

"No, not quite," he said. "My name is Donald McCain, and I'm the hotel manager here. We have several complaints about this room."

Nikki immediately twisted around and yelled: "Hey, Hellen! Some people would like to speak to you!"

"Did you say something?" she tried to yell back, if you wanna call it that.

Without replying, Nikki opened the door wide enough so Hellen could see the angry folks at the door.

"Oh, shit!" Hellen panicked, letting go of my throbbing manhood. "Turn down the music! Hurry up!" She then rushed to the door, leaving everybody behind.

"Miss Baker?" Donald asked, still trying to get some type of confirmation, looking up to her.

"Yes." Hellen wiped her mouth. "I'm Miss Baker. How can I help you?"

"Well, I'm the hotel manager. I'm here because our front desk received several complaints regarding this room and about some visitors of yours." He paused, hoping to read the expression off her face. Then added: "I must advise you of our hotel policy, we don't tolerate our guests running through the hall semi-nude or disrespecting other guests at any given—"

"Hey!" Kevin interrupted him, pulling the door wide open, while wearing nothing but a towel wrapped around his waist. "Y'all didn't say anything about older folks were gonna be at this party too?"

"That's the heathen" —Ms. Betty pointed her finger in his face— "I was telling you about!"

Kevin cowered, then quickly relaxed himself.

To which she added, "And he had the nerve to show me his shriveled up wiener!"

"Stop lying!" Kevin snapped back at her. "Because I didn't show you a muthafucking' thing! You old misandry bitch!"

Ms. Betty turned to Donald and Sister Mary. "Did you hear what this filthy heathen just called me?"

Kevin went on to ask her, "Why are you bothering us? What the hell is your problem?"

"Well, for one," she twisted back to him, "my problem is not only with you!" She looked over his shoulders, pointing her finger at us. "But, all of you heathens in here!" She rested her hand on a Bible. "You all live like the devil's emissary, running around here doing his evil deeds!" She then threw her hand up in the air again, jerked her upper body and shouted: "O' Lord Jesus! Help me!" She jerked her upper body again. "Whew! O' help me, Lord! The devil is using his children to commit sins against you oh, Lord! Deliver me the strength, O' Lord! Glory hallelujah!" She jerked again. "Send them all to hell!"

We all stared at her—speaking for myself, I thought she was possessed by some sort of demonic spirit—wondering if she was all right.

But then again, I should have known better: she was faking. She was a Christian.

Then my mind changed to something different: I was puzzled for a brief moment because I didn't have the sightless clue as to what this harridan was talking about until it suddenly dawned on me. I almost laughed. "I know this nigga didn't show her his dick," I mumbled out by mistake.

"You weren't even there!" Ms. Betty snapped at me. "So you can't say anything about it, but keep your trap shut. You filthy heathen!"

Damn....

She just stood there at our door, chewing me and Kevin up, saying some bullshit like we were defiling God's day by doing the devil's deeds.

After what seemed to be a long moment, I cut her off with, "Don't blame the devil for this day. Just remember your supposed lord had made this day. It's only right for us to be glad and enjoy it."

"Don't use my Lord's name in vain, you dirty heathen!"

Just when Donald was about to get in the middle of our dispute, Hellen cut him off: "Excuse me sir, may I speak to you in private please?"

"Sure."

They both stepped away from us.

I shot Ms. Betty an impetuous stare, letting her know that if she got out of line, I was going to slap the shit out of her.

"Nigga, please!" she said. "You don't scare me with that look."

"Sir," **Hellen began**, "my best friend Bridgette is having her bachelorette's party before she jumps the broomstick tomorrow—"

"You can call me Donald," he told her, trying his damnedest not to look at her cleavage. It was right there in front of him. Two huge water melons.

"Okay, Donald," she said, while a conniving smile started to grow on her face once she knew he was locked onto her breasts. "I like that name, Donald." She paused for a brief second, if that. "But Donald, maybe you wouldn't have the tiniest clue how it feels to be young and fresh, and wanting to unleash a certain energy within...."

Oh yeah, that did it. Donald was lost in his bewildered mind. He started bobbing his head. "Uh-huh, uh-huh, I know exactly what you mean." He unconsciously licked his lips, slightly distracted by her 38 double D's. "I was once young too, you know."

There was another pause. A very short one.

"Okay," he said, after considering the situation. "You all can continue y'all party. But just make sure that you keep your visitors inside your room with y'all. Okay?"

"Sure. Anything you say, Donald. You're the man in charge here."

"Yeah," he seemed to like the sound of that. "I'm the man in charge here."

"DONALD!" Ms. Betty yelled from across the hall, shocked by the leering smile that he had on his face. "What has come over you?!"

Donald came back to his senses. "Everything is under control," he told her with a slight turn of his head. "You and Sister Mary can go back to your room now."

But Ms. Betty insisted: "Get them outta here!"

Donald hesitated for a moment. Not for long. It was no more than a second or two, then he walked over to her. He wrapped his arm around Ms. Betty's shoulder and led her and Sister Mary back to their room. "Now, now Sister Betty," he began soothingly, "how long have we known each other?"

Ms. Betty shrugged. "I don't know. Probably fifteen or sixteen years now." She gave him a suspicious look. "Why are you asking me this? You ought to know that already."

"Exactly. I have known you long enough to know that you have a forgiving heart. And besides, we were young just like them once. So why don't we allow them to have some fun, okay?"

Donald stood out in the hall, about three doors down, talking intensively to Ms. Betty.

"My nigga, what's that hoe's problem?" Kevin asked me over my shoulder as we watched Donald trying to calm her down.

"I don't know. But I just hope you don't grow old and bitter like that nagging bitch over there."

"Never that."

We laughed.

As Donald was still running off at the mouth to Ms. Betty and Sister Mary, they looked over his shoulders and saw us standing by our doorway, clowning on them.

I threw a puerile look on my face, hoping to antagonize them.

And it worked.

"Eh, look out!" Kevin tried to push me aside while holding his towel around his waist. "Let me get up there."

I cleared a path for him.

He smiled at Ms. Betty and Sister Mary, but they never smiled back. They shot him a death stare instead. Their eyes were cold and hollow looking.

That was understandable.

Kevin then whipped his towel open. He had his arms spread wide, flashing the both of them with his naked body. I was shocked! Kevin wiggled his hips from side to side while Donald had his back turned towards us.

Kevin definitely showed them his manhood this time. I saw it myself.

Ms. Betty's jaw dropped. "There he goes again!" she yelled at Donald, pointing her finger over his shoulder. "He did it again and the Lord is my witness. That black muthafucker just showed me his.... His fucking dick!"

Donald twisted around to see what she was talking about. But by the time he looked, all of us had already ducked back into the room, leaving Hellen by herself. She stood there at the doorway, looking more innocent than the first time he set his eyes upon her.

Donald smiled at Hellen; she smiled back.

Damn, she's fine, he must have been thinking, judging by the way that smile stretched further across his face.

Hellen waved good-bye and went back inside the room, showing him her perfect T-string through her lingerie.

Mmmm-mmm....

Donald turned back to Ms. Betty with a smile. "Everything is gonna be eh-o-kay," he tried to reassure her, placing his hand on her shoulder, hoping to sugar coat it.

"Don't you dare touch me!" She jerked her shoulder away from him.

"Don't you ever touch me again! You, you, you Undercover Heathen!" Then she guided Sister Mary into their room, stepped inside, and slammed the door in Donald's face.

He stood there for a hot second before he walked away. Then, all of a sudden, he stopped. He turned back around, lurking toward

Room 512, and just as he was about to knock on the door, Ms. Betty's door, right across the hall from him, swung open.

"Ah-Ha!" she accused. "I've caught you in your filthy act! So how dare you try to defile the Lord's sanctified day? You filthy-minded heathen!"

"What are you talking about?" he came up with a quick one. "I thought I heard some loud music playing in there again. And I just wanna make sure all of you on this floor are having a good-night's sleep."

"Oh, sure you do." Ms. Betty looked at him, knowing he was lying to her. "Vengeance is mine, saith the Lord. And I can't wait to see you all burn in hell!" She threw her hand in the air and jerked her upper body. "Glory hallelujah!" She slammed the door in his face again.

"You frustrated bitch!" Donald stormed away, heading toward the elevator. "What you need to do is try to go get a life of your own and leave other people alone."

Kevin ran over to the boom box and turned the music volume back up before running back to the center of the impatient females. "This my shit right here." He got directly behind Vanessa, right up against her ass, and whispered in her ear: "Girl, you make a nigga wanna stick this dick up inside of you and bust off."

Vanessa twisted her head around and smiled. "So, what's stopping you?"

He smiled back, then led her to the king-size bed.

I had Bridgette, the bachelorette—the soon-to-be bride—up in the bathroom, doing my own little thing with her: gyrating my body in front of her face with my speedo brushing against her chin.

"Ooooh," she dragged with a whisper. "Pull it out for me and let me kiss it for you."

"Now you know I can't do that." I kept dancing with a steady squirmy pace. "And besides, you're getting married tomorrow. So don't do anything that you'll probably regret for the rest of your life."

"Regret?!" Bridgette's facial expression changed. "Fuck that nigga! He probably be out there with that same frog face bitch I caught him with last week." She paused, then zoomed in on my pouch again. "Just let me see it then."

Well, on that note, I pulled my underwear aside so she could get a good look at my combat souljah.

Meet Goliath.

She got wide-eyed and spread her legs open. "Oh, yes," she moaned softly. "Oh, yes, give it to me…." She then stuck two fingers inside her and started playing with herself for about three minutes straight. Nonstop. "Uh, fuck! She fiddled her fingers inside her love hole even faster this time. "I'm about to cum…."

I broke free from her grip and sat her on top of the bathroom sink. I smiled, then crouched in and parted her labia lips. For a dark skinned shawty, her pussy hole was fluorescent pink. That pretty color pink. I just had to taste her.

She moaned for me not to stop.

And I didn't.

When I stepped out of the bathroom I noticed the room wasn't as crowded as it had been before. It was down to the foursome now with Kevin lying in the center of the bed. He was with the three broads who had stayed behind.

I laughed to myself when I saw that freak Bridgette—yes, the same one who I just got finished knocking off in the bathroom— taking turns with Hellen, slobbering on Kevin's dick. I grabbed my duffel bag.

Jasmine stopped kissing on Kevin's chest and extended her hand to me. "Why don't you join us?" she asked, hoping that I would jump in the bed with them. "I promise, you won't regret it. Actually, you'll enjoy every bit of it."

"Nah, I'm all right." Any other time I would have joined them, since she bore a close resemblance to Jennifer Lopez. And besides, she had that nice spread before she twisted around to me. Her ass was up in the air, looking beautiful and plump. Tempted, yes. I wouldn't mind tasting her sphincter. It's not so often that I come across an albino chick. But since I decided to call it a night, I didn't mind leaving Kevin there by himself so he could get his freak on with them. But in all truth, I needed to have some time to myself to consider what Aunt Enid wanted to tell me tomorrow afternoon.

"Are you sure about that?" Jasmine asked me, then began to gnaw on her bottom lip.

"Oh, what the hell." I smiled. I had plenty of time to think about what Aunt Enid had to tell me tomorrow. I took my shirt off and got in the bed with them. I pulled Jasmine close. I kissed her, while laying her flat on her back in the kitty-position. Then I worked my way down to her mound.

She moaned.

I parted her yellow lips for easy access. I lapped it once; then twice. She spread her legs wider. I lapped her again and felt her hands on the back of my head. I went to work on her, stretching her pussy lips out, eating all that I can eat.

When I parked my car in Aunt Enid's driveway, I saw a bunch of children, from toddlers to teenagers, swarming up and down the street like pesty rag-rats. I got out of the car and scanned the block.

Carol City was nothing like it used to be. It used to be more organized. For real. You can even go ask Shelby Rushin from 99 Jamz about it. Because I remembered growing up on this same block, on 179th street, with Aunt Enid, the neighbors were more friendly back then. They used to look after one another like a real community. It was once clean around here. But now ... there was trash everywhere you looked. The neighborhood had changed, drastically. It was criminally infested with drug dealers, wanna-be pimps, thieves, prostitutes, and crack-heads. And if you think that's something, check this out: at least half the houses needed to be renovated, or even better yet, demolished for safety reasons. Most of the people who lived in or visited the neighborhood, walked up and down the block like lifeless zombies. And I swear, I had been trying to persuade my aunt to leave this rat-infested neighborhood for years now. But she has always put up a fight and declined to do so since she felt like she build her whole history on this ghetto ass block.

I, however, was taught—by an old schooler, back in the day—that it is always best, in the match of tug and war, to release your arms for a short moment before you pull on the rope again. So on that note, I know she would eventually break weak and I would get my wish to move her from this government ghetto war zone for Blacks.

I walked inside the house and found it full of life and plenty of kids romping and running throughout the rooms. I strolled straight into the living room, which looked more like a little day care center with a complete set up for a nursery.

You see, my aunt not only ran a day care center from inside her home, she operated a foster home in there as well. And just like always, she kept the youngest child at her side.

"Hey, baby," she whispered over to me. "I'll be right with you in a moment. Gimme a second." She was in the process of rocking that young child to sleep.

I looked around the room. For wonderful reasons, I smiled. I remembered certain moments from my childhood days that unconsciously flashed through my mind: moments of great joy that I would always appreciate. Memories of myself as a young boy in this same room with Aunt Enid, listening to her hum the rhythms of different church choir songs. Then I thought of other times when Aunt Enid used to pamper me in the same manner. Sorta like what she was doing to that little youngster now. And at that moment I realized how much I missed her and this old house; especially her core value that she stood firm on: "Spare the rod, and you will spoil the child", she would always say.

I quietly laughed to myself. Those were the good old days when I used to—

"Okay, I'm done now," she said, interrupting my joyful memories. "Let's go in the kitchen so I can fill you in on everything before tomorrow."

And she did just that when we went inside the kitchen. She explained everything to me in detail.

"And you're sure this can't be a mistake?" I asked.

"No, I doubt it. But we'll find out when we drive up there to Tallahassee tomorrow."

"I just hope this shit ain't some prank."

"Boy, tame your tongue while you're in my presence!"

I accidentally sucked my teeth, and the palm of her hand went straight for the back of my head.

I didn't know what to expect when I got up to Tallahassee with Aunt Enid, so—to be on the safe side—I invited Carlton to come along with us. And besides, I needed his assistance. It was an eight hour drive.

When we arrived at the Family Court, it had a subsection building where the state kept its Family Services Department. We went inside.

But once inside, it was nothing like what I had thought it would look like. It was totally the opposite from what I have seen on TV: a large office area with about twenty-five cubicles where the caseworkers were at hand, ready to assist you upon arrival. But oh no, not this spot: it was the flip side of everything that you could have imagined. Like, besides the waiting area being ridiculously cramped, there was a swarm of children with their guardians, looking as if they didn't have a bit of self-control. Some children were crying while others were enjoying themselves, running up and down the hallway, as if they were at Miami Metro Zoo.

Unbelievable....

All night while driving up to Tallahassee, I had spent my time pondering a course of action regarding this child. I knew what I had to do wouldn't be easy for some people. But, in my case, it would be simple. Very simple. I had planned on walking straight in there and then walking straight out of there, denying any responsibility for that child.

Who?

Jessica, who?

No, I'm sorry. I don't believe I ever met a person by that name before, I planned on saying. But deep down I know I couldn't lie like that in front of Aunt Enid. She knew the truth.

I suddenly recalled the momentous event that took place back in the day that made me pause for a moment.

One night when I was about 13 years old, while eating dinner at Aunt Enid's house, a neighborhood friend came over, unexpectedly.

With the eccentric anger that I had developed after my mom's death, I asked Kevin, "What you want over here at this time of the night? Don't you have your own house to go to?"

"DASHAWN!" Aunt Enid flipped the script on me when she heard me say that to him, then got up from the table and strode over there to where we were standing. "Don't treat your friend like that. He must have a good reason for coming over here."

Close call, I thought she was about to pop me upside my head.

Kevin seemed relieved. "I just came over to see whatchu were doing," he answered my question, then looked over my shoulder to the dining room table.

Aunt Enid noticed. "Baby, do you want something to eat?" she asked him, resting her hand on the side of his ashy face. "Because we have enough food for you, if you want some?"

"Yes, ma'am." He quickly nodded his head. "May I have something to eat?"

"Sure you can, hon."

His smile widened. "And my sister…," he stammered. "Can my sister eat with us too?"

I looked up at Aunt Enid and shook my head, but she didn't pay me any attention.

"Oh, sure," she told him. "She can have something to eat too. So go ahead and get her for me. And in the meantime, I'll set up two plates for both of you."

Kevin smiled; it seemed like he was about to run from the doorway to get his sister, but he didn't. He just stuck his arm outside, around the bend of the door frame, and pulled his sister Keisha inside the house with us.

I was ticked off!

Aunt Enid told them to have a seat at the table, then turned to me. "Honey, follow me in the kitchen and help me prepare two plates for our friends here." Then she walked away, heading toward the kitchen.

I dragged my feet behind her.

Inside the kitchen, I stood in silence. Aunt Enid couldn't help but notice that scorching look I had on my face.

"You know there are two different type of people in the world," she said while preparing the two plates of food. "Those that are fortunate enough and those that aren't so fortunate."

"Why are you telling me this for?"

She placed her hand on my cheek and smiled. "Because you're fortunate enough to be loved by me, and to be taken care of. But then, there are other people who aren't so fortunate, like your friends out there: Kevin and Keisha. And the sad thing about that is, the both of them are young and innocent, and it's not their fault. So it's our duty to look after those who aren't so fortunate, and help them during their time of need—"

"But you're my auntie. I'm grateful for that. So let them find their own auntie to be grateful for."

I remembered that day just as if it was yesterday because Aunt Enid pondered my anger for a moment, then slowly shook her head and hit me with one of her reach one, teach one mottos: "I'm everybody's auntie around here, hon. But for you, you're more than just my nephew: you're my world. But just imagine for a moment here that I wasn't your aunt and you were like one of those hungry kids out there who was in need for a nice warm meal to eat." She paused. Then added: "How would you feel then?"

I shrugged my thin shoulders. "I don't know," I remembered telling her as I cut my eyes to the kitchen floor. "Probably sad."

She lifted my face back up to look at me. "Okay then, since you're fortunate enough to have me as your aunt, show somebody else, like your friends out there, who aren't so fortunate, that they are also loved by someone who is fortunate enough to care about their well-being."

I embraced her, wrapping my arms around her wide body. "I love you, Auntie."

"I love you too. So come now, let's go eat because our food is getting cold."

At the dining room table, Aunt Enid asked Kevin to say a prayer for all of us before we ate our supper. And he did. Although he gave a short, deadbeat prayer that night, we still enjoyed our meal. The following day, as I learned later down the road, Aunt Enid went over to Kevin's house to visit his mom and attempted to enlighten her on the priority she needed to have for her children's welfare. But Aunt Enid didn't accomplish anything that morning because Kevin's mother was too far out there on drugs. She had a neighborhood drug dealer over at the house, giving him a trick-for-a-treat. In other words, the drug dealer gave Kevin's mother a piece of crack-rock for a sexual favor.

A blow-job.

From then on, Kevin and his sister Keisha stayed over with us until they were old enough to support themselves.

But this is now, not back then when I was much younger.

During the drive up to Tallahassee, I had made up my mind. I would inform the caseworker this has to be a big misunderstanding because I practiced celibacy. No! The idea of me being sterile was better, I thought. So it would be impossible, if not ridiculous for the alleged child to be mine.

I couldn't wait to get this shit over with!

"How long is this gonna take?" I asked Aunt Enid. "Because I have other things to do back home, other than just sitting around here doing nothing."

"I don't know." She gave me a scornful look. "I guess when they call us."

Carlton got up and went to the water fountain. When he came back, he tried to taunt me by knocking his knee against mine.

"What's your problem?" I asked.

"Which one of these lucky kids do you think is yours?"

"Man, fuck you!"

Aunt Enid nudged me with her elbow. "DaShawn! Watch your mouth when you're in front of me."

"I'm sorry."

She cut her eyes away from me.

A moment later a young boy who looked to be about six years old—maybe seven years old, and that's pushing it—walked up to

Carlton and tapped him on his knee. Then asked, "Are you my daddy?"

"Oh, hell nah!" Carlton proclaimed, then quickly flicked his thumb at me. "He's your daddy."

I went with my first instinct: I hammered my elbow straight into Carlton's ribs.

He crunched down a bit, gasping for air.

I swear, I had literally tried to break one of his fucking ribs for trying me like that.

"My nigga," Carlton barely got his wind back when he twisted to me, looking upset, "you knocked the air outta me, you stupid ass."

I ignored him.

The young boy then turned to me with a smile on his face. "So are you my daddy?"

I was taken by surprise. Yeah, I was prepared to tell the caseworker a white lie, but not to a little youngster like this. So with the little compassion that I had in me, I barely shrugged my lazy shoulders and told him the truth: "I don't know."

"JUSTIN!"

The little boy turned around; I looked in the same direction to see who called him.

It was a Hispanic female in her mid-thirties who was dressed in white spandex pants, tight-fitting. And she looked all right, too. She had wide hips, heading straight towards us.

"Didn't I tell you not to move from there?" she asked the little boy as she approached him. "And what did I tell you about talking to strangers?" She grabbed him by the hand and jerked his arm a bit.

"But he's my daddy," he said, probably to lighten the burden upon himself. "He told me so."

This Hispanic female cut her eyes to me and asked in a cold manner, "Did you tell my son that?"

"Of course not. I just told him that I didn't know."

"Excuse me? You said that to him?" She paused, looking me up and down. Then quickly added: "You didn't know?"

"Yeah, that's all I said to him."

She turned to Justin. "Sweetie, cover your ears for me."

And the little shit-starter did, using both his hands. She turned back to me and unleashed a Hillary Clinton: "Where in the fuck do you know me from?"

"I don't. Well, at least I don't think I do."

"Alright then! So why in the hell did you tell my son some bullshit like that to get him confused about who is his father?"

I felt like an idiot. "Nah. I didn't mean it like that, ma." I tried to keep it real with her. "I only told him that because I didn't know if he were—"

This Spanish bitch snapped again. "¡Enfermo, hijodeputa!" she shouted at me, among some other stuff from her native tongue—as if I had a slightest clue as to what the hell she was saying to me— before she strode away upset, dragging her son behind her.

"Mr. DaShawn Powell?"

I turned to see who had called me.

Damn!

It was an older white lady standing down the corridor at a doorway. I swallowed hard. Fear showered me. I knew this was the beginning of everything: my wretchedness. I managed to say, "Yes," as I slowly got up from my seat, then looked at Aunt Enid for some sort of support.

She got up, and so did Carlton.

This old hag met Aunt Enid, Carlton, and me halfway down the hall, holding a blue folder against her breasts. She looked to be in her seventies, if not in her eighties. But not only her age, though: It was her skin. I mean like, whoa..., her skin was wizened badly. Full of wrinkles. And to top it off, she had a regrettable mole on the side of her face near her aquiline-looking nose.

"I'm Ms. Pattie-May Butcher, the caseworker over your case," she said with a pure Southern accent. "Now which one of you boys is Mr. Powell?"

"That would be me, ma'am."

Ms. Pattie-May smiled at me. "You're a fine looking lad. I can see where your child got the resemblances from."

"Yeah, that's what I need to talk to you about."

"You don't need to say anything more. Y'all just follow me in here so we can get down to business." She started to lead us to her office. "So how is the weather down yonder, in Miami?"

"Just beautiful," Aunt Enid said.

Ms. Pattie-May stopped at her office doorway, smiling over at us. "Well, I guess I hafta go down there and get me some of those beautiful sun rays on South Beach. I hear that it's a wonderful place down yonder." She paused for a second. "I have this two piece bikini that I have always wanted to wear."

"Eeuw!" Carlton murmured under his breath.

I could only imagine what he was thinking: Who was she trying to fool?

"I beg your pardon?" Ms. Pattie-May asked him. "Did you say something, cutie?"

Oh, my goodness. He better not! I cut back to him.

"I said, yeah, you would love South Beach," he straight out lied to her. "So whenever you're down there, I wouldn't mind showing you around town."

Ms. Pattie-May flashed her big brown eyes and blushed. "I might take you up on that offer," she said, then walked us into her office.

Ms. Pattie-May's office was decorated with children's paintings and toys. Old toys. Stuff like from the eighties. She invited us to sit in some shabby-looking chairs on the other side of her oak wood desk.

I grabbed the chair on the far left and sat there gathering up my thoughts. My mind couldn't get away from the thought of this alleged child of mine; then it hit me.

Fuck this shit! I couldn't wait another second; I jumped right to it. "Ms. Pattie-May," my tone was a bit straightforward, "I would like to be honest with you and get this over with as soon as possible."

"Of course, Mr. Powell. It's only a few things I have to go over with you first. And before you know it, it'll be all over with. You will have your child with you in a bit."

I took a deep breath. "You see, that's my problem. How do I know if this child is actually mine or not?"

Ms. Pattie-May stopped flipping through her blue folder; she paused. "Oh, my," she said with her doddering fingers over her mouth, slightly shaking her head in disbelief, then stopped. "Son, are you just saying this to avoid your responsibilities, or are you really not sure if this child is yours?"

"I don't really know the truth." I admitted to her. "You see, I used to be in a relationship with this child's mother. But she disappeared eight years ago after she told me about her pregnancy."

"Oh," Ms. Pattie-May let out, as she slowly bobbed her head. "But did she ever tell you that you were the father?"

"Yeah. But then again, no." Moments from my past relationship with Jessica flashed through my mind again: Moments that we shared together up until that last conversation we had regarding her pregnancy. And then I thought about all those moments after that when I was caught in limbo because she left me without any explanation.

"Okay then," Ms. Pattie-May said, interrupting my thoughts. "If you don't mind, can you tell me the time period that you were with this young gal, Ms. Anderson, so we can start drawing some conclusions?"

"Sure." I gave her all the dates she need to know about the time frame I shared with Jessica.

"Now, if you're certain about the time period when you were with this gal, before and during the beginning stages of her pregnancy, my calculations show that there's a strong possibility that you are the biological father of this child."

"But still," I contested, "that doesn't prove that I'm the father."

Ms. Pattie-May seemed to agree with me on that point, because she took a moment to herself before she made eye contact again.

"Okay then, I can do this for you," she suggested. "I will request a paternity test from the court and recommend that this child be placed under foster care until the test results come back."

Hell, yeah! I smiled. "We can do that." I quickly nodded my head to show my gratitude. "That would be—uggh!" I was saying before I got hit in my ribs by Aunt Enid. "What's that for?"

"Boy, are you that stupid, or you just don't have a bit of sense in that pea-brain of yours?"

I didn't answer that: it was a Catch-22.

Aunt Enid kept her eyes on me. By the look of things, it seemed like she wanted to pop me upside my head. She had her hand cocked back. But then she turned to look at Ms. Pattie-May, then back to me. I guess she changed her mind.

"But Auntie, I don't even know if this child is mine or not."

"But what if he is?" she shot back. "What then? Would you really allow your child to sit up in some youth facility until the court decides on the outcome of some blood test?"

I wanted to say Hell, yeah, but I decided to keep my mouth shut. She still had her palm opened.

"My nigga, that's true," Carlton said to me. "You can't do something like that."

Aunt Enid turned her attention on Carlton now, giving him an evil stare. "What did I tell you about using that N-word in front of me?"

"But I didn't use the N-word in front of you."

"So you gonna tell me in my face that I didn't hear you use that N-word in front of me?"

"I swear to God I didn't." He seemed serious about his reply. Then he looked to Ms. Pattie-May for some sort of support. "Can you tell her I didn't use that N-word a second ago?"

"But you did use the N-word, son."

Carlton sucked his teeth at her, then said, "You must think I'm stupid or something. I know I didn't use the N-word in front of y'all. She musta put you up to say that about me."

"Of course not."

Even under these circumstances, I couldn't help but laugh.

Carlton spread his hands in the air in a helpless gesture, then dropped his hands hard against his lap. "What can I do?" He turned back to Aunt Enid. "Because I'm convinced that y'all are lying on me. I know what I said to him. And if I did slip up and said something like that in front of you, I don't be using the N-word with an R, like the one they," —he beckoned his head toward Ms. Pattie-May— "used behind our backs. I used it with an A. It's different. A big difference. Here, just hear the difference for yourself..., Nigga. Not nigger."

Aunt Enid immediately raised her hand at him. She almost lost her composure, but I guess she knew it wasn't worth it. He's a weed-head, she was probably thinking when she said, "We have a more important issue right now. We're talking about a child here, and we have to be more concerned with this child's welfare."

"You're right," Ms. Pattie-May said, "But there's something else that I can do." She paused, then looked at me. "Since you're listed as the biological father...."

Okay, I must admit, this old bitch got my attention again. So I asked in a casual tone of voice, trying to downplay all my lack of concern for this alleged child of mine: "And what might that be?"

Ms. Pattie-May took a deep breath, looking across her desk at the three of us. "Lemme tell y'all the reality of this," she said, then turned her attention straight to me. "I have the authority to send this child back under the State's foster care until a paternity test is administered. But given what you have told me so far regarding the history between you and that gal Ms. Anderson, I strongly believe son, this child is yours. And I would have to agree with your mammy here—"

"Aunt," Aunt Enid corrected her.

"Pardon me," Ms. Pattie-May said. "But I would have to agree with your auntie here. Sending this child to a foster home isn't a good idea, if you're the biological father."

I opened my mouth because I wanted to make my objection known, but I closed it back until she got finished saying whatever she had to say.

"However," she began to add, "on the other side of this, I can also allow you to have custody over the child for the time being until we confirm our paternity test result. But again, this is all up to you...."

I actually felt lost right there. But I still managed to glance over at Aunt Enid, then back to Ms. Pattie-May. "Well, I don't see any problem with that then, if that be the case. But how long before I can take this paternity test?"

"Soon. All I have to do is set up an appointment with one of our sister offices down yonder in Miami and have them contact you as soon as possible."

"That would be excellent."

"And oh, just one more thing," Ms. Pattie-May said. "Since a paternity test is pending, I will have to assign a family caseworker from Miami to oversee your case file until this matter is resolved. And if you have any problem, you can discuss it with the assigned caseworker, or perhaps you can call me here at my office."

"Sure, I can do that"

Ms. Pattie-May leaned over the desk, placed several sheets of paper in front of me and said, "All you have to do is sign these forms." She pointed her finger at the space for my signature. "Yeah, right there. And I'll take you to see little Dee-Jay." She smiled. "I had that little cutie sent to my office early this morning to avoid y'all the trip across town. Actually, Dee-Jay is just a few doors down the hall with some other kids."

I hesitated a bit when I was signing the custody release forms. And when I had finished, I looked at Ms. Pattie-May, wishing I had the strength to tell her what was going through my mind about this bullshit! But still, the irritation flashed: Who in the hell they think I am? Some desperate muthafucker who's in search of a fucking kid? And if that's the case, they all have it twisted then. Because I'm not!

I tried not to show my outrage, but I had one question for Ms. Pattie-May: "If you don't mind me asking: Whatever happened to Jessica Anderson?"

Ms. Pattie-May covered her mouth with her fingers again and took a deep breath. "Oh my, I didn't tell you?"

Hell nah, you didn't tell me. I shook my head. Tell me what? I was all ears.

Ms. Pattie-May continued: "That poor gal caught the Acquired Immunodeficiency Syndrome. The AIDS virus. She passed away about three weeks ago." She looked as if she wanted to cry. "It's just a pity that little child had to go through such a bad experience watching—"

"What?!" I cut her off. "She died of AIDS?" Suddenly my mind was paralyzed. My heart skipped a beat. Maybe two. For a moment I began to wonder if I had contracted the virus, too. And if I did, I thought, that bitch gave it to me! But then, when my brain started working again, I remembered I had taken an HIV test a few months ago and it had come back clean.

Ms. Pattie-May remained silent, but she did nod her head slowly.

Damn … Jessica caught the virus, I mulled. "But what about this child of hers?" I began to ask Ms. Pattie-May, "was the virus passed on …"

Ms. Pattie-May beat me to the punch: "To the little one?"

I barely nodded. "Yeah."

"No. Of course not! My records reveal that Ms. Jessica Anderson caught the AIDS virus about three years after she gave birth to her child."

Oh, that was good to know. For the child's sake, that is.

Ms. Pattie-May got up from her chair. "Well, come on, let me take you to see this cutie," she said, as she led us out of the office and walked us down the corridor to a locked, guarded door.

The door was huge with a red and white warning sign on it that read: "THIS IS AN UNAUTHORIZED AREA – STAFF MEMBERS ONLY."

"Hey, Charlie," Ms. Pattie-May said to the security officer who was posted at the door.

"Hi, there. How's your day?"

"Just fine. But it could be a little better," she said with a suggestive wink.

Charlie laughed at her attempt to flirt with him. "So how can I assist you today?"

"Well for starters," her face seemed to have taken on some sort of life form from somewhere, "these fine folks came all the way up from Miami to pick that young child that I had brought over here early this morning."

Charlie knew exactly who she was talking about when he went on to say, "That child hasn't spoken to anybody or moved from that window all day. Just stood there looking out the window as if it were some kinda cartoon show on TV." He opened the door and walked us inside the room.

And I'm like daaaamn … who would have expected this room to be so humongous? Despite its size, it was filled with children. Some kids were running around playing, while a few of them stayed to him- or herself.

"Over by the window," Charlie said, then nodded toward four motionless children who were standing there with their back facing us. "You see, just like I'd told you: looking out the window all day."

"Dee-Jay!" Ms. Pattie-May called out from across the room as she led us toward the window.

I tried to act like a parent. I scanned the four kids who were standing over there by the window, but I didn't have a clue. "Which one of them do you think is he?" I whispered over to Carlton.

He shrugged. "I don't know, my nigga. But if anything, I hope he's the one on the far left with that black shirt on."

"Dee-Jay!" Ms. Pattie-May said again, as we drew near to the window.

Then two of the four children turned around, saw that we were approaching, and walked away. The other two youngsters stayed behind: the kids in the black shirt that Carlton was betting on, and another one who was wearing an old baseball cap.

"Dawg, it's him, I can feel it." Carlton got excited. "It's him."

I smiled. What the hell? I can work with him, I though. But as soon as we arrived at the window, the little youngster in the black shirt looked up at us and walked off to some other part of the room.

My smile disappeared.

"Dee-Jay," Ms. Pattie-May said, in a soft tone as she tapped the remaining child on the shoulder. Dee-Jay cocked around, looking frightened by Ms. Pattie-May's tap.

"Now, now cupcake," Ms. Pattie-May said. "You don't need to be afraid because, look what we have here. You have some fine folks who came a long way to see you." She paused, then placed her hand on Dee-Jay's chin and raised it a bit. "You're such a cutie."

How in the hell could she say some shit like that, I thought, when that worn-out baseball cap nearly covered Dee-Jay's whole face? The cap looked like it was once blue, but now it was old and faded.

Dee-Jay was small, with a thin figure and a light skinned complexion. And his overall appearance—to me—looked shabby. His pants were dingy, his shirt was ruined, and I shouldn't go in depth about his tennis shoes either because they looked like something he had found hanging from a telephone pole in the slum of Miami.

But when I saw that gold chain hanging from his neck I immediately recognized it. It was the same chain medallion that I had bought Jessica on her twenty-first birthday from a jewelry shop in 183rd flea market in Miami. It only cost me about $400. And on the back of the medallion, I had something personally engraved on it.

I cut my eyes from the gold chain back to Dee-Jay again, hoping to get a look at his face. But that dirty cap was in the way. And I couldn't help but wonder, Does he looks like his mom or what?

I grew impatient.

"Hey dawg, let's get a look at your face." Without any thoughts about it, I snatched the cap off his head and immediately leaped back when I saw Dee-Jay's hair tumble out from under the cap, hanging just below the shoulders.

"Oh, shit!"

I cut to my left and looked at Carlton. A smile began to stretch across his face, after sounding excited.

Oh, hell nah! I cut back to Dee-Jay.

What the hell is going on here! I screamed in my head.

Dee-Jay wasn't a boy at all. He was a damned girl! A goddamn girl, for crying out loud.

This shit can't be happening to me, I mulled. I didn't care if Dee-Jay had this girlish, pretty looking face. And I damn sure didn't care if her eyes were watery and swollen from crying all night; or even worse, since she learned of her mother's death. This shit ain't gonna work!

Dee-Jay ducked her head and cried some more.

Uh, fuck y'all!

Y'all could say what y'all wanna say.

Like I said before, I didn't care. So go fuck off if you don't like it!

"DASHAWN!" Aunt Enid shouted. "What's the matter with you?!"

But before I could respond to her, Carlton cut me off: "You have a baby girl.... Gahhhh, damn! Wait till the homeys see her."

I fixed my eyes on Ms. Pattie-May with a cold stare. I just hope this old bitch was telepathic, because I wanted to tell her that players don't have girls, we play girls. But when I got my voice back I settled on something more demeaning.

"What the hell is this?!" I asked her, flipping my hand open toward Dee-Jay, as if she were sitting inside some sort of showcase. "He ain't a boy! He's a she.... I damned girl! Oh, hell, nah! This wasn't part of our agreement. I'm not taking her with me!"

Dee-Jay snatched her baseball cap from my hand and placed it back on her head. She gave me an ugly stare, then continued to cry.

So? I don't care—I swear, I didn't—so go ahead and shed all the tears you want.

Aunt Enid drew Dee-Jay close to her, trying to console her.

So, like really, as if I really gave a fuck!

Ms. Patty-May had the nerve to act like she was confused. "What are you talking about, Mr. Powell?" she asked me. "Of course Dee-Jay here is a gal. She has always been one. And what sorta agreement are you talking about? I'm definitely lost here."

"What agreement?!"

"Yes!"

I pointed my hand at that little ragamuffin again and nearly shouted: "This! This is what the hell I'm talking about!"

"Please calm down," she tried to tell me, as if this shit was easy for me to swallow. "Let's go back to my office to discuss this."

Damn right we have to discuss this! I followed right behind her.

While walking back toward her office, Aunt Enid murmured something under her breath. She seemed pissed. I could see that she was upset with me. But at this point, I didn't give a damn! She could go ahead and say whatever she wanted.

Then it hit me. It felt like a Mike Tyson power punch slammed straight into my chest. I couldn't believe what I was telling myself. Aunt Enid was the one who raised me when I didn't have anyone, and I loved her for that. She has to know that too. But I'm a man now, so she has to respect my position.

I glanced over at her, and quickly looked in front of me to watch where I was walking. I was still upset. But then again, I didn't want her to be upset with me either.

"What's your problem?" Aunt Enid blew under her breath, as we trailed behind Ms. Pattie-May. I looked at her. Then she continued with, "I didn't come all the way up here for you to embarrass me like this in front of these people."

"I'm sorry Auntie, you have to believe me," I whispered back. "But she's a girl, and I'm not gonna be able to handle this. You know what kinda occupation I have?"

She sighed. "I know she's a girl. But just remember something too: You were a little snotty-nose boy when I took you in under my roof. Yes, a boy. And I thought I couldn't handle you either back then."

I didn't respond to that. How could I? She was right.

After that, everything seemed to come a little clearer. I had to decide the path I wanted to choose: to be a part-time father until that fucking paternity test comes back or to continue to live my life without any obligation to this child? And I felt something else stirring around in the bottom of my soul: a vague thought of Jessica running through me as if she were looking down to see what I was going to do.

Well, if that's the case. Fuck you too, bitch!

After all, she was the one who created this crisis. Ms. Pattie-May led us back into her office. "Come in and have a seat," she told us, then walked around her desk and sat her flat ass down. "I don't think Dee-Jay should be in here to hear this." She hit the button on the intercom, and a voice came over it.

"Good afternoon, Ms. Pattie," the voice greeted her. "How can I help you?"

"Jane, can you please step in my office for a second?"

"Sure, I'll be right over."

It became uncomfortably quiet inside her office. But within seconds a thin female in her late 30's walked into the room.

"Can you please assist me by taking this young gal with you till I call for her?" Ms. Pattie-May asked.

"Sure, I can do that for you." Jane reached for Dee-Jay's hand and escorted her out of the office.

It was about this same time I started to feel a little nervous.

Ms. Pattie-May cleared her throat and looked directly at me.

"Now tell me, what seems to be the problem?"

I played it off. I looked to my right side to Aunt Enid. Nope, she wasn't talking to her. I twisted to the left side to Carlton. Nope. Not him either. Then I turned back to Ms. Pattie-May. "Who me?" I suspiciously asked while pressing my finger against my chest.

"Yes, you. Now tell me, what seems to be the problem?"

I glanced at Aunt Enid again, then back at Ms. Pattie-May and shook my head. "I don't have a problem. I only have concerns and issues, if anything."

"And what kind of concerns and issues might those be?"

Bitch! Slow down a bit. I wanted to stall a little to think it out: If I contest Dee-Jay and argue that I didn't want to have any responsibility for her, would Aunt Enid forgive me, I wondered. Which I doubted. So I chose my first words carefully. "Well, we all know that, ummm … Dee-Jay is a girl, right?"

"Uh-huh. And your point?"

"And my point is this," I said slowly, trying to buy a few more seconds to come up with the right words to say. "Just what if she has to use the restroom or something? Or even worse, take a shower? What am I supposed to do then?"

Ms. Pattie-May seemed relieved now. "Are those your main concerns?"

"Yeah," I lied.

She laughed. "Oh, that's nothing, hon. You won't have to worry about that because she's potty-trained. And she can shower on her own, too"

"So my concerns are solved then," I told her another lie.

Ms. Pattie-May smiled, displaying her coffee-stained teeth. I fired back with a politician's smile. But who in the hell could my Hillary Clinton smile fool? I'm a male stripper who entertains females for a living. So, what now? Dee-Jay is supposed to follow in my footsteps and become a stripper at Rolex's nightclub when she grows up?

"All righty then, we're set to go." Ms. Pattie-May pressed that button on the intercom again, and told Jane to bring Dee-Jay back into her office.

Aunt Enid raised her hands in the air, in a gesture of praise, and looked at the ceiling. "Oh, thank you, Lord! Thank you! Thank you for putting some sense into his thick skull!"

Jane walked into the room with Dee-Jay.

Then Ms. Pattie-May said to Dee-Jay, "These fine folks right here wanna take you home with them until we get some things straightened out. Okay?"

Dee-Jay kept quiet.

"Hi, Dee-Jay," Aunt Enid said in a cheerful, friendly tone, resting her hand against Dee-Jay's arm.

Dee-Jay turned and looked at her.

Then Aunt Enid proceeded with: "How are you doing?"

Dee-Jay remained silent, but she kept her eyes on Aunt Enid.

I wanted to play my part as well. "Dee-Jay." I tapped her on the shoulder; she looked at me. Then I added: "You'll be coming home with us. Wouldn't you like that?" I waited for a response but she didn't say anything back to me either. "So what is it? Did the cat steal your tongue?"

Dee-Jay ducked her head down and started crying again.

"Now look what you've done!" Aunt Enid said, as she drew Dee-Jay near to her. "Don't listen to that big-head dummy. He just doesn't know any better."

"But," I asked Aunt Enid, "what did I do? I didn't even say anything wrong." I looked to Ms. Pattie-May. "I swear, I didn't."

They both shot me with that shame-on-you look.

After the meeting, Ms. Pattie-May and I tarried a little behind at the exit to the building while Aunt Enid, Carlton, and Dee-Jay were walking to the car.

"I believe once she starts to feel more comfortably around you," Ms. Pattie-May began telling me, "she'll start talking to you. I haven't heard a peep outta her mouth yet. But from what the people said around here, she can speak just fine. It's just that that poor gal went through so much about her mama's death."

"Yeah, I can imagine so," I said, thinking about Jessica. "Her mother was a true sweetheart...." Then I fell into a little trance when

I saw Aunt Enid from a distance trying to get Dee-Jay inside the car. But all Dee-Jay did was shake her head. I guess she didn't want to go with—

"I know this might be a little difficult for you at first," Ms. Pattie-May added, breaking up my thoughts. "But before you notice it, you'll be a professional parent. And a proud one too."

"Yeah, right," I said doubtfully. "Just imagine that." I shook her hand and thanked her for her time.

She went back inside the building.

As I headed for the car, I noticed Dee-Jay was carrying a yellow duffel back, no bigger than a regular size book bag, with different colored flower designs on it. She had it strapped around her shoulder, while refusing to get in the car.

"Wow," I gushed with enthusiasm, believing that might work. "That's a pretty bag you have there. Do you want me to put it with the rest of your stuff?"

Aunt Enid looked at me as if I were an idiot. "That's the only bag that she has," she said, then walked around the car, opened the back passenger's door and got in. "So try a different line."

"What do you mean that's the only bag she has? What about all her clothes and stuff?"

"That's all of it," she said before shutting the door behind her.

I turned back to Dee-Jay and politely tried to take the bag from her. But she held onto it as though I was a known purse-snatcher. "Okay, then," I tried a different approach. "Do you wanna sit up here in the front with me?"

She slowly shook her head, then walked away to the other side of the car.

"Where are you going?" I lingered behind her.

Without answering, she stopped at the back passenger's door and knocked on the window. Aunt Enid opened the car door and Dee-Jay got in.

I stood there for a few seconds, wondering what the hell I had gotten myself into.

Carlton blew the car horn. "Dawg, come on. Let's go. You're holding us up!"

"All right." I got inside the car.

He drove off in the bright midday afternoon. The heat was terrible out there, so I started playing with the AC controller and turned it up a bit. After a while, I got it straight. Although I wasn't driving, I reset the rearview mirror and watched Dee-Jay for a while. She was looking out the side window, still gripping onto her duffel bag with both hands.

"Yo, my nigga," Carlton whispered over to me. "Go ahead and get some sleep. I got you."

Aunt Enid cleared her throat with her eyes closed. I guess to let Carlton know that she wasn't asleep. I swear I thought they were about to go at it again, but they didn't. So I allowed my body to relax and let my mind drift off. I mulled about my sweet ol' Jessica when I used to be with her back in the day.

And to tell you a little secret: only a few months after I met Jessica, we'd become lovers. That ineffable love I felt for her back then, I haven't experienced a love like that for anyone else since then. I could honestly say she was my everything. My foundation; and I was madly in love with her. A love which I would freely have given my own life for. I'm dead serious. Yeah, I know it might sound a bit crazy, but it's true. As young lovers, we shared our dreams with one another. Get this: our dream was to be married one day, having a white picket fence and maybe two or three kids running through the house.

I exhaled, deeply.

I can't believe how I poured my heart out to her. I told her how much I longed to be a fashion designer and how one day I was going to have everybody wearing my clothes. But, in all truth, my dreams were shattered into tiny pieces when she dropped the bomb on me in the nightclub about her pregnancy. I actually felt like my heart exploded that day with a stack of dynamites leaning against it.

Don't get it twisted, it's not like I didn't want a child with her: having kids was a part of my own childhood fantasy. I wanted a child, but, I wasn't ready for that type of responsibility then. Or even now for that matter. And there was one other reason that discouraged me the most. You see, in Miami, I had seen plenty of guys who were on top of their game, but once a child popped up in their lives, their whole world started crumbling down—right before their eyes.

No! Let me correct that: their whole world started crumbling down right before our eyes. Now that was something I was afraid of, because I didn't want that to happen to me, too.

I shut my eyes and feel into a deep, relaxing sleep while Carlton drove, hoping that when I woke up from my sleep, this whole thing would turn out to be nothing more than a nightmare.

When Carlton pulled up in front of Aunt Enid's home, I woke up.

I twisted around and looked at Dee-Jay. It seemed that she was wide awake, looking at the new scenery. Amazing, I imagine. It took Carlton a little under seven hours to drive back to Aunt Enid's house. He must have sped all the way here.

Some of Aunt Enid's foster children were hanging out on the front porch in spite of the time. It was a little past nine o'clock at night, and they knew they were supposed to be inside the house at eight o'clock. But still, they ran up to the car when they saw Aunt Enid opening the back passenger door. They greeted her with hugs. And when those little rag-rats got close enough to see Dee-Jay, they seemed dumbfounded. They all started whispering to one another.

"Get y'all damned hands off the car!" Carlton demanded from them before I did. "I'm sick and tired of y'all doing that. It's like every time I come over here, y'all be doing the same—"

"What's happening, dawg?"

Carlton quickly cocked his head to the left side.

It was RaDaze, a young kid from up the block, leaning against the window frame. "What've you been up to?"

"None of your damn business!" Carlton snapped on him, too. "And how many times I'm gonna tell you not to holla at me anymore: until you gimme by damn money back?" He took a short pause. Then blew under his breath: "Trying me with that fucking oregano."

"Damn dawg, you act like you never got to me before." RaDaze parried a forget-you-then with his hand and walked away.

By this time, Aunt Enid grabbed her purse from the backseat. "Honey, I'm going to go inside to take a shower," she stated to me, "before I get these kids ready for bed." As she advised me about that, she must have noticed Dee-Jay wanting to get out of the car with her, because she immediately added, "No-no-no, sweetie, you're going home with him: to a different house."

I twisted around and looked.

Then Dee-Jay looked at me.

"Yeah," I smiled, trying to amuse her, "to a much better house. Where you're gonna have a lot of fun at."

Dee-Jay grabbed hold of her duffel bag—tighter.

I looked at Aunt Enid. "So I'll see you later then. I'm just gonna go home and make her something to eat."

"Okay."

We all said our farewells—except Dee-Jay of course, she just kept her mouth closed—and Carlton pulled off.

About twenty minutes later, when we drove up in our driveway to a complete stop, I had to practically drag Dee-Jay out of the car by pulling that dingy bag of hers. Hey, what the hell you expect me to do? That was the only way I could get her to move. And the saddest thing about that was, she didn't say a word to me while I was dragging her along the way. Not even a "Stop it!" I'm not lying. I strongly believed this little girl was mute or something. I was sure of that.

When we approached the house, the front door abruptly swung open as Carlton was about a unlock it. We leaped back, going on our impulse.

It was Uncle James with a Chucky E. Cheese smile on his face, standing in front of the doorway and looking down at Dee-Jay. She hid behind my legs. To which he said, "I'm your uncle.... Uncle James!"

Nothing.

But Carlton exploded on him: "You stupid asshole! What the hell are you trying to do? Give a nigga a fucking heart attack or something?" He paused, then pushed Uncle James aside so he could enter inside the house. "You nearly scared the shit outta m—, her!"

I walked into the house too and went straight to the kitchen. Dee-Jay trailed directly behind me. And of course, Uncle James was right behind us, analyzing Dee-Jay as if she were some weird science project.

"I'm starving." I opened the fridge door. "I'm gonna make us two plates of food. Hamburgers and some French fries. I know you have to be hungry too."

No comments from her. She just stared at me.

Then Uncle James butted in: "Oh man, I'm hungry, too. So you might as well make that three plates instead.

"You have a better chance on hell freezing over than to see me making you that plate of food. Because for you, I don't remember me asking you if you were hungry or not!"

Uncle James cut his eyes to Dee-Jay, forcing me to look too. Then he tried to play an aggressive role on her: "Whatchu smiling about?"

Without a word, she boldly pointed her finger at his face.

I swear, you should have been there to have seen it yourself.

Uncle James got ticked off and left the kitchen upset. I turned back to Dee-Jay with a smile. Because, truthfully—how can I say this without exaggerating about it here—I was touched by her action; more so, impressed to see how little she was, and still she stood up against Uncle James' intimidating question.

I took a short moment and thought about something silly: I remembered back when I first moved in with Aunt Enid and was approached by Uncle James in the same manner. I remembered when I had that same boldness in myself too. So there was a little similarity between Dee-Jay and me. We were both tough. I could see that. But that still didn't prove anything to me though. She just wasn't my child.

I made us two plates of food: Hamburger and French fries, as promised. And to show me her appreciation for the meal I cooked for her, she ate everything I put on her plate.

I do mean like, everything.

Later on that night, I made up the couch for her (with a bed sheet and pillow) to sleep on. That was only for temporary until I straightened out the back room for her.

So, until then, welcome to the Powell family.

Life isn't sweet and neither was that hot ass weather that I had woke up to this morning. But by the afternoon, it became a glorious day and I took advantage of it, washing my Audi coupe in the driveway.

And BAM!

About twenty minutes later, for a strange reason, I looked back at the house and noticed Dee-Jay peeking out the living room window, watching me. I smiled at her. She didn't smile back. But then again, she probably forgot how to smile after her mother's death. She needed to lighten up a bit and get out of that nutshell she was in.

People die, sweetie. So get over it.

I beckoned my hand for her to come outside with me. But all she did was walk away from the window, shoving me off.

I played it off in a cheerful mood, showing a stolid interest in her evasion. But in all truth, it would be hard for any alleged father not to be bothered by such behavior. Despite the fact she had arrived at the house three days earlier, I had not heard her speak a single word yet. I kid you not. She even refused to inquire about the simplest things like "What's this?" or "What's that?" as young children her age normally would ask when they are exploring new things in life.

But not little Dee-Jay, though: She went without asking about anything.

So, in a way, I felt relieved that she kept to herself and out of my way for the time being. She would lock herself in the bathroom most of the time. What more could I ask for?

Absolutely nothing at all.

I smiled to myself and almost fell into a trance until I heard someone called my name. I looked to my left, then to my right.

"Behind you, silly!"

I twisted around.

It was Amanda, the neighborhood hoe who lived directly across the street from me. She stood a short distance away, giving me the opportunity to get a look at her buxom figure. She didn't look bad at all, even though she looked to be in her early forties. But I knew she was much younger than that, though. I knew a few guys who ran through her as if she was a shopping mall on Black Friday, after Thanksgiving Day. I'm talking about the whole work: head, anal, ménage à trios, gang bangs, et cetera. You name it—she had done them all. And her body? It was nothing much to brag about. She was still doable, and that's all that count. She had nice hips with a wide ass. Her hair, long and curly, pushed back into a ponytail for a guy to grapple onto with a tight grip, while pounding her from the back. Especially in her ass. The word has it on the block, that's how she likes it most of the time.

And from the look of things, it appeared that Amanda had just come from a long jog because she looked semi-drenched. Her perspiration soaked all the right areas. And she had the nerve to wear spandex shorts that nearly looked like something from Victoria's Secret naughty lingerie collection. Something I could only imagine Lil' Kim to wear. They snuggled Amanda's crotch area, displaying that camel toe inside her shorts—straight down the middle—over her nookie. And I'd be damned if it didn't look meaty and fat to me.

I couldn't help but look at her pussy. It was right there in front of me, flaunting hello. I wanted to wave back. Or at least stick my hand down there and ask Amanda, "Can I touch it, just once?" But I couldn't play myself for this hood rat. I just couldn't. I fought hard to keep my eyes off her nookie. Very hard. But still, that didn't last very long because immediately thereafter I got distracted by her sagging melons. She wore a gray worn-out T-shirt that transparently displayed her swollen nipples from her areolae, as if her nipples were looking forward to being sucked on.

"So whatchu doing?"

"Just washing my ride," I said, while trying to avoid looking at her titties now. "But what's up with you, though? I haven't been seeing you around lately."

She smiled and moved closer to me. "Why? Were you looking for me?"

"Nah. Not really."

She took another step closer. "Oh, yeah—"

"Amanda!"

We both looked across the street.

It was her man—some gullible idiot—standing at his doorway. He looked Spanish, but he was from one of those terrorist states in the Middle East.

"What the hell I told you about disrespecting me in from of my house like this?!" he shouted, trying to sound American. "Just bring your ass back in the house! I'm hungry!"

"I'm coming, dear!" Amanda twisted back to me. Then whispered: "I just gotta catch you on another day when that fool ain't around. Because I would like to continue this conversation with you."

"Alright."

She swaggered off in a slow motion, slinging that ass back to the house.

That clown of hers stood in their doorway, waiting on her.

"Mmmm!" I thrummed loud enough for him to hear me because I wanted him to think that I was interested in sexing his girl if it came down to it. But, truth be told, unlike him, I don't fuck with sloppy leftovers.

When Amanda reached her doorway, she turned her head around as if she knew I would still be looking at her. And what could I say, she was right. I watched her ass wobble the whole way there. She waved good-bye; I waved back.

Then her man barked at her: "Get your ass in this fucking house before I kill you out here!" He then looked at me with a poisonous stare.

I laughed at him, because I knew what I could do to this clown.

He slammed the door.

Later on that night, while Carlton was watching The Matrix in the family room, Dee-Jay posted herself at the doorway, wanting to get a peek at Morpheus and Neo's no-holds-barred karate match on each other.

It was the best part of the movie.

Carlton noticed her standing there. "With all this damned room on this couch," he began to tell her, "why don't you come in and have a seat? You're distracting me." But since she just stood there with her hands in her pockets, shaking her head, he went on to add: "Suit yourself then. Because I'm not gonna beg you."

She tightened her face up, giving him an angry look.

"What!?" he paused. Then added some more: "You gonna tell on me?" He tried to antagonize her with a little sarcasm, because he knew she hadn't spoken a word since she arrived. "So go ahead and try to tell on me if you can."

She walked away.

When I balled up another one of my sketches—from my clothing designs collection—I caught a glimpse of Dee-Jay across the table, standing by the den doorway watching me.

I shot her with a smile.

Then she walked away.

That wasn't cool at all.

About five minutes later I took a break from my project and went into the kitchen to grab me something to snack on. I found the fridge door open and Dee-Jay standing there with a large drinking glass in her hand, reaching for something.

"Hey! Let me give you a hand."

She quickly cocked around with a frightened look on her face when she saw me standing behind her.

"What are you trying to get outta here?" I asked.

She slowly shook her head.

"You can have anything you want." I said, pretending like I had known her since birth. "Just point it out and I'll get it for you."

After a short moment, she broke.

"Oh, you want this?"

She nodded.

I grabbed the carton and poured her a glass of milk. And just when she was about to put the glass to her mouth, I stopped her.

"Hold up for a second." I went to the cabinet and grabbed the chocolate syrup.

Her eyes looked excited.

As I poured the Hershey syrup into the glass and stirred it into the milk, she hesitated a bit when I handed the glass to her. It seemed like she wanted to smile but she didn't. I just watched her guzzle the chocolate milk down her throat. And just when I thought she was about to break the ice, the phone rang and ruined the moment.

I snatched the phone off the wall on the forth ring. "What is it?"

It was Kevin. "Whatchu doing right now?"

"Nothing. Why?"

"Because I lined us up with those Spanish hoes again."

"What Spanish ho—" I froze, remembering Dee-Jay was in the kitchen with me. Then I tried again, taking it down a notch: "What Spanish broads are you talking about?"

"Those Brazilians who we met at IHOP the other night. Man, tell me you didn't forget about our date with them already?"

"Nah. I didn't forget about it." Actually, it slipped my mind, though. "What time we supposed to meet up with them?"

"Later on tonight."

"Tonight?"

"Yeah, tonight. I see you musta forgotten about it already." He paused. Then immediately went on to say, "If you can't go, just let me know from right now because, if anything, I can call Mikey to take your place."

"Nigga, stop tripping. I'm coming."

"Alright, go ahead and get ready. In the meantime, I'm gonna give them a call and tell them that we'll meet up with them at the movie theater."

"At what time tonight?"

"My nigga, I just told you to get ready. That means, right now."

"At what time?"

"We're trying to see the ten o'clock flick. Are you happy now?"

I looked at my wristwatch. It was a quarter to nine. That was more than enough time to get ready. I turned back to Dee-Jay with a genuine smile on my face; and for the first time, I saw a trace of anger in her eyes.

"What's the matter with you?" I asked her. "You want some more chocolate milk?"

She walked away, pouting her bottom lip.

I paused for a moment to gather up my thoughts because I didn't understand why she would—

"YO!" Kevin screamed through the phone. "Are you listening to me?"

"Yeah! Now, what were you saying again?"

"Man, just get ready. I'll be over there in a few." He hung up without saying good-bye.

A short moment later, while I was drying myself off, I could have sworn I heard a knock on my bedroom door while I was in my bathroom.

Then I heard it again.

"Yeah?!" I stuck my head out into my bedroom. Then yelled, "What is it?!"

Nothing.

I waited a few seconds for a response, but there was nothing. I didn't have any time to waste, I started to get dress. I slid my pants on; then I heard those annoying taps again. I trudged to the bedroom door and snatched it open. "What?!" I roared, but when I saw Dee-Jay standing down there with tears in her eyes, I felt my heart sink. "What happened?" my voice broke weak. "Did one of them out there say something mean to you?"

She just stood there and wept.

"Uh, you don't have to cry. Come in here with me."

When she entered my bedroom, I know the fresh fragrance of my scented oil kissed her on the nose because her face gave it away. She took a good look at me, then dropped her head again and cried.

I threw my shirt on and picked her up. I sat her at the edge of the bed, and she looked up at me again. She had her mother's eyes, for sure.

I reached over to wipe a few teardrops from her cheeks, realizing that I should at least say something to her. But I couldn't find the right words to start off with.

She started sobbing this time.

And it was about that moment when I noticed that chain again around her neck. "You know," I began to say, hoping I can cheer her up a little, "I gave that necklace to your mom on her birthday. A long time ago. And if you look behind the medallion, it reads, 'Forever—"

"True love," she cut in and finished it off with me: "DaShawn and Jessica."

"Holy shit!" I was shocked. "You can talk?"

She lifted her head and looked at me.

"I can't believe you're finally talking." My heart was crushed yet filled with joy. "But I don't understand. Why are your crying?"

Dee-Jay didn't answer me. She just sat there and allowed her tears to run down her face.

"You have to tell me why you're crying if you want me to help you."

She sobbed a little more, then spoke in a sweet angel's voice: "I don't want you to leave. I want you to stay here with me."

"But I'll be right back. I'm only going out for a little while."

"No, you're not."

"Yeah, I am. I'm going to see a friend of mine. And right after that, I'm coming right back."

She opened her mouth as if she wanted to say something else, but she shut it back. Then her bottom lip began to quiver again.

"Okay," I tried to have a little compassion here, still thinking about that Brazilian mami Kevin had hooked me up with. "You don't have to cry." Think. But nothing good was coming to mind: "Is there something, anything you want me to do for you?"

She immediately looked at me. "I want you to read me a bedtime story and sing me a song." She wiped her tears away with the back of her hand. "My mommy used to do that for me."

"Oh, she did, huh?"

"Uh-huh, every night."

"Every night?" My brain nearly hit the ceiling. I just hoped she wasn't expecting me to do the same thing.

She nodded her head.

Damn! I had to open my big mouth. "Well, I don't see a problem with me reading you a bedtime story. But that singing stuff is gonna be a problem though. That's not gonna work."

She appeared to agree to my term; she smiled.

"Now, that's what I'm talking about." I wiped the rest of her tears away. "Because baby girls don't cry: they exultize."

"Huh?"

I thought about it. "Uh, never mind." I got up and walked over to my little bookshelf beside the bed. "Let me find a good book to read her," I whispered to myself while combing through my book collection of various authors: Harlan Cohen, Eric Jerome Dickey, Nikki Turner, Trista Russell, and some other good novelists.

"Hey, what about Dreams from My Father by Barack Obama, our president?" When I spun around to see what Dee-Jay had thought about my choice, she was gone. I felt stupid. I veered the room in search of her, but she was nowhere in sight. "Where in the hell did she go to?" I quietly asked myself, getting up from the bed. Then I yelled out: "EH, DEE-JAY!"

There wasn't any response.

I waited some more.

Nothing.

I then walked to my bedroom door and shouted her name again, but she didn't respond. Now I felt a little annoyed by her not answering me. As soon as I turned toward the bed, I got hit from behind.

It was Dee-Jay.

She had run into me by accident. "Here you go," she said, passing me a book. "Read me this one."

"All right." I held her book—33 Strategies of War—in my hand and decided not to even question her about her selected choice, because I had something more bothering on my mind. "But before I start reading this book, let me ask you a question first, sweetie: Why didn't you answer me when I called you a few seconds ago?"

"I didn't hear you call me."

"Are you sure about that?"

It seemed like my question amused her. "Yeah, I'm sure," she said between giggles. "Why?"

"Because I was screaming your name out and you didn't answer me. So you can tell me the truth. I'm not gonna be mad with you."

"But you weren't calling me. You were calling Dee-Jay. Not me."

It felt like my chin had hit the floor. "Your name isn't Dee-Jay?"

She shook her head. "No."

"Hold up! Don't they call you Dee-Jay?"

"No."

"So, what do they call you then?"

She gave me a scrutinizing look and said, "They call me by my name, silly." She laughed.

Okay, I'm confused here. I should have read the custody release forms.

Then she said something that made my mind feel at ease: "My mommy named me, Destini."

I had a great idea.

While I was reading Destini her bedtime story, I decided to slow down my reading pace and lower my voice to a lullaby tone. And my strategy was working here. Little by little, her heavy eyelids began to blink sluggishly. I continued reading in the same manner until both of her eyelids dropped and never came back up. And then—Oh, man—I heard the cutest sound ever: a slight, baby snore. I paused for a second to examine her deep relaxation.

She was asleep, for sure.

I slowly got up and before I could click the light off, somebody started ringing the damned doorbell!

I oughta go out there and—

Shit!

Destini managed to open one of her eyes, and then the other one. "Uh-huh, and what happened next?" she asked me in a weary tone.

"And they all lived happily ever after," I said, hoping she would believe me and go back to sleep.

But it seemed like she was fighting it.

"Okay now," I whispered. "Go ahead and keep your eyes closed. I want you to go to sleep, sweetie."

"Okay."

It seemed like it was working up until Kevin popped up in front of my bedroom doorway. "My nigga! What the fuck's taking you so—"

I cut him off, parrying my hand at him to get-the-hell-away from the room.

He did, only after he told me to Go fuck off!

Destini opened her eyes again, but shut them back.

Thank goodness. I reached over and hit the switch on the lamp.

"But you have to sing me a song too," she said, trying to stay awake, "so I can fall asleep."

Who are you kidding? "Sing you a song?"

She nodded again. "Uh-huh."

"Alright then, I'll be right back." I rushed out of the room, ran through the hall to the front door and yelled out to Kevin. "Just give me another minute! I'm coming!"

"So hurry the fuck up then!" he shouted back from inside his SUV. "We're gonna be late!"

I ran back to the bedroom. "Okay, I'm back," I told Destini. "What kind of song you wanna hear me sing for you?"

She tried to shrug. "I don't know."

"You don't know, huh?" I echoed, then thought for a moment until it dawned on me. "I have a nice song for you."

She showed me a half smile.

I cleared my throat and tried to sing "If This Word Was Mine" by Luther Vandross. My voice didn't sound much like his, though. If anything, I was off key as if I was singing from a karaoke machine. But get this: when I was midway through the song, Destini fell asleep. I watched her for a short moment, then smiled when I heard that slight snore again. I killed the lights and walked to the family room.

"Yo, Carlton!" I waited until I got this attention off the movie. Then said, "I'm about to head out. So make sure you check up on her now and then for me. All right?"

"Who?" He turned back to his movie.

"The little one."

"Oh, alright. I got you. But what time you'll be back?"

"I don't know. Probably sometime before morning, if I get lucky."

"Alright then."

I was about to walk away, but I turned back around. "And yo!" I tried to get his attention again. "Don't even think about bringing your boys over here while I'm gone to smoke that bullshit in the house. You hear me?"

He waved me off. "Alright."

As soon as I stepped out of the house, I could have sworn I heard him say some fly shit out of his mouth. I thought about it for a quick second, and had a change of mind. I shut the door behind me, then headed over to Kevin's SUV.

"Yo, this shit is driving me crazy!" I tried to vent, while taking the passenger seat of Kevin's SUV. "They just needa hurry up with this paternity test so I can have my life back."

"Man, I don't wanna hear that shit!" He looked at his watch. "It's already a quarter to ten. I can't believe how you had me waiting on you like I'm some fuck-ass hoe out here!"

"The hell with that! What's up with those Spanish mommies?"

"For all I know, they probably went out with some other niggas instead."

"Give them a call to see if everything is still on."

And just as Kevin was punching in the females' digits into his cell phone, I heard some sort of tapping sound.

"What's that noise?"

"What noise?" Kevin paused to see if he could hear something. But there was nothing unusual. Then he added: "My nigga, you've been cooped up in that damned house too long. You're losing your—"

"Shhh! There it goes again." I held my hand up a bit for him to be quiet.

But he heard it this time too. "It's coming from your side." He turned the music volume down.

The tapping grew louder.

I looked out the passenger's window, there was no one standing out there. Well, at least to my knowledge. Then I caught the vibes not to investigate it further. But my stupid ass rolled the window down and stuck my head out there to get a look.

And to my surprise, it was Destini with tears in her eyes.

"What's the matter now?"

Destini whined, "I can't sleep." Then she started sobbing again. "You have to sing me a song."

"I did that already."

"You have to sing me another song then, because the other one didn't work. You can't see I'm still up?"

I couldn't believe this shit! I twisted back to Kevin, hoping to show him what I was up against.

He saw the frustration painted on my face and before I blew my cool, he told me, "Why don't you just go ahead and stay home tonight. We can get up with those shawties at another time."

I knew what he meant by that: Get the hell outta my rider because you're holding me up!

I gave it some thoughts and reminded myself that this issue would soon be over with once I take that paternity test. I glanced over at Destini, then back to Kevin. "All right then. I'll catch up with you later." I got out of the SUV and walked Destini back to the house.

Carlton seemed surprised. "You're back already? And what's she doing outta bed? I thought you wanted me to watch her for you?"

I ignored him and walked Destini back to my bedroom. I had no other choice but go for another round to see if I can put her to sleep again.

She lay underneath my bed sheet as I started reading that unusual bedtime story to her. Not even a minute has gone by, before she interrupted me: "You can lay right here"—she scooted over a bit—"and finish reading me my bedtime story." She then patted her hand in the empty space where I could lie down.

I was a little astonished by her thoughtfulness; I smiled. "Oh, what the hell." I lay beside her, then picked up where I had left off from earlier.

"Can I have some milk?"

"Shh," I tried to control the situation. "Pay attention. This part is interesting."

She then plugged her ears with her fingers. "I want some milk. Chocolate milk!"

Now, that's a whole lot of ass right there!

Well, at least, that's what Kevin thought when he held the door open for Vida and Samara, checking them both out as they were exiting Aventura's Movie Theater off Biscayne Boulevard.

"I wouldn't mind watching that "Blackout" movie again," Vida said to Kevin as they headed for his SUV.

"It was alright, but I rather watch a Black flick instead."

"What kind of movie is that?"

He shot her a confident smile. "A movie you would enjoy."

"You freak!" She playfully hit him.

He laughed; then they both laughed together.

As they got to the SUV, Samara took the backseat.

Vida started playing with the radio dial. She settled in on HOT 105, with Freddie Cruz, playing the Quiet Storm. That was the type of music she liked when she was in the mood to get her groove on.

"Hey!" Samara got their attention. "Y'all can drop me off at Veronica's apartment. I'm gonna hangout with her for a while."

"Okay." That sounded like a good idea to Vida.

Right after that Kevin jumped back in, telling Samara, "I'm sorry that my homey couldn't make it. He wanted to be here with us. But like I told you before, he had to babysit."

"Yeah, okay. If you say so. But you don't have to make up a story for your friend. I do understand: He's your friend."

"I'm dead serious. He's home right now babysitting."

She didn't believe him.

I was neither asleep nor awoke. But I could tell you this, though: I was tired than a muthafucker after reading Destini about thirty-five pages from that book of hers. I swear, I was so weak, I laid on the edge of the bed with my eyelids closed, not having the strength to push Destini's hand off my face.

Then the phone rang.

It startled me. I glanced over at the clock on the night table. It was nearly one o'clock in the morning. I wanted to ignore the ringing sounds, but I couldn't. I snatched the phone off the night table on the third ring. As soon as I heard a female's voice, I snapped.

"Who the fuck is this?"

"Oops! I'm sorry."

It sounded like the phone was tossed somewhere. Then, seconds later, Kevin's voice came over the phone line: "My nigga, what's happening?"

My mind became clear, yet clouded with frustration. "Man, hold on for a second," I murmured as I snuck into the bathroom. "Yo, why would you have some bitch calling my crib at this time of the night, knowing I have a little kid in the house with me?"

"Damn, that's my fault! It slipped my mind. But hey! That was that little Spanish mommy you were supposed to meet up with tonight. She didn't believe me that you were babysitting."

"Who?"

"Samara, stupid!"

"Damn, that was her?"

"Yeah."

"Yo, put her back on the phone so I can holla at her."

"Alright. Hold on."

After a few seconds, a soft voice shot through the phone line: "Hello."

"First of all, I would like to apologize for my manners, for what'd happened a second ago," I told her in a pleading tone. "It's just that I have a child in the house with me and it's kinda late. You feel me?"

"I understand. But I think I should apologize to you instead. I told Kevin not to call, but he insisted."

Kevin shouted in the background: "She's lying!"

"No, I'm not!" Samara laughed, then turned her attention back to me. "But I'm truly sorry if I woke either one of y'all up."

"Don't worry about it. I know it was Kevin's fault, if anything."

She laughed; I laughed back.

We spoke for the next few minutes until she reached her destination. Somewhere in Hialeah. We ended up exchanging our phone numbers and setup another date—just for the two of us—for Thursday evening at the China Grill restaurant on South Beach.

"Okay then." She tried to sound sweet.

"All right. But don't be afraid to call me in the meantime."

"I won't."

We hung up after saying good-bye.

I smiled. Samara sounded all right, I thought. "I can work with that," I whispered under my breath as I stepped back into my room and noticed Destini still sleeping.

I had a change of mind: I decided to give her my bed for the night. I went to the family room to crash there instead.

Within a minute later, if that, Destini came staggering in the room with a sheet and pillow in her hands.

The following morning Carlton was in the kitchen making Destini breakfast: it consisted of sunny-side-ups and a bowl of cheesy grits.

"This one right here is your daddy," he joked, as Destini stood near him, observing his creative cooking. He decorated two eggs in the frying pan with chopped green peppers as imaginary eyeballs and hair.

She laughed. "Whew," she dragged between giggles. Then said, "I'm telling on you."

I walked in the kitchen and saw Destini standing in a chair. "Get down from there before you hurt yourself." I then headed to the table. "And what are you whewing about?"

She stepped down from the chair and said, "Nothing."

I looked at Carlton. "Why are you smiling?"

"You didn't notice that she's talking now?"

"I know that already. We spoke last night."

Carlton quickly twisted to Destini with a foolish look on his face. "I thought you said I was the first one to hear you speak?"

She laughed at him.

I sat in a chair, elbows on the table, massaging my temples. "Yo, Carlton," I got his attention. "Can you make me a cup of coffee? This damned headache is killing me."

"Alright. I got you." He made it for me. Then he turned to Destini. "I have the magic touch." He winked at her. "He likes the way I make his coffee: Dark and sweet with no cream in it. It makes him feel better."

Of course, that was a lie. I rested the cup in front of me.

"So you can start making me chocolate milk in the morning too," she said to him and sat at the table with me. "Because I think I feel a headache coming." She started rubbing her temples, trying to mimic me.

"Girl," —Carlton grabbed the frying pan— "I oughta bust you in your face with this. I'd already made you two glasses of chocolate milk this morning."

She laughed again.

"Oh, shit! That just reminds me, Destini." I waited for her to look at me. Then proceeded with: "We have to go see the doctor today. And—"

"Why?" she interrupted me. "Are you sick?"

"Nah. We have to go take our physical."

"Oh."

"And after that," I continued, "I'm gonna take you over to Auntie's house for a little bit. Okay?"

"Why?"

"Because I have to take care of some business."

"Oh, okay."

We heard Uncle James shouting something from the front door as he stepped inside the house. I guess he smelled the brewing coffee, because he walked straight to the kitchen and leaned against the door frame.

Then he asked me: "What the hell are you shaking your head for?"

I ignored him.

So he went on to Carlton instead. "Boy, make me a cup of coffee!"

"Go make your own shit! You don't see any slaves up in here."

But before Uncle James could reply back to him, Destini cut in with a suggestion: "Why don't you ask Yo to make it for you?"

Uncle James looked at her with a smile. He probably was taken by surprise that she could speak. But his astonishment disappeared when he asked her, "Yo, who?" He quickly cut to Carlton, then back to her. "Who's that?"

She wore a mischievous smile on her face and said, "Why don't you make it Yo-damn-self!"

Carlton and I burst out laughing. We gave Destini high fives.

Uncle James didn't find anything amusing about that, since the joke was on him. "Ha, ha, ha," he said in slow motion, while wobbling his head at her from side to side. "Isn't, that, funny?" He refused to put a smile on his face as he walked over to the coffee maker. "That corny-ass joke," he murmured to himself. "I'll make my own damned coffee then."

We burst out laughing again, and Uncle James quickly turned around and gave Destini an evil stare.

Our laughter came to a standstill when we heard several taps—out of all places—on the kitchen window.

"Who is it?" I asked.

"It's me!" a man's voice tried to whisper.

"Who?"

"It's me, Ricky! Hurry up and open the door. This shit is getting too heavy!"

When Carlton opened the door, Ricky, the neighborhood crack-head, tramped inside the house with an object that was wrapped up within a white bed sheet.

I rested my cup on the table.

"Close the door," Ricky said. "Hurry up!"

Carlton did. Then asked: "What the hell you have there?"

"Something you need," he said, while placing the concealed object on the table. Then, about a second later, he snatched the sheet off of it and shouted, "Wa-La! An Apple Computer…. I don't know how to hook it up, but this sh—" he quickly paused when he saw a child in his presence. Then he cranked back up: "This joint right here is bad as hell. It even talks to you and let you know about certain things. But there's only one problem with it, though."

"And what's that?" I was curious to know.

"It doesn't know how to shut up when you tell it to."

Let me give you a little rundown about Ricky. He was a scandalous-ass nigga in the neighborhood. But he was the only person you could depend on to get about anything you need off the streets. You see, there wasn't anything out there he couldn't steal to support his drug habit. Stealing was his profession and he was the best at it.

Although Ricky was a thief, he respected majority of the neighbors on the block. Not because he knew us, but rather because we knew about him. If there were any break-ins or anything missing from our homes, the finger would be pointed at him. So, for that reason, based on what I have been told by others, he only broke into those white folk's houses in the neighborhood.

Carlton seemed puzzled. "Whatchu mean by a talking computer?"

"I'll tell you exactly what I mean," he said. "When I came across this one house up the block, it had of the prettiest rooms I'd ever saw in my life. And y'all know that I'm really good when I'm doing my thang. But this time I made a mistake. I dropped all the silverware on the floor because when I stood in front of this computer, it came on, telling me 'You have mail. Beep! You have mail.' I'm not stupid, I know it sensed me in there."

Carlton kept his eyes on this idiot. "And that's what it said to you, huh?"

"Hell, yeah! I even tried to shut it up, but it wouldn't listen to me. So" —Ricky jerked his hand backward, forcefully, to demonstrate that he had snatched something out of a socket— "I unplugged it and took it with me just in case it was a hidden camera built in there. I didn't want it to show Ms. Murphy that I came over there and stole some of her stuff."

I cut in: "You're not talking about that little, old white lady, Ms. Murphy, who lives three houses up the block?"

"Yeah! Oh, you know her, too?"

I practically lived out here my whole life. So who didn't I know around here? I refused to answer that. I started sipping on my coffee, pretending like I didn't have any interest in that computer. Because, deep down inside, I wanted it. "So how much you want for it?"

He shrugged. "I don't know. How much money you got in your pocket?

"What?" I knew he didn't just ask me that.

"How much money do you think it's worth then?"

That's more like it. I pretended like I didn't know. "I guess about a hundred fifty dollars. But I really don't know. Just give me a price?"

"Tell me this then. How much you bought that Xbox from me last week?"

"I don't remember. Probably about a hundred, I think."

He placed his finger on his lips as if he were pondering about something, while mumbling out some wild figures under his breath. Then he had the nerve to say, "Give me three hundred for it."

"Three hundred dollars? You must be sick!"

"Okay, okay. Just gimme two-fifty then."

"Two-fifty? Where am I gonna get two hundred and fifty dollars from?"

"My nigga!" —Ricky tightened up his face— "don't play with me! I know you be shaking your thang up in these clubs around here and getting paid for it. So don't even try me like that." He paused, looking disappointed. Then added: "Well, how much you got on you right now?"

"About two hundred."

"That's all you got?"

"Yeah."

"Not even an extra dollar on you?"

"No."

"Alright. Let me get that then."

I smiled. "That's a deal."

Later on that afternoon, Destini and I were sitting in the waiting room of the Children and Family Services in Miami on Southwest 184th Street. Children were running all over the place.

I looked at my wristwatch—it was nearly three o'clock. We had been sitting here for the past hour, and out of all the things that could possibly go wrong, a young boy showed up and appeared to be lost.

Damn!

The little youngster who looked to be about five years old homed in on me, then tapped my leg. "Did you see my mommy?"

"Nah." I shook my head. "I don't know your mommy."

"Why don't you know my mommy?"

All of this sounded too familiar to me. How could I forget about the episode that went down in Tallahassee? So to avoid any more arguments with some frustrated bitch, I tried to get rid of him.

"Shoo!" I motioned my hand to brush him away. "Run along and play with the other kids over there."

He looked to the corner, then back at me.

"Yeah, over there." I was dead serious. "Go! Get the hell outta here before I pitch you."

But he wouldn't leave: He just gave me a repulsive stare, then switched it to an ineffable smile. "Do that hurt?" he asked.

"What the hell are you talking about?"

Destini cut in: "Don't answer that."

I looked at her, then back to the little knuckle-head. I thought I could handle this on my own. "What are you talking about?" I asked him. "Does what hurt?"

"Does this hurt?!" the little youngster said, as he kicked me on my shin and quickly ran off.

"You son-of-a-bitch!" I accidently said in front of Destini, while grabbing my lower left leg. "God dammit! That little muthafucker!"

About the same time, an older black lady from the Family Services' medical contractor stepped into the room and shouted: "Mr. DaShawn Powell!"

I stood up, holding back the pain.

She smiled. I tried to smile back, as Destini and I approached her.

This medical contractor had a great personality and a name tag that fitted her name perfectly: Debbie.

I finally smiled. My first thought was, How I can wheedle this broad to get what I want from her. Because if I succeed—and Kevin said I would—everything would be back in order again.

She wore a heavy perfume scent that filled the air as if she had bathed herself in a rosebush all day. Her medical shirt was slightly opened and her cleavage—Oh, man, those playboy titties—was looking beautiful. I kid you not. She looked to be in her mid-fifties, but her features were acceptable for any late night action. She was built like a porn star; kinda looked like that Congresswoman from Texas: Sheila Jackson. She had a wide ass.

"Can you please follow me?" she asked Destini and me, then led us through the hallway to what seemed to be an examination room. "This is only gonna take a few seconds."

"Only if you get yours off first," I mumbled.

Debbie looked at me. "Boy, I heard that," her voice was rather deep but in a sweet way. "Don't you think I'm a little outta your league?"

I kept quiet. I pretended like I didn't have a clue as to what she was talking about.

She shook her head with a little smirk before she turned to Destini, holding a large swab stick in her hand. "Okay, cutie," she said, "open up for me." Then she placed the swab inside of Destini's mouth and collected some saliva.

I felt compelled to ask: "What's that? A big Q-tip?"

"Sorta." She wore a vamp smile. "It's just that technology is steadily advancing. We don't have to draw blood samples for DNA anymore, unless it's requested."

"Ohh...." I didn't know that. "But is that just as good?"

"Most certainly." She carefully packaged Destini's saliva and sealed it inside a white envelope. She then turned to me. "You're up next, cutie. Open up."

And I did. "So how long before I hear something back from y'all regarding these results?"

She shrugged. "Can't really give you an exact date, because it can range from a few days to a few months. But usually, it takes from three weeks to a month before you'll be contacted."

I kinda got nervous. It was the now or never moment for me. I felt stuck. What if she didn't bite the bait, I thought. I swear, if she's willing to do this shit for me, I would beat her fucking back out whenever she wanted me to. I kept my eyes on hers. She had bedroom eyes with a nice sex appeal to them. Or at least, that's what I wanted to believe. And, on that note, I went to my playbook and remembered the first rule: When in doubt, give it all you got.

"Okay." She gave us the cue to leave. "When we receive the results back, you'll be contacted."

"Well, thanks for your time. But if you should hear anything soon or just about anything else for that matter" —I passed her my info— "don't be afraid to call me."

She looked at the business card; then smiled back.

"I see that you're very persistent in going after what you want."

I merely smiled with her. "It doesn't have to be that way if the doors are open for me to explore. It just might be a journey worth your while."

She playfully rolled her eyes up, like, expressing Whatever.

And since we were finished here Destini and I were the first ones to walk out of the examination room, with Debbie following a little way behind us. I noticed she stopped trailing behind us when she arrived at the doorway. Right at her left foot was a small trash can. I watched her for a few seconds to see what she was going to do with my info—but when I saw her sticking my card in her bra—I twisted back around and kept walking.

"Mr. Powell!"

It worked. I stopped to see what time she was willing to link with me.

Hopefully tonight.

I was somewhat lost in their conversation. But then again it turned out to be a wonderful visit thus far.

Aunt Enid was astonished that Destini had opened up to us. They had a good conversation, even though Destini's responses were short and simple: "Uh-huh", "Uh-uh", "I don't know", and "I think so". But still, Aunt Enid was pleased with Destini letting down her guard for us.

I cut in: "Auntie, may I speak to you in the other room, please?" I motioned my head toward the kitchen.

"Sure." She turned to Destini. "Just give me a second. I'll be right back with you." She then went into the kitchen with me.

I went straight to the point: "Can you watch Destini for me, for a few days until I get a couple of things back in order?"

"No!" Her smile vanished. "That's your responsibility. Not mine. You have to learn how to look after her on your own. We have already discussed this."

"It's only for a few days, just till after the weekend."

"No."

"What about just today and tomorrow?"

"DaShawn, I said no already. So leave it alone. You have to learn how to deal with your own responsibilities and stop asking others to work them out for you."

I kept quiet, trying to put my thoughts together.

Then Kevin arrived. He stepped into the kitchen and gave Aunt Enid a kiss, then opened the fridge door. "Damn, I'm hungry," he announced, speaking to no one in general. Then he grabbed a slice of an apple pie and sank his teeth into it. "Now, this what I'm talking about." He took another bite. "It's delicious."

I stood there speechless.

Aunt Enid turned her attention back to me. "One day you're gonna thank me for this."

Probably so, but not in this lifetime. I kept quiet, holding my thoughts to myself.

Then all of a sudden we were pulled in Kevin's direction where he was rummaging through the fridge. He stopped when he grabbed the bottle of milk, then started guzzling the milk down his throat.

Aunt Enid popped him upside his head.

"What's that for?" He wiped the spilled milk from his chin.

"What did I tell you about drinking anything outta my fridge like that? Now, go get yourself a drinking glass to drink out of."

I had heard that same argument before. I looked at my wristwatch. "Yo, Kev. It's four-thirty. Let's hit the mall before it gets too late."

"Yeah, alright. But what's up with little mama out there?"

"We might as well take her along with us. I needa get her some extra clothes anyway." I gave Aunt Enid a kiss, then headed for the kitchen doorway.

As Kevin was about to exit with me, Aunt Enid yanked him by the ear, drawing him back to her. "Are you forgetting something?"

I laughed.

He looked at me, then back to Aunt Enid. "I'm a little too old to still be getting slaps, Auntie." He whined a bit, then gave her a kiss. "What would the fellas think, if they knew I still be getting pops?"

"Boy, get outta here before I pop you again."

We walked out of the kitchen.

When we pulled up in Dade Land Mall's parking lot, it was nearly packed with cars—even more than usual. We entered the mall through the west entrance.

"Destini, just make sure that you stay close to me, okay?"

"Okay." She turned her head from me and started looking at some teenagers who were laughing about something as we walked pass them.

After about two hours of shopping for outfits, for Destini and a few other items for myself, we were casually browsing through the mall when I saw this new clothing store.

"Hold up for a second. Let me check this spot out." I entered the store first, and by the time Destini and Kevin caught up with me, I already had a shirt I wanted to purchase in my hand.

"Yeah, that's you right there."

I turned to Kevin. "Word?"

"Hell, yeah," he said, "You should get that green one, too."

"Yeah?" I reached for that one as well.

"Hell, yeah."

Then it dawned on me. "So" —I threw the shirt at him— "you might as well go ahead and buy it yourself then!"

"For what?!" He threw the shirt back at me. "When all I have to do is borrow it from you when you're not wearing it."

"Exactly! That's why I'm not getting it." I placed the shirt back on the clothes rack.

"I'll get it myself then!" As he reached for the shirt, he suddenly panicked. "Oh shit!" He ducked into the clothes rack on my left. "You didn't see me."

"What the hell are you talking about?" I cut my eyes from him and tried to see who got him spooked.

"I'm talking about Vanessa," he whispered, pointing his finger in the direction behind him. "She's over there."

"Which Vanessa?" I asked him. But then I immediately spotted her and her friend Kenya, looking dead at me. I tilted my head downward a bit, trying not to be obvious about it. "Stay down, they're coming this way."

"DaShawn!" Vanessa shouted when she saw me about to walk away.

I stopped.

"Oh, my God." She walked over there to me. "Speaking of the devil. How are you doing, gorgeous?"

"I'm doing all right. What about yourself?"

She smiled and shook her hips from side to side, while spinning around for a complete circle. "What? You can't see for yourself?" she replied with an inviting smile. "I'm doing fine."

I then twisted to Kenya and greeted her, too.

But before she could say anything back to me, Vanessa cut her off. "Tell me something, DaShawn," she began to ask. "Where's your cousin at?"

"Who? Kev?

"Yeah," she seemed irritated by my procrastination.

"Oh. He hasn't been feeling good lately. So he's been laying low."

"Ohh," Vanessa dragged with a look on her face that she didn't buy my story. Then said: "Well, can you tell him that I'm looking for him?"

But before I could say, Sure, I can do that for you, Kenya suddenly leaped back from the clothes rack—from where we were standing—with a loud shout: "What the fuck is that?!"

They both zoomed in, realizing it was Kevin.

He was busted. "Hey-eeee, baby," he said to Vanessa in a phony tone while getting out of the clothes rack. "What's happening?"

"Don't you baby me!" she snapped at him, swaying her head from side to side, acting ghetto as hell. "Why haven't you been calling me back?" And since he didn't respond fast enough for her, she added, "I don't mean to bust your bubble, boo, but you ain't all that."

"C'mon, baby, don't say awful things like that," he told her, then looked over at Kenya and me, then back to Vanessa. "It's just that I have so much on my mind right now. And if you feel like cursing me out, just go ahead and do that. I sorta deserve that."

"What's on your damned mind?" She seemed like she wanted to know.

I did too. I was all ears.

Kevin looked at me, then at Kenya, then he threw his arm around Vanessa's shoulder and stepped aside. "You see, baby...," his voice faded as they walked away from us.

Kenya broke the silence: "I haven't seen you since we were at the hotel. So who are you hiding from?"

"Hiding?" I almost laughed at her. "I'm not hiding from anyone." And if she felt like putting me to the test, I would fuck her in the dressing room right now, if push comes to shove. A quickie wouldn't hurt anybody. "But seriously, I have been babysitting for the past several days."

"Babysitting who?"

"My little missy right—" I froze when I didn't see Destini beside me. I literally felt my heart skip a beat. Better yet, a few beats. I panicked. "Where did she go?!"

"Who?" Kenya asked me as if I were making up a story. "I didn't see anybody over here with you."

To hell with her insinuations! I strode away from her. I had a more important issue on my mind: "DESTINI!" I yelled across the store.

Nothing.

I yelled out her name again. And again. And of course, again. But still, there was no response.

When my shouting caught Kevin's attention, he jerked his head up toward me.

I spread my hands in the air to indicate helplessness and yelled: "I don't know where Destini's at! She's missing!"

I searched the entire department store, from section to section, and I still couldn't find Destini anywhere. I ran out of the store into the mall walkway.

People were everywhere.

Shit!

I yelled out, "DESTINI!" and waited for a response.

Nothing.

I shouted her name out again. And still, no luck. I got scared and started asking pedestrians if they had seen a little girl walking on her own. But they all shook their heads, looking confused. Probably because they didn't understand the English language.

So welcome to Miami, Cuba.

Kevin strode up to me. "My nigga, let's report this to the po-po before it gets too late. At least they can post an Amber Alert for us."

That sounded like a good idea. We rushed to a nearby security officer, who was standing at Steve's Pretzel stand.

"Excuse me! Officer!" I got his attention, nearly all out of breath.

But this officer looked somewhat irritated by the interruption. "Whaaat?" he dragged, while trying to enjoy his hot pretzel. "What do you want?" He took a hard swallow. Then added: "This better be good."

"I lost a little girl and I can't find her anywhere!"

"You don't lose little girls." The officer seemed like he was not taking my situation seriously. "You lose stuff like a bag, a wallet, or some money here and there, but not a girl, fella." He had the audacity to take another bite of his fucking pretzel, mocking me with that ugly-ass smirk on his face.

I held back my anger but I couldn't say the same thing for Kevin, though. He snapped on the mall security, "You fuck-ass busta! He didn't ask you all that fuck-shit! He just told you that he lost his daughter—"

"Ho-hold up, Kev!" I held my hand against his chest, because it seemed like he were about to slap the pretzel from the officer's mouth. Then I twisted back to the officer. "All I'm asking is if you can help me out here. I need you to help me find this little girl before somebody snatches her up." I paused, fighting my fear from taking over me. "If that didn't happen yet."

The officer stopped chewing on his pretzel and cut his eyes from me to Kevin, then back to me. "Give me her name, description, and age." He then reached for his notepad. "And where was the last location you saw her?"

I told him everything I knew, step by step.

"Yeah, that should be about everything I need," the officer said, still holding onto his pad. "But one more question, just a rough estimate, how tall is she?"

"She's about four feet tall."

Kevin jumped in: "No she's not! She's around four and half feet tall."

"Dawg, are you stupid?" I contested, looking around for someone of a similar stature as Destini. "She's about his height right there." I pointed at some little Spanish youngster who was walking by with his mother, I guess.

"You have to be kidding me," Kevin disagreed. "Because if I believe that shit, you might as well say that I'm about five feet tall then."

The officer looked at me. "You don't know how tall your daughter is?"

"Yeah…. No!" I stammered defensively. "I mean, they're saying she's mine, but I'm not actually sure about that yet."

The officer looked confused.

Only if he knew how I felt about it then. But then again I had no reason to explain anything to him. My eyes cut from him and began searching again for somebody around Destini's height. "She's about—" I started, then stopped. I couldn't believe this shit! "There she goes right there!"

"Where?" Kevin asked.

"Right there," I said, striding to K.B. Toys' store.

Kevin followed.

I felt my blood boiling inside me. As I entered the department store, I noticed Destini was in the company of a female who looked to be much older than she. They were browsing through the water gun shelf together.

Kevin caught up with me, and we both walked up to Destini together.

I snatched her up by the arm. "What the hell is the matter with you?" Even though she seemed to be safe, that didn't change the fact that she walked out of my sight without telling me anything. "You had me worried-sick about you!" She looked scared, but I didn't give a damn. "Just supposed something would have happened to you? What then?

The young lady who was kneeling beside Destini finally stood up, wearing a baseball cap low over her forehead. "I'm sorry," she said. "It was somewhat my fault. But I assure you, she was in safe hands. I wasn't—"

"But" —I cut her off— "that still doesn't make a difference here. She wasn't supposed to walk away like that." It was then that I got a good look at this shawty's face. "Don't I know you from somewhere?"

"No. I don't believe so."

There was a pause. It was neither a long pause nor a short one.

I kept my eyes on her. Think...

America's Most Wanted?

Nah....

Somebody at the club?

Could be....

Then within seconds, we both said, "IHOP!"

Kevin looked at me, then at her.

I nodded. "Yeah, that's it. You were the one who bucked on paying your bill."

"I know you don't believe that."

Of course I did, but for the sake of it, I said, "Only you would know the truth behind that. But what brings you out here?"

"Here?"

"Yes, here?"

Her facial expression changed to something mischievous. "To be honest?"

I nodded.

"I'm here to see if I can boost something."

I knew it!

She laughed. "I'm only joking. I'm just browsing around."

Oh, sure you were.

Kevin stuck his hand out to her and said, "I don't think we were properly introduced. My name is Kevin, and it's nice to meet you."

"Likewise." She shook his hand. "My name is Naomi."

"So are you from around here, Naomi?"

"No. Not really." She combed her fingers through Destini's hair, then jumped the topic off of her. "So, whose little princess is this?"

"She's mine."

Although Destini was playing with a water gun, she suddenly stopped. She looked at me.

Kevin cut back in, speaking directly to Naomi. "So, my new found friend," he tried to sound a bit too smooth. "What are you doing after this? Because I was wondering, since you're not from around here, perhaps I could show you around town."

"That won't be necessary. I'm a big girl now. And besides, I'm not gonna have any problems browsing around here before I call it a night."

I wanted to laugh at Kevin, but instead I turned to Destini. "All right sweetie, go ahead and put those back so we can leave."

Destini hesitated. She looked at the water gun, then back to me.

I knew what that meant. I didn't have to be a rocket scientist to figure that one out. Perhaps at any other time I would have bought them for her. But now.... Hell, nah! She doesn't deserve anyone of them. She was out of line for walking away from—

"Hey, Destini!" Naomi butted in. "Wouldn't you like to have that?"

Destini quickly nodded her head.

"So, what are you waiting on? Bring it on, I'll buy it for you, since your daddy lost his wallet."

Destini smiled. Instead of carrying just one water gun, she brought two of them along with her: A triple-gauge water shooter and a regular squirter, a Glock 40.

"Don't worry about it," I whispered to Naomi. "I'll take care of it."

"Oh, child, please." She unzipped her purse and grabbed for her checkbook. "I had already told her that I would buy it for her. And besides, I can at least do this for her since you paid my bill the other night."

I refused to argue against that.

Kevin and I headed for the outskirts of the cash registers, waiting on Naomi and Destini to get through. Naomi grabbed a stuffed toy monkey from the side of the cashier's lane and started dangling it in front of Destini's face.

Destini burst out laughing, then looked at me.

You might think this sounds silly, but I think they may have been making fun of me.

After Naomi purchased those few items for Destini, they approached us.

"Well, it was a pleasure to have met you again," I told Naomi. "And thanks for brightening up my little girl's day with your gifts."

"Don't mention it. The pleasure was mine."

Kevin cut in: "So why don't you gimme your digits so I can holla at you, at a later time?"

"I'm sorry, but I don't give my number to just about everybody I encounter."

"But what about me?" Destini shook Naomi's leg. "Can I call you?"

Naomi hesitated, then finally said, "Sure, you can have it."

She reached for her pen and jotted her phone number down on a sheet of paper. "Here you go. But make sure you don't give it away to anybody."

Destini nodded, "Okay."

"So what about me?" I had to ask. "Can she give it to me?"

Naomi sort of smiled. "That's for her to decide."

We all shook hands and Naomi departed, disappearing into the crowd. And that's when I realized we hadn't eaten a decent meal all day. Literally, I felt like one of those homeless-ass vets, coming back from the Afghanistan war. I was starving. So I could only imagine how Destini's tummy felt when we hit that corner and saw Piccadilly's restaurant.

"Let's get something to eat outta here," I recommended.

They didn't object.

Just before we walked into Piccadilly's, Kevin asked Destini for Naomi's telephone number and she bucked by reminding him that, "Naomi told you no already."

Then when I looked at her, she must have thought I was going to ask her for Naomi's phone number too: She stuck the paper inside her pocket, eyeballing me from the corner of her eye.

Oh, hell nah! I know she didn't try me like that.

I grabbed her by the wrist. "Gimme that number, since you wanna act like that!

"Okay, okay." She pulled the number out of her pocket, then immediately stuffed it inside her mouth.

"Ow!" She bit my finger.

By Thursday evening the house was a total chaos.

Destini came running into the family room with her stuffed monkey in her hand and saw Carlton and Uncle James were already in there, watching "The Antichrist" on DVD.

"Y'all always watching this movie," she told them, taking a seat beside Carlton, hoping he would change it to something else.

"So?"

"So? So I don't wanna watch this!"

"Well, just shut your eyes then, dummy!"

Uncle James laughed at her from a nearby recliner.

Destini looked at him, then back to Carlton; she whacked him with her toy monkey, who she eventually named, Abu.

"Alright now. Don't make me punch you in your face."

The phone rang.

Destini quickly answered it before Carlton did.

"Hey!" It was Kevin. "What's up?"

"Whatchu want?"

"Hey, little mama," he said, hoping she would lighten up on him. "Where's your daddy at?"

There was a pause.

"Hello?" he said.

She broke the silence. "I'm not a little mama."

Kevin laughed it off. "You're so funny. But for real though, where's your daddy at? It's important."

As soon as I got out of the shower and set foot in the bedroom, I heard somebody knocking on the door.

"Yeah, who is it?" I was drying my back off with the towel.

"It's me," Destini said. "Kevin's on the phone. Do you want me to tell him to call back?"

"No." I ajar the door, just enough to reach for the phone. "Thanks, sweetie." I shut the door back and answered the call.

"Yeah, what's up?"

"Oh! So that's how it is now?"

"What the hell are you talking about?" I started drying between my toes.

"I just got off the phone with Vida, and she told me that you and her girl Samara supposed to go out tonight."

"And what's the matter with that?" I got off the bed and walked over to my dresser.

"Everything!" he began to explain. "When have I ever went out with one of these hoes around here without inviting you to come along?"

"Damn, that's my fault." I started rubbing some of that new Jordan's deodorant underneath my armpits. "I'll hook something up for us on the next one. Alright?"

"Don't even worry about that shit anymore, because I can look out for myself. But on a serious note, what time you trying to head out there anyway?"

"I don't know. Probably about half an hour from now. Why?"

"Alright then. I'll be right over. I set it up for us already. We're going out on a double date."

A double date?

But before I could respond to that, that douche bag hung up on me. Then it dawned on me: The latest news about him coming along with me wouldn't be bad after all. Because, if anything, he could coax his shawty up a bit so Samara could feel comfortable around me.

What a brilliant idea.

"Yo, Shawn!" Kevin shouted from the family room while everybody was laid back, chilling. "Why don't you hurry the fuck up? We're running late!"

Uncle James immediately cupped his ears the moment Kevin shouted in the room. "You damn dummy! What are you trying to do? Make us all deaf in here!"

"My fault."

"Damn right it's your fault! Marching up in here like it's some sorta pimp convention going on. Now get your ass outta my way, because you're blocking my view."

Kevin stepped aside and joked: "I'm gonna knock your old-ass out one day. Just keep it up."

"My nigga," Carlton butted in, "hold it down around the little one."

Kevin placed his hand on top of Destini's head and said, "It ain't like she hasn't heard those type of words before?"

She shoved his hand away.

"Hey-ee. Don't be so mean, little mama."

She cut her eyes back to the TV.

"What's up with you anyway?"

"None-yah."

He smiled. "None-yah business, huh?"

She hesitated before she twisted back to him and said, "Nope!"

"So none-yah, what then?"

"This right here" —she wildly waved her hand around and about her face— "is none of your concern."

He shook his head with a smirk.

"I see you have met your match," Uncle James said to Kevin with a slight laugh. "None-of-your-concern... How could you fall for that one? You have to be a complete nincompoop."

Carlton twisted to Uncle James, looking at him with a hypocritical stare.

Uncle James stopped laughing, then gave an embarrassed cough before he went back to the movie.

Not to brag on myself, but when I stepped into the family room, I was looking really good. It felt like I was walking the red carpet in Hollywood.

Destini—my first entourage—ran up to me and asked, "Where are you going?"

"I'm going out for a while." I picked her up and carried her back to the couch, praying that she wouldn't wrinkle my outfit up. "Carlton and Uncle James are going to watch you tonight. Just until I come back."

"But who gonna read me a bedtime story?"

"Either one of them."

Destini took a quick look at Carlton and Uncle James, then back to me. "Can they read?"

Carlton snapped: "Girl, I oughta knock your ass out for saying that!"

I cut back in: "Of course they can read."

"But it won't be the same."

"Yeah it will." I then reached for that monkey she was carrying. "Do you see this right here?"

"Who, Abu?"

"Yeah. You see Abu, right here?" I waited a second or two, up until she nodded her head, before I went on to continue: "Well, when they're reading you your bedtime story, just imagine Abu is me. And I want you to pretend like I'm the one who is reading it to you."

"But it won't work." She pouted.

Okay, to make a long story short, I had to convince her—after about five minutes straight—to allow me to go out with Kevin, and of course, I wound up promising her that I would make it back up to her.

"So you're coming back home, right?"

"Of course," I told her. "I live here."

"Promise me then."

"I promise," I whispered, wondering why she didn't believe me. "I'll be right back home before you even realize I'm gone."

She smiled. "Okay, I'm realizing you're gone already. Does that mean you're gonna stay home now?"

"Huh?"

She giggled. "I gotchu. I'm only playing."

I smiled with her and gave her a kiss on her forehead. "So be good now. Okay?"

"Okay."

Kevin broke in: "Alright, my nigga. Let's go before we be late." He went for the door and we walked out.

Once we were outside, Kevin asked me, "Why don't we just take one ride instead of two, since we're going to the same place anyway? We could save some gas money. You feel me?"

"Yeah, we can do that." I headed for his SUV.

"Nah dawg. Let's take your ride instead," he said, while walking toward my Audi coupe. "My shit be guzzling my gas up."

I should have expected some shit like that from him. As soon as I deactivated the car alarm, my cell phone started to vibrate. I checked the caller ID.

"Who's that?"

I took the driver seat, and said, "Nobody."

"So what the fuck you smiled for then?" he asked. Then immediately added before I could respond: "Who was it? A bitch I know?"

I cranked the car up; then came clean: "Yeah, sort of. It was that RN chick from Family Services."

"Who, that hoe Debbie?"

"Yeah. She has been blowing my phone up since I put it down on her last week. But I have been avoiding her calls ever since."

Kevin laughed. "You musta ate her pussy out?"

I refused to answer that.

He laughed some more. "You did. Didn't you?"

I cut to the left when I saw two little youngsters from up the block went inside Amanda's house; she closed the door behind them.

"So, did you?"

I cut back to Kevin with a smile. "What the hell you think?"

Destini peeked through the living room drapes and watched the Audi coupe drive away. Her countenance dropped. She strolled back to the family room and stood at the entranceway.

"Come over here and have a seat." Carlton was the first one to notice her there. "This is the best part of—"

Uncle James intervened: "Did your daddy leave yet?"

She barely nodded her head.

"Okay then. Go get me a glass of water. Hurry up! I'm thirsty."

She sighed, then walked over to Carlton and sat beside him. "You can get it yourself."

"What?!" Uncle James raised his voice. "What the hell you just said? You didn't hear me?"

"Uh-huh, I heard you." She looked innocent. "Why? Are you really thirsty?"

That's more like it, he seemed to have cooled down when he told her, "Yeah. Now go get me some water."

"So, go get it yourself."

Uncle James leaped from the chair. "What the hell you just said?!" He started to unbuckle his belt. "I'm gonna whoop your little ass for disrespecting me like that! And you can run and tell your daddy about it once he gets back."

Carlton cut in: "Why don't you leave her alone."

Uncle James paused. Not for long. It was just long enough to look at the both of them. "I'll go and get my own damn iced water then," he murmured under his breath, giving Destini that menacing stare as he headed out of the room. "You needa learn some damn manners, because you're messing with the right one. I'd be the right one to give you that ass whooping you're looking for."

"Oh man, my nigga," Kevin said, just a few blocks away from meeting up with our dates. "I can't wait till we get there. But I just hope your bitch doesn't fuck it up for me though."

"If you stick to my plan, she won't."

"I just hope so, because I'm trying to beat my hoe for some head tonight."

"Is it like that?" I made a right turn on Washington Avenue.

"Is it?" He kept his eyes on me. "I swear to God, I rate that bitch within my top ten."

"Word?"

"Hell, yeah!"

"Does she swallow?" I was dying to know the character of this trick.

"Does she?" he repeated. "That fuck-hoe sucked me up the other day like a muthafucking vacuum, leaving nothing behind."

I glanced over at him and chuckled. I knew birds of a feather flock together. I sped up, curious to know what Samara had to offer me.

Carlton tried to pass Destini a bag of barbecue potato chips while they were sitting in front of the TV, but she declined to have any.

"So, suit yourself then," he told her.

She kept quiet.

"Hey!" Uncle James got Carlton's attention. "Lemme get some of those."

Carlton tossed him the bag.

Uncle James poured himself some chips onto his shirt. "Here you go!" He tossed the bag back.

Destini seemed irritated, looking over at Uncle James. "Can you watch how you throw that bag? Because it hit me on my head."

"You shoulda ducked then," Uncle James retorted, while gobbling on his chips.

Carlton held the bag out in front of her again. "You sure you don't want some?"

She shoved the bag away. "I said no already."

"I wasn't gonna give you none anyway."

Destini didn't respond. She kept her eyes on the TV screen. About a minute later, while they were still watching OWN channel network, Destini seemed disturbed about something. She glanced to her right side at Carlton and saw him sitting there, watching TV. She quickly shifted her head to the left to Uncle James, and he was doing the same thing, watching For Better or Worse.

Then Carlton asked her, "Is everything alright with you?"

She turned to him and nodded her head to let him know that she was okay. But then, all of a sudden, a cascade of crumbs came hurtling down her face out of nowhere. She panicked! She waved her hands over her head to brush the particles away, most of them landing on her lap. And that was when she realized it was crushed barbecue potato chips. She suspiciously looked back at Carlton.

"Are you sure you don't want some chips?" he asked, taunting her. "Because it looks like it's written all over your face that you want some."

Uncle James guffawed a bit. "It's written all over your face," he said, pointing his finger at her. "Do you get it, potato-head? It's written all over your face. Get it?"

Destini finally broke her silence, tittering right along with them, giving them a mischievous smile.

It was about time!

We finally reached the China Grill restaurant. The fluorescent light in front of this spot looked nice. And there were our two beautiful Spanish mommies, waiting for our arrival. I quickly parked the car and we got out.

Vida and Samara looked stunning. Their buxom figures looked astonishingly appealing. Breathtaking. They wore bright sun-dresses, one lime-green with flower designs on it and the other one was yellow; both of them wore matching wedge shoes.

Toes looked lovely.

"Now, this is a wonderful sight to look upon," Kevin said to me as we approached them. "Two beautiful, secret gardens."

"Okay, boo." Vida started to blush. "Don't overdo it now."

"But I'm not." Kevin took her by the hand and led her through the front entrance.

Samara and I lingered shortly behind them. I looked at Samara's backside when I allowed her to step through the door before me. She had an ass like Nicki Minaj. It was nice and phat. And I can't wait to—

Fuck!

She spun her head around and caught me eyeing her ass; she smiled.

"You look beautiful," I quickly whispered to her, hoping to throw her off, before she figured out what this was all about.

"Oh, thank you." She tried to act cute. "You look nice, yourself."

"Thanks."

We stood behind Kevin and Vida, waiting on the hostess to arrive.

Samara glanced down at me, then slapped a naughty look on her face. She mumbled something tasteful under her breath, which I would rather not repeat. It might jinx me. But I could tell you this though: She brought a smile on my face.

The hostess arrived and ushered us to our reserved table. I took another peek at Samara's backside again. I didn't see any pantie lines.

Destini leaned toward the coffee table and grabbed the glass of Hawaiian Punch.

"Remember, don't drink too much of that," Carlton told her while sitting beside her on the couch. "Because I don't want you to be pissing the bed tonight."

"Okay." She gave him a roguish smirk. "May I have some tato chips?"

"Yeah, you can have some." He twisted toward the night table to grab the bag of potato chips for her.

"I'll get it!" she quickly said, while leaning over him with a drink in her hand and accidentally spilled all of it on him.

"You idiot!" He leaped from the couch.

"Oops, I'm sorry."

He looked down at his chest, finding his shirt and pants soaked with fruit punch.

Uncle James started laughing at him,

Carlton looked at him, then back at Destini. "Oops, huh?" he asked her, believing there was some sort of foul play involved.

"Uh-huh" —she nodded her head with an impassive look— "but it won't happen again. I'm sorry."

"You're sorry, huh?"

She nodded again.

He left the family room without saying another word to her. Then, about three minutes later, he came back in the room with a pot of water in his hands.

Destini immediately tried to make a run for it, but he blocked her from exiting the room. She panicked and ran over to Uncle James for his protection.

"Oh, hell nah! Don't you dare bring your little ass over here beside me!" He tried to push her back toward Carlton.

She froze, then cut to the other side, trying to get away from them.

"How does it feels when the rabbit got the gun?!" Uncle James shouted at her. Then cheered Carlton on: "Wet her ass back!"

Destini didn't pay any mind to Uncle James: She was more concerned about getting away from Carlton. She saw an opening—an escape route—straight out the room. She went for it.

Splash!!!

Her back got soaked with cold water. She ran out of the room.

"That's showing her." Uncle James praised Carlton. "An eye for an eye and a tooth for a tooth, as the Good Old Book says it. You got her little bad ass!"

Destini could hear them laughing from behind the bathroom door. But she knew this was far from being over with.

She smiled again.

Sometimes it's best not to overdo it.

"I hope this one is true," Vida said to Kevin, holding a thin strip of paper that she had just pulled out of a fortune cookie, as we were waiting for our meal to arrive. "It reads, Your dreams are in the process of being fulfilled." She paused. Then asked him: "Are you a part of my dreams I'm about to fulfill?"

"Well, I don't know about you." He grabbed her hand and gently brushed his lips against it. "But, I'm living my dreams now."

Yeah, right! Just one word: Lame.

Vida lowered her head. "Boy, you are off the chain."

Oh, sure he was, because he was killing my character.

Samara looked at me, probably wondering why I hadn't tried to spark a conversation up with her yet. But then again, before I knew it, she broke the ice herself, "So, how is she?"

"How is who?"

"Your little girl," she said. "You remember her, don't you?"

I felt like an asshole! "Of course. You just threw me off with that one. You're talking about Destini."

She nodded significantly with one eyebrow raised higher than the other one, looking at me as if I were a complete dunce.

"She's doing fine." I admitted. "My cousin is babysitting her for me right now."

"So how does it feel to be a dad?"

I almost laughed. "You know, at first, I thought this whole parenthood thing was going to be a serious problem for me. Being new to this father role and all. But come to find out, Destini makes it seem so easy. She doesn't ask for much. She just a little sweetheart." I paused for a moment. Maybe a second or two. Then continued: "So, what more can I ask for?"

"She sounds really sweet. She musta gotten that from you then."

"Yeah, she probably did." I shot her a politician's smile.

Destini got up from underneath the dining room table and peeked into the family room to see what Carlton and Uncle James were doing.

They were still watching OWN.

She reached down and hid something behind her back. Then, she went over to the entranceway of the family room and faked a cough. It worked: Carlton was the first one to look at her.

He gave her a sardonic smile, then cut to Uncle James. "I told you she wasn't—" he started, but then immediately ducked his head. The water balloon missed him by an inch, if not two inches, spattering against the wall.

Uncle James laughed.

She threw another water balloon, but this time at Uncle James.

Splash!!!

It slapped him across his face.

"You dirty little runt, you!" He got up from the recliner and yelled: "Get your ass over here!"

She stood motionless in the doorway, then when Carlton and Uncle James drew near to her, she threw a cup of toilet water in their faces and ran. They chased after her. She cut to the left, then made a quick right, and ran through the dining room. Then, as planned, she pushed a chair down—stretching a shoelace from one chair to the dining room table—and Uncle James stumbled.

First there was a BOOM, then a SPLASH!

His face landed square in the mop bucket filled with dirty water. "That's it!" he yelled. "You dunnit now! I'm gonna whoop your fucking ass, you little shit!" He got up and continued his pursuit after her.

But Destini was nowhere in sight.

They split up and went on a little search party. Carlton went to the back end of the house, while Uncle James went to the front.

"Destini!" Carlton called out for her. "Where are you?! Why don't you come out? Everything is over with! I just wanna show you something!"

"Yeah!" Uncle James shouted from the front end of the house. "Come out! I have something to show you too, god dammit!" Then suddenly his eyes were drawn to the china cabinet: He went over there. "Ah-HA!" He snatched the lower cabinet doors open. "I gotchu!"

Nothing.

She wasn't in there.

Uncle James pouted. About a minute later he met up with Carlton in the hallway.

"Where in the hell can she be at?" Carlton asked him "She has to be somewhere in here."

No comment. Uncle James shrugged, showing a sign of helplessness. His eyes explored his surroundings. Then something clicked! His eyes shot straight to the hallway closet. His rough-looking face painted on three expressions: revenge, frustration, and satisfaction.

At the same moment, Carlton gazed at the same closet door. He pointed to it, feeling certain she was hiding in there. They were sure of it as they tiptoed down the hall.

"If she tries to run out of there," Uncle James whispered, as they approached the closet door, "just grab her for me. I'm gonna give her an ass whooping that she won't forget about."

Carlton reached for the doorknob and slowly began turning it just before he yanked it open and yelled: "I GOTCHU!"

She wasn't there.

Again, their curiosities pounded them: Where could she be?

They were clueless. Just as they decided to give up on their search and go change their clothes, a door further down the hall swung open.

It was Destini, standing there with a triple gauge water gun in her hand, pointing it at them. The same water gun that Naomi had bought her from K.B. Toys' store. But Carlton and Uncle James thought Destini was bluffing when they took a step toward her.

"Say hello to my little friend, you little cockroach," she said in a broken-English accent, with her finger on the trigger.

They froze....

Then she sprayed them furiously. She started with Carlton. She wanted to even the score with him first. She squirted him square in his face. He dropped on the floor, balling up in fetal position. But Uncle James was bold enough to challenge Baby-Scarface. He rushed toward her with his hands stretched out, screaming from the top of his voice, "Aaaaaahhhhh..."

She immediately went for the Glock 40 (water gun) and changed position for her new target. She got down on one knee, aimed, and shot Uncle James dead in his eyes. He was temporarily blinded, but he kept running directly at her with his eyes shut, stretching his hands out even further this time because he was determined to get his hands on her.

She reached over and yanked a string as he got near. He fell for another booby trap. His legs wobbled when he tripped over the string, then he flew like a young bird, departing from its nest, flapping his useless arms back and forth.

BAM!

Uncle James' head slammed against the door. It probably felt like a Mike Tyson punch. He was down for the count. He had blood leaking from his nose and mouth.

Destini held her Glock 40 in position with her finger still on the trigger. She knew it could be a trick. She exercised caution when she eased over there to check him out, using her foot to poke him a few times. "Are you okay?" She kicked him in the ribs this time. Then again.

But he didn't respond. He laid there motionless.

Carlton unfolded himself and raised his head. "What's the matter with him?" He began to get up off the floor. "Is he still alive?"

Destini shrugged. "I don't know."

It was about time! The waitress finally arrived with our entrées. I sat there at the table and listened to Kevin entertaining Samara and Vida with corny-ass jokes as we were munching down on our meal.

They laughed; I laughed too, to keep the atmosphere excited.

"Okay, okay," Kevin chuckled a little more, "but here's the best part though."

They were tuned in.

Then he went on to add, "My ex-girlfriend's mom was so freaky that, when I took her on a job hunt, she came across a question on the job application that asks for 'Position desired', which her stupid ass wrote, 'I don't mind giving head, as long as you don't cum in my mouth. However, I prefer to do doggy-style.'"

"Get outta here?" Vida couldn't stop laughing.

"I'm dead serious."

"Did anybody hire her?"

"Did they?" He allowed the suspense to build for a hot three seconds, then let it rip: "Hell, yeah! They hired her right there on the spot, after a little demonstration. She has three jobs now, and putting in overtime."

She laughed some more.

I dipped an egg roll in the duck sauce, trying my best to be a part of the circle.

"May I have that?" Samara asked me.

"This?" I glanced at my egg roll, then back to her.

"Yes, that one...."

I reached over the table, thinking she was going to use her hand to take it from me. But instead, she opened her mouth and craned her neck towards me. I held my breath as her lips blanketed my fingers.

She slowly pulled away, chewing the egg roll with a smile, giving me that look. That I-wanna-fuck-you look.

It was on now.

Carlton walked over toward Destini and pressed two fingers against Uncle James' neck to check for a pulse. "He's still alive," he whispered, then reached down to grab him. "C'mon. Help me sit him up against the wall."

She helped him.

Then Carlton yelled at Uncle James, while filliping his fingers a few times in front of him. "Wake up!"

Nothing.

Carlton then shook Uncle James a little, rocking him back and forth.

Uncle James' head slouched over.

"Slap him," Destini recommended. "I think that will work."

"Are you crazy?"

"Okay, I'll do it then." She got in a striking position and went for it. Wapow!

She slapped Uncle James across his face. But he didn't budge. Not even a little bit. She looked at Carlton again for answers.

No comment.

She turned back to Uncle James and slapped him again and again, gradually picking up speed on every smack.

Carlton thought she was crazy up until he recalled all the ass whipping he had gotten from Uncle James back in the day. It penetrated his mind: Destini was having all the fun, slapping Uncle James, and he wasn't.

Then Destini stopped for a moment, feeling the need for a break. Only a short one. She wiped the sweat from her forehead, then cocked her palm back up—as far as she could take it—and swung after Uncle James' face again.

Carlton stopped her in time, grabbing hold of her wrist. "Let me give it a try."

She gave him a suspicious look as she stepped aside.

He then leaned over to set up for his target. He raised Uncle James' chin and turned back to Destini. "Do you think he gonna remember this?"

"I don't know," she said. Then changed course: "I mean" —a smile started to grow on her face— "I don't think so."

Carlton looked at Uncle James again, and gave it a try.

WaPow!!!

His smack sent a frightening sound through the hall.

Destini's eyebrows shot up! She placed her hand on the side of her face as if she was the one who just got slapped.

Carlton smiled at her, then went ballistic on Uncle James' face: slap after slap, repeatedly.

Uncle James slowly began to regain consciousness. He managed to raise his left eyelid, and then the other one. But it was too late: Carlton's furious palm was a just tenth of a second away from the bull's-eye, and Uncle James couldn't stop it.

WaPow!!!

It seemed like everything in the house, even the old clock on the wall, had stopped.

"Eh!" Uncle James became hysterical, throwing his arms over his head. "What the fuck's going on in here?!" He tried to look up at Carlton, but got distracted when he felt one of his teeth popped out of his mouth. He looked down at it, then back at Carlton. "What the hell is your problem?!" Then another tooth fell out of his mouth. "You son-of-a-bitch!" He tried to get up and fight, but fell back down.

Carlton attempted to pick him up. "Destini, gimme a hand."

She hesitated at first, but felt obligated to help.

"What happened?" Uncle James asked, as they carried him to the family room. "What the hell were you slapping me for?"

"You passed out in the hallway, and we tried to wake you up."

"How the hell I passed out?"

Destini panicked.

Carlton sorta shook his head at her, hoping that she wouldn't say anything. Then he told Uncle James, "We were playing around and you ran into the door, slamming your head against it."

"Oh, that explains why I have this lump right here. It's killing me."

"Just sit right here," Carlton told him, while helping him to the couch. "I'll be back. I'm gonna get something for your head."

Destini stayed in the room with Uncle James. She kept quiet, looking at the lumps on his face. One on the forehead and the other just below his eye.

About two minutes later Carlton came back into the room with aspirins, medical gauze, and some ice cubes in his hands. "Eh, Destini!" he said while wrapping Uncle James' head up with the gauze. "Go get him some water so he can take these aspirins."

She ran off to the kitchen. Within seconds she was back with a glass of faucet water in her hand. "Here you go!" She tried to pass it to Uncle James, but he freaked out.

Apparently, the glass of water brought his memory back. At least some of it.

"Get her away!" He folded up like a coward. "Get her away from me!"

"Chill the fuck out!" Carlton nearly snapped on him. "She only got you some water to wash down your aspirins."

"I don't care." He stayed in a fetal position. "Just get her away from me!"

"C'mon, Destini. It's getting late anyway. You might as well sleep in your daddy's room for tonight."

"But it ain't school tomorrow," she said, putting the question up for debate. "And my daddy said I can stay up late till he gets back."

"Girl, bring your little ass on." He gave her a little shove, walking her straight to the bedroom. "And stop lying like that, because it'll make you grow old and ugly."

"That's why you look like that?"

"Shut the hell up, and get in there!"

A few minutes later Destini was lying on the bed, tucked under the sheets. She reached for Abu and covered her ears. "Stop it! That's not singing!"

"Girl, gangstas don't sing. We rap."

"But I can't sleep if you don't sing for me."

"Well, you're outta luck then. I'm not singing for you."

Destini drew a frown on her face as tears began to build up. "I want my daddy," she cried.

I know I wasn't all that great, but when it comes down to entertaining the ladies, I knew I was a little better than Kevin, though.

"I don't believe it!" Samara said to me, looking surprised. "How did you bend that fork just by telling it to?"

"It's easy. It's mind over matter. But really though, it's the energy that lies deep in us. We all have the same energy source. You just gotta find out where your energy source lies."

Kevin cut in: "Yeah, I could believe that, because I know where my energy source at." He looked down to his private area and smiled.

Vida nudged him. "You freak!"

I turned to Samara. "So where you think your energy source lies?"

She thought about it for a brief moment, then laughed. "I'd rather not say," she said with a giggle. "Because I don't want you to get the wrong impression about me."

"Nah" —I held my smile back— "I won't. I'm open-minded about things like this. You can tell me."

"If you give me another one of your energy sources, I'll tell you mine."

"You wanna hear another one, huh?" I nearly whispered as a smile stretched across my face. "Well—" I paused when I felt my cell phone vibrated for the fourth time. "Hold up for a second." I reached for my phone and looked at the front screen to see who was buzzing me. It was from home. "Yeah," I answered it. "What's up?"

"My nigga, Destini can't sleep," Carlton said. "She's crying over here, saying that she wants you to come home and sing for her."

"Man, you have to be kidding me. I'm in the fucking restaurant right now. Eating! So why don't you do it for me?"

"Because she ain't my damn—"

Uncle James cut in. "Is this Shawn?" he asked through the other phone line in the house.

"I can't believe y'all called me for this bullshit!"

"Well," Uncle James growled over the phone, "you needa teach that little girl of yours some damn respect then! Because she was over here running through the house thinking she was some goddamn John Mohammad!"

"Who?" Carlton and I asked about the same time.

"The D.C. Sniper!" he shot back at us. "Carlton knows what the hell she did to me. Tell him, boy!"

I snapped before Carlton had a chance to explain. "Get the fuck off the phone and put her on! I can't believe y'all call me for this bullshit!"

Within seconds Destini's shallow voice came over the phone line: "Hello."

"What's the matter, sweetie?"

She didn't respond as quickly as I wanted her to, but when she did, her voice came out crackly with a little sobbing sound. "I want you to sing a song for me so I can go to sleep"

There was a long pause. My heart sank. I looked at everyone who was at the table with me. "Eh, y'all have to excuse me for a second." I got up from the table and went to the restroom to finish off my conversation with Destini. "Now, where were we?"

"I can't sleep," she dragged with a little whine. "Are you coming back home now? Remember, you promised me."

"I can't come back right now, but I'll be there shortly." Then I thought of something: "What if I sing you a song over the phone in the meantime? Would you go to sleep until I get back?"

"I don't know. I think so. But you're still coming back home, right?"

"Yeah, of course I am. I promised you that already. Didn't I?"

"Uh-huh."

"Okay then. What about if I sing you By Your Side by Sade?"

"I don't care," she said in a soft voice.

I didn't know all the lyrics to that song, but I gave it my best shot. Even before I was finished singing to her, I heard a slight, breathing snore. "Destini," I whispered through the receiver.

No response.

She must have fallen asleep, I thought. I ended my phone call about the same time when some Spanish elderly lady set foot in the men's restroom, pissy drunk. She brushed up against me.

She grabbed my dick and smiled.

I smiled back, because she sorta looked like that Congresswoman, Nancy Pelosi, from California.

She reached in for a kiss.

I returned back to the table and told my friends about the lullaby that I gave Destini over the phone to help her fall asleep, without mentioning anything about what went down with me and that older chick in the restroom in stall three a short moment ago.

"For real?"

"Yeah."

"I didn't know you could sing."

I looked at Samara. "I didn't know either."

We all laughed.

After our meal, we went for a walk down Collins Avenue and Kevin was acting very gentleman-like. I was impressed. He was following the instructions I gave him earlier. He had his arm wrapped around Vida's neck, whispering something in her ear.

She giggled and tried to whisper back to him: "You so nasty."

Samara seemed a bit jealous of the progress her friend was making. "It's a little chilly out here," she said, then hooked her arm around mine, falling right into my trap.

That was elementary stuff. But I played right along with it. I broke my arm loose from hers and wrapped it around her neck, pulling her close to me. She gave me a warm, fetching smile. I smiled back.

Vida skipped a beat in her step. "What are your plans tonight after you're through here?" she asked Kevin, wrapping her arm even tighter around his.

"I really don't know," he tried to be smooth with his reply. "Other than going straight to the crib and taking a hot bath with some of that new fragrance that I bought from Victoria's Secret the other day, I was thinking about watching a movie or two. Why?"

She smiled. "Because that was the same thing I had in mind."

"Well" —he kissed her on the forehead— "we might as well spend the rest of the night together then."

"Yeah, I think you're right." She leaned her head against his arm.

I wanted to laugh.

Kevin stopped walking. "My nigga," he said, spinning around to me. "What y'all about to do?"

"Why, what's up?"

"I feel a little tired and I was gonna have Vida to drive me home. I don't wanna mess y'all night up, when it seems like y'all having a good time together."

But before I could respond, Samara cut in and asked me, "Do you mind taking me home?"

"Nah. I don't mind."

And I guess that was good enough for Kevin, to hear because he immediately told me, "Good looking out, dawg. I'm gonna holla at you tomorrow,"

"Where you live again?" I asked Samara inside my car, setting the radio dial to 103.5, the BEAT.

"On East Seventh Lane, in Hialeah."

Minutes later, while driving through Miami, I glanced over at Samara because I couldn't help but notice how she was rubbing her thighs.

They were thick, chunky, delicious looking. I loved them!

There's no doubt about it, my dick got hard. It was like I was checking out a chick at the red light district in Amsterdam. I couldn't help it: I had to take another peek at her.

And she caught me.

A smile grew on her face. "Is it cold in here, or is it just me?" She kept rubbing her thighs, knocking her knees against each other.

"Here. Let me turn the thermostat on for you." I then busted the heat on her.

When I finally arrived at her house, she had that come-fuck-me look painted on her face. "Would you like to come in and have something to drink?"

"Sure." I stepped out of the car, feeling positive that I was going to get me some pussy tonight. "I wouldn't mind having a cup of coffee. But I just hope you have enough sugar in there to boost my energy. I like my coffee really sweet."

She smiled back. "I promise you, I have more than enough sugar in there to keep you energized, if not satisfied."

"You promise, huh?"

"Yes," she sounded sexy as hell. "But only if you promise me that you'll behave."

"I promise." Then it dawned on me. "Damn!" I looked at my wristwatch, then at her. "I'm sorry but we have to take a rain check on this. I had promised Destini that I was gonna head back to the crib right after I was finished dining out with y'all. And it's already after one."

"You know, she probably won't mind, if you just stay a while."

"I can't." I had to be honest with her. "If I don't keep my promise to her, she'll probably hold that against me and doubt everything else that I'll tell her in the future."

When Samara finally realized that I was serious, her seductive look disappeared. "Alright then. We can continue this on another day."

"Most certainly." I gave her a hug. Then added: "Just hit me up and let me know when you wanna go on another date. I promise, it'll be so much better next time."

"You promise?"

"Of course." I gave her another hug and left.

When I got home, I wanted to go straight to my bedroom and hit the sack. But when I opened my room door, I saw Destini sleeping on my bed.

I wasn't sure what to do: Should I toss her on the couch to sleep or allow her to stay?

I stood there at the doorway for a moment, wondering how in the hell did I get myself into this situation. I was tired. And I was just about tired of all of this parental bullshit, too! But I knew it wasn't her fault, even though she played the major role in my improbable dilemma.

And just when I was about to walk away from the doorway to go sleep on the couch, Destini kicked the sheet off of herself; I stopped. She wasn't covered properly, and I couldn't leave her like that. I may be arrogant, but I'm far from being thoughtless. I walked to her bedside and pulled the sheet over her chest. I stood there, taking a good look at her. She looked so innocent, so beautiful; so happy, as a visible angel, sleeping in my bed. I almost smiled. Then I became lost in my thoughts for a moment. I can't say if it was a long one or a short one. I wasn't keeping up with the time. But then again, I do remember thinking how my mother used to look at me after tucking me in bed when I was about Destini's age. I shot out a little scoffing sound, then gave Destini an ineffable smile. I shook it away. It was too much for me to bear. I left the room and went into the family room to slumber there for the night.

Moments later while I was halfway asleep on the couch, Destini came stumbling into the family room with Abu in one hand and a bed sheet in the other. She cuddled up on the other couch across from me, looking as if she was trying to read my thoughts. I made a funny face, pretending to be mean and tough.

She smiled.

It was quite obvious that there was tension in the kitchen's atmosphere. Uncle James kept his eyes on Destini, sitting across the table from her and Carlton, feeling angry about the events that took place the night before.

She caught him eyeing her while she was trying to enjoy her bowl of Cap'n Crunch cereal. The blueberry kind.

"Whatchu looking at?" He tried to pick an argument with her, tossing his spoon inside his bowl. "You lost something over here?"

"No."

"So, what the hell you looking at then?"

She smiled. "At something ugly," she admitted, then giggled. "You musta lied a lot when you were little."

Carlton accidently spat cereal from his mouth when he laughed.

Uncle James jolted a bit as if he wanted to leap from his seat. "I oughta come around this damned table and give you some of this ugly-ass whooping right now, you rotten runt!"

"So, what's holding you?"

"What?!" Uncle James leaped from his chair.

"What's all the commotion in here?" I asked, walking into the kitchen, approaching the counter-top to make myself a cup of coffee.

"It's nothing I can't handle myself," Uncle James mumbled under his breath, cutting his eyes back to Destini and taking a seat at the table.

"God dammit man! What the hell happened to you?" I took a good look at his face. "It looks like you caught up with Aunt Esther."

"No, it was much worse than her," he said, while keeping his eyes on Destini. "It was more like a little devil instead."

Destini gave Uncle James an evil look and showed him something at her side.

I craned my neck over to zoom in on it. And I'll be damned! It was the butt-handle of her water gun tucked inside her shorts.

Uncle James snapped, raising himself up with both hands on the table. "You dirty little—"

I cut him off: "What the hell happened to your front teeth?"

Carlton laughed.

"That's what the hell I was trying to tell you about last night!" Uncle James tried to explain, pulling his top lip up, showing me his gums. "Just look what the hell this little—"

The doorbell rang.

Destini ran out of the kitchen and Carlton chased after her.

"No! Don't answer it!" Carlton told Destini, low enough so she could hear it. "It might be the po-po."

It was too late: She opened the front door.

Carlton immediately pulled back, trying to avoid being seen by whomever was at the door. Then seconds later he heard an older woman's voice, asking Destini for somebody. But he really couldn't catch what she was saying. He walked a little closer toward the front door to get a better understanding. When he was standing just a short distance away, he was able to hear a little clearer. It was a woman's voice he heard for sure: it sounded friendly but cold.

"That's cute, my little one," the lady's voice traveled to where he was hiding. "But can you call your father or any other adult who's in the house with you?"

"Okay," he heard Destini say.

Then immediately afterward, he heard a rumbling sound. He stood still.

"Oops!" Destini apologized for running into him. "I'm sorry."

"Shhh, keep it down. She might hear you, stupid!"

"Somebody wants you at the door."

"Get your hands off me." He tried to shove her away.

"HELLO!" the lady's heavy voice echoed to where they were standing.

"Do you see what the hell you did?" Carlton murmured to Destini, then straightened himself up, while trying to look presentable. He cleared his throat. "Yeah!" he shouted back to the lady at the front door. "One second, please!" He cut his eyes from Destini before he strolled into the living room to see what this lady wanted.

Destini followed behind him.

"How can I help you?" he asked the elderly looking lady from a short distance away.

"Yes, my name is Ms. Betty Brady," she said. "I'm from Family Services here in Miami, and I was assigned to be the caseworker for this wonderful child right here." She rested her hand on top of Destini's head. "Are you Mr. Powell?"

"No, ma'am. My name is Carlton Hall. But Mr. Powell is my cousin though. I would be happy to call him for you, if you want."

"Can you, please?"

"Sure. C'mon in."

"Oh, thank you." She stepped inside the house.

"No sweat," he said to her, then turned to Destini and tried to be discreet about it. "Go get your daddy, since you wanna answer the damn door."

Ms. Betty's eyes browsed around the living room. "You have a nice home, and I do admire your oil paintings on the walls."

"Thanks. I try to do my best to keep up with the fashion world." He gave her a politician lie, knowing he didn't decorate any part of the house.

I walked into the living room and asked, "Is there someone asking to speak to me?"

"Yes, that would be me," the elderly woman said, turning toward me with a smile on her face. "Ms. Betty Brady from Family Services."

It felt like I got hit with a monkey wrench across my forehead. My body jerked on its own. I didn't mean to. I tried to de-emphasize my shock. I smiled, but it was a phony one. I just couldn't believe it: It was that same nagging bitch—yes, the same one who complained to the hotel manager about me and Kevin at the Holiday Inn—from the bachelorette's party the other night.

"Oh, how are you doing?" I tried to play it cool.

I tilted my head to the side a bit and tried my best to avoid any eye contact with Ms. Betty. I wanted to run but I held my composure. I took a deep breath. Just deny everything, I told myself, if she asked. I even went as far as to conceal my accent, changing my voice up a little so she wouldn't recognize it.

But Destini tried to expose me when she asked, "What's the matter with your voice? You sound funny." She giggled. "You sound like you have a cold."

For goodness sake, whose side are you on? "I feel fine." I twisted back to Ms. Betty, trying my hardest to be polite to her, even though I would have preferred to kick her out of the house—ass first! But I rolled with my ad-libbed script anyway.

We conversed for a while, chatting about parenthood and, yes, my unexpected new role as a father. I could honestly say this: she seemed really astonished by my acceptance of the situation. She kept her eyes on me the whole time while I was yakking off at the mouth. But then she started looking at me differently, as if she were analyzing something I had on my nose. So I kept talking, hoping that might throw her off. But she waited for the perfect moment to ask me a crushing question.

"You look familiar to me. Have we met before?"

"No. I don't believe so. But I hear that question quite often."

"Oh." She was persistent. "But have you ever attended Solid Rock Baptist Church on 142nd Street?"

I shook my head again, hoping she wouldn't narrow it down to the Holiday Inn. "Oh, my goodness!" I looked at my wristwatch to throw her off. "It's already two o'clock. I'm running late." I cut back to her.

"Oh, I'm sorry if I'm holding you from your appointment," Ms. Betty said, while getting up from the couch. She looked at her wristwatch. Then added: "Well, I believe I have everything I need to know."

"That's good to know." I walked her to the front door.

As soon as she stepped outside of the house and felt the heat slapping her across the face, she said, "It sure feels like the devil is having his way out here today."

I had heard similar metaphors before. And believe me, I hated every single one of them. So, on that note, I allowed my words to come out easy, but hard on this close-minded bitch!

"You shouldn't be blaming the devil for this terrible heat out here," I said it in a way to put her in check without realizing what the hell I was saying to her. "Because just remember that your Lord had made this devilish-day, so you should be happy in it."

Ms. Betty looked shocked.

Damn! I think I fuck'd up!

After my remark, her mood changed to something unpleasant. It seemed like she wanted to say something but she closed her mouth back. She cut her eyes from me and walked away from the door, mumbling something under her breath. She headed towards her car. A silver Ford Taurus. Then she suddenly stopped, halfway there, and twisted around and gave me an evil stare once more before she quickly turned toward her car again.

I pushed Destini back inside the house and shut the door.

Thank goodness that bitch was gone!

I watched Ms. Betty—through a small opening in the living room curtains—drive away and disappear. When she made that first right up the block, I felt relieved.

I turned to Destini with a little chuckle. "What's the matter with your voice?" I tried to mimic her with a joke. "You sound funny. Do you have a cold?"

She kept quiet, just standing there looking at me: clueless, of course.

I laughed. "What were you trying to do" —I playfully shoved her shoulder a bit— "get me caught?"

She smiled and immediately swung Abu at me.

"Oh, you wanna play, huh?" I snatched her up in the air, with my arms stretched high.

The phone rang and Carlton answered it. "Yeah, holla?" He paused for a brief second and said, "Hold on." He then tossed the phone on the couch. "It's for you!"

"Who is it?" I put Destini back down.

"I don't know," he said. "It's some hoe asking for you."

I smiled. I was certain it was Samara, since she promised to give me a call today. "Hello."

"DaShawn?"

"Yeah." I heard a female's voice but it wasn't Samara's. "This is he. How can I help you?"

There was a short pause. Then, the female's voice came back over the phone line: "A couple of friends of mine are planning to put a party together. And we were hoping to have a couple of strippers to come over and shake their—"

"How did you get my number?" I cut this bitch off! "This is a private line! You have to call me on my voice mail, then I'll get back to you on that. But you can't—" I paused when I heard a click. "Hello?"

Nothing.

So I hung up.

Ms. Betty pressed the END button on her cell phone.

"What a small world," she mumbled to herself as she coaxed the car engine to start; then drove away.

About a week later the heat was so intense outdoors that it could literally melt the drawers off a brotha's ass if he stayed outside too long.

Well, at least, that's how I felt while rubbing Armor-All on my car tires. Then, all of a sudden, I felt my car jolt a bit. I stopped; I stayed still.

Then my car jolted again.

I looked up and across, and saw Mikey sitting on the hood of the car, bobbing his head to DJ Suicide's free-style bootie mix.

"YO!" I yelled over to him. "Get your ass off my muthafucking car before you put a dent on it! And go rest your ass somewhere else. I just got finished washing the shit!"

"What are you trippin' about? It's only a friggin' car, bro."

"Yeah, and it's my muthafucking car," I mocked him. "Bro!"

But before he could respond back to that, Kevin popped the driver's door open, blasting my speaker to an old rap song from the late Uncle Al. Then shouted: "This that shit right here!" He got out of the car, mimicking alongside Uncle Al's rap lyrics.

"Hey, fellas!" Amanda, my neighbor from across the street, yelled out to us; then waved.

We waved back.

Mikey asked me, "Who's that?" while checking Amanda out.

"You might as well forget about her. She's married to an overprotective coward, who's guarding that pussy like it Fort Knox." I twisted back to him.

"How old is she?"

"I don't know. I would say she's about in her early or mid-forties. But she could be younger than that though. Why?"

Mikey didn't answer my question. He just kept his eyes on Amanda. And she caught him eyeing her; she fiddled hello. He smiled and blew a kiss at her. She smiled back.

"My nigga!" Kevin said, bringing Mikey back to our world. "What's up with you and all these older chicks?"

"What are you talking about?"

"I'm not trying to get in your personal life and shit, but I've noticed you don't be messing around with chicks our age. And I don't understand it either, because the broads you be going after could be old enough to be your mom and shit! What's the deal on that?"

"It's like what you said, you don't need to be in my personal life, because it's none of your business. And out of respect, let's keep my mom out of our conversation when we're talking about females. Can you at least do that for me?"

"You got that. I didn't mean to get you in your feelings and shit!"

"Stop the bullshit!"

"What the fuck you talking about?"

"You know exactly what I'm talking about. Why are you looking at me like that?"

Kevin refused to answer that. "I'm through with this, my nigga. You're overreacting off of nothing."

Mikey acted like he wanted to respond to that, but I cut him off: "Why don't you chill out! He didn't mean any harm asking you that."

Mikey ignored me; he kept his eyes on Kevin, as if he was trying to study his face. "And don't think I'm stupid either, because I know what the hell you're trying to insinuate here," he said, then cut his eyes to me. "Oh, hell nah! You, too?!" He shook his head. "Now, that's messed up! That's what my friends think about me behind my back?"

"Homey," I thought of a quick one, "don't drag me into y'all shit! I'm not thinking about anything other than what the hell is going on with you?"

"You must really think I'm stupid. But I'm gonna tell y'all" —he glanced at Kevin, then back to me— "before y'all start getting the wrong impression about me, as if I were some sick perv who was tampered with at a young age by my parents. Because if that's the case, that's not true."

I looked at Kevin and gave him that look, I-told-you-so.

He parried my gesture away.

"But," Mikey went on to add, drawing our attention back to him, "before I tell y'all anything: y'all have to assure me first that y'all won't tell anybody what I'm about to say to y'all."

Kevin and I nodded; we both moved in closer.

Then Mikey asked, "Do y'all remember when I told y'all that I used to fuck with a chick by the name of Monica, about two years ago?"

"Yeah." I nodded, hoping he would go on with it. "I remember her."

"Well, about a year ago, I heard that she caught the package. And I thought she probably—"

Kevin cut him off: "What kind of package?"

"The AIDS virus."

"Ohhh." Kevin took a step back.

"Well," Mikey went on anyway, "when I heard that Monica caught that shit, I almost went crazy. I didn't know if she gave it to me or not. So to be on the safe side, I went to the clinic for a checkup."

Kevin cut back in: "Damn my nigga, you went in for a checkup? Yo, y'all white muthafuckers are crazy, for real!"

"Crazy about what?" he asked. "I just wanna make sure that I didn't contract the virus from her. Because, if anything, if it weren't too late, I didn't want to pass it to my new girl."

Kevin looked dumbfounded.

"But let me finish telling y'all everything," Mikey said. "So after I found out that I was straight, the doctor told me that it was a good thing that I came in for the checkup; and then recommended that I should do periodically, like every six months on a regular visit. Not only for the virus but for everything else to be on the safe side. And that's when he told me a little more about the AIDS virus."

I don't know about Kevin, but I didn't see what this had to do with him being sexually attracted to older females, so I had asked him, "What did he say?"

"He sorta revealed how I can avoid contracting that AIDS shit when he mentioned that the AIDS virus was higher among the age group between fifteen and fifty. So when I asked him about my chances of catching the virus by having unprotected sex with females over fifty, he told me that my chances were less."

Kevin and I shrugged with confusion, hoping to get a better understanding.

"Soooo," Mikey dragged. Then said, "To be on the safe side, I'm not fucking anything under fifty, unprotected anymore. I'm trying to live."

It all made perfect sense now: My homey was just straight out crazy.

"So let me know this then?" Kevin asked him.

"What?"

"So you're into older broads now?"

"Yeah!"

"Damn my nigga, you're a sick-ass cracka! You needa seek some help. Or at least try to get some sorta counseling or something. Because I've seen you with a lotta older females who looked to be in their sixties and shit...."

Mikey didn't respond.

"Oh, hell nah!" Kevin seemed bothered, if not disgusted by Mikey's silence. "You're gonna rot in hell for that shit!"

"Well" —Mikey smiled— "it'll be well worth it then."

I sucked my teeth. "Yeah, right?"

"I swear to you."

Kevin cut back in: "Nigga, you're lying. I know it ain't all that good.... Is it?"

"If I'm lying, I'm dying. It's better than most of the females' pussies that I had fucked around here."

"Barbara's"

"Better!"

"What about that cute shawty Jessica?"

Mikey made a serious face. "Be real," he said to me. "I fucked an older chick the other day who was about seventy years old and whose pussy is about ten times better pussy than Jessica's."

Kevin laughed. "But what that shit feels like?"

"Like hot tight pudding. And it even taste like it sometimes."

I burst out laughing, because it reminded me of Debbie's pussy. That medical chick from the Family Services who used to blow my cell phone up until I changed the number on her. She was an animal.

A cougar with claws. Someone with plenty of life and energy. That was the main reason why I had to let that feral cat back out in the wild. She was a little too much for me to handle. So yes, I could somewhat relate to what Mikey was saying about older females. Because not only Debbie was a good fuck in bed, she had some good tasting pussy too, to be fifty-four years old. And for me, she was a bedroom superstar. We did about everything in the bedroom, from doggy-style to 69-position, with her on top; not to mention, even that one time with me hitting her from the backdoor.

"Get the fuck out of here!" Kevin made an ugly face at Mikey.

"They don't call me Mikey for the fun of it! Shiiiit, my tongue eats it all. It doesn't discriminate. It's a cannibal. You should have seen it on your girl last night."

Kevin punched him in the chest, jokingly. "You're a nasty-ass cracka," he said between a laugh. "I don't know how you can even do that shit!"

Mikey laughed with us. "Because it's easy."

"But how, though?"

Mikey wiped the sweat from his forehead. "Tell me this," he said, then paused for a quick second. Then added: "Which older chick you know or know about, that you would fuck right now if it comes down to it?"

I immediately thought about Madonna. I know I would love to get her in the bedroom to tear her ass apart!

"Shiiit," Kevin dragged before Mikey. Then said, "If I have to fuck an older broad, I would have to say, it has to be someone like Oprah Winfrey then. Because I know there are some benefits behind it."

"Okay then, that's how you'd do it. Just pretend."

"But how, though?"

"Look! The next time you come across an older chick and she acts like she wanna give you the pussy, just go ahead and accept it from her. Just pretend like if you were fucking Oprah." He smiled. "Just look what I had to go through before I got to enjoy this shit! I had to imagine as if I were busting up that broad Martha to get me into—"

"Who?" Kevin interrupted. "That lady who went to jail before?"

"Yeah, but never mind that," he said. "The next time you come across an older chick, just pretend like she's Oprah and bust her ass up."

Kevin laughed. "I'm gonna try it out one day to see what the hell you're talking about."

"There you go right there," Mikey said, while looking over my shoulder. Then finished telling Kevin, "Your day has just arrived."

We both twisted around and saw Mrs. Murphy, the older white lady who lived down the street, stepped outside of her house to check the mailbox.

"Oh, hell nah!" Kevin looked like he tasted some sour milk. "That hoe looks like she's about eighty years old!"

"That makes the odds even better for you then."

Mrs. Murphy saw us looking at her.

Mikey smiled. He was the first one to wave at her; she waved back.

"Dawg, you're sick." I was dead serious when I told Mikey that.

"Just watch my work." He walked away from us.

Kevin shouted behind him: "My nigga! You ain't allowed to come to our auntie's house anymore! I'm dead serious!"

Mikey brushed us off and headed over towards Mrs. Murphy's house.

Then I had to ask Kevin, "Where the hell are you going?" as he began to walk away from me.

"To see if I can get me some of that hoe's pussy over there while her man is at work." He twisted back around, heading across the street to Amanda's crib. "C'mon, let's see if we can run a train on her."

"Nah, I'm alright."

Then, within a matter of seconds, Amanda stepped out of her house with a white robe on. It hung open and loose just below her hips. She wore black panties, no top. She saw me looking at her, as Kevin made his way across the street. She smiled. I smiled back. Then she slouched over to pick up her newspaper at the door, giving us a little show. I enjoyed it. I saw her nipple.

"Yo, Kev, wait up for me!"

I felt like I was entering into my midlife crisis already.

And to make matters worse, today was Friday and I had no one to look after Destini for me while I was supposed to be at work tonight. I had already asked about everybody I knew, starting from Aunt Enid down to Uncle James, to babysit Destini for me but they all claimed to be busy, doing their own things. So I had no other choice but stay home and watch Destini's favorite movie with her again ... for the hundredth time!

While we were halfway through the movie, I made a call to Domino's Pizza and ordered a Meat Lover's. I was advised that our pizza would be delivered within half an hour. I was delighted to know that. He hung up. And just when I was about to lay the phone down, I decided to give Samara a call. And I'll be damned, she picked up on the third ring.

"Hello."

I hesitated at first, but then came out with it: "I'm surprised to have caught you home at this time of the night. I was just pushing my luck to give you a call."

"Who is this?" A second passed by. Maybe two. Then she added: "DaShawn?"

"Yeah."

"Oh, my God! I swear, I was just thinking about you, boo. You're definitely gonna live long."

"Well, I hope so. If anything, I can live my days out with someone like you."

She giggled.

It seemed like I had her where I wanted her. "What're you doing?"

"Why? What do you have in mind?"

Other than going straight to the point and asking her for some pussy, I said, "Nothing really," then paused. I took a short breather, not even for a second. Then: "I'm over here chillin' with Destini, watching a movie. And I was kinda bored." Okay, that one slipped out by mistake. I waited for her to say something since I used the bored word on her, but she kept quiet. So I continued: "You know, we ordered pizza, and I was just wondering if you weren't doing anything would you like to come over and join us?"

There was another pause.

I was just about to say something else when she said, "I would be happy to come over. But can I ask you something?"

"Sure."

"I'm not saying this to blow your head up and all. But guys in your occupation don't usually be staying inside the house on days like these. Unless y'all have other things on y'all mind." She then gave me a half laugh over the phone. "So, should I bring my—. But waita second! Why aren't you working anyway?"

"I can't." I wasn't ashamed to admit that.

"Why?"

"Because I couldn't find a babysitter for Destini."

"Well, I haven't made any plans for tonight. I can babysit her for you until you get back."

I had to think about that for a moment. "Nah, that's alright. I don't wanna burden you with my responsibilities."

"But you're not. I just said I wasn't doing anything."

"Are you sure?"

"Yeah, I'm sure. Where do you live at so I can come over there?"

Now, that was something I couldn't refuse. I gave her my address.

"Oh, I know exactly where that area is at. I'll be over in a few."

"You're a lifesaver. Thanks."

"You can thank me later. I'll see you in a bit." She hung up.

I felt somewhat relieved. But a part of me was worried about how Destini was going to react about somebody she didn't know babysitting her.

I had no other choice but take my chances.

I went back to the family room and didn't waste any time. "Sweetie, one of my friends is coming over here." I waited until I got her attention. "I know you're gonna like her. She's really cool."

Destini shrugged her thin shoulders. "I don't care," she said. "Whatchu telling me that for?"

"Because I need her to babysit you I'm at work."

Destini acted like she wanted to say something but her mouth never cracked open. She pouted instead and turned back to the TV, tucking her hands underneath her armpits.

About twenty minutes later, the doorbell rang.

Destini flinched at first, as if she wanted to get up and answer the door, but I stopped her. "Let me get it." I got up instead. "And besides, I don't want you to be answering the door at this time of the night anyway."

The doorbell rang again.

"Hold up!" I yelled, while gathering up a few dollars. "I'm coming!"

The doorbell rang again for the third time.

"You stupid muthafucker," I murmured, then snatched the door open. To my surprise, it was Samara standing there with a fetching smile on her face.

"Hey, boo." She tried to sound sweet. "I'm here."

I smiled back. "Oh, man, I thought you were the pizza boy. But I'm surprised, you got here really quick."

Her eyes then gave me that are-you-going-to-let-me-in-or-just-allow-me-to-stand-out-here look.

"Oh, excuse me. Please, come in."

She stepped inside the house and greeted me with a warm embrace; along with a light kiss on the cheek.

"Thanks for coming."

She sorta smiled. No comment.

As I was about to shut the door I noticed the pizza man was pulling up in front of the house. "Perfect timing."

"I'm starving." She wrapped her arm around mine. "I think I can eat a whole horse right now."

I laughed because my seven inch dick came to mind. I wouldn't mind cramming it down her throat. It's fat and meaty. She laughed back. I then paid for the Meat Lover's and walked her straight to the family room.

I called out to Destini the moment I set foot in the room and said, "The pizza's here!"

Destini twisted around and when she saw Samara standing beside me, her face grew cold.

"Sweetie, this is my friend, Samara.... The one I was telling you about earlier," I said in a soft tone, hoping that could lighten her up some.

"Oh, my God, DaShawn!" Samara started walking toward Destini. "She's beautiful.... She definitely has your beautiful features and looks."

I looked at Samara because she was ego-stroking Destini's confidence in order to gain her trust.

Smart move.

Samara extended her hand out to Destini. "My name is Samara and it's a great honor to meet you: I have heard so much about you."

Destini didn't say anything. She just stared at Samara, not wanting to shake her hand.

"Oh, my...." Samara then cut to the television set. "That's Scarface. This is one of my favorite movies." She accidentally bumped Destini when she sat beside her. "I can't believe this."

When I saw Destini's facial expression changed for the worse, I quickly said, "That's Destini's favorite movie too. It seems like y'all both have something in common."

Destini glanced at Samara, then back at me, then shook her head to disagree.

Samara nudged Destini on the arm. "Is that true, cutie? Do we have something in common?"

Destini flinched, as if she held back a flash of pain, just before she said, "I don't think so," then furiously elbowed Samara back.

"What's the hell the matter with—"

"You know," I cut Samara off before she went off on Destini, "we better eat this pizza before it gets cold. Because I know I can eat this whole thing by myself. It's Domino's!"

"Uh-uh!" Destini leaped from the couch and rushed to the pizza. "I don't know about you, but I want my half."

Samara got up from the couch and came over to where we were. She grabbed herself a slice of pizza. Destini gave her a death stare, making sure Samara didn't touch her side of the pie.

As we were eating, Samara tried to tuck the remainder of the pizza crust in her mouth.

Destini laughed at her.

Samara looked puzzled, with a specious smile, she asked Destini, "What's funny?"

Destini pointed at the tomato sauce on Samara's cheek, then giggled some more.

"Oops." Samara wiped the sauce off her face. "My bad."

We all laughed.

When we were nearly finished with the pizza, Samara and I started up a casual conversation about various clothes. Versace, Giorgio Armani, Louis Vuitton, and so on. Who's hot; who's not.

I guess Destini felt left out because she intervened between us, saying, "My mom used to dress nice. She used to wear a lot of expensive clothes, too."

"Oh, really?" Samara responded without a hint of concern. "That's nice to know." Then she twisted back to me.

I, on the other hand, was annoyed by the comment. I tried to ignore my past relationship with Destini's mother, for the most part. Because in a way I felt betrayed by Jessica when she just got up and left me without any explanation, then metaphorically threw a child at my front door. I didn't mean to express that contemptuous thought out openly, but I did.

"Well, where your mother's at right now, I doubt it if she can wear those expensive clothes you're talking about."

Destini gave me a heart-crushing look, not saying a word. Within seconds, her bottom lip began to tremble, then her eyes became watery.

Damn! I felt terrible when I saw the first teardrop. "I'm sorry, sweetie. I didn't mean that."

Destini got up from the table and ran straight to the bathroom. The door slammed.

I called out for her, but she ignored me. What a father I am, I thought. I needed to do something.

And just when I was about to go to the bathroom to go check on her, Samara stopped me. "Let her go. She has to let it out, one way or the other."

That made a lot of sense. I kinda agreed with her on that.

Then she added: "Just go to work. I'll take good care of her while you're gone."

I had second thoughts about that. I felt like staying home now. But Samara convinced me to do otherwise when she said, "She has to learn, boo. We were once her age. She just needs a little time to herself." She paused. Then added: "You just go to work, everything is going to be alright."

"Are you sure?"

She nodded.

"All right." I got up from the table. "Let me get ready." I walked to my bedroom to get dressed. And once I was finished there, I strolled back down the hallway, realizing Destini was still in the bathroom.

It felt like I was back to square one with her all over again.

"Destini." I knocked on the door, but she didn't respond. So I took the initiative to apologize to her again, hoping it might change the situation. But she never responded.

"Just go to work, boo," Samara suggested, sneaking up behind me. "I got her."

I looked at her, then at the bathroom door again. And after a short moment, I gave in. "Okay, sweetie," I spoke toward the door. "I'm going to head out to work now. Samara's gonna look after you while I'm gone. Okay?" I waited.

But still there was no response.

And just when I was about to walk away, Destini swung the door open and ran up to me, holding on to my pants leg. "You can't' leave me here with her! You have to take me with you."

I kneeled on one knee, smiling because she was talking to me again. "I can't take you with me: It's not a place for young girls your age. But Samara's gonna watch you until I get back."

Destini looked at Samara and gave her a contemptuous stare. "Look at her," she tried to whisper to me. "She looks like a serial killer."

"I promise you she's not a serial killer. You don't have to worry about that." I held her hands in mine, then drew them to my chest.

"I'm only leaving for a short while. That's all. I just have to go to work tonight, so I can pay some of these bills around here." I paused because she gave Samara that deadly stare again. "And you can bet your life on it…." I was hoping that she would look at me, but she didn't. I continued anyway: "I'll be right back before you notice it."

Then she finally faced me. "I don't have to talk to her, do I?"

"That's on you, sweetie. But do you have a good reason not to speak to her?"

"Uh-huh. I have a good reason."

I chuckled a bit. "You're such a character." I gave her a kiss on the cheek; then, I headed towards the front door with Samara.

Destini lingered behind us.

"Eeuw!"

I looked at Destini. I guess she disapproved of the hug I was giving to Samara. I smiled and reached down to give her a hug, too. "Be good while I'm not here. Okay?"

"Only because you said so."

When I stood back up, I turned to Samara. "She's not a bad kid," I whispered. "Once she breaks the ice with you, she's adorable."

She looked at Destini; Destini back at her. And before Samara could make a comment, Destini raised two fingers to her mouth, acting as if she was zipping her lips shut.

Samara looked back at me. "I guess she won't be speaking to me tonight."

"Don't pay that any mind. She will eventually open up to you once she gets used to you. I went three days like that with her."

"I see it's gonna be a long night."

"It'll be all right."

"I just hope so."

It was nearly eleven o'clock when I left the house; Destini and Samara stood at the doorway and watched me drive away.

"Destini!" Samara shouted in the hallway. "Where are you?!" She strode down to the bedroom and saw Destini on the phone.

"Oh, really?" Destini said into the receiver, while lying on the bed. "I wanna go there, too." She paused. Then added: "Did you have fun?"

"Destini!" Samara still had her hand on the doorknob, looking ticked off with her. "I have been calling for you, for the last ten minutes! Why are you ignoring me?"

"Hold on a second," Destini said into the receiver, then turned her attention to Samara. "Did you say something?"

Samara wouldn't dare open her mouth. She kept it shut. She was too afraid of what might lash out on Destini. But her face showed it all. It looked like she just stepped into some wet dog shit with her favorite shoes on.

And since Samara didn't respond to Destini's question, Destini continued to speak into the receiver again. "Oh, no," she said. "It's this old lady my daddy met on the street last week and asked her to watch our house for us until he gets back."

With those words in mind, Samara felt a surge of frustration building up in her. She stomped away from the doorway before she did or said something stupid to Destini.

"So," Destini proceeded over the phone with a high pitch, knowing Samara could hear her down the hall. "I'm gonna see you tomorrow?! Just ME, my DADDY, and YOU! RIGHT?!"

Samara was bothered by the fact that Destini might be bad-mouthing her to someone over the phone. It was boiling her, inside out. She felt like marching back in the bedroom and confronting

Destini about her manners, but she stopped herself when she glanced over to the telephone beside her.

A thought came to mind....

She hesitated at first, but then went for it: she gently picked up the phone in hope to eavesdrop on Destini's conversation. But to her surprise, once she listened in on Destini, all she heard was a busy dial tone.

"Uh-huh!" Destini said, speaking to no one in general but herself. "My daddy thinks about you all the time...."

Samara gave a sigh of relief before putting the phone back into the cradle.

It was usually packed at Club Space with many party goers—even more so like any other nightclub on South Beach—but tonight it was swarming with females, everywhere you look.

A huge audience stood in front of the dance platform, screaming and literally trying to grab hold of me when I stepped on the stage, dancing under the soft rhythm of "12-Plays" by R. Kelly.

Shit was getting hectic in here.

This one cute blonde-headed chick, who looked a little like Taylor Swift, grabbed my hand and led it between her legs. It felt soft down there. And I loved every bit of her. I reached in and kissed her. She grabbed me.

I broke loose, raising my index finger in front of her. "Hold up, ma."

She opened her mouth. I rested my finger inside there. She sucked it.

I smiled, watching her work her jaw muscles. What a tight grip. I reached in and kissed her again, then stepped back. I wore my tan leather cowboy outfit, chaps and vest, with my black colored G-string on.

The music stopped and so did I. Then suddenly—just as I had planned it—the club deejay spun one of Trick Daddy's records, and I hopped my yellow ass all over the stage area, on my tippy-toes, as if I were prancing on a wild rodeo horse.

"You go, boy!" I heard someone shout. "Now, come over here and saddle me up!"

I kept my pearly whites showing; I wound my left hand in the air, as if I were about to throw a lasso, and with my other hand I immediately snatched my chaps off. The crowd started screaming louder now. Believe me, I'm not conceited but I do consider myself an excellent performer. One of the top male strippers in South Florida—so I have heard. The Chippendales don't have shit on me! Unlike them, I could entertain about any type of crowd. What can I say? I was blessed with a magnificent gift below, and I'm not a homo.

I made the crowd excited; they loved me. Even when my dancing segment ended they seemed like they wanted more from me. But Mikey was up next. After a while, the crowd forgot about me because Mikey's performance turned out to be great, too. He snatched his G-sting off, giving then something to kill that bosh stereotype about his race. Every bit of his eight-inch manhood.

Inside the dressing room I started to get dressed when Kevin walked in.

"Damn, my nigga," he said. "You're leaving already?"

"Yeah, I have Samara over by the house watching Destini for me. And I don't wanna hold her up, if anything." I gave him daps and bounced out of there.

It took me less than a half an hour to reach my crib.

Once I stepped inside the house, I looked into the family room for Destini and Samara, but they weren't there. I strolled down to my bedroom, expecting to see both of them in there, but I only found Samara sleeping in my bed, with my black T-shirt on. I quietly shut the door back, wondering about Destini's whereabouts. I cut to the left and went farther down the hall, looking in room after room until I finally came across the end room that I was planning on fixing up for her.

She was sound asleep. I stepped in the room and covered her with a blanket which was nearby. I headed back to my room to take a shower.

About fifteen minutes later I stepped out of the bathroom with just a towel wrapped around my waist, tiptoeing to the dresser to snatch out one of my boxer shorts. As I was shutting the dresser drawer back, Samara woke up.

"Hey, baby," her voice sounded hoarse. "When did you get back?"

"A few minutes ago."

There was a long pause.

Then Samara whispered in a soft tone, "Come here for a second," while using her elbow to raise herself up.

I proceeded to walk to her when she kicked her legs off the bed, licking her lips. I kept my eyes on them. They were gleaming from the bathroom light. I couldn't believe it: she slowly inclined her head as I got closer to her. She sat at the edge of the bed for a better position.

I kinda felt intimidated; I froze.

Samara reached for my towel and slowly pulled it away from my waist, dropping it at my feet. My dick hung freely. She looked up at me. I didn't blink. I couldn't. She wore a seductive look in her eyes, while gnawing on her bottom lip.

I swallowed my spit to breathe a little better. I looked into her hypnotic eyes, attempting to read her very thought: Come a little closer, they seemed to be saying to me. I plodded my left foot forward, then my right. I couldn't control my rising nature. It grew strong in front of her. It stood straight up. Then she grabbed my dick and wrapped her lips at the head of it, caressing her tongue along the shaft. It felt weird, but in a good way. I stretched my neck to the side to get a look at her because she started guiding her tongue all over it.

I closed my eyes and swallowed hard this time. She started sucking on my dick, while changing her position on the bed. Her mouth felt good. I combed my fingers through her hair. As she leaned forward, rocking her head back and forth, giving me the most pleasurable time of my life, I slowly started pumping my dick in and out of her mouth.

I tilted my head upward to feel the ecstatic pleasure. "Ohhh, yeaaaahh," I groaned while feeding her my meaty Polish sausage. "That's it…. Don't stop…."

I guess she looked up and tried to make eye contact because I felt her head incline, but then she went back into regular position, bobbing her head up and down under my dick. This shit feels too good to be true, I mulled. Then she did the unbelievable: she released her hand from around my manhood, hooked her index finger at the bottom of it, opened her mouth wider, and nearly shoved the whole thing down her throat.

God dammit, man!

I had to catch my balance.

She started pumping her head—back and forth—making that slurping sound. It made the scene feel ... tabooish. I'm like, fuck it! There's no other word that could describe it better. She picked up her speed and started sucking my dick faster and faster, sorta gyrating her head in a circular motion.

I wasn't used to this type of shit!

Of course, I moaned out, "Ohhh, fuck!" I tried to control myself, but I couldn't. She was too good. My face and mouth contorted on its own, taking on a different form—similar to those frightening characters in that scary movie 'Scream'—that I wouldn't know how to describe. "Shit!" I rested my other hands on the other side of her head and warned: "I'm about to cum! I'm about to cum...."

She ignored my warning, even after I shot a monster load in her mouth. And sure enough, she kept sucking on my candy stick for a little while longer; only letting go of it when her jaw muscles began to ache.

Well, my dick was known to be related to a Jaw Breaker candy: The red one.

I crouched in and gave her a kiss. She kissed me back, then eased over to the center of the bed and pulled her T-shirt off. She was naked. No bra, no panties. I saw her baldness down there. Just how I liked it. Now, I didn't have to worry about any of her pubic hairs getting caught in the back of my throat. She opened her legs wide, then ran two of her fingers along the side of her pussy lips, rubbing against them. My mouth watered. I licked my lips to get them wet. I admired her breasts. I smiled. Her nipples stood tall like the former Twin Towers.

They were beautiful.

I layed on the bed and placed my head straight between her legs. I took a really good look at her pussy before I parted her labia lips with my fingers. I felt her pelvic area pumped upward and then resilience back. I reached in and gave her a kiss on the opening. She slowly gyrated her hips and rested her hands on the back of my head. I gave her pussy another kiss, then locked my arms around her thighs. I parted her pussy lips again, pulling them farther apart from one another; then gave it a lap along the center of her pink hole. Then I lapped it once more. She shot out a loud grunt and I went to work.

I flicked my tongue against her clitoris bud for about five minutes straight, periodically, grinding my mouth in her pussy with a little pressure. I felt her legs tightened up on me again. I kept flicking my tongue. It seemed like she was trying to hold back from cumming, so I went to plan B: I released one of my hands from around her thigh and stuck two fingers inside her while my tongue kept punching against her clitoris bud, as if it was a boxer's speed bag. I had a nice coordination, nonstop. Punch after punch. She started rocking her pussy back and forth in my mouth again, but it was too late for that.

I found her G-spot.

I shook the tip of my finger over it for a few seconds, then started playing on it. I began to follow a swirl pattern, in small circles, over and over again.

"Ah, fuck!" She grabbed both of my ears, applying pressure against her pussy.

I almost laughed when she started fucking my mouth. I kept flicking and sticking my tongue in her.

She shot out a loud moan: "Here it come! Here it come!" She panted heavily, not wanting to stop, rocking her pelvis faster and faster. "Eat this pussy! Eat it, muthafucker! Eat it!"

I kept going. Then I felt her legs lock up and got stiff on me—only for a hot second—before she squirted in my mouth and allowed her body to go into a convulsion. I slowly broke my tongue down to something more of an easy pace for her to handle, while I slurped on her juice. And only when her twitching stopped did I climb on top of her in a kitty-position and went straight for her oil-well. Well, at least, that's what her nana felt like to me.

It was soft, slippery, wet. I couldn't ask for anything better than this. She tensed up when I slid my dick halfway in her. But, from the look of things, it appeared like she was willing to take the other half of it. The whole shebang. My seven inch Goliath. It was swelled up as if it did about a thousand push-ups. It was nice and thick, with veins pumped in certain areas, as if it was rocking sex-pearls under the surface. So I slowly ground my dick inside her. Her pussy felt warm; she blanketed me.

I threw her legs up and over my arms. I was able to stick my whole thing inside of her.

"Ohhh yessss!" she cried in a whisper. "I want you to fuck me, baby. I want you to fuck me good and hard. Don't stop. Fuck this pussy. It's yours." Her teeth clamped down on her lower lip, then released it. "Harder... a little harder, baby. Harder... That's it. Harder!"

I started pounding on that pussy for the love of god before I changed our position. I flipped her over on all fours in a doggy-style, hitting her from the back. And it felt even better now.

I shoulda videotaped this shit!

Her ass-cheeks were spread beautifully. No lie. It looked like a Valentine's heart—upside down. I thought of Nicki Minaj with all this ass in front of me. I couldn't hold back the temptation any longer. At first I wanted to suck her asshole out from the back just like that, but I stuck my thumb over her bootie-hole instead and rubbed against it. And she pushed back and half of my thumb slipped inside her. On the following pump, the whole thing. It felt slushy in her, yet in a good way. I left my thumb there as I worked my rod in her pink paradise.

"Oh, yes!" she shouted, throwing her ass back and forth on me, probably because I had both of her holes on blast. "Don't stop! Don't stop!" She threw it on me a little harder this time when she felt me beating on her back wall. "I'm about to cum! I'm about to cum again! Don't stop! Oh, yes! Don't stop!"

When I pulled my thumb out of her ass, her sphincter got the last kiss. I wanted to kiss it back, but I grabbed her waist instead, fucking her with all I had. For three minutes straight, she moaned and screamed as if that were the first time that somebody finally fucked the shit out of her. But I knew better than that: She's from Miami.

"Oh, don't stop! Don't stop!" She took a short pause before she started pumping her ass back towards me with a little more force. "I'm about to cum! Oh, shit! I'm about to cummmmm." She gave out another loud moan. Then yelled: "I'm cummmmmmiinnngg...." Her pussy muscled gripped around my hard-on when her body went stiff. Then a few seconds later her body gave way, dropping her face flat on the bed—with her ass still in the air—looking satisfied.

I felt her vagina muscles twitched with a few powerful spasms, as sweat poured down from us. She began gyrating her hips in little circular motion. "I haven't felt like this in a long time."

I smiled. I knew I had put my work in on her. But I wasn't quite finished yet. I kept stroking in her, slowly, hoping that I could coax her up a bit. Or at least have her to participate a little more. But then she dropped flat on the bed and rolled over on me, giving me the universal sign that she wanted to stop.

Damn!

While lying on her back, in a kitty-position, she started caressing my chest. Sweat still dripped from us. She lowered her head, breaking eye contact with me. "You were wonderful.

I whispered back: "So were you."

It was at that precise moment when she saw me stroking my manhood. It was still hard and I wanted to get another nut off. She sat up, leaning her back against the headboard. I saw her entire nakedness, watching me, watching her.

She looked sexy like that. I wanted to ask her for a second session but I didn't want to seem too desperate. So I left it alone. I just laid there, admiring her beautiful titties, slowly yanking on myself.

And after a hot second of that, it seemed like she had read my mind because she placed her hand back on my dick and said, "I don't usually do this." Then immediately, she ducked her head down and started sucking on my dick again.

She was sensational great. The way she was working her mouth over and around my dick made me think of heaven. I was on Cloud Nine. I swear, I wanted to say something—Yes, I believe, I believe— but I didn't want to interrupt her performance. She bounced her mouth up and down over me as if her head was jumping on a trampoline. A cartwheel here, a back flip there, front flip, front flip, and then a high ballerina split. And she had the nerve to say that she doesn't usually do this, I mockingly recalled.

Yeah, right!

She was sucking my dick like a professional.

But I knew two things for certain and one thing for sure: Lil' Kim doesn't have anything on this hoe.

Samara was a freak; a stone, cold freak. And she was mine. She was someone I could definitely work with.

Ho-hold up!

My mind changed to a caution alert.

Waita second!

Stop!

What's that?

I threw my hand on the back of her head, trying to prevent her from making that slurping sound because I thought I had heard something outside my bedroom door.

Oops!

Samara nearly choked.

The following week was just like the last one: I needed Samara's help to babysit Destini for me again, which she didn't mind. And as a small token of my appreciation, I blessed her lovely—for nearly three hours straight—when I came back from work.

And you best to believe it I would have put in four hours on her last night, but she couldn't take it: I popped a Viagra pill.

While Samara was in the kitchen preparing us brunch—scrambled eggs and turkey sausages—I checked her out from the table.

"Would you like to have some butter biscuits, too?" she asked, standing by the stove, shuffling the sausages in the pan.

"Nah, that's alright." I kept my eyes on her backside. "But if anything, the only biscuits I want are those same ones that I had last night before you took them away from me."

"Damn, right!" she giggled, then turned back to the frying pan. "If I didn't stop you in time, you probably woulda damaged something."

"I will be careful next time."

"I don't think so."

I got up from the table and snuck behind her, wrapping my arms around her waist. "Do you forgive me?" I kissed her on the neck.

"Nope!" She stuck her ass out a bit, forcing me to move back.

"You should have done that for me last night, and stop faking." I joked back, swiping two fingers between her ass cheeks.

"Because you know—"

"Boy!" She jokingly swung her hand at me and laughed. "Suppose somebody walked in on us and saw you pulling my shirt up?"

I laughed. " So allow me to take you to a place where they won't be able to see anything." I headed back towards the table. "In the

Garden of Eden, where I'm able to nibble on that forbidden fruit back there again."

"Boy, you have issues," she tittered, then tried to get serious when she went back to cooking. "You might as well call Destini for breakfast because it's almost finished."

I changed route and went to the kitchen doorway instead. Then shouted: "DESTINI! COME EAT YOUR BREAKFAST!" I went to the table again.

Within seconds, Uncle James stopped by the kitchen doorway. "Did you call for me?"

"You know damn-well nobody call you in here."

He ignored me, cutting his eyes to Samara. "Whew-weee! That sure smell good. Do you think you have enough for this old buzzard here?"

"Sure." She tossed the sausages into a large serving bowl. "I have enough for you. Actually, I made enough for everybody in the house."

"Oh, bless your heart, young lady." Uncle James went over to the dish rack to grab himself a plate. "My nephew should have met you a long time ago."

And just when I was about to shout Destini's name again, she barged into the kitchen. She cut her eyes from Samara, then looked at me. "I don't want any eggs for breakfast: I want some cereal."

"Do you want me to make it for you?"

"No, I can do it myself." She walked over to the cabinet and grabbed a large cooking pot, then poured some Coco Puff's in the pot and drowned it with milk.

As she was about to walk out of the kitchen with her cereal, I told her, "Nah, come over here and sit at the table with me."

She acted like she didn't want to, but she did anyway.

Samara went to the coffee maker and asked me, "How would you like your coffee?

Just when I was about to tell her, somebody started tapping on the kitchen's window.

We all looked.

"Who is it?" Uncle James went over there to check it out, since he was the closest one to the door. He waited for a response but there wasn't one. He snatched the door open.

"Eh!" It was Ricky; he was acting paranoid, looking over his shoulders. "What's going on in here?"

"It's none of your damn business!" Uncle James said. "Now, what the hell you want, crack-head?"

"Damn, old man" —Ricky stepped inside the house, uninvited— "why are you always tripping with me for?" Then, he looked at me and added: "Eh, there were some people sitting in their car, a few houses up the street, watching your crib, and—" he froze, setting his eyes on Samara. "Mm-mmm! Those sausages sure look good."

"Yo!" I cut in: "You said some people were watching my crib?"

"Yeah, up the street."

"When?"

"I don't remember, probably about two hours ago."

"Two hours ago?"

"Yeah, it was something like that."

"So, why are you telling me this now?" I got up from the table.

"Because I forgot. But they ain't there anymore." He cut his eyes back to Samara with a smile. "And who might you be, Miss Lady?"

But before she could answer him, Uncle James cut in: "Boy! So what the hell they wanted?"

"I don't remember." Ricky did that thing with his shoulders, then looked back at Samara. "Are you from around here?"

She didn't respond, but she did give him one of those bent-looking faces that only meant, I-know-you-didn't-try-me-like-that.

"But," I broke Ricky's concentration when my words slipped out a little hard, "why the hell would somebody be watching my house?"

He turned to me. "How I'm supposed to know that? They only said something like, they heard there were some guys who lived over here, who can show them a good time. That's all. And they musta been talking about you and Carlton, because I know they couldn't have been talking about James here. He sure can't show anybody a good time but show them a good bottle of rum to drink from." Then he tried to laugh to his own joke.

"You dirty, crack-head!" Uncle James snapped on him. "You can go to hell!"

"I'll meet you there, if you don't beat me there, wino."

I cut back in and asked Ricky, "So how do you know what they wanted?"

"Who?"

"Those folks you said who were watching my crib?"

"Oh, that's right. How do I know?"

"Yeah?"

"Because they asked me."

Is he fucking stupid? "There were people asking you about some people who lived up in here and you didn't come over here to let us know about it?"

"What do you think I'm over here now for?"

"But you're two hours late." I just couldn't understood that. "So what did you tell them?"

"What I told them?"

"Yeah."

"Uhhh, since I knew they weren't your type, I told them that you were usually booked with a lotta girls, doing shows at strip clubs and other places; in which...," his voice faded.

"In which, what?"

"In which I could show them a good time too, since we're like family."

Samara and Uncle James burst out laughing. Destini joined in too, although I knew she was clueless as to why there were laughing at him.

After all was said, Uncle James kicked Ricky out of the house so we could enjoy our brunch.

A moment later, Destini ran from the table to the family room. And since I was about finished too, I walked Samara back to my bedroom so she could retrieve her belongings.

"So, hey," she began to ask me, "you wanna go out to a movie or something else before you go to work tonight?"

"Sure, I wouldn't mind." I watched her put her bra on, then something crossed my mind. "Nah. Not tonight because I have to go to this meeting later on before I head out to work.... However, we can still do something afterwards."

"Like what?"

"If nothing else" —I thought about a late night booty call— "we can hang out here after I get off from work tonight."

I guess she knew exactly what I had in mind because she slapped an inviting smile on her face.

Then, it hit me.

Shit!

I just remembered about something else. I wrapped my arms around her. "Sweetie, I need a favor from you again."

"Like what?"

I came straight out with it: "Carlton wanted to borrow my car later on tonight to go do something. So I was gonna have him to take me to my meeting, then drop me off at work afterward." I paused for a short moment, waiting for her facial expression to ease up a bit. I guess, she knew where I was going with this. "So can you watch Destini for me until Carlton comes back to the house?" It seemed like she had to think about it, so I added before she made up a lame excuse as to why she couldn't babysit for me: "It's only for about, at the most, three hours."

One of her eyebrows went higher than the other one. "Are you sure it's only gonna be for three hours?"

"I swear, it's no more than that." I gave her a kiss, hoping that would seal the deal.

The room grew quiet for a moment until she broke the silence. "Yeah, I can do that for you. But can you make sure Carlton won't forget about these three hours?"

"I promise you he won't forget." I assured her with another kiss. "Thanks."

After I stopped fawning over her, she slowly shook her head. "You shouldn't have to be taking so much of this parental mess by yourself."

"But what can I do?"

"There is a lotta things you can do," she quickly pointed out. "You can put Destini in some type of summer camp or something. She needa be around kids her own age. I know there're plenty of camps around here that she can go to. So—"

"I don't wanna go to a camp!"

We looked toward the doorway. It was Destini. And I don't know about Samara, but I knew I had a guilty look painted in my eyes.

"I hate you!" Destini said to me before running away from us.

Samara grabbed my arm, trying to prevent me from running after Destini. "Let her go," she said. "Don't baby her. That's all she wants you to do. She has to learn, boo."

Learn about what, I thought.

Yeah, I can be open-minded at times, but I had no interest in her thoughtless theory. Because, for one, Destini was a little too young to be going through so much. She's a human being, not some fucking rag doll! And to top that off, she grew up without a father—and who's to say that I'm not the pathetic sperm donor, honestly?—and not to mention that she lost her mother to a tragic illness. So apparently, Samara must have overlooked this critical info before saying some shit like that! So really, how much does Destini have to go through to learn something?

Perhaps, a helluva lot to Samara then!

I appreciated her off-the-wall suggestion, but I totally thought it was a bunch of bullshit!

"Let me go!" I shook my arm loose. "I can't do that. I have to go to her."

Samara's face looked troubled. "Okay then. I'll see you later on when I stop by."

I gave her a kiss, and she left.

When I walked into Destini's bedroom, I found her curled up in a fetal position, crying. And that shit crushed me! No lie.

I sat at the edge of the bed and gently rested my hands on her. "It's not what you thought you've heard, sweetie," I said in a soft tone, hoping that she might stop crying. "We were only talking about whether or not you should go to—"

"Don't call me Sweetie!" She brushed my hand off her, then covered her face with a pillow. "I know you don't want me here with you. I'm not stupid!" She cried some more. This time, heavily.

Damn! My heart collapsed somewhere within my chest. I opened my mouth, closed it, I rather wait.

Okay, I could admit it: she was kind of right. But not a hundred percent right as she believed. Of course I didn't mind her staying at the house with me. At least until the paternity test proved otherwise that I wasn't her biological father. But the flip side of this same coin is that she came into my life at the wrong time. And I really mean at the wrong time. I was living wild and free, running through every good opportunity that came my way.

What...? That's understandable.

I'm a man, so I thought. But not in this case.

I slowly shook my head, putting my thoughts in order. I pulled the pillow away from her face. Now, if you thought my heart had sunk before, it sank even further this time.

"C'mon, sweetie," I whispered while combing my fingers through her hair. "Now, you know that's not even true. So, don't even allow that negative vibes to make you believe that." I paused for a few seconds to see what else I could honestly say to cheer her up. Then, suddenly, something creative clicked in my mind and I went for it: "Now, if that was true, who am I gonna have around here to run Uncle James crazy?"

She seemed to be somewhat soothed by my remark. At least she stopped crying, then looked at me.

Then I added to clarify myself, "No one could run him crazier than you, silly."

She got it now, because I saw a hidden smile fighting to stay down.

We both fell into a silent storm of our own private thoughts. As for myself, I was actually thinking about how the both of us met up on this same path in our lives. Perhaps it was for a good reason. I guess that's why Jessica named her Destini. But ... who knows? There must be a good reason behind it, I thought. Everything in life ~~does~~ happens for a reason.

Destini slightly shook her head in disbelief with a tiny smile on her face. "What I'm gonna do with you?" she asked with a little bit of humor in her tone.

"Just work with me on this, I'm new at it."

"You're a bubble-head," she said in a joking manner as she began wiping the tears from her eyes. Then she had the audacity to lie: "I hate you."

"Of course you do," I mocked her back, while helping wipe her tears away. "That's why you have that big-ass smile on your face now?"

She ducked her head under the pillow and giggled.

For the following thirty-five minutes straight, I listened to the whole ordeal of her life story and the loss of her mom. She poured her heart out to me, crying in between. In a way, I could somewhat relate to her situation. I'd also lost my mother at a young age, too, and never got to know who my father was. I'm afraid to admit it, but my mother was much like Jessica from what I had gathered up so far. She played both roles as a single parent. So yeah, like I said before, I could somewhat relate to Destini's situation. I understood what she was going through. Shit, even at the age of 31, I still dream of my mother occasionally. Basically, the same way how I used to remember her when I was a young boy, being catered by her love and support, and that inspiring hope that gave me the strength to move forward.

Oddly enough, it was at that same moment that I realized how much I missed my mother's guidance and—

"Are you okay?" Destini asked, interrupting my thoughts and bringing me back to where we were.

"Yeah." I shook my reverie away. "I was just thinking about something."

"Do you ever think about my mommy?"

"Your mom?" I wished she never asked me that.

She barely nodded, watching my eyes.

I hesitated at first, but I kept it real with her. "Yeah," my voice broke weak in front of her. "I still think of her…. That's probably the reason I still dream about her, too. She was everything I once believed in…. My life."

"For real?" her voice dropped low, as if Jessica had lied to her all this time.

I nodded. I had nothing to hide from her.

And it seemed like she wasn't ready for the truth because her smile disappeared and her eyes became watery.

"You know what?"

She looked at me. "What?"

"I'm in the mood for some ice cream. What about you?"

Her eyes widened. "Dairy Queen!" she managed to smile again, wiping a teardrop from her face. "I'm in the mood for Dairy Queen ice cream." She then licked her lips.

Yeah, she made me smile: She forced me to. And if you were in my predicament, you would have done the same thing, too.

I slowly nodded my head and kinda whispered at a level that I knew she could hear: "Yeah, me too."

The phone rang.

"**You sure love** some chocolate," I joked with Destini while we sat inside of Dairy Queen's ice cream parlor on 67th Avenue. "Don't you?"

"Uh-huh!" she mumbled while munching down on her ice cream. "I love chocolate. It's my favorite."

"So I have noticed." I kept a smile on my face, admiring her appetite for the multiple chocolate confections—like, chocolate sprinkles, chocolate fudge, and several pieces of chocolate Hershey's Kisses—and get this, over chocolate ice cream. "And there's no doubt about that either."

Destini acted like she wanted to laugh but she didn't. She shot me a smirk instead; and even that changed into a smile when she took another spoonful of ice cream into her mouth.

I smiled back, then suddenly became sidetracked when I heard an unusual squeaky laugh that grabbed my attention. I looked over by the front entrance of the parlor and noticed a small group of people—four of them in total—who had just walked in, heading toward the customer's line.

"Damn," I accidentally whispered out by mistake. "You sure get around."

"Who, me?" Destini asked.

"Nah. Not you." I tilted my head toward the cashier counter. "I'm talking about that woman over there who we met in the mall the other day. The one who bought you—"

"Who?" Destini twisted around to see who I was talking about. Then said: "Naomi!"

"Yeah, I think it was something like that—" I was saying before Destini leaped from her seat, running over to the customer's line; I got up.

And about a few seconds later, if that, Destini was deep in conversation. I don't know what was actually asked, but I did hear Destini say, "My daddy," among some other stuff.

Then Naomi said, "Oh, there you are," when I approached them. "I'd thought perhaps, she'd run off from you again."

"Nah, not quite." I twisted to Destini and wiped some chocolate fudge off her cheek.

One of Naomi's friends, the one with the big-ass smile on her face, looked at me, then back at Naomi. Then asked us, "Do y'all know each other?"

Since Naomi hesitated, I jumped straight at it: "Yeah, you could say something like that. We've had our little run-ins."

Then Naomi cut in and tried to introduce me: "Eh, y'all, this is...."

"DaShawn." I helped her out.

"That's right," she said. "His name is DaShawn."

I ended up meeting and greeting Ciara, Davon, and Bruce with handshakes.

Then Naomi added, "This is the guy I was telling y'all about: The one who paid for my bill at IHOP and wanted me to go home with him for the night."

"That's not true." I felt cheap, especially in front of her friends. "It wasn't anything like that."

"I'm only joking. But you did eyeball me when you came out of IHOP, as if you were expecting something in return."

"Nah. Actually when I saw you out there alone, I was only wondering if you were going to be alright or not. So excuse me for having a little concern about a stranger."

Ciara raised one of her eyebrows and quickly thrummed a sound. Davon nudged her in the ribs.

I cut my eyes from them and noticed Destini and Naomi tittering. "What's so funny?"

Naomi throttled her laughter down to a smile.

I cut to Destini, for some sort of explanation.

But she kept giggling and had the nerve to say, "Nothing."

Yeah, right.

Naomi never took the smile off her face, then extended her hand to me. I cocked my head back a bit, then stood still. She was the one who was violating here. Not me. And that's when I felt her thumb running against my cheek.

Ohhh...

She wiped a small portion of syrup off my face and asked, "Why are you so jumpy?" then cleaned her thumb off on a napkin. "You need to relax."

I didn't respond to that because I was wondering why that dude, Bruce, didn't find that to be disrespectful.

And it seemed like Naomi had read my mind when she openly said, "Bruce is my friend. He's a transgender."

Damn, for real? "I didn't know that," I said. "I just thought he was your man."

Bruce playfully cut in. "What?" he dragged, sounding a bit feminine now. Then said: "I'm supposed to advertise it for you that I'm gay?"

"Nah. It's none of my business, fo' real." I was dead serious about that. "But I just thought she was your girl because you looked to be straight."

He then shot me with a piercing look as if I had said something wrong to him. "First of all," he began, leaning back a bit, "I'm straight!" He quickly paused, as if he wanted to snap his fingers two times. Then added: "Just because I'm gay doesn't mean I would bend over for you."

Okay, I tried to laugh it off as a joke. Because in all truth, I don't play that homosexual shit! So I decided to kill the conversation right there before I said something to offend this fucking faggot! "Well" —I quickly turned to Naomi— "it was nice meeting you again."

"Likewise." She returned with a handshake, then gravitated toward Destini and whispered something in her ear.

"Okay." Destini smiled. "I'll do that."

Of course my curiosity rose, wondering what the hell Naomi had said to her. But then again, I decided to leave it alone. It was a waste of time to even ask Destini about it, knowing she had lied to me already about the syrup on my cheek. "C'mon, you little liar." I criticized her when we walked out of the ice cream parlor. "Nothing, huh?"

She smiled.

"Hey." I turned the radio volume down a little and looked over at Destini in the passenger seat. "I'm gonna need a big favor from you." I put my eyes back on the road. "But I'm really gonna need your support on it though. Okay?"

"Okay." She nodded. "What is it?"

"I'm supposed to see somebody later on tonight before I go to work, and I had asked Samara to watch over you for a little while until—"

"But why can't someone else watch me?"

"Well" —I tried to be persuasive here— "Carlton is actually gonna watch over you tonight, but Samara has to watch over you first till Carlton gets back. It's only gonna be for a little while. That's all."

Destini sighed, looking uncomfortable. "But," she muttered, "I still don't have to talk to her, right?"

"Nah. You don't have to. But I can't see why you don't want to."

"Okay, you're pushing it now."

I laughed at her facial expression and continued to drive home without mentioning anything more on the topic.

"But," Destini began to say once I pulled up to the house, "can I ask you something?"

"Sure."

"What do you see in Samara?"

I cut to the house, then back to Destini again; then to the house again.

Carlton stepped outside.

Destini leaped from the couch, then sat back down, scrunching her face while playing UFC Undisputed against Carlton. And just when he was about to demonstrate a fatal move on her action fighter, the doorbell rang.

Destini sprung from the couch to answer it; and as she drew near to the door, she shouted, "Who is it?!" But when she heard a female's voice on the other side of the door, she walked away and went back into the family room.

"Who was it?" Carlton asked her.

"Uh, nobody," she stammered with a slight hesitation. "I think somebody was playing on—"

The doorbell rang once more, cutting in on her.

"There it goes again," he said, then got up from the couch. "Well, whoever it was, they musta come back."

Destini gave him that blistering look, while picking up the joystick. "It must be nobody important then."

Again: "Ding-Dong."

"Hold up!" Carlton shouted. "I'm coming!" And when he opened the door he found Samara standing there with her arms folded over her breasts, looking upset. She didn't even greet him. So, on that note, he gave her the fuck-you stare of disgust. "DaShawn just got outta the shower," he informed her. "He'll be with you in a second." He then headed back to the family room.

She stepped inside the house and walked down the hall.

"Yeah," —Carlton sat beside Destini— "you were right," he whispered while picking up the joystick, then looked over his shoulder to make sure the coast was clear, then back to the TV. "It was nobody, but a stank hoe...."

"What's that?"

"What's what?"

"A stink hole?"

Wow! Carlton felt like everything in his mind had shut down. But then he thought of a plan to cover his choice of words in front of her. "So, whatever I tell you, you can't tell anybody. Alright?"

She nodded.

"Alright then," he began to lie, "a stank hoe is when a girl thinks she knows it all, when in fact, she doesn't know a damn thing because she has a hole in her brain for being so stupid."

"Oh, for real?"

"Yeah," he nodded his head. "That's right. But just remember you can't tell anybody what you have learned today."

She barely nodded her head with a smile.

"And that especially goes for your daddy, too. Alright?"

"Okay."

I was thrown off guard—preoccupied on which casual dress shirt I wanted to wear—when someone snuck up behind me and blanketed my eyes with their hands.

"Guess who?"

"Uhhh.... Stacy Dash?" I got excited. "We have to hurry up before my girl gets here!"

Samara playfully shoved me from the back of my head and said, "You ain't anything good, but a damn dog!" She then tried to sit on the bed.

But I stopped her, pulling her close to me. "Girl, you know I was only playing." I gave her a kiss. "Thanks for coming."

"Don't mention it. But just make sure your cousin comes back in time, because Vida and I are supposed to do something later on tonight."

"He'll be back in time. I had already holla'd at him about that." I paused, contemplating on those two shirts in my hands. "So, which one do you think I should wear?"

"The beige one."

That was a good choice, but I went with the cream shirt instead. When I got dressed, we walked to the family room and found Carlton and Destini going at each other on a video game.

"Carlton, let's get outta here: I don't wanna be late for my meeting. It's nearly nine o'clock already."

"Alright."

When Carlton and I were about to drive away, Samara and Destini waved good-bye. I waved back. They watched us disappear when I made that first right up the block.

Samara looked at Destini, hoping to break the ice with her. But just before Samara could say anything to her, Destini sighed and walked away, heading back to the family room.

"You little heifer," Samara blew under her breath, "you can pout all you want to."

Well, let me keep it real: "I just hope everything works out for me at this meeting." I glanced over at Carlton, then to the road again. "Because I sure need to get a foot in the door, you know?"

"Don't sweat that shit, my nigga," he tried to encourage me. "I know you got this one, fo' sure. I can feel it."

"Well, I just hope so."

Destini did not hate all adults: she just disliked the ones who didn't respect her.

You see, Destini's mom was raising Destini with on all the love and support that she needed to have in life. But, as you know already, all of that came to a tragic end when Jessica passed away a few months ago. And just before then, Jessica was teaching Destini everything she needed to know about life, because she knew life could be unfair at times, especially for a young black child in America. And the first principle that Jessica taught Destini was the most critical one that Destini had to respect herself before she could respect anyone else.

Indeed, Jessica knew the odds would be stacked up against her daughter once she left the physical plane due to her declining health. That's why she taught Destini not to allow anyone to take advantage of her kindness, for weakness, under any circumstances. And Destini lived up to her mom's teachings. But unfortunately, after her mom's death, a piece of Destini died with her. But don't get it twisted, though: Jessica was nowhere near as an angel, as it appears. Not at all. Not even by a long shot. She had a dark side to her which some might call it bipolar, because she was known to get ghetto on a muthafucker—really quick. She had that Harriet Tubman, with a pinch of Angela Davis, fight in her. She would blast your ass if it came down to it. And because Jessica wasn't there to direct Destini through life, Destini absorbed certain practices from Jessica that she shouldn't have learned. She mirrored certain traits from her mom when standing up for herself. She didn't fight water with water: she fought water with an ocean; a wind with tornado; a fire with an inferno.

As Destini sat in front of the TV—playing a video game—Samara stood at the family room entranceway watching her until she felt the urge to ask Destini, "Why don't we do something together" — Samara then stepped inside the room with her— "until Carlton gets back?"

Destini looked at her, then after some consideration, she said, "Okay, we could do something together." She turned back around, concentrating more on her video game. "Why don't we both try to mind our own business until Carlton gets here?"

"I know this little heifa didn't," Samara murmured out by accident just before she stormed out of the room down the hall to the bedroom. She sat at the edge of the bed, then blanketed her body flat over it and tried to relax with her arms sprawled. "Why me?" she soliloquized, then glanced over to the night table and noticed a little black notebook beside the phone.

A crazy thought ran through her mind.

She grabbed the notebook and tried to flip through the pages before Destini walked in on her. She froze. "Monique?" She acted like she couldn't believe it. "This nigga knows this bitch too?"

She exhaled heavily, then started scanning the room for something more before she focused on the dresser in front of her.

Bingo!

She snatched the top dresser drawer open and couldn't hide her shock: "What's this muthafucker doing with these?"

Patience is only learned from perseverance when somebody has the tendency to wait like a fucking fool!

And I don't know about Carlton, but I felt like a moron when I found myself sitting in the lobby of the Hilton Hotel, waiting for nearly an hour, for some fashion design agent who goes by the name of Martin for our scheduled meeting.

"So how long this fuck-nigga gonna take to come down to see you?"

I tried to give Carlton a smile but I couldn't. "Let's give him another ten minutes" —I glanced at my wristwatch— "and if he doesn't come down by ten thirty, we could bounce then. Alright?"

The ridges of Carlton's forehead began to fade away.

Jesus Christ! Samara had found a stack of nude photos of females buried deep inside the dresser draw. Underneath a pile of socks and underwear.

She stopped combing through the photos when her cell phone started to ring; she answered it.

It was Stacy. "Girl, whatchu doing?"

"Nothing really. But I was just about to call you once I got finished here."

"Why, what happened?"

"You won't believe what I found underneath this nigga's mattress?"

"Whose mattress?"

"This nasty bastard! DaShawn!"

"Uh-uh. What did you find?"

"Some fucking nasty hoe's panties, underneath his mattress!"

"Oh, I know he didn't." Stacy tried to encourage Samara's rage.

"Oh, yes he did. But I got something for his ass once I see him. And he won't hear the last of it."

"I don't blame you. You gotta get his ass back! I know I would, if I were you."

"I am. Watch!" She paused. Then added: "I don't even wanna talk about this lame-ass nigga anymore. So what's up?"

"Nothing that I can't control myself. But I was just calling you because that fine brother from If Loving You Is Wrong is on right now."

"Oh, shit! I'd almost forgot about it!" Samara ran out of the bedroom to the family room and changed the TV station to OWN.

"Hey!" Destini nearly had a heart attack. "What you doing?! I wasn't even finished playing my game yet!" She then snatched the remote control out of Samara's hand and switched it back to channel three.

"It's only for a little while."

"I don't care if it was only for two seconds! I'm gonna finish playing my game first!"

"You're outta line!" Samara shut the TV off. Then said, "Go to your room! It's past your bedtime anyway."

Destini shot her with a look of disdain.

But Samara seemed like she was up for the challenge: She stared back. "You could look at me like that until your eyeballs pop outta your head, like I care! But I can tell you this though, you're still not playing your video game up in here tonight."

Destini snatched Abu from the couch and pouted, heading straight to her room.

Samara put the phone back to her ear. "That little girl has issues," she told Stacy; then turned the TV station back to OWN to finish watching her weekly reruns. "She just needa good ol' ass whooping to straighten her out." She paused. Then: "That brother looks fine as hell. It's a shame they don't make them like that around here anymore. And if they did, he gotta have some stinking-hoe's panties underneath his mattress."

Stacy laughed.

Samara cut back in with, "But on a serious note."

"What? What is it?"

There was a slight pause. Then she spit it out: "Did you ever take some nude pictures for DaShawn?"

Stacy hesitated. "No. Course not. Why?"

That ten minute deadline I had given Carlton, for Martin to show up, had finally arrived.

"C'mon" —I got up from my seat— "let's get the hell outta here."

"The hell with that fuck-nigga," Carlton said, and we headed toward the exit.

"Mr. Powell!"

I twisted around; so did Carlton.

The lady at the front desk was pointing her finger at me to let some guy know who I was. I guess he must be Martin then, I thought.

Carlton and I walked to the desk to meet up with this bama.

My assumption turned out to be correct when he introduced himself to us and went on to say, "Please excuse me for the delay. It's just that I hadda handle a little personal matter before I came downstairs." He smiled, then looked a short distance away at a cheap looking floozy who he probably met in some back alleyway up the street, then back to us. "Y'all understand, y'all dig?"

Hell, nah! I didn't understand that bullshit! He could have at least advised the receptionist at the front desk to info me that he was going to be late or something. But then again, I smiled right along with him anyway and lied: "Yeah, we understand. Pleasure always outweighs pressure."

Martin started bobbing his head. "Young blood, I like that one. I see that you're a playa-playa yourself, huh?" He smiled. "I gotta use that line one day. But in the meantime, let's grab a seat over there so you can show me what you got there."

Destini didn't care it was long past her bedtime, she strolled down to the kitchen anyway because she wanted to get something to drink. She could hear Samara chatting over the phone in the family room while watching TV.

Destini sighed, then pulled the fridge door open and her eyes lit up like 4th of July celebration.

She no longer wanted a glass of Hawaiian Punch, as planned: she made herself a large glass of chocolate milk instead. And just when she was about to walk out of the kitchen with her drink in her hand, she noticed that the kitchen door—the one that led straight into the garage—was ajar. She saw something interesting inside there.

A mischievous smile grew on her face.

Meanwhile back in the family room Samara was still watching her program. "About one o'clock?" she said into her cell phone to Stacy. "Yeah, I'll be there…. Shiiit, two of us can play at this game."

There was a pause.

Samara raised her eyebrows. "Oh, my God! Oh, my God!" She got excited, directing her attention back to her TV program. "There he goes again!" Another pause. Then: "Girl, I wanna start a fire so I can have that brother to come over here to put this flaming pussy out for me."

They both laughed.

Then the whole house went pitch black.

"I don't believe this shit!" Samara seemed agitated.

"What happened? I musta missed it."

"No, you haven't missed anything." She slowly got off the couch, stretching her hand out in front of her. "The electricity shut off on me. And now I can't see shit in here!" She paused again. But it was only for a split second before she shouted: "DESTINI!"

"Well," Martin started off on an easy pace before he went in for the kill, "I love your work but I'm sorta looking for something catchier."

For something more catchy?

You son-of-bitch! You shattered my dreams!

Then he had the nerve to add: "But don't give up on your hope though."

What a fucking joke! I reached for my drawings and started placing them back inside my portfolio. When I got up from my seat, I wanted to tell him to Go fuck off, but I kept it to myself. A few females walked by and waved hello. I gave them a head nod. Then turned back to Martin, forcing myself to smile.

"That's all a part of life," I told him. "What won't kill you, will only make you stronger." I shook his hand. "Well, I do thank you for your time anyway."

"Likewise."

Carlton extended his hand out to him as well. But just before their hands touched, he quickly pulled his hand away and shot Martin with a middle finger instead. "Don't give up on your hope either, because this can be a little catchy too."

I wasn't a bit surprised by that. We left Martin standing there like a fool.

I looked at my wristwatch, I couldn't believe it. "Yo, we needa hurry up. It's nearly twelve o'clock and I'm late for work already."

"DESTINI!" Samara shouted again, tottering in the dark hallway with her hands groping in front of her while hoping to avoid from colliding into something. "WHERE ARE YOU?!" She waited for a response.

But there wasn't any.

Destini was in bed, pretending to be asleep under the bed sheet, conversing on the phone, tattletaling, so to say. "And she said that if I don't go to bed, she was gonna beat me up," she whispered; then paused. She thought she might had heard something outside her room. "Uh-huh.... Okay, but what if she—"

Click!

It was at that precise moment that the lights inside the house were turned back on.

Destini panicked. "Okay, I'm sleepy now. Can you sing me a song before I go to sleep?"

Within seconds Destini's bedroom door swung open and Samara strode to her bedside. "I know you're not sleeping!" she shouted, then snatched the bed sheet off of Destini.

But Destini lay there with her eyelids shut. She pretended as if she had fallen asleep already, with the phone glued to her ear.

"You must think I'm stupid or something! I know you were the one who shut the damned light off! And when I see your daddy, I'm gonna—"

Destini quickly sat up with the phone at her side, cutting Samara off, "I DIDN'T DO ANYTHING!"

"Stop LYING, because I know you did it!"

"It ain't nobody in here who can say they saw me do anything!"

"So how the hell did the power switch get shut off in the garage when it's only me and you in here? How?!"

"How I'm supposed to know that?! I thought you did it when I was on the phone."

"Don't lie to me!" Samara almost lost it. "You don't think I know you be talking to your imaginary friend on the phone?"

Destini then placed the receiver back to her ear. "See, I told you: this hoe always messing with me.... Why? But—"

Samara felt a towering rage building up inside of her. "What the fuck you just called me?"

Destini kept quiet.

So Samara went on to say, "No, you have it wrong, you little bitch!" She wore an angry facial expression, not to be fucked with. "Your mama was a hoe! A two dollar, cum-drinking hoe, bitch!"

Destini leaped from the bed, balling a little fist at her side. "You don't know my mommy!" she said in a strong yet broken voice as tears began to build.

"Yeah, I don't know your mama," Samara barked back. "But I know an apple doesn't fall far from its tree. She can't be any different from your little spoiled, bad ass!" She snatched the receiver off the bed, slammed it into the cradle, and started walking away.

"I HATE YOU!"

Samara stopped when she got at the door and twisted around to face Destini. "Yeah, that's good to know, because I don't like you either. So basically, that makes us both even, you damn little brat!"

The phone rang.

Samara went back to the night table and snatched the phone up with a little animosity in her tone: "Hello!" But as soon as she heard a female's voice, she added, "Whoever you're looking for isn't here!"

"Well," the voice said through the phone line, "I was hoping to speak to you first; then afterward, I would like to speak back to Destini once we get—"

Samara cut her off: "Who is this?"

"That's all irrelevant right—"

"I said who this is before I hang up on you!"

"This is Naomi.... Destini's imaginary friend."

When Carlton and I pulled up in front of Cristal Nightclub, I got out of the car and reminded him again: "Just make sure that you shoot over to the crib and babysit Destini for me."

"Yeah, yeah, I gotchu." His eyes were locked on a few females who were standing by the club entrance.

"Yo!" I tapped the roof of the car to get his attention. "Don't forget!"

"Dammit man!" he snapped, breaking his focus from the females in line. "Stop making it seems as if it's a big ass deal! I've told you that I got you already. Fuck!" He finally drove away.

Samara sucked her teeth, tossed the phone on the bed and stormed out of the bedroom in a snit.

Destini picked the receiver up and started crying the moment she heard Naomi's voice.

After all, Destini wasn't familiar with the street terminology of the word "hoe". She was in the blind, stuck on the misconception that it only meant an 'air-head'. If anything, it was Carlton's fault for misleading her about the true meaning of the word. And Destini had given it to Samara raw and uncut when she called her a "hoe".

I walked past the bouncers and headed straight inside the club.

"Ehh, Goldieeee...."

I twisted to my left.

It was a cutie: a plus-size white chick. Mid-to-late forties, I guess, with huge titties.

Although I didn't know her, I still gestured hello as I wrestled my way toward the bar-counter. "What's up, Amber?" I grabbed a seat. "Let me have a Long Island."

"Sure." She made me one.

Even though I wasn't a connoisseur of cocktails, I knew my drink was terribly weak. Actually, it tasted more like a Mystic Iced Tea than a Long Island iced tea. It was nothing like the other stuff I was used to. So, of course, I was forced to order another drink to get that woozy feeling I was looking for.

When three females walked past me, one of them—the one on the far right with the pinstripe suit on—grazed her hand across my private area and smiled. I blew a kiss to her; she blew one back and kept walking.

Then I saw Dang-a-Lang with a white chick who looked like Paris Hilton's clone.

"Yo!" I stopped him. "Have you seen Kev around here?"

"Yeah." He craned his neck, scanning the area. "Uhhh ... the last I time I saw him," he said, while pointing his finger toward the back of the club, "he was somewhere over there."

Then that same white chick, who was standing beside him broke loose from his arm and stumbled into me. She'd had a little too much to drink. I smelt it on her breath when she leaned forward. And if she were Paris—Oh, man—I think I would have tried to steal her away from him. Because, in a way, I liked her: She was sexier than a muthafucker! She had the whole shebang; that whole bedroom come-fuck-me look painted in her eyes. I would love to have her to stay for the night. At least to fuck the dog-shit out of her and show her how a real nigga could get down. But then again, it wasn't Paris. We were face to face, staring each other in the eyes. Up and close.

I smiled.

She smiled back, stretching her lips across her face. Then she had the audacity to ask me with a slur, "Are you ... Are you comin' to the party with us? I wouldn't mind, you know?" she paused. Then turned to Dang-a-Lang. "Can he come along with us? He's an old friend of mine." She twisted back to me, winked, and then gave me another smile.

But before Dang-a-Lang could respond, I cut in: "Y'all go ahead and I'll catch up with y'all later."

She shot me a bigger smile this time. "Well" —she rested her hand against my face— "we'll be waiting on you, handsome. So don't take too long because you're gonna have a lotta catching up to do."

I did the math.

Dang-a-Lang was silent, giving me that suspicious, puzzled look, as he never knew that I get down with a dirty threesome.

"Alright then," he said to me. "We'll see you in a bit." He strolled away with his little snow bunny at his side.

And I was like, Damn, she even smelled like Paris Hilton: Sweet.

I stood there for a while, sipping on my Long Island until I spotted Kevin a short distance away: He was performing for a few females. I turned to Amber. "Let me have another one, ma. But make it a little stronger for me this time."

She gave me a weird look. I guess she knew what I was talking about because she started pouring me a combination of alcohol shots in a plastic glass. Then when she passed me my drink I immediately tried to take a swig of that crazy shit!

"Whoa!" I clinched my eyes tight, trying to shake it off. "God dammit, man! This shit is strong!"

She raised her eyebrows and did that thing with her head and shoulders to suggest that I had asked for it.

Well, I guess I had then. I smiled back, paid for my drink and headed to the dressing room to get ready for work.

Samara was still pissed off!

She began pacing through the hallway, back and forth, murmuring to herself about the altercation she'd had with Destini earlier. She couldn't help but wonder where Carlton was.

Destini opened the door and stood in the doorway.

Samara stopped pacing when she noticed Destini standing there, watching her.

Destini wasn't a bit intimidated by her stare. "Do you know when my daddy will be coming home?"

Samara rolled her eyes at her and walked away. She headed back to the family room. When she stepped inside the room, she felt her cell phone vibrating. She answered it.

It was Vida. "Girl, why you ain't here yet? We're about to go out to the club?"

"I can't go right now."

"Why?"

"Because that bastard threw his kid on me, and now—"

"Who?" Vida interrupted.

"That muthafucker, DaShawn! He asked me to babysit his daughter for him: only for a little while till his cousin get back. But he hasn't showed up yet."

"Girl, I don't even know why you're putting up with that shit! I told you already that you were picking up that busta who has a lotta issues. You just needa dump his ass! He's playing you."

"He ain't playing me. If anything, he's playing his damn-self!"

"I feel you."

Samara took a breather, only for a second or two. Then said, "Hey, lemme make a couple of calls to find this sorry muthafucker! If I hear anything, I'll give you a ring back."

"Alright."

When they ended their phone call, Samara immediately dialed a number and it picked up on the first ring.

"Today at Club Cristal," the answering machine started to announce, "it's ladies' night! With the hottest male dancers in the M-I-A...."

Samara hung up.

On the other side of town, Carlton was doing his own thing from inside the car. Well, at least, that's what he thought.

"All I'm asking for is an ounce of weed on credit."

"I can't do it today," the weed-man said, barely shaking his head. "I'm kinda low right now."

"Damn, my nigga, you gonna try me like that, knowing I be buying that bullshit from you like every other day. And now you're telling me you can't look out for a brother?"

"Nigga, you used that same line on me yesterday."

"So you're telling me you ain't gonna look out?"

"My nigga, read my lips…. No!" The weed-man got out of the car and took a step away, paying more attention to the scenery on the block. Then he got distracted. "Eh, ma!" he called out to a hoochy-looking mama from across the street. "When are you gonna holla at a nigga?!"

She rolled her eyes at him.

"Alright then," Carlton called him back. "Give me a dub sack."

The weed-man cut back to him. "My nigga, I said no already. So you might as well forget about it and pull the fuck off! You're hotting the spot up!"

"Nigga!" Carlton stuck a twenty dollar bill outside the passenger's window. "I got the money right here!"

"I thought you said you didn't have anything on you?" The weed-man did the exchange. "You're a lying ass nigga."

"Nah, I'm not a lying ass nigga. It's just that your cheap ass weed ain't worth my money, nigga."

"Fuck you!"

"Nah, fuck-you! Hoe-ass-nigga!"

The weed-man reached for something.

Carlton quickly pulled off.

Three shots were fired; one shot hit the taillight.

Samara slammed the receiver into the cradle for the tenth time: The answering machine kept picking up on her. "You know what?" she murmured to herself. "The hell with this shit!" She strode down the hall and shouted: "DESTINI!"

But there was no response.

She then barged into Destini's bedroom and snatched the bed sheet off of her. "Get up!" she barked. "We gonna meet up with your sorry-ass father!"

Destini wanted to smile, but instead, she quickly jumped out of the bed. She threw on her sneakers.

I ordered my second glass of Hurricane Andrew because those Long Islands weren't doing the trick for me. And if I didn't know any better, I would have sworn Amber had dropped something in my drink. Because, not only was I tipsier than an average muthafucker on South Beach, I felt a little spaced out when a middle-age broad (I wasn't sure if she was either White or Latina) approached me with a cajole smile on her face.

I smiled back.

She slid her hand in my speedo underwear. "I like this," she said, while fondling on my dick. "So are you working tonight?"

"I don't know." I allowed her hand to stay there. "It all depends on what you have in mind."

"Well, a couple of my friends and I are trying to enjoy ourselves tonight. And I was wondering if you would like to visit our table and entertain us?" Before I could respond to that, she added: "You'd be paid abundantly for your time and services."

On that note, I guzzled my drink down my throat, and told her, "Take me to your table."

She led the way.

"Go ahead and put your seat belt on," Samara ordered Destini as she backed out of the driveway.

Destini did what she was told.

And Samara drove away with her.

"I would like to borrow this for an hour," a Hispanic lady said to me in broken English, while gently rubbing the palm of her hand over my private area.

You must be crazy, I thought. Borrow? I looked down at my growing muscle, gyrating my hips in a slow motion.

"What if I give you a hundred dollars then?"

I ignored her, keeping the flow of my motion.

"Two hundred?"

I look at her aging lips and gestured my head up for her to bid higher.

She did: "Three hundred dollars and that's my final offer."

I looked over my shoulder to an empty spot in the corner of the club and smiled.

Carlton pulled up in the driveway, not giving a damn who's Honda Civic had just driven away.

When he got out of the car his mind was concentrating on one thing, and one thing only: that thick-ass shawty who had just got out of the car with him. She was built like a thoroughbred. At five three, one hundred fifty-four pounds, she had all the perfect swerves and curves. She had little titties, but with a pretty phat ass like Serena Williams'.

He walked her inside the house. "So feel at home and help yourself in the kitchen, if you like. I'll be right back. I have to go take a piss!" He exited the family room, and went straight to the bathroom. Once inside there, he popped a Viagra and an ecstasy pill together, flushing them both down his throat with some faucet water. A perverted smile grew on his face when he went to the toilet and pulled out his flaccid muscle. "I need you again, Champ."

About twenty minutes later, Samara had double parked in front of Cristal Nightclub and ordered Destini to "Stay right here till I get back."

Destini kept quiet.

Outside of the nightclub, the line was wedged tight with mostly females trying to get in. Samara strode up to the front of the line, hoping to avoid the wait. "Can you call a friend of mine who's working here tonight?" she asked one of the security guards. "His name is DaShawn Powell."

He acted as if he didn't understand her.

So she added, "He's a male stripper."

"Oh." He must have heard that same line about a million times before. He threw a smirk on his face and said, "Yeah, okay. I could do that for you. But in the meantime, just stand over there for me."

She looked over her shoulder, then back at him. "Where?"

"Back there."

Her voice changed to something cold with a hint of agitation. "Back where?"

"In the back of the damn line!" He then used his hands to muscle her aside. "Because you're not any different from the rest of them. You have to wait your turn like—"

"Get your muthafucking hands off of me!" Samara cut him off when she jolted her arm away from him. "And don't you ever put your hands on my again, you punk muthafucker! You just don't know who you're fucking with. I could get your rental-ass fucked up! You—"

"Bitch, fuck you!" he cut her back off. "Now, go get whoever you wanna get! And after I finished whooping his ass, he gonna whoop your ass for getting him fuck'd up!"

She didn't seem a bit intimidated at all. "You soft ass faggot! You ain't gonna do shit but go off at the mouth. Because if he were right here, you wouldn't be talking all that fake-ass-gangsta shit to me right now!"

They both started exchanging offensive words for a good hot minute before another security guard who was standing nearby, whose name was Rex, tried to control the situation by kindly asking Samara to step aside for a moment so he could speak to her.

She did.

"Now, come on," he said. "Was all that called for?" He waited a second before he continued: "Now you know you don't need to be out here screaming and using those type of words out of your mouth."

"But I told that faggot over there, I didn't wanna go inside the club. All I wanted him to do for me was call my boy—" Samara quickly paused to correct herself. "I mean, my ex from outta there so he can come get his child. I have things I gotta do, too! That's all!"

"Alright. I can do that for you. But I can't promise you anything though. I'm gonna let him know that you're out here, looking for him. Okay?"

She felt a bit relieved.

"So what's his name?"

"DaShawn Powell, he goes by the name of—"

"Goldie Lox, right?"

"Yeah."

After Rex stepped away, Samara walked back to her car and stood beside it. She acted like she didn't want to be in the same car with Destini anymore.

Which Destini didn't mind.

It took Rex about three minutes to walk in and walk out the nightclub; Samara met him halfway when she saw him heading toward her.

"DaShawn says that he's busy right now," Rex informed her. "And he'll holla at you later on once he gets off from work."

"Oh, really?" She strode away from him, then went to the car. She then told Destini, "C'mon. You're gonna meet up with your sorry-ass father!"

When Destini got out of the car, Samara grabbed her by the wrist and sort of dragged her to the front of the nightclub. She drew near to Rex. "Here!" She handed Destini over to him. "Ask that bastard in there if he's too busy for her, too!"

But before Rex could say anything, she stormed back to her car and drove away.

"Are you sure?" I asked one of the waitresses inside the nightclub, after being notified about Destini.

"Yeah, Rex told me that he left her up front with Karen at the cashier's booth."

I was confused. I thought Carlton was home babysitting Destini for me. He gave me his word on that. So, there had to be a good explanation for this bullshit!

But looking for an explanation from him right now became the least of my worries when I walked into the foyer and saw my living nightmare.

Out of all the people in the world, it was the devil's helper in person, along with her fallen sidekick, standing at the cashier's booth.

I could honestly say I was face to face with it. No! Better yet, let me correct that: I was face to face with them. And my words came out flat yet with a scary tone.

"Oh, my goodness.... Ms. Betty Brady."

"Mr. Powell," Ms. Betty began to say to me, "it's a pleasure to know exactly what you do for a living."

My eyes accidentally locked on to hers while I tried to search for a suitable explanation.

But Ms. Betty's friend, Sister Mary, broke my damn concentration with her sarcastic remark when she said, "It's so funny how we keep meeting in these unusual places. From the Holiday Inn, all the way here to the devil's den. And only God knows where next!" She then threw one of her hands in the air with her eyes shut, acting as if she was possessed by some demonic spirit, jerking her upper body in a very unusual way. "Whoa!" she shouted. "Oh, thank you, Lord! Oh, thank you, O' Lord Jesus!" Her body jerked again. "Save me from this world!" She jerked again. "Glory Hallelujah!" She hopped forward with one hand raised in the air, and then hopped back. "O' glory Hallelujah! Praise God!"

What a hoax! I began to wonder if all Christians pretend like this, too. I swear, I wanted to ask her, but I decided not to. It would probably make matters worse. However, I went with something else instead. "It's not what you think," I tried to justify myself with a wicked lie. "I don't work here. Actually, my boss is having a company party here tonight."

Ms. Betty gave me a phony chuckle, as she pulled a pen and a small writing pad out of her purse. "Oh, really?" she asked, paying close attention to her writing.

"Uh-huh." I nodded. "You see, it's all a misunderstanding but it can be cleared up."

"It can, huh?" Ms. Betty mocked me as she kept jotting something down on her pad.

"Yeah, of course." I looked at the both of them for some sort of mercy, but I couldn't find any.

Then Ms. Betty stopped writing, shooting me a suspicious look.

I couldn't help but wonder why.

"Have you been drinking alcohol, Mr. Powell?"

"Of course not!" I lied, taking a step back. "It's just that somebody accidently slipped their drink on me." I looked at my bare chest and arms. Then added: "That idiot!"

"Oh, so that's why you don't have any clothes on?" Ms. Betty asked.

But before I could respond, Sister Mary slid her two cents in: "And that's why you have that towel wrapped around you too, huh?"

"Yeah." That's it. "But of course." My alibi was suddenly established, thanks to her. "That's why I'm not wearing my clothes."

"You filthy heathen!" Ms. Betty snapped at me, trying her damnedest to embarrass me in front of everybody who was standing in the foyer with us. "We were already informed by your cousin earlier today you'll be dancing at this club tonight."

That two-timing traitor! My own damn flesh and blood sold me out to these bitches! "I can't believe Carlton would do this to me," I blurted out by mistake.

"No! It was your other cousin," Ms. Betty threw at me. "Ricky! Freaky Ricky, as he called himself."

"Ricky?" I was confused. "But I don't have a cousin—" I began to say until the thought of the neighborhood crack-head flashed through my mind. That son-of-bitch! "He ain't my cousin!"

"Well, whether he is or not, that's all irrelevant right now, because he gave us credible information about your workplace today."

"But I have a good reason for this...."

She gave me her full attention, grabbing her little yellow notepad again.

At this point, I decided to come clean and tell her the truth. I tried everything in my power to explain myself for her. The whole reason as to why I had fabricated a story about my place of work. But she didn't accept it. She seemed to be ticked off with me even more when I brought the incident up about the Holiday Inn. So basically, from what she told me, she would be filing her complaint with Family Court early Monday morning.

And just out of curiosity she asked, "Since you're here, who is babysitting Destini for you?"

"Oh, no!" I immediately remembered what Lisa had told me about Destini: My eyes began to scan the area where we were standing.

"Is everything alright, Mr. Powell?" Ms. Betty asked me.

"Yeah, yeah. But of course." I tried to relax.

"And Destini?"

"What about her?"

"What about her?" she retorted with sarcasm. Then she spat out: "Who's watching over Destini while you're here, doing the devil's deeds?"

"Oh…. That's what you meant by that." I tried to stall for some more time to get my story straight. "Well, my cousin Carlton is babysitting her while I'm here. Actually, I just got finish speaking to her a few hours ago, just before she went to bed."

At that precise moment I heard Kevin's voice cut in, directly behind me, when he said, "Eh, my nigga! Guess who I found by the bar?"

But before I could turned around to see who he was talking about, Ms. Betty burst out with, "Good Heaven!"

And I would be damned: that's when I saw him carrying Destini in his arms.

Ms. Betty shouted: "I can't believe this!" She then turned to me. "Are you outta your mind?!" She didn't give me a chance to respond before she added: "What's she doing here in this sort of place; especially in these wee hours of the morning?"

I couldn't answer that. How could I?

"Mr. Powell!" Ms. Betty said in a cold, bitter way. "You have drawn the last straw here!" She started writing in her pad again.

I felt bad. "Let me explain everything to you."

Sister Mary cut in: "You'll have enough time to explain everything to the judge, young man." She looked to her left. "Tell him, Sister Betty."

A group of females swaggered up to the club entrance and observed Ms. Betty writing something down in her notepad. "You go granny," one of them said. "Get your groove on."

Ms. Betty stopped writing in her pad and evil mugged those three—. No, now four females, as they entered inside the club. Then Ms. Betty turned back and poured all her anger out on me. I kid you not. That old bitch chewed me up as if I were a stripe of gum—any cheap brand you could think of—and spat me out on the sidewalk to be stomped on by others.

At this point there was so much distraction in the foyer that the security guards asked us—Ms. Betty, Sister Mary, Destini, Kevin, and me—to step out of the club and away from the doorway. Not only were we blocking the entrance, according to him, but we were also drawing too much attention to us.

We stepped aside.

"Here you go," Rex said, giving me a club logo T-shirt to wear.

"Thanks."

Ms. Betty started going off at the mouth again. She claimed that she was about to call an officer to take Destini to the Youth Detention Center, until Monday's court hearing, where she would make a recommendation to send Destini to a foster home. Because according to her—get this—I was unfit to be a parent.

An unfit parent out of all things.

Now that was fucked up!

It felt like I was in a sort of no-holds-barred grudge match. And the main event ... me: up against this old, nagging bitch! It seemed like I was in a no-win situation. She had the upper hand over me. So I gave up. She won. Fuck it! I dropped my guard. If this bitch wanna take Destini away, I thought, just go ahead and do it then. Because, if anything, Destini had been nothing more than a problem for me since she came into my life. So basically, you'll be doing me a favor, you old—

Oops!

Ms. Betty pierced at me with an ugly look when I accidently belched in her face.

And I think that set it off for the worse because she told Kevin, "Let me have her, please." Then she turned her attention to Destini and spoke in a soft, specious tone: "You be coming with me, dear."

Destini became wide-eyed with fear; she kept her distance, shaking her head, refusing to go to her.

Ms. Betty took a step toward her, but Destini pushed off from Kevin and hid behind me. Then Ms. Betty took another step with her hands out to grab Destini, but she stopped. I guess Ms. Betty didn't want to cause a commotion out there in front of everybody. Her facial expression gave an indication that she seemed uncertain about something before she came to her decision.

"Listen, Mr. Powell," she said, with a regretful yet strong tone. "I have changed my mind for now. But we all know Destini cannot be in this type of environment, especially in these late hours of the night." She paused for a split second. Then added: "You only have two options here. You can either call somebody to come pick her up, someone who's trustworthy, or have a designated driver to take the both of you home...."

I was astonished that she had changed her mind. But before I could say anything, Kevin threw in his suggestion: "My nigga, give Carlton a call and have him to come pick her up for you."

That was a good idea. I immediately started pat-searching myself for my cell phone. But when I realized I wasn't wearing my pants, Ms. Betty loaned me her phone.

I called home.

Carlton's shawty, LaTonya, grabbed the cordless phone off the night table of the fifth ring and slung it across the room, slamming it against the wall: It was breaking her concentration from reaching her climax. She was at her peak, and she wanted to cum. She rode Carlton like a world rodeo cowgirl.

Some hard-core, gangsta shit you could only find on an underground sex flick at www.extremebooty.com.

"Oh, yes!" She took one last bounce before she flipped over on her back in a missionary position. "Fuck me! Fuck me!" She swallowed heavily. "Uh, yes! Yes! Yes! That's it! Fuck me! Harder! Fuck me, harder!"

By all means, Carlton was giving her everything he had, enjoying every moment of it. Sex had always been a strong craving for him. He loved that shit! Let the truth be told, he had experienced his first encounter with sex at the age of five with his Cousin Diana, while playing House. And since then, he had gained a passion for it. He had slept with well over 120 females in his lifetime. He could remember every piece of pussy that he went up in: tight pussy, loose pussy, deep pussy, sloppy pussy, stinky pussy. Basically about every color piece of pussy you could think of, from different ethnic backgrounds, all over South Florida. Each of them was memorable. But when it came down to his shawty, LaTonya, she was his favorite.

She was the pick of the litter.

She knew how to work her pussy muscles perfectly. And good at it, too. The top of her class as a ghetto chick. A red-bone. And that's why he had been pounding on her pussy for nearly an hour straight.

"Ohhh, yes! Oh, yes.... Yes!" she cried out with her hands wrapped around him. "I'm about to cum again! I'm about to cum again!" She swallowed heavily. "Take off your condom! Take it off!" She started rocking back on him. "Hurry! Take it off! I want you to cum with me. Oh! Cum with me. Oh, fuck! I'm about to cum! I'm about to cummmmm...."

Yeah, Carlton might be a weed-head, a little slow here and there, but he wasn't retarded. With all these man-made diseases in Black communities, he knew better than to take his condom off. He just ignored her and continued to long stroke that good piece of pussy until she came for him.

Of course, I didn't stay on the cell phone long: I hung up the moment when I heard a female's voice screaming in the background due to some sort of sexual pleasure.

"I'm just gonna call a cab instead," I told Ms. Betty. "I think my cousin has fallen asleep."

"Oh, okay."

Destini grabbed my hand. "Why don't you call Naomi?"

"Nah. Don't worry about it. I'm gonna take you home instead. And besides, I don't know her number anyway."

"Whew! I know it! I know it!" She immediately snatched the phone out of my hand and dialed Naomi's telephone number.

I looked at Kevin, helplessly.

Within seconds, Destini got excited over the phone: "Hi, Naomi! It's me.... Destini!" There was a pause. Then Destini shrugged her thin shoulder and said, "I don't know." There was another pause. She unconsciously nodded her head. "Uh-huh, it's a lotta people out here. How you know?" There was a brief pause this time. It was nothing like the other ones. It was much shorter. "Right here." Destini pointed at me.

Another pause...

I believe Naomi asked Destini a tough question because Destini looked around as if she were analyzing her surroundings before she asked me, "Where's right here?"

"Let me speak to her."

She passed the phone to me.

"Hey, Naomi," I immediately apologized. "I'm sorry if I woke you from your sleep at this time of the night. I don't know how to say this. But ... if you don't mind, I'm gonna need your help on something."

"Don't worry about it. What can I help you with?"

But before I could say anything, Destini had shouted, "Hurry up and come get me!" loud enough so Naomi could hear her through the receiver.

"Did she say what I think she said?" Naomi asked.

"Uh, she wanna know—. I mean, I wanna know if you can pick Destini up and take her home for me?"

Naomi became quiet, and after a short moment, she said, "I don't have a problem with that. But if you don't mind me asking, why can't you take her home?"

"I can't explain it to you right now." I glanced over at Ms. Betty, then turned to the side. Then whispered, "But I'll tell you about it later."

There was a brief moment of silence. A sorta long one, too. Then finally she asked me, "Where are you?"

"Cristal Nightclub."

"Cristal?!" She acted as if she couldn't believe me. "What is she doing—." She paused for a quick second. Then continued: "I'll be there in a few minutes."

Thank goodness.

Once I hung up, I passed the cell phone back to Ms. Betty and thanked her for allowing me to use it.

Nothing in return.

Silently, she stared at me in disgust with her arms wrapped across her heavy breasts.

Yeah, whatever....

Less than ten minutes later Naomi pulled up in front of Cristal Nightclub, driving a black Nissan Maxima. A 2008 model. She parked. When she got out of the car, I greeted her with a friendly light hug. Just a little something to throw Ms. Betty and Sister Mary off. Naomi shook Kevin's hand too, and then gave Destini a hug. One of those nice, warm hugs.

"Girl, what are you doing out here?" she playfully asked Destini.

I smiled, but before Destini could reply, I quickly introduced Naomi to Ms. Betty and Sister Mary.

After they shook hands, something clicked there. Ms. Betty's personality changed instantly while she got caught up in a conversation with Naomi. It wasn't a long one, but it was long enough. In fact, Ms. Betty didn't seem worried about Destini leaving with Naomi.

Ms. Betty looked at Kevin and me, then back to Naomi. "You surprise me that you would know these types of people."

"He's not so bad." She looked at me, then back to her with a smile on her face. "It's easy to tame a lion."

"Yeah, with a shotgun and a shovel, to bury it out in the backyard afterwards."

She laughed.

"Hey." I didn't find anything funny about that. I walked over to them. "It's getting late and I think Destini needs to start heading home now." I turned to face Naomi. "May I please speak to you for a second?"

"Sure." She stepped aside with me.

"Hey, thanks for coming. You're definitely a lifesaver here."

"I told you already, it's nothing. But let's just say this: you owe me one."

I smiled with her. "I most definitely do. Whatever you want. I got you."

After what seemed like a long moment of silence, she said, "Let me have the address to your house."

I gave it to her. "And check it. If nobody answers the door, there's a spare key taped underneath the mailbox."

"Okay"

From a short distance, I guess Ms. Betty saw when Naomi shook my hand because she waved good-bye and said, "All right, Ms. Bryams, it was nice meeting you! Perhaps we'll meet again!" She paused, fluttered her fingers at Destini, and said, "Bye-bye, sugar dumpling!"

Destini shot her a grimace and grabbed Naomi's hand. Naomi and I waved back at Ms. Betty to throw her off. And surprisingly it worked. She waved back at Naomi, but then rolled her eyes at me.

When Ms. Betty and Sister Mary strode across the street to their car we heard a group of guys taunting them with, "Mmm-mm! Work it, granny!"

Ms. Betty and Sister Mary tilted their noses up in the air—looking flustered by the fellas' comments—as they got into the car and sped off quickly, leaving tire streaks on the pavement.

I smiled as I watched Naomi and Destini drive away, too. I felt relieved. One problem was solved, but another one was at hand. I had to get back to work. Kevin and I headed back to the nightclub as if nothing had happened a moment ago. As soon as after we entered through the club foyer, we were swarmed by a bunch of carnal-minded females.

Nymphos.

I shook my head playfully, because one of them squeezed my ass. I turned around with an ineffable smile.

They all smiled back.

"Euw!" My smile vanished when I saw their huge Adam's Apples below their chins. I felt violated. I twisted back around and tried to walk away, but one of them copped another feel.

I snapped!

Naomi pulled up in front of the house and parked. She looked over at Destini and noticed that she was a little bent out of shape, if not tired.

As they got out of the car and approached the house, Naomi rang the doorbell. She waited a bit. Nothing. She retrieved the hidden key from underneath the mailbox and unlocked the front door. They went inside.

"You wanna see my room?"

"Of course."

Destini led the way.

"Okay," after Naomi received her little tour, she told Destini, "You're taking a shower before you hit the sack. You stink!"

"No, I don't! I don't stink. I can take a shower tomorrow."

"I think not." Naomi gathered a few items for Destini before she led her back out of the bedroom. "C'mon, you're taking a shower."

"Okay." Destini gave in. "But you have to wait outside the bathroom."

Naomi agreed.

Destini went into the bathroom and shut the door behind her.

After a short time, Naomi heard Destini squeal, "It's co-ol-old," just after the shower faucet was turned on. She smiled and walked away. She went back to the front of the house to browse around until Destini got finished. And as she roamed through the living room, she admired the family portraits on the wall. There was one particular photo that caught her attention: It was a family reunion picture with a lot of people in it.

She smiled....

Then suddenly her eyes caught as shadow floating past the doorway, heading down the hall.

"Destini!" she called out. But there was no response. "It's impossible for her to be finished with that shower already." She walked out of the room in pursuit; straight to the kitchen.

Ah, ha!

Naomi saw the refrigeration door open, and it was blocking her view. "Destini, it's too late for you to be drinking at this time of the night when you're supposed to," she started, while snatching the fridge door back to confront her, but froze. Naomi immediately looked away as she twisted around. She caught a glimpse of something she didn't supposed to see. At least not like this. But it was just dangling right there in front of her, waving hello. She felt embarrassed. "I'm truly sorry. I thought you were Destini."

"Nah. Don't sweat it." Carlton stood there, wearing nothing but a used condom—an ultra-thin kind—while sinking his teeth into a glazed doughnut. "It ain't like you never saw a man before. But who are you though?"

"I'm a friend of DaShawn and Destini," she said with her back facing him. "DaShawn asked me if I could take Destini home for him, and I didn't mind."

"Oh, I was wondering where that little girl was at." He then shut the fridge door and walked around her, heading back to his bedroom.

Naomi quickly strode back into Destini's room. Within minutes she was tucking Destini in bed.

"Can you sing me a song before I go to sleep?"

"Sure."

Destini slid over and patted the available space on the bed to invite Naomi to either sit or lie beside her.

Naomi accepted the invitation. She lay down and began to sing "Fly Like a Bird" by Mariah Carey.

Look at this, my nigga," Kevin sat beside me with a bundle of cash in his hand. "I made over twelve hundred dollars tonight." He paused. Then tried to taunt me: "So, how much did you make?"

"I don't know." I slid on my shoes.

"Well, count it then. Whatchu waiting on?"

"Nothing! But I'm gonna count it once I get home. I have a little headache."

"Yeah, right. A headache, my ass!" He obviously doubted me.

Mikey and two other dancers walked into the dressing room about the same time Kevin made his comment to me. They called it quits for the night, too.

"Eh, dawg!" Kevin went straight to the punch line, asking Mikey, "How much money you made tonight?"

"About fifteen hundred. Why, what's up?"

"Nah. It's nothing. I was just wondering. That's all."

Mikey shot him a curious smile, then jerked his head up a bit.

But Kevin pretended he didn't know what Mikey meant by that. He nodded back at Mikey, trying to throw him off.

Mikey followed up with a question instead: "So how much you made?"

"I don't know." Kevin stuck his money back in his pocket. "I was gonna count it when I get home. I'm feeling a little light-headed."

I turned to Kevin and gave him that you-got-to-be-kidding-me look.

"So," Mikey got our attention, "y'all wanna go out and grab something to eat?"

"Nah, I'm alright." Kevin threw on his shirt. "I had already made plans for the night."

"Well, what about you?"

"Nah, I have to pass too." I could barely hold my eyelids up. "I needa go home and check on Destini."

"Alright." Within minutes, Mikey left with a few friends of ours.

And as soon as they stepped out of the room, Kevin asked me, "Do you think that muthafucker really made that much money?"

"Who?"

"Mikey," he said. "I think his ass is lying. What you think?"

"That's our homey you're talking about."

"So?"

I shook my head and got up. "C'mon, let's go." I grabbed my duffel bag. "It's getting late, and I need to start heading home."

"Yeah, me too."

A moment later, while Kevin was inside of his SUV waiting on me, I found myself trying to help a group of people locate a friend of theirs.

"She's about my height," an ivory-complexioned female said, "with blond hair, just little past her shoulders."

"Yeah, I know who you're talking about. She looks a little like Paris Hilton."

She kinda smiled at me, then to her friends, then to me again. No comment.

"Please tell me that wasn't her."

She didn't want to answer my question.

Damn! I missed out on the party. I shoulda taken the offer when she gave it to me.

"So, do you know where we could find—."

Kevin blew the horn from across the street.

I turned toward him, raising my index finger in the air. "Hold up! Just give me a second!" As soon as I was about to get back to the conversation with them, Kevin started honking the horn like a madman; I twisted back around to him. "Just give me a fucking second!"

"Eh, y'all!" He ignored me, snapping on them instead. "Why don't y'all let my homeboy go! I'm trying to get the fuck outta here!"

They kept quiet.

"Hey" —I turned back to them— "I'm sorry about that. But let me get out of here before he catches a nervous breakdown over there."

"Okay. But you're sure you saw my friend?"

"Yeah, a few hours ago. But the last time I saw her, she was with a friend of mine who goes by the name Dang-a-Lang. They both headed toward the back of the club. So if I were you, I'd check the restroom out. The last toilet stool in the back."

"Thanks."

I finally reached the SUV and hopped into the front passenger seat.

"It's about time!" Kevin said. "You acted like you wanted to stay out there with them—."

"I don't wanna hear that shit!" I cut him off. "Because you don't be seeing me trippin' like a bitch whenever you be holding me up, trying to holla at every piece of pussy that comes your—."

"Eh, eh, eh!" he cut me back off. Then motioned his head toward the backseat. "Meet Janine."

I twisted around and saw a Caribbean looking chick back there. I shot her a head-nod; she smiled. I twisted back around and kept quiet the whole ride home.

"Alright then," Kevin broke the silence when I stepped out of the vehicle. "I'll holla at you tomorrow."

"All right."

He pulled off and made a left turn up the block.

As I entered the house and approached Destini's door, the lights inside her room nearly blinded me. I got my focus back when I saw two sleeping beauties lying in bed together.

I smiled.

Destini was underneath the bed sheet, tucked in, while Naomi wasn't. She was just lying there beside Destini—flat on her back.

I zoomed in on Naomi. She had a book propped open, resting against her breasts. She must have fallen asleep while reading Destini a bedtime story, I mulled. So, instead of waking her up, I walked over to the bed and gently removed the book from her bosom.

I was impressed. I admired her C-cup. A perfect size. I covered her with a nearby blanket. And just before I walked out, I flicked the lights off, then immediately cut them back on. I saw Naomi roll over on her side with her backside facing me.

Good heavens!

I hit the lights again and copped a feel before I exited the room.

Naomi smelled the cooking aroma well before she woke up from her sleep.

It smelled good to her.

She took another sniff while stretching. A nice, long stretch. Then she popped her eyes open, realizing that she wasn't at home. She panicked. The sunlight fought its way through the window blinds. She cut her eyes to the left side of the bed where Destini had slept last night. But now Destini was gone.

"Shit!" Naomi leaped from the bed, gathered up her belongings, and ran out of the room. She turned right, then left, and ran straight into the bathroom.

I swear, I wanted to rest a little longer, but I couldn't. The smell of Taster's Choice coffee pinched my nose.

With my eyelids still shut, I took another noseful; then exhaled. I smiled. Then, all of a sudden, I heard a loud piercing scream.

"What the hell?" I jumped out of bed and ran toward the shrilling cry.

It was coming from Destini. She was crying on the kitchen floor with her T-shirt soaked with steaming coffee.

I immediately scooped her up and rushed her over to the kitchen sink. "What happened?!" I asked, feeling a bit terrified while spraying her stomach with the faucet hose.

But she didn't answer me.

Her face twisted in anguish as she blubbered and cried. And just when it seemed like she was about to tell me something, I heard a shout behind me.

I looked.

It was Naomi; she rushed over to us.

What she is still doing here, I wondered. But then again, I was more concerned about Destini. "I think she was making herself some coffee," I gave Naomi a wild guess, "and accidently burned herself with it."

Naomi watched Destini wince and cry for a brief moment, then told me, "She probably needs some medical attention. Let me get my car ready."

"Dammit, man!" I didn't expect the emergency room at the hospital to feel like an unemployed department. "How long are they gonna take to come out to see us?"

Naomi shrugged and tilted her head to the side to indicate that she didn't know.

Every chair in the ER's waiting room was taken by those who were either on Medicaid, Medicare, or the lame-ass Obamacare. So basically, the medical assistance wasn't worth shit! But this was the nearest hospital from the house.

What a joke!

I could honestly say this, though: the best thing that had happened so far—something that took me by surprise—was when an elderly man gave his seat to Destini. Yeah, that was very charitable of him to do so, but Naomi and I had to stand for the next twenty minutes until other seats became available. On the other side of the room. And if you think that was something, wait until you hear this: it took about two additional hours before Destini, Naomi, and I were finally escorted into sort of a triage room where Destini was then given a gurney to lie on. And we still ended up waiting there for another forty-plus minutes until a nurse entered our cubicle and placed a wet towel on Destini's stomach, with crushed ice on top of it.

"You're a little too young to be making yourself a cup of coffee," the nurse told Destini in a cheerful manner, while taking her blood pressure and temperature. "I have heard that cocoa is better."

Destini didn't seem amused by her remarks.

Neither was I. "Do you know when the physician is going to see her?" I kinda snapped on the nurse, not intentionally, but rather for the lack of medical attention we were receiving from them. "Because we have been waiting to see a doctor for the past four hours now, and one has yet to come see us. And if that be the case of what you're doing now, I could have easily given her some ice myself to save us the trouble from coming to this damned hospital."

"I'm sorry about your wait, Mr. Powell. But since there's a shortage of doctors and nurses at this hospital, we are trying to do our best with the little manpower that we are currently working with. However, I do assure you, a doctor will be with you very soon."

I felt ashamed.

I guess she accepted my guilty apology when I kept my mouth shut. She smiled just before she stepped out of the cubicle.

But, then again, that "very soon" she assured me of just a short while ago ended up being an additional half an hour to our already excessive wait.

"Miss Powell, the young coffee-maker," an older man said to Destini in a playful tone, as he pulled the curtains aside and entered the cubicle with us. "My name is Doctor Sanders, and I'll be your healer today." He smiled at her, then at us, and then back to her. "So, how are you feeling?"

"I dunno," Destini barely opened her mouth.

"Well," he continued, "I promise you'll be up and running again in no time."

Destini's eyes lit up with a smile.

"Just look at that! You're getting better already."

"Fo' real?"

"Yup!" he assured her in a childish way, then turned to Naomi and me, and apologized for the delay. He went on to tell us that there had been a terrible car collision on I-95 in which all the doctors and medical personnel had their hands full until recently. "Seven made it, four didn't."

I swear, I felt like some shit!

"So," Dr. Sanders turned back to Destini, "let's take a look at your tummy."

"Oww!" Destini flinched.

"What's the matter?" Dr. Sanders asked, removing his hand from her stomach. "Did that hurt you?"

"No! But your fingers are cold!"

He scoffed a short laugh and said, "You startled me for a second there."

When I was about to ask him about the seriousness of Destini's burn my cell phone began to ring.

"Yeah." I answered it. "Hey! What happened to you last night?... Yeah, but I told you Carlton was gonna relieve you once he got back home.... Oh, he didn't.... But damn" —I turned away from the examination table, facing the opposite direction for a little privacy— "you didn't have to drop her at my damned workplace like that. What the hell were you thinking?"

It was at that precise moment that Destini started moaning as if she were in serious pain, turning and twisting her head, screaming, "Ooooww, it hurts! It hurts me! Please make it stop!"

"Hey, listen up! I can't talk right now," I told Samara through the cell phone, then looked at Destini. Then back into the phone: "Because I'm at the hospital with a doctor.... Nah, it's Destini. She got scalded this morning while trying to make herself coffee. I think there's some sorta problem right now.... I don't know. It seems like she's in pain.... I don't know.... Hey, listen up! I can't talk right now.... Yeah, later on once I'm finished here.... All right then.... Yeah, later." I hung up.

Then, all of a sudden, Destini stopped groaning.

"Does it hurt right here?" Dr. Sanders asked her while lightly palpating around her stomach area.

She shook her head. "Nope! It doesn't hurt anymore. I think you fixed it."

Dr. Sanders gave her a wary look, then turned to me and explained that the coffee burn wasn't as serious as it appeared. I was only a slight irritation that would heal within a short time— probably a day or two. I was happy to know that. He finally released us, recommending that Destini stay out of the sun for a few days.

"Oh. Okay. That shouldn't be hard." I shook his hand and we left.

"Can we go to Dairy Queen and get some ice cream?"

I had to really look at this little knuckle-head. "No, not right now, Destini."

"Pleaseeee...."

"It's me," I announced, stepping inside the house with Destini in my arms; Naomi trailed behind me.

Uncle James looked suspicious about something as I entered the family room. It seemed like he was confused about which way he wanted to run: left or right. Then he froze like a deer on the side of the highway.

"Clear the couch off for me," I told him. "I need to lay her down."

He did, then asked Destini in a taunting tone, "Now, what you got yourself into?"

I cut in: "She burned herself while making coffee this morning."

"That's all?" he murmured.

"What you said? I didn't catch that."

"I said that's awful." Then he immediately changed the subject: "You know, you have several messages on the answering machine?"

"From who?"

"I don't know...."

And just when I was about to walk off to check the answering machine, Naomi asked me if she could help herself to something to drink.

"Yeah, but of course. You can have anything you want. The kitchen is down the hall, on your right."

"Thanks." She walked away.

Uncle James had a silly look on his face, but before he could inquire about who Naomi was, I asked him, "Have you seen Carlton this morning?"

"No."

I pressed the PLAY button on the answering machine. "You have … seven … recorded messages," it played out for me. "To review your messages … press the pound key now."

I pressed the pound key. The first message was from Ms. Betty, the caseworker, informing me that she had reported last night's incident to her supervisor. The second message was for Carlton, from a female by the name of Natasha. The third message was from a man who worked for a fashion design agency, who informed me that our appointment had been rescheduled for a later day. And the fourth, fifth, sixth, and yes, the seventh messages were all from Samara. All of her messages had a great sense of urgency: "We needa fucking talk!"

I picked the receiver up to call her back.

"DaShawn."

I turned around.

It was Naomi: "May I speak to you in the other room for a second?"

"Yeah, what's up?" I put the phone down and walked to the kitchen with her.

Then she showed me the disarray scenery. "I think Destini was making us breakfast this morning before she got burnt," she said, while looking over the evidence.

I noticed the three servings of egg omelets, a cup of coffee, and a half a glass of chocolate milk beside it. "You don't really believe she was making us breakfast, do you?"

"Of course I do. Just look." She pointed toward the floor. "There's a coffee mug right there and another one is on the table. I can only assume one of them was for you and the other cup was for me."

Good observation…. It made plenty sense.

"But she didn't have to go through the trouble." I was dead serious. "I could have easily made us some breakfast this morning when I got up."

"I know. I believe she knew that too. But instead she wanted to do the same thing for us this morning."

I stood there dumbfounded. We waited a few minutes in the kitchen, cleaning up a bit before going back into the family room.

"Here you go, sweetie." I passed Destini a cold glass of chocolate milk. "Is there anything else you'd like before I make us something to eat?"

Destini looked at me with her slanted eyes, probably hoping to catch a hint of what I was thinking. She shook her head, then with a slight hesitation, raised the glass to her mouth.

"Do you feel comfortable?" I rose her legs and placed a pillow under them. "Do you need me to get you something before I start cooking?"

"Okay!" Destini stopped drinking. "What is it?"

"What are you talking about?"

Then Naomi offered to help me out of the ditch. "It's nothing to get wary about, Destini. He's just being courteous to you because of all you have been through today. That's all."

Destini hesitated. "Are you sure?"

"A hundred percent sure, sweetie."

"Oh, because I thought he was trying to pamper me to have that ugly girl to watch over me again."

"What girl?" Naomi asked.

"Samara!"

"Oh, shit!" I almost forgot about her. I went straight to the phone to give her a call.

Samara picked up on the second ring. Her tone was melodious at first until she heard my voice. Then her voice immediately became cold and moody as if she were rehearsing for an internship at the White House. "What the hell you want?"

"**What the fuck's** the matter with you?" I asked Samara over the phone.

"It's none of your damn business anymore! But like I said, what do you want?"

"I want you. And I need you to stop trippin' for a minute."

"Stop tripping?" she snapped again. "What the hell took you so long to call me back?! Huh? Just tell me that!"

I felt kinda forced to explain everything to her about what happened to Destini. It was only then that she lightened up on me.

"So what about our date we had planned for tonight? Have you forgotten about that too?"

"Nah. I didn't forget." I lied between my teeth. "It's just that I was tied up at the hospital all day and didn't get a chance to find a babysitter to watch Destini for me yet.... Yeah, but—." I paused for a moment when I heard Destini started moaning again.

"... my belly hurts.... Oowwwww!"

I shot her a suspicious look because I had just seen her joking with Naomi; she pouted back.

Uncle James started clowning on her. "That's why he caught your little lying-ass!"

Destini's eye cut to the flower vase.

Water!

She tried to reach for the vase; Naomi caught her because it appears that Destini almost slipped off the couch.

Uncle James nearly shitted on himself.

"Hey, DaShawn! I wouldn't mind babysitting her for you while you go out on your date."

I paused with the phone in my hand when I heard Naomi's suggestion: It sounded good. "Are you sure about that?"

"Of course I am. I wouldn't mind" —she smiled at Destini— "watching this little princess for you."

"Yeah, right!" Uncle James objected. "The princess of darkness maybe."

I smiled at Naomi and said, "Thanks." Then I jumped right back on my phone conversation with Samara, telling her that a friend of mine was going to babysit Destini for me while we went out on our date.

"Who are you talking about?" Samara asked, probably because I kept saying this and that about my friend. "Naomi?"

"Yeah," I was astonished. "Do you know her?"

"No! I don't know that bitch! And she damn sure doesn't want to get to know me either!"

I was shocked! Samara kept shouting in all different kind of cuss words, acting like she didn't have any plans on shutting up—even though I practically begged her to. And I knew Uncle James could hear her chewing me up from where he was sitting. I caught him looking at me just before he cut his eyes toward the wall. So I exited the room, searching for the right words to slow her down.

"You stupid bitch! Why the fuck are you screaming in my ear like you don't have any fucking sense?!"

Destini looked at Naomi, then at Uncle James. But he shot her with that What-the-hell-are-you-looking-at stare, then got up from his seat and ran over to the doorway to eavesdrop. Destini got up and ran over there beside him: She wanted to hear, too.

Naomi twisted toward the doorway, taking a seat on the couch. "Destini," she called out to her. "You shouldn't be doing that. That's wrong. You shouldn't be listening to your father's conversation."

"Shhh!" Destini parried her hand to Naomi to be quiet. "He might hear you." She then eased closer to the doorway, nearly on Uncle James' back, to listen in.

I couldn't believe this shit! "And what if I'm fucking her too! ... You ain't gonna do a muthafucking' thing! ... Oh, yeah! ... Well, fuck you too! ... Bitch! Fuck you! If you wanna give your pussy up to him, just go ahead and do it! And I bet you I won't lose any sleep over it.... Fuck you too, bitch! I don't have to hear your shit!" I hung up on Samara.

Damn....

I tried to shake the rancor off my shoulders before I headed back into the family room. "What the hell is this?" I found Destini and Uncle James on all fours with their ears facing the hallway. "What are y'all doing?"

Uncle James tried to play it off. "You see, right here?" he ignored me, talking to Destini instead, pointing his finger at the door frame. "Now, pay close attention, kid. Do you see how that paint—"

"Get off the damn floor! And stop being so damn nosy!"

"Whatchu talking about?" He got up to his feet; so did Destini.

I ignored him and turned to Naomi. "You don't have to babysit for me anymore. I had a change of heart about going out tonight."

"Okay." She got up. "So, I'll be heading home then."

"But you know, you don't have to leave if you don't want to. I'm ... I'm about to prepare something to eat. And I would like it if you can stay."

At first, she hesitated but then explained that she needed to go home and take a shower. "Perhaps another time."

Destini threw in her help: "You can take a shower here," she suggested to Naomi. "And you could wear some of my clothes."

"I can't fit in your clothes, they're too small for me, boo."

"Well" —I went for the kill— "you could wear something of mine then. Just temporarily. Perhaps a T-shirt and sweat pants. In the meantime, I could just throw your clothes in the washer for you, if you'd like."

She just kept her eyes on me, pondering the offer. Then said, "I don't know about that."

"Oh, yeah you do!" Destini jumped back in our conversation. "How can you not know about that," she said to Naomi. "Well?" She waited a second more. Then added: "I'll answer for you then." Destini turned to me and said, "Yeah, she gonna stay with us."

Naomi's facial expression changed, giving Destini an amused, confused, puzzled look.

"So what is it?" I asked Naomi, wanting for her to confirm it. "Are you staying?"

She looked back to Destini again, then back at me, "Yeah...," she finally broke. "I could stay for a while."

"All righty then." I smiled with Destini. "Let me get you something to throw on in the meantime." I left the room.

Naomi looked at Uncle James, then back to Destini. "Why are y'all so anxious for me to stay for dinner?"

Uncle James was the first one to answer her. "Because that boy doesn't usually cook," he said. "But when he does, his meals taste like Pattie LaBelle smothered in spicy bacon gravy.... Mmm-mm! I could just taste her now."

Naomi faked a cough, hoping to bring him back.

"Oh, excuse me. I just got a little carried away," he claimed. "But his cooking is really good. One of the best ever."

"Oh, really? So I see I'll have to invite you to try one of my main courses, one day."

Destini quickly asked: "What about me?"

"Of course you, too. You'll always be invited."

Within minutes, I returned back to the family room with the whole hook-up for Naomi: a towel, wash rag, red Polo T-shirt, and gray sweat shorts. "So when you get ready, just kick your clothes out of the bathroom for me and I'll wash them for you. Okay?"

"No, that's alright. You don't have to."

"But I insist."

She smiled; then immediately asked, "Why are you being so kind to me?"

"Why"

She nodded.

She wouldn't understand if I told her the truth. How can she? She's a woman. And a woman doesn't have the slightest idea how a man can control his emotions, especially when he gets into a heated argument with his old lady—just like the one I had with Samara a few minutes ago. Because, let the truth be told, the first thing that came to mind to help me relieve some tension off my back was to engage in a good fuck!

What else a man like myself can ask for under such pressure? A psychologist?

I think not, because I rather stick my dick in just about any pussy hole right now to help release some stress off my back than to have some psycho with a fucking PhD—a Pure hater Degree—to tell me what's good for me.

Like I said, I couldn't tell her the truth, so I told her a boldface lie. "There isn't any particular reason why I'm being kind to you. I'm just showing you my appreciation for what you have done for me so far. That's the least I can offer you."

"Oh." And on the note, she disappeared.

About ten minutes later, Naomi stood behind the bathroom door, probably naked when she cracked the door open and slid her clothes out to me. I held onto them and started walking up the hallway until I heard a heavy hissing sound; I stopped.

It was Uncle James. "Over here," he tried to whisper from inside the closet, then motioned his hand at me.

I went over there. Then he started combing through Naomi's clothes as if he had lost something in there.

"What are you looking for?"

"Her panties stupid-ass!"

"Man" —I snatched her clothes away from him— "you needa go find some fucking help, you sick bastard!" I walked away from him, striding straight for the laundry room.

A moment later, while Destini was laying on her back playing a video game, Naomi walked in the family room as if she were on a Jerry Springer's make-over show.

Uncle James' mouth gaped.

Uncle James couldn't believe it.

Naomi had the sweat shorts that she was wearing, rolled up at the top so they could grip around her hips for a better hold; she had tied a knot in the back of her Polo shirt to make it fit right.

And it did.

"So what the hell happened to you in there?" Uncle James asked her.

"What are you talking about?"

"This!" He motioned his hand up and down, scanning her body. Then added: "Whew-wee! You sure look like a sweet grape on a vine bush ... just waiting to get plucked!"

Naomi looked shocked, if not offended.

Destini sat up; and Naomi immediately took a seat beside her.

"Do you wanna play against me?" Destini pushed the joystick at her.

Without a word, Naomi grabbed the gizmo and hunched over a bit, with her elbows resting on her knees to take the pressure off her nipples, since she wasn't wearing a bra.

Unfortunately, Uncle James had noticed that fact, getting a glimpse of the shaded areas that showed faintly through the shirt.

Naomi felt his eyes lock on her breasts; she felt violated. She threw the towel around her neck, allowing it to hang freely over her shoulders.

But Uncle James had all the time in the world to wait on more nipple exposure. Either one of them will do. So he waited. And waited. But there was still no nipple exposure. Not even a damn titties shot. Her towel was blocking the view. He wiped his forehead and said, "God-lee! It's sure hot in here."

Naomi made the mistake of glancing over at him.

"Is it just me," he began to ask her, "or is it just hotter than a devil's fart in here?"

"It feels quite fine to me."

"Oh, does it?"

She nodded, trying to avoid any eye contact.

"So, you're telling me that you're not even thirsty for something to drink?"

She turned to him and gave him an empty stare; then a thought came to mind: "Come to think of it, I am thirsty."

"Yeah, me too. So while you're getting yourself something to drink, why don't you be kind enough and bring me back a cold glass of lemonade from outta the fridge? Thanks."

Her plan had backfired: She wanted him to leave the room, not her.

He smiled.

She tried to smile back. "You're welcome."

He kept his eyes on her breasts; and if that fails, he could at least get a view of her backside.

She got up from the couch and twisted to Destini. "Sweetie, would you like to have something to drink while I'm in there?"

"Uh-huh, some orange soda," Destini said, keeping her eyes on the video game, while twisting and jolting her upper body along with the joystick in her hand.

"Do you mean orange juice, sweetie?"

Destini sighed. "See what you made me do? You made me mess up. I told you orange soda, not juice."

Naomi left the room without responding. She headed straight for the kitchen.

"**I know they** gonna love this," I mumbled to myself, while flipping chicken breasts over the gravy in the saucepan.

"Mmmmm-mm.... Now, that smells good."

I was startled at first until I looked over my shoulder. "Oh, it's you." I turned back around to finish cooking, then immediately took another good look at Naomi. I was like, Wow! I was impressed. It's not so often that I come across an authentic chick like this, with no makeup on. Some real Erykah Badu shit, like the time when she exposed herself in the Window Seat video: accept her or reject her for being real and unadulterated. But in my case, I had to play my cards right. I started bobbing my head to let her know that I liked the look she had. "If I didn't know you were inside this house, I almost didn't recognize you."

"Not you, too."

"What are you talking about?"

"Nothing." She stepped away from me. "Where do you keep the drinking glasses?"

I motioned my head to the side. "Over there in the cabinet.... Top shelf."

"Thanks."

And as she was about to finish pouring her drinks, I asked, "Can you do something for me really quick?"

"Like what?"

"Can you grab me a flat pan from outta the cabinet, underneath the sink?"

"Sure." She got the pan for me, then began to walk away.

"Hold up for a second. I need your help on something else too."

She stopped and drew near. "What else you need me to do for you?"

"Place that pan over there" —I motioned my head to the side since my hands were occupied— "so I can put the chicken in there."

She did it and complimented my cooking with, "That sure smells good."

"Good?"

"Oh, I'm sorry," she corrected with a joke. "I meant, it smells scrumptious. Now, does that sound better for you?" She laughed. "I can't wait to taste your cooking."

I scooped a little gravy onto the wooden spoon. "Here you go, taste this to see what to expect later."

She leaned in.

"Girl!" I yanked the spoon back from her mouth. "You better blow on it before you burn yourself.

"Girl?" she mocked me back.

I smiled. "Now, you know I didn't mean it like that, in that kinda way, Woman!"

She laughed. "Ohhh.... Boy!"

I smiled back. And that's when it happened, all in slow motion: She stuck her lips out, forming a tiny hole directly in the center of her mouth—like a perfect tight o –blowing softly on the spoon. I stared at her pretty lips and fell into a trance. Then, a déjà vu blindfolded me. It sorta felt like I was here before. Perhaps in another lifetime. But then, moments from my previous relationship started running through my mind. Memories of a remarkable time when I used to be in love with Jessica. I thought about the few times when she used to share her dreams with me, about how she wanted to be so much like Oprah Winfrey; have a family; and have my children. Then, I thought of a different time when we used to cook those quick meals for each other: fish and grits or shrimp pasta. And it was at that same moment when I realized how much I missed my past. I guess those were the good old—

"Mmmmm...," Naomi exclaimed, interrupting my thoughts. "This tastes delicious.... I'm really impressed, he wasn't lying."

"He?" She threw me off with that one. "Who wasn't lying?"

"Your uncle, but that's not important. When are we going to eat? You made me hungry."

"I made you hungry." I sorta laughed.

"Yeah." She laughed back.

Just when our conversation started to escalate, Destini ran in the kitchen. "Where's our drinks at?!" she asked, sounding a bit dehydrated but full of energy. "I'm thirsty!"

Naomi stood silently with a smile on her face.

To which I cut in and told Destini, "I see you're up and running again."

Then, in a wink of an eye, she had the audacity to transform her facial expression to something painful while placing her hands on her stomach, and moaned: "Ow-owww, I think I'm gonna die."

"Girl, stop lying." I almost laughed at her cheap performance. "And since you're feeling better now, go set the table up for us."

"I knew I shoulda stayed in there." She headed for the kitchen cabinet but when she heard the doorbell, she took off like an illegal alien, running for the border.

The doorbell rang again.

"Waita second, I'm coming!" Destini finally unlocked the front door.

It was Carlton. "What did I tell you about answering the door?" He stepped inside the house with a box of bootleg DVD's in his hands.

She shrugged. "I dunno."

"You don't know, huh?" he mocked her as he headed toward the family room. "One day, when you keep answering this damned door, you're gonna regret it. Watch!"

Destini didn't pay him any mind. She just ran back into the kitchen.

When I saw Naomi from the side, I was impressed. She had nice thighs, something I truly admire in a woman.

And Destini caught me looking at Naomi.

So I told her, "Why don't you grab the juice outta the fridge for me?"

"Why?"

"Because I said so, that's why."

She frowned. "Why we always gotta drink juice?"

Naomi looked at me.

I looked back at her, then at Destini. "You don't wanna drink any juice?"

She slowly shook her head. "No...."

"Oh, alright then. If you don't wanna drink any juice, you don't have to. And to make you feel better, we're gonna drink whatever you're drinking. Okay?"

She smiled. "Fo' real?!"

"Have I ever lied to you before?"

"No. I don't think so."

"Okay then, we're gonna have whatever you're drinking," I told her, believing that she was going to grab the orange soda from out of the refrigerator, or perhaps even the Sierra Mist. But she didn't: She pulled the milk out instead and placed it on the table. I looked at Naomi again; she back at me. We stared at each other for a considerable amount of time. A sorta long one. I just couldn't believe this.

Destini turned to Naomi, then pointed her tiny finger at the cabinet. "Can you get the chocolate syrup for me?" she asked in a way that it would be hard to refuse.

"Sure."

I looked at Destini. This is some bullshit! I thought. I didn't want any chocolate milk for dinner. And it seemed like Naomi knew what I had on my mind when she looked at me. She smiled to loosen me up some.

It worked.

Then, all of a sudden, Naomi did something silly: She started wobbling her head from side to side, as if she were sitting on top of a dashboard, to imitate me with her eyes slightly crisscrossed. "We're gonna drink whatever you're drinking, sweetie," she even tried to mimic my voice, but then her facial expression changed as though she had thought about something else.

I just kept my eyes on her.

"You're a great dad," she said.

I gave her a half smile, because I didn't think so.

Destini broke in between us: "Can we have cookies and ice cream too?"

I turned to answer her, but before I could respond, Naomi beat me to the punch: "Hon, not tonight."

"But everybody eats dessert after dinner. They show it on TV."

Naomi and I burst out laughing because Destini had shot us a look that you could only find on one of those Little Rascal characters: looking innocent, but mischievous as hell.

"Yeah," I finally broke weak, "you can have some dessert. But only if you finish everything I put on your plate."

Destini agreed.

When Carlton walked into the kitchen and saw me and Naomi laughing, he greeted me with a "What's happening" then looked at Naomi. "Don't I know you from somewhere?"

She nodded. "Yeah, from last night."

He seemed lost.

So she added, "Here, in the kitchen: Last night."

"Oh, yeah, that's right!" He then approached the fridge and took out the pitcher of lemonade. "You looked a little different from the last time I saw you. I thought you were a dude last night at first until I saw your chest.

Chest?

Naomi cocked her neck back a little, probably feeling a bit thrown off by his remarks.

But who could blame her? Guys are known to have chests, females have breasts.

"But you never know these days," Carlton went on to say, raising his drink near his mouth. "We have a lot of weirdos out here on the streets who can just go into any cosmetic surgery joint and buy themselves a set of boobs. And you would never know the difference unless you check out their high school yearbook." He tipped the glass to his mouth and took a swig. "So," he paused for a brief moment, looking at Naomi's breasts, "are those—"

"Yo, Carlton!" I cut him off. "What are you doing tonight?"

"I don't know." He turned to me. "Why, what do you have in mind?"

"I cooked dinner and we have enough food here for you, if you wanna plate."

"If I wanna plate?" He gave me a fake laugh. "Hell, yeah, I wanna plate of food. That shit sounds stupid as hell, my nigga! Don't a farmer needa chicken to pluck and a Catholic priest needa young boy to fu@*—!"

"Destini!" Naomi yelled over Carlton's comment. "Can you let your uncle know that dinner is ready for me?"

"Do I have to?"

Oh, hell nah! I stepped in. "Destini, go get Uncle James! And stop giving people your lip!"

She pouted her way out of the kitchen.

A short while later we all sat around the table to enjoy our meal. When we were about halfway through it, the phone on the kitchen wall began to ring.

"Lemme get it," Uncle James said since he was the closest to the phone. He answered it on the fourth ring, listened for a second, and then said, "Uhhh.... I don't know. I just stepped inside the house. Let me go check for you. But, who should I say is calling?"

There was another pause.

Uncle James seemed alarmed when he looked at me.

This foolish nigga must think I'm retarded or something, Samara thought, when Uncle James covered the phone receiver with his hand.

It was so obvious.

She snapped with a strong, "Hello!"

But Uncle James didn't respond to her, at least not when she wanted him to.

She barely shook her head out of frustration and unconsciously gave an evil stare at her friends, Vida and Stacy, while they were getting dressed to go out to a club tonight.

Vida shot her with curious look, wondering if everything was all right. But Samara wasn't in the mood to explain anything to her, or to anyone else for that matter—at this moment.

Uncle James came back over the phone line. "Nah, he's not in anymore," he told her. "He musta stepped out a minute ago. But as soon as he gets back, I'll tell—"

"So," she interrupted him with, "who is that I hear in the background?"

"Huh?"

"I said, so who's that I'm hearing in the background?" she semi-repeated herself, growing more frustrated. "I can hear his voice in the background. I'm not stupid, you know."

"Oh, man! He just stepped back in the house. Hold on."

Samara noticed that Uncle James tried to cover the receiver again, but he accidently left a small gap between his fingers. She heard everything he said: "She heard you; she know you're here...."

Then, Samara got distracted by the noise Vida and Stacy were making in the background. She stormed out of the room to the bathroom with a black thong on.

Within seconds, Uncle James came back over the phone. "Hey, Samara!" he said in a phony tone. "DaShawn said—"

"I heard what that muthafucker said!" she interrupted him again. "He must have one of his bitches over there with him! Just tell that short-dick muthafucker that I said to get the fuck on this phone!"

"Hold on."

Samara pressed her ear closer to the receiver to listen in on him. Then she heard him say, "She said she wanna talk to you." Then, immediately afterward, she heard a click.

"That bastard!" She was really ticked off now. She called back, and Uncle James answered the phone on the third ring. "Lemme speak to that muthafucker!"

"Hold on for a second," he told her. Then said to someone else, without covering the mouth piece on the phone this time: "It's her again."

Samara lost her cool. "I don't think you know who the hell I am."

"Huh, did you say something?"

"Man!" I kept it real with Uncle James, "just give her the third degree and hang up on her again!"

I guess that was all Uncle James wanted to hear, because he gladly put the receiver back to his mouth and said, "Samara, are you still there?" There was a short pause. Then he went on to say, "I told DaShawn what you wanted me to tell him and.... Yeah, waita second so I can tell you first.... Uh-huh, but.... Hey! Stop cutting me off! ... Thank you. Well, I wanna tell you he has a young fine, dark Easter Bunny at his side, chillin' over here with him.... Yes, right now.... Uh-huh.... No, I'm not gonna tell her that: she has class. More class than you could possibly have." He winked his eye at me. Then continued with his phone call: "Yeah, yeah, yeah, I have heard worse than that before.... But.... But, listen up for a second!" He snapped. "We can sing together, but we can't talk at the same time. Just hear me out first, because there's something else I wanna tell you regarding— ... What is it? ... Sure thing, that's what I'm telling you, but you keep cutting me off.... Thank you. Well, do you remembered when you said that my nephew DaShawn has a small weenie, right?"

I felt embarrassed. She couldn't have possibly said that about Goliath, I mulled.

Uncle James continued: "Yeah, yeah. Exactly. I just wanted to paraphrase it a bit, that's all.... Well, has it ever crossed your mind that his Mr. Johnson ain't exactly small at all, but it's the other way around?" He paused. Then went on to add, "What's the other way around? ... That's simple. The other way around is this, you stupid nincompoop! Have you ever thought that YOUR SLOPPY PUSSY IS JUST WIDE AS A LAKE AND DEEP AS THE SEA, Beeech!" he shouted, then slammed the receiver into the cradle, looked at me and Naomi with a delightful smile on his face. "What a third degree, huh?" He walked out of the kitchen.

I was speechless. I wanted to say something to hide my shock, but I couldn't think of anything. So I tried another route: I lifted my untouched glass of chocolate milk to my mouth and started guzzling it down my throat.

"Well," Naomi took the initiative to spark up conversation, "if that was the third degree, I absolutely don't want to know what the first and second degrees are."

I almost spat my chocolate milk out of my mouth.

She continued under her breath: "Wide as a lake, deep as the sea.... I mean like, whoa...."

I had no other choice but give her that innocent look, with a light head shake, as though I didn't know what Uncle James' third degree was all about.

"Yeah, right!" She burst out laughing. "I just hope I never receive a degree like that from y'all."

I waited a few seconds before I said, "You're too much of a lady to receive any type of degree like that." I got up and started cleaning off the table.

"Let me give you a hand."

"Thanks."

After Naomi was finished cleaning off the counter-top, she placed the dishes and eating utensils into the dishwasher. I grabbed the broom near the closet door and started sweeping and that's when it felt like I had another flash of déjà vu visiting me again. I smiled. I felt like I had known Naomi longer than I actually did. Perhaps I knew her from another lifetime—many, many years ago. Probably during the first empire of China, I thought. No! Better yet, what about in the nineteenth Dynasty of Egypt?

Yeah. Back in Akhetaton's day in 1347 BC when Black people were strong and mighty before the invasion of others.

That's where I could imagine Naomi, running around practically naked with her sort of transparent, see-through dress on, with her titties hanging freely, and her being my... I think I might be pushing it here.

"Why are you looking at me like that?"

"Huh?" I broke my reverie from her.

Then she repeated: "Why are you looking at me like that?"

Naomi and I strolled into the family room and found Destini and Carlton playing with the Xbox, as expected.

"All right, Destini." I stood in front of her. "That's about enough of the video games. You need to go take your shower and start getting ready for bed."

"But it ain't my bedtime yet."

"Destini, what did I just tell you?"

"That's not fair!" She got off the couch. "How can you stay up and I can't?"

"Because I pay the bills around here and you don't." I then pointed toward the hallway. "Now go take your shower. And please, don't make me repeat myself."

She mumbled something under her breath as she walked out of the room.

I felt relieved. Uncle James disappeared without a trace; and I can't say where Carlton went to, because he dipped out of the room when I told Destini she had to get ready for bed. So now, it was just the two of us, Naomi and me, all alone. At last. The scene looked perfect.

"Well," this was when Naomi made the record scratch, bringing an irritated squeak to my ears when she said, "I think it's time for me to be heading home now."

"You know you can stay a little while longer, if you want to." I practically begged her without saying pretty-please.

She looked at her wristwatch. "No. I can't. It's getting late and I have a lotta catching up to do."

"BUT WHO'S GONNA SING ME TO SLEEP, IF YOU LEAVE?"

Naomi and I spun toward the doorway. There was no one there.

I shouted, "Destini!" Then, I waited for a response.

After a few seconds she shouted back, trying to disguise her voice: "She's in the bathroom, taking a shower...."

"Oh, yeah?!" I started walking up the hallway with Naomi.

"Yeah! SHE'S, IN, THE, SHOWER!" Destini's voice sounded much clearer than before.

I snuck up on her and caught her laying on her stomach in the hallway. "Girl, get your ass of the floor!" I yanked her up by the ear, forcing her to stand up on her tippy-toes. "Didn't I tell you to hit the shower already?"

"Ow-ow-ow-ow," she yelped with her ear facing the ceiling. "That hurts! That hurts! You're gonna pull it outta the socket!"

I released her ear. "Why haven't you taken your shower yet?"

"But I did already. I did."

"So you're telling me that you took your shower already?"

"Uh-huh."

"If that's true, why are you still wearing the same clothes then?"

She shrugged her thin shoulders. "I dunno." She looked at Naomi, then back at me. "I didn't ... have ... anything else to wear...?"

"So why do I see chicken grease right there?"

She looked at her arm and hesitated for a moment. "I musta forgot to wash that part when I took my shower." She then rubbed her arm on her pants. "But look at this arm. It's clean. Look!"

"Girl—" I started to put her in check, but I decided to go with something else: "What do you want from me?"

"Nothing."

"So why are you not getting ready for bed yet?"

"I am ready. I just wanted Naomi to sing me a song before she leaves, because I don't like how you sing anymore."

I was about to say something to that, but Naomi cut in and told her, "If I agree to sing you a song, will you be good and do what your daddy tells you to do?"

Destini hesitated. "Does that mean everything he says?"

"Girl!" I nearly flipped on her.

"Okay, okay, okay." She nodded; then looked at Naomi. "Yeah."

Then, Naomi took back over: "Go take another shower for me, and I'll be with you shortly to sing you a song that I know you would like. Okay?"

"Okay!" Destini ran to the bathroom, and we heard the door slam.

Naomi and I looked at each other; she was the first one to smile.

"Please allow me to show you something while you're waiting on her to get finished." I led her to the den where I spent most of my leisure time.

The den was more like a mini Chinatown sweatshop. There was a sewing machine, a drawing board, two mannequins, and all those other miscellaneous stuff that dress shops have in their workrooms. I showed her my art designs and told her all about my dreams of being this well-known fashion designer one day.

She seemed to admire my vision when she told me, "You have to follow your dreams, and when you capture them, never let go of them."

I stared at my drawings for a moment, digesting her words. Then said, "But how can I when no one wants to give me a chance?"

"Yeah, I know what you mean. That sort of remind me of this one time, about three years ago, when my best friend Ciara—." she paused. Then added: "Oh, my God! My friend Ciara! She works in the fashion industry. Maybe she can help you out."

"How is that? Is she an agent?"

"No, not really. But she's a secretary to Decorous' Fashion World. I don't see a problem with her helping you get a foot in the door, with an interview that is. But the rest would be on you."

"Yeah, I'd appreciate that if you could hook something up for me."

With that being said, she immediately made a call and asked Ciara if she could set me up for an appointment with Decorous'. After a few seconds, Naomi smiled and gave me her thumbs ups, then spoke back into the receiver. "Okay, I'll speak to you later.... Okay. Ciao." When she hung up, she kept that same smile on her face.

I smiled back. "So, what'd she say?"

"She said she's going to pull a few strings for us."

"Thanks."

Then all of a sudden Destini came running into the den. "I'm finished now!" she exclaimed, trying to give Naomi a hint that she was ready for bed.

"A two minute shower, huh?"

"You can say whatever you want. Just look! The grease is gone now." She stretched her arm out to me. "And I changed my clothes too."

"Well, I believe you if you say so."

Naomi took over and started to lead Destini up the hall. As we reached Destini's bedroom door, Naomi asked her, "Why's your hair still dry?

I just walked away when I saw Destini's animated-smile vanish from her face.

"I dunno." I heard the little rascal say when I bent the corner. "It probably got dry already."

Minutes later, Naomi was singing Destini a song by Anita Baker: "My Angel". But she altered the song a bit by sliding Destini's name in it.

Destini was loving it.

The atmosphere was wonderful. Destini was laying on her back with her eyes fighting to stay open. The more she fought to stay awake, the more Naomi's voice softened to a smoother tone.

And it was working.

As I stood at the doorway watching them, I smiled. The scene was a Kodak moment, for sure. Destini had her hand cocked up on Naomi's left ear, twirling it between her fingers. A few seconds later Destini took about four heavy winks and before she knew it, on the fifth wink, her eyelids never came back up.

We snuck out of the room and went outside.

The air was cozy with a nice tropical breeze as I walked Naomi to the car. "You know," I began to advise her again, "you can stay a little while longer because the night is still young, and I can offer you a casual conversation over a good hot cup of coffee. Just the two of us. I swear, nothing more, nothing less. I promise."

She looked tempted to stay, but shook her head. "Perhaps on another day." She opened her car door. "I have to go home and get some work done. Like I told you before, I have a lotta catching up to do. I'm kinda behind schedule."

"So when am I gonna see you again?" I tried to sound cute. "Soon?"

She smiled. "Perhaps." She got in her car and shut the door behind her.

And as she was backing her car out of the driveway, I shouted out: "When?!"

She stopped and rolled the window down. "Let's allow destiny to play her role."

"Oh, you want me to ask Destini?"

"No, I'm talking about the other destiny.... Fate!"

"Ohhh." I felt moved. She was playing hard. I smiled back and watched her drive away.

When I stepped back in the house, I strolled straight to Destini's doorway and stood there for a long moment—lost in my thoughts—watching her. A smile slowly grew on my face. She's a wild one, I noticed. She was squirming in bed like a worm, probably trying to find a comfortable spot. So I decided to walk away before my presence woke her.

I strolled back to the den to touch up on a few of my art works, because I wasn't quite ready to call it a night yet.

My cell phone vibrated; I looked at it.

It was Jennifer: some white chick who I had met at the gas station the other day.

I smiled and took the call.

Naomi felt at ease: Everything was running smooth for her.

She scrambled through the radio dial to find something casual to listen to on her way back home. To her surprise HOT 105 was playing "My Angel" by Anita Baker.

What a coincidence, she thought.

Then she began to think back on the previous few hours spent. There was that one moment when she remembered running into the kitchen and seeing Destini screaming and crying over the kitchen sink after she got scalded with a hot cup of coffee. She also remembered seeing tears filling Destini's eyes, running down her face.

"Oh, Jesus!" Naomi remembered saying just before she ran to the sink while Destini was being sprayed with the kitchen water hose. "What happened to her?"

"I think she was making herself some coffee, and accidently burned herself with it."

It was at that same moment when Destini's screams turned into a whimpering cry. "Oww … I'm gonna die," she said between her weeping. "I'm gonna die. I don't wanna die. I'm too young to die."

"Girl, you're not gonna die," Naomi remembered assuring her. "You only got burned with hot water, so stop saying that. You're getting me scared!"

Destini kept her eyes on Naomi and sobbed. "Before I die … I wanna let you know something."

"What?"

"You are my best friennnnnnd.…"

"Don't cry and worry yourself. You are not gonna die. Just believe me, sweetie." Then Naomi remembered saying, "She needs medical attention. Let me get my car ready."

Other than the radio playing in the background now, Naomi's mind had a moment of silence. The silence didn't last long. Not long at all. It only last for about five seconds. Then she thought about how the evening had ended from singing Destini to sleep up until the time when she was about to get in her car, about to leave.

Then her recollection echoed: "You know you can stay a little while longer, if you want to. Because the night is still young. And I can offer you a casual conversation over a good hot cup of coffee. Just the two of us. I swear, nothing more, nothing less. I promise."

Naomi smiled unconsciously to herself, breaking up her reverie, and made a complete stop at the yellow light—long before it turned red.

I got up from my chair, looked out the den window, and started gathering up my art materials, placing them back in a neat pile. Then I suddenly heard someone knocking on the front door.

It was sort of like those tiny knocks. The ones you could barely hear.

I looked at my wristwatch. It was 10:20 p.m., and the thought of Naomi came to mind. I smiled. I headed for the living room, feeling certain it was her. I opened the front door without asking who it was.

And I'll be damned!

It was Samara. She was just standing there with her arms wrapped across her breasts, looking extremely pissed-off!

"What the fuck do you want?" I just stood there with my hand on the door.

"What do you mean by what I want?"

"Yo, check this out: I'm through with all your bullshit! You needa take that shit somewhere else."

"Oh, I see it. You musta found yourself a new bitch to be with now, huh?" Seeing that I wouldn't reply to that, she added: "So you just fuck me and kick me to the curb once you're through with me. Is that it?"

"Are you fucking crazy or something? Because the way I recall it, you were the one who was screaming at the top of your lungs, saying all that bullshit about you didn't know why you were fucking with my sorry-ass!"

"Yeah," she tried to sound seductive in a coaxing way, "I said that because you had said my pa-nanny was big like the sea, remember? You hurt my feelings, boo, when you said that about me."

Finally, I was convinced she was one of those loonies who flew out of the cuckoo's nest. And just when I was about to argue the facts of the matter, she threw her tongue straight in my mouth.

I swear, she caught me off guard.

I tried to push her away, but she held on to me with both hands wrapped around my back. I gave in on the third shove and kissed her back. Within seconds I immediately caught a hard-on. I pressed my meat against her stomach. I went for her shirt and ripped it off—straight down the middle. She ripped mine off too, then stuck her hand inside my pants. She pulled my dick out. I couldn't take it any longer. My adrenaline was pumping fast. I picked her up a bit, just high enough to slide my rod inside her; she saddled up, straddling her legs around my waist. I carried her to my bedroom.

There was something about her femininity that caught me off guard every time she threw herself on me. Her sweet, phat ass was like bait, and I bit after it every time I had a chance. It was irresistible. I sorta felt like Chris Brown when he accepted Rihanna back: Weak! But what made this moment different from any other time was the fact that she had tried to belittle my manhood: She had called Goliath small.

Of all sizes ... small.

The nerve of this bitch, I thought. Goliath had a fat, retarded head and stood seven inches long, with a gangsta lean.

I laid her on the bed in a kitty-position, straight on her back, with me on top of her. She opened up for me and I started fucking the hell out of her. Believe me, every man has an ego to live up to; and I had my God-given-right to live up to mine, too.

"Oh, yes!" she moaned in my ear. "Oh, yes! Uh! Oh, yes! Yes! But not so hard, baby.... You're hurting me."

Hurting you?

I added a little flavor to the scene: I dropped one of her legs flat on the bed and threw her other leg over my shoulder. Her pussy was stretched vertically tight—and just right.

"Uhh, yes," she moaned some more. Then said, "Yes baby, fuck me! Fuck me, baby!"

"Take this dick." I kept long-stroking this bitch with an undulated thrust, straight to her back wall.

"Uh-uh. Hold up, baby." She rested her hands against my chest, "You're hurting me! Hold up, stop. Stop! Stop for a second...."

And I did, only for a quick moment, until I remembered what this trick had said about my dick being small. I cranked myself back up, giving her everything I had.

"Uh-uh-uh, stop!" she nearly screamed in my ear. "You're hurting me!"

"Hold up, I'm about to cum," I told a damn lie so I could finish ramming my souljah inside her.

"Uh, stop! Ow! Hold the fuck up! Ow! Sto-stop! Stop it right now, you're hurting me! ... I said, STOP! I mean it!"

Damn near every major city has a liquor store in the heart of the ghetto where patrons tend to use as a stomping ground.

But Mr. Yin—the owner of Paul's Liquor which was located on the corner of 183rd Street—didn't like the fact that winos hang out in front of his store, looking for some sorta handout from the patrons who were walking in and out of his establishment. It was bad for business, as he always tried to tell them. However, he found himself repeatedly telling the same people over and over again to leave the premise after they purchase something from his store, but it seemed like no one would take heed to him. But this night was sort of different from any other night.

Out of all people who were standing outside of Mr. Yin's store, there was one loafer who got under his skin.

"You buy, you leave!" Mr. Yin said in broken English, while holding a broom in his hand. "No more, in front of store.... I call police.... Leave now!"

"You just waita second there, Mr. Yin," Uncle James said, while holding himself up against the store window, drunk. "You just waita second there." He tried to put his twisted thoughts together.

"Wait, what?"

"No-no-no, Mr. Yin." Uncle James slowly swayed his finger from side to side. "Don't you mean, Wait for what? That's the problem with y'all illegal aliens, who be sneaking over here in this country: Y'all be fucking the English language up."

"You tell him James!"

Mr. Yin looked at Albert, then cut back to Uncle James. "You mudda-fuckah!" he snapped. "I say, Wait for what? I know what I say. I call police now!" He then went for the door handle.

"Okay, okay." Uncle James stumbled forward and grabbed Mr. Yin's arm, trying to get serious. "I'm the police. How can I help you, sir?"

Albert and a few other loafers laughed aloud.

"You no police! I know police. I call now!" Mr. Yin broke his arm free from Uncle James' grip.

"Ho-ho-hold up, Mr. Yin! Lemme show you my proof." Uncle James raised his shirt just high enough to show Mr. Yin the butt handle of Destini's water gun, which he had tucked in his pants.

The loafers laughed again.

"Oh, oh, you got gun! I got gun, too!" Mr. Yin then tore his way back into the store, reached over the counter and grabbed a M-16 assault rifle. And by the time he came back outside, the whole crowd had dispersed.

There wasn't a soul in sight. Everybody scattered in their own separate direction; especially Uncle James, he was the first one to get the hell out of there.

"COME BACK!" Mr. Yin shouted. "COME BACK! YOU MUDDA-FUCKAH! ... I GOT GUN TOO! MUDDA-FUCKAH!" He then pointed his M-16 in the air and busted off three shots. "YOU BITCH! COME BACK!"

I flipped Samara over on all four.

So who has a small dick now, I pondered, while pounding my monster tool inside of her. Who has the small dick now?!

"Oh, yes!" Samara tightened her face, but in a porno way, with her mouth agape. "Oh yes, fuck me! Fuck me! Fuck me, harder. Fuck this pussy! It's yours!"

And that was exactly what I was going to do until I thought I heard several knocks coming from the front door. I stopped.

"What's the matter, baby?"

"It's nothing," I told her, but I kept my ear on alert. "I thought I had heard something out there. But I guess my mind was playing tricks on me." I put my dick back in motion and started fucking that gushy pussy some more.

"Oh, yesssss.... Yes, baby." She threw one hand on the headboard, while the other hand stayed on the bed as she pumped back, picking up speed. "Fuck this pussy! Give it to me. Give it to me!"

The doorbell rang twice.

Who in the hell can this be?

I stopped, all out of breath. My heart pounding. I looked at the alarm clock on the night stand. It wasn't even 11 o'clock yet.

I slid my dick out of her and got out of bed. "I'd be back in a second," I said, while sliding on my boxer shorts. Then I patted her on the ass. "So keep that pussy hot for me till I get back." I strode to the front door and looked out the peephole to see who was out there. But I didn't see anybody. Just when I was about to head back to the bedroom, I heard Uncle James blabbing off at the mouth, from the other side of the door.

"Oh, yeah, I like how you feel. You can hold me up any time you want to, sweetie-pie."

I turned back around and opened the door for him. And when I did, he fell directly into my arms. "Dammit man! You smell like a fucking drunk!" Then I tried to get a better grip on him.

"Guess who I found on my way—" he started to say before I let him go. He landed dead on his face.

"Naomi!" I said, not quite believing my eyes. "What are you doing here?"

"I think I would like to take you up on that offer." She stood outside with a cute smile on her face.

"Now?" I stepped out of the house, trying to conceal my surprise, closing the door behind me.

"Of course, right now."

"Well … I mean," I stammered. "… It can't be right now. I was just about to go to bed. But what about tomorrow?"

"Oh, I'm sorry," she managed to say before she took a step away from me, wiping the smile off her face. "I didn't know you had a visitor over."

I tried to find the right words to explain everything to her. But the only words that came out of my mouth were, "Nah. It ain't what it looks like."

She stopped. Her smile began to grow back. She was all ears. I felt pressure to lie to her—if I wanted anything to do with her—so I just went ahead and said, "I wish I did. But I don't have anybody over here with me—"

"Is everything okay out here, baby?"

I twisted around about the same time I saw Naomi's smile disappear.

It was Samara, standing by the door, wearing that same T-shirt I had on earlier today. The same one Naomi complimented me in.

"Yeah." I couldn't believe this bitch, Samara! My face was painted with outrage. "Everything is alright. I'll be inside in a minute."

"Okay, baby, I'll be in bed waiting for you."

Fuck! That was the nail in the coffin!

I turned back to Naomi, and before I could say anything, she asked me, "Who's that? Samara?"

I'm not sure, but I think I kinda nodded my head. "Yeah, that's her. But please, allow me to explain everything to you."

She raised her hand, indicating that I should stop talking.

I did.

Then she went on to say, "You don't owe me any explanation." She headed back to her car and got inside. "But I do apologize for coming to your home unannounced, without asking you first."

I wanted to say something to her, but I couldn't. She looked crushed. I had been caught in a lie. A horrible lie. So I just stood there in the middle of the street with my boxer shorts on, no T-shirt, watching her drive away until her taillights disappeared.

I went back inside the house, straight to my bedroom, and found Samara laying on the bed, waiting on me. And I do mean waiting on me: She had her knees raised and apart, rubbing her finger along the line of her pussy lips. "Look what I have for you," she said.

At any other time I would have been tempted. But now, "I'm not in the mood anymore." I just laid on the bed, giving her the cold shoulder.

But it seemed like she wanted to convince me otherwise when she reached for my dick and said, "Well, I just gotta see about that then."

She lowered her head to it.

I was like ... whatever.

I even went as far as to get my mind off of what she was doing to me by thinking about my light bill.

Then she stuck my dick inside her mouth.

I immediately shifted my thoughts to my car payment.

She worked her tongue around the head of my dick.

Ohhh, man....

I blinked a few times, fighting to keep my eyes open, shifting my thoughts to a book—The Templar Revelation—that I had recently read. It mentioned about how Jesus had his supposed sexual relationship with a chick named Mary Magdalene. Which...

Oh, man, that felt good.

I looked at Samara, then at the ceiling again.

Just focus.... Focus!

I went back to thinking about Jesus again, which I couldn't help but wonder if he got his....

Ohhh, shit! Samara was sucking the hell out of my dick.

She left her head up, then started flicking her tongue on the head of my dick; then buried her mouth over it again.

I had no other choice but close my eyes this time, getting the feel of her mouth working its way down on me. It felt tight and slimy. And I don't know why, but I thought about Mary Magdalene again. Probably because it felt original. I opened my eyes to make sure it was Samara. Oh, yes! It was a beautiful sight. It was her, but I thought of another female. A white chick I would love to fuck! I took another look at Samara, then fantasized. Her head was swerving and oscillating over my dick, up and down, inching down deeper and deeper. It didn't take long for my rising nature to grow stronger in her mouth. This shit was feeling too good to be true. I felt too relaxed. I took my mind off of Britney Spears and thought of nothing else but the blow job Samara was giving me.

I rested my hand on the back of Samara's head and allowed my hand to go on a vertical joyride while getting my dick slobbered on. No lie. She sucked my dick about ten minutes straight before I grabbed her back up to me and started kissing her again. She then slid her hand down to my dick and wiggled it between her pussy lips until the head of it slipped in her.

It was soaked down there. But in a good way.

I watched her ease her body straight up in a sitting position, straddled directly on top. With her knees on the side of me. Then she started to ride me in slow motion, twisting her hips from side to side, all sort of directions, going up and down. Believe me, she was like that: she knew how to work her pussy muscles. Really good. I held her breasts, twirling her nipples with my fingertips. She seemed to like how I was pinching on them. She got excited and started riding me with a little aggression, taking herself all the way to her climax. And when she released, she released heavily; and it wasn't long after I skeeted inside of her.

Well, she did say she was on the pills the last time we spoke on this subject. So, I kept pumping her pussy because I wanted to go for another round. But within seconds, something distracted me.

I stopped.

"No-no-no, keep going, baby..." she practically begged, while rocking her pelvic bone on me. "I wanna cum again. Don't stop."

"Shhh... I think I heard somebody outside my door."

"I didn't hear anything out there. That's your mind messing with you." She kept rocking, throwing in a few twirls, here and there, then going back to her rocking motion again, "C'mon, baby, don't stop. I want you to keep going for me."

I guess she was right, so I started working in her gushy pussy again. "Ho-ho-hold up!" I stopped moving. "There it goes again. I know you heard it that time?"

"Heard what?" She tried to listen for herself, while slowly gyrating her hips on me.

I thought I heard another squeak.

Samara stopped without me telling her to. "I heard it."

The next morning Uncle James was in the family room laying on his back, knocked out on the sofa, sounding like a roaring grizzly bear.

Then he suddenly stopped snoring; then twitched his nose. Whatever it was, it only irritated him for a second. Maybe for two seconds. He wasn't counting. He fell back asleep.

One Mississippi; two Mississippi; three Mississippi; four—. There it goes again, Uncle James felt something. He twitched his nose again. And again. But the tickle irritation wouldn't stop. Those damned flies, he probably thought when he parried his hand over his face to get it away from him.

Good! It was gone now.

Then within seconds, under another three seconds Mississippi count for the fifth time, that annoying tingle feeling came back again! But this time it irritated the hell out of him. It pushed him over the edge that he almost lost control over himself. It felt like it was about to crawl inside his nose.

He swung after it.

WHOP POW!

He slapped fire across his face and immediately leaped up, hoping to find the little bugaboo. He veered his head to the left, then to his right side. But there was nothing and no one in sight. He gave up and dropped his head back onto the sofa pillows. Within seconds, he was out for the count again.

As soon as he fell asleep, Destini came up from the other end of the sofa: A hidden spot where Uncle James' eyes couldn't see her. She wanted to laugh, but then again she didn't want to expose herself. Uncle James might wake up and realize it was her. She held her laughter back, quietly giggling to herself, with her hand over the mouth. Then, out of the blue, she smelled a sweet aroma.

Food!

She sped off into the kitchen, hoping to find Carlton there.

But it was the last person she expected it to be.

It was her archenemy, Samara, cooking breakfast.

"Whatchu doing here?" she asked Samara, immediately losing her appetite. But when Samara didn't answer her question, she tore her way down the hall.

"Daddy! Daddy! Daddy!" was all I heard in my sleep. It was more like a nightmare though, because I was being chased in my dream in some dark alleyway in Liberty City, near the Pork and Bean Project.

But the voice I heard sounded familiar to me. I stopped running.

"Daddy! Daddy!" Destini seemed to be panicking, rocking me back and forth. "Daddy! Get up! Hurry! Get up!"

That was when I realized it wasn't a dream after all. It was much worse: it was a new version of Nightmare on 176th Street. I forced one eye to open, and then the other one. Hold up! Did she just call me, Daddy, I wondered.

She most definitely did.

I was astonished. As I was getting up, she began to search around the room.

"What's the matter?" I asked, raising my head off the pillow.

"Where's my gun?" She ran pass my bed.

"What gun? What's going on?"

She then stuck her head out of the closet. "My water gun. Where is it?"

"I don't know."

She went back in the closet and said, "I've lost it. And I just found a robber inside our house, stealing our food! I gotta shoot her before she gets away from—"

"What?!" I leaped from the bed. "There's a thief inside the house?"

"Yeah!" She stepped out of the closet. "So help me look for my gun! Hurry up!" She looked under my bed. Then added: "We need it!"

To hell with that! I went for the baseball bat instead. "Where's he?"

"She's in the kitchen. Cooking!"

Hold up! "Did you say, she was in the kitchen, cooking?" I felt a bit confused. "Are you sure about that?"

"Yeah, I'm sure." She ran over to the other side of the bed, looking for her squirt gun. "It's Samara! And I'm gonna shoot her before she gets away because she ain't supposed to be here. She's stealing our food!"

"Sweetie." I sat at the edge of the bed before lying back down. "I know she's here."

Destini looked confused. "You know she's here?"

"Yeah, she slept over last night."

"In this house?"

"Yeah."

Destini became hysterical. "How could you do this to me?"

"Do what?"

"How could you bring her inside this house after what she has done to me? I hate her!"

"Okay, that's enough!" I took my stand. "Don't ever say that again. Because she hasn't done anything to you but tried to be your friend. So watch how you use your tongue around here."

"I hate her!" she cried out. "And nobody can change that! I hate her."

"Okay," I was just about to lose it. "Just give me one damn reason for hating her?!"

"She called my mommy a two-dollar-come-drinking-hole, and my mommy ain't no dummy! ... She doesn't know my mommy—"

"What?!" I cut her off. "What the hell did she call Jessica?"

"A two-dollar-come-drinking-hole...."

I felt like marching into the kitchen and confronting Samara, but then I considered the credibility of Destini's story. "Are you sure she said that?"

"Yeah." It seemed like she was about to cry.

I sprang from the bed, a little hotheaded. "Lemme get to the bottom of this bull—"

And it was at that same time the phone at my bedside began to ring; I snatched it.

It was Kevin. "My nigga," he began, "you ain't gonna believe who I bumped into last night."

"Yo, let me call you back in a few minutes because I see that I have to put this" —I just remembered about Destini's presence in the room with me— "this ... witch in check right now!"

Destini's eyes widened. "I knew it!" She started looking for her water gun again.

"Damn!" Kevin got my attention. "What happened?"

"This silly-ass broad said some crazy shit to Destini about her mom."

"Who said something about Jessica?"

"Samara!"

"What she said?"

It took me a few seconds to explain everything to Kevin.

"Damn, if she said that, that will be fuck'd up for real, dawg! But that's a little hard to believe though. Samara doesn't seem to be the type of hoe who would say some fuck-shit like that. You know?"

Yeah, I knew that too. "In a way, that was the same thing I was thinking.

Then the phone line became silent for a brief moment.

To which Kevin said, "My nigga, you know little-mama could be making that shit up about Samara because you're probably not giving her your full attention over there and shit."

I started bobbing my head: I kinda agreed with him on that. I looked at Destini, then told her, "Sweetie, let me speak on the phone in private. I need to speak to Kevin about something. I'll be with you in a second. Okay?"

Destini didn't say anything. She just walked out of the room, looking perplexed, probably because of my sudden change of emotion.

And after she left the room, I totally changed the conversation to a different topic. "Dawg," I tried not to get excited, "my hoe got some fire head!"

"Word?"

"Hell, yeah!" I couldn't keep it to myself. "And I punished her ass last night too!"

"Damn my nigga, when you gonna let me get a piece of her? We could do the closet thing on her."

"Whenever you let me hit your shawty first."

"Which one?"

"Sandra?"

"Yeah, right! Just picture that shit!"

I laughed.

"So what's up," he began to ask me, "are you still gonna go to work tonight or what?"

"Yeah, I'm going. But just make sure you come over to pick me though."

"Alright. I got you."

I headed to the kitchen after freshening up. Samara was cooking breakfast in my orange Louis Vuitton T-shirt.

And I'll be damned....

She looked sexier than a King of Diamond stripper in that shirt. I snuck up behind her and kissed on the side of the neck.

She cowered a bit. "I see you're up."

"Yeah, I just got up a minute ago." I peeped over her shoulder. "Those potatoes and eggs look good; not to mention, how good they smell. I can't wait to sink my teeth in them." I paused for a quick moment. Then added: "But I know they don't taste as good as you were last night." I gave her another kiss on her neck.

She smiled and poked her ass out a bit to push me away from her. "Breakfast will be finished in a little," she said between a light giggle. "So, you might as well call Destini so she can eat with us too."

"Yeah, all right." I flirted back with her before I strolled to the family room to inform Destini that breakfast would be ready soon. "So, you might as well get ready to come in the kitchen and eat."

"I'm not hungry." She kept her eyes on the TV screen, watching a cartoon. "I ate earlier this morning before you got up."

"You sure you don't want some potatoes and eggs? They look good."

Destini turned from the TV and gave me a cold stare. "I said I'm not hungry. I ate already." She cut her eyes back to the TV.

All righty then.

I strode back to the kitchen.

"So where is she?" Samara asked me as soon as I sat at the table.

"She said she ate breakfast this morning."

"Oh, well" —Samara shrugged a bit— "that means there's more food for us then." She filled my plate up.

"Mmm ... this taste good. What'd you put in this?"

"It's my family's secret receipt; I would have to kill you if I tell you."

I laughed. "Well, I think it might be worth it then." I took another spoonful of potatoes in my mouth. "But hey! What are you doing tonight?"

"... What?" She looked as if she were about to choke on her food.

"What are you doing tonight?"

"Oh.... My girls and I made some plans for tonight. Why?"

"Nah, it's nothing really. I just wanted to know if you wanted to meet up later, so we could take care of some unfinished business."

She hesitated. "Sure, we could meet up later if my friends and I decide to cut our night short."

"That's cool." I smiled at her while taking another spoonful of potatoes in my mouth. "Until then, I'll keep my fingers crossed, hoping that I get my wish to see you later."

After we were finished eating, we headed back to my bedroom so she could get dressed. But get this: When she pulled off her T-shirt, she wasn't wearing a damn thing. I mean like ... absolutely nothing in my bedroom.

I smiled when she bent over to grab her clothes off the floor. I swallowed hard. It was a pretty sight to see. She had a chunky pussy back there on display. It was nice and phat; about the size of my fist. She took a seat at the edge of the bed, trying to slide her skirt on— no panties. She stood up, looking at me.

"Why are you smiling at me?" she asked in a puzzling manner yet in a humorous way, while wiggling her hips inside her skirt.

"No reason. But hold up for a second." I drew near to her. "Let me help you with that." But instead of jacking her skirt upward, I began to pull them down.

"Nooo. Not right now, boo. Let's do this later."

"Shhh, somebody might hear us." I laid her on the bed and gently pulled her skirt off, then tossed it over my shoulder.

She moved toward the center of the bed to position herself.

I almost melted when I stuck my dick inside her.

About half an hour later Samara was ready to leave again.

While I was walking her out, she stopped in front of the family room and said, "Bye, Destini."

But Destini ignored her.

I felt embarrassed. "Destini, Samara said good-bye to you. Aren't you gonna say something back to her?"

Nothing.

Now that shit right there pissed me the fuck off! Destini was ignoring me, just lying in front of the TV, watching her stupid-ass cartoon program again.

Samara tapped me on the shoulder. "Don't worry about it. She'll grow out of it soon. One way or the other."

"Yeah, you're right." I walked Samara to the front door and she gave me a lingering kiss, then broke free from my grip. "Let's go back to the room so I can tease you with my tongue."

She probably knew I wasn't faking because she bucked, forcing her way out of the house.

So, on that note, I let her arm go and walked her to her car.

"Damn! I forgot my purse!"

I smiled.

Later on that night, Carlton and Destini were having their little grudge match over a game of UFC-undisputed.

Destini wasn't at all worried about Carlton's competitor skill anymore. He wasn't any match for her, as she put it. And, in a way, he must have known that too, judging by the way he nudged her arm, hoping that she would lose control of her joystick and mess up.

She glanced over at him and slid a few inches away.

But he slid over toward her again. But this time, he rested his arm against hers, applying a little pressure to it.

"You can't do that!" she leaped from the couch, laughing. "You're cheating! You're cheating!" She took a swipe at him, going back to her battle match. "You're cheating!"

Then the doorbell rang.

"Why don't one of y'all answer the damn door?!" I shouted from my bedroom.

No response.

So I stormed out into the hallway, walked to the front door with only a towel wrapped around my waist.

It was Kevin. "My nigga, what the fuck's your problem?" He seemed to be in his feelings, as he budged his way pass me. "I was out there for ten fucking minutes! Just what if someone was chasing me and I needed you to bust the door open for me? I'll be a dead muthafucker right now!"

I walked away from him and went straight to the family room.

"Are y'all deaf in here?" I tried to get either Carlton or Destini's attention, but they wouldn't look at me. "I know y'all heard me calling y'all..."

"Huh?" Carlton's eyes were locked on the video game. "Hold up for a second, my nigga. Let me see if I can get her right here."

I just turned to Kevin. "Give me a minute so I can throw my shit on." I walked back to my bedroom, got dressed, and headed back to the family room with a duffel back in my hand. It wasn't heavy at all. It was just the basic stuff I usually carry with me when I go out to work: my chaps outfit, condoms, a different set of clothing and a Black Tail magazine to get my dick aroused, if necessary.

"And it's about time!" Kevin leaped from the couch. "I thought you had forgot about me out here—"

"Eh, Destini!" I cut him off, paying more attention to her. "I'm about to leave."

She shrugged her thin shoulders, as if she didn't care.

"So you're not going to say bye to me?"

No comment. She remained silent.

"Eh, Carlton." I waited for him to look before I continued: "I'm about to head out, so make sure that she goes to bed soon. Alright? And besides, it's already past her bedtime anyway."

"Alright dawg, I got you."

"C'mon, my nigga," Kevin said, as he started to walk away. "We're gonna miss out on all the money." He walked out of the house and left the door open.

I lingered a few feet behind, shutting the door behind us.

"I thought you said," Kevin started, as he approached his SUV, "that little mama in there was a little sweetheart? She was in there trippin' on me and shit, saying that she didn't want me talking to her anymore...."

I didn't respond to that. I just looked back at the house.

"My nigga, you don't have to go to work tonight if you don't want to."

"Nah, I'm going," I said, twisting to him. Then I quickly twisted back to the house. I thought I had seen someone at the window, watching us. But when I took a closer look, there wasn't anybody there. "Come on, let's go."

"Oh, I thought so."

Destini stopped peeking through the living room curtain when Kevin drove away.

"Are they gone yet?" Carlton shouted from the family room.

"Yeah," she barely said as she walked back inside the room.

"What's the matter with you?"

She felt like he wouldn't understand.

"I know you ain't trippin' about that curfew shit!"

Just what she thought: He wouldn't understand. She kept quiet.

"Well, just to let you know, you don't have to worry about any curfew up in here while I'm in here with you."

As if she didn't know that already.

"So go ahead and grab yourself a movie off the shelf, and let's watch it."

Destini looked up at him. Usually a smile would appear on her face. But this time, it didn't. "What about Scarface?"

"Again?" He gave her a firm look. "You gotta be kidding me?"

She smiled finally.

"But you already saw that movie about a million times already?!"

"So?"

He pondered on it for a moment, then decided: "Alright, you can watch it. But you better hurry up and get that shit before I change my mind. I don't even know what the hell you see in that movie anyway? You're a little girl." He paused; then went on to say, "But don't even worry about it though, because I gotta trick for your ass...."

She didn't care what he was talking about, she just grabbed the Scarface movie and stuck it inside the DVD player.

"So you better enjoy this movie for the last time because after we get finished watching it, I'm gonna break that shit up! Watch!"

She sat back down, looked at him, and then cut her eyes to the TV. And just before the movie was about to start, she turned to him again, opened her mouth, then shut it. She turned back to the picture screen.

"Spit it out."

"Spit what out?" She looked back at him.

"Whatever you gotta say?"

After a short pause, she did: "I wanna know if I can ask you a question?"

"Yeah, go ahead. But make it quick though. The movie is about to start."

She hesitated at first, then came out with it: "What's a two-dollar-come-drinking-hole?"

He wanted to laugh, but then again he controlled himself. "Nah," he lied to her. "I don't know what that one means." He wore a suspicious smile on his face. "But where did you hear that word from?"

"My daddy's girlfriend said that my mommy was that."

His smile slowly disappeared. "How you know she said that about your mom?"

"Because she told me that."

"What?!" He seemed to have gotten upset now. "So why didn't you tell DaShawn about this?"

"I did."

"And what the fuck he say?"

Destini slowly shook her head, feeling a bit intimidated, and said, "Nothing...."

Carlton never came back with a follow-up question. He just kept his eyes on her, lost in his thoughts.

But Destini on the other hand had never seen him react like this before. So she asked him, "Are you mad with me for asking you that question?"

He got up and walked away from her.

The party was at Club NV.

Just like any other nightclub in South Florida, this one was packed with freaks and weirdos. The females outnumbered the males by far: 15 to 1. So, most definitely, this was the spot to be at.

As Kevin and I swaggered through the front entrance a hand grabbed me and pulled me close.

"Mmmm," it was Rita. "Take it off."

"Hey, baby." I kissed her on the cheek. "Now, what are you doing in here?"

"I probably came here to see you."

"Girl, the last time I remember it, you supposed to have gotten married to someone."

"What that's supposed to stop me from coming out here to see you?"

"Of course not." I pulled her close to me. "If you put it like that, we can go over there in the back, in our usual corner and do our little thing in a more secluded area. Just like old times."

"Ohhh, God," she whispered with her eyes closed. "I miss those days."

"Who can say those days are over with? We can always finish off what we've started." I kissed her glossy lips.

She welcomed it.

Kevin mumbled: "My nigga is back."

Back? I think not, because I hadn't gone anywhere.

After Rita walked away with her friends, Kevin and I headed toward the dressing room with no worries on our minds. But then, all of a sudden, someone yanked him back.

It was Ms. Ginsberg: an older white lady, with heavy bags under her eyes. "I want you to visit my table once you get settled in," she demanded for his services. "And you'll be paid handsomely."

"Oh, hell nah! I have several other tables that I have to visit first. But" —he then pulled me close to him— "I think my friend Goldie here is gonna be free though."

A perverted smile appeared on her face. She grabbed me by the pants, pulling me close to her. "I'm paying very well. And I'll throw in a little extra in it for you if you're packing down there." She then looked at my private area.

I sorta laughed. "I don't know about that, you're a little too much outta my league. But I know the right person for you."

"Well," she seemed curious, "send him over to me!" She began rubbing her hands together like a fly, then tilted her head to me. "Is he packing down there?"

"Is he packing down there?" I wanted to build some sort of suspense with her.

She quickly nodded her head.

"Hell, yeah! So I have heard."

A dangerous smile grew on her face now. "So whatchu waiting on?" she slid me a five dollar bill. "Go get him for me!"

Kevin and I walked away, laughing.

"Who you gonna get for her?"

I gave Kevin a quick, mischievous smile as I pushed the dressing room door open. "Yo, Mikey!" I called out to him. "There's a broad out there who's looking for you."

"Where?"

"On the other end of the bar. You can't miss her. She's wearing a light blue dress, with a white bonnet."

"All right. Thanks."

"Don't mention it." I sat down, dropping my duffel back in front of me, smiling.

Kevin whispered, "You're some shit."

"Whatever," I joked back, pulling my leather chaps out of my bag. I took my pants off and placed then inside the bag; I did the same with my shirt.

The door swung open.

It was Fabulous. "Eh, Goldie!" he got my attention when he said, "I think your homeboy needs your help out there."

"Who?"

"Your homey, Mikey!" Fabulous then pulled his shirt off. "It's some old dame out there, chasing after him."

I looked at Kevin with a smirk, then went back to Fabulous. "He'll be alright."

Minutes later, Kevin and I walked out of the room and ordered two cocktail drinks at the bar. A Long Island for me and a Tidal Wave for him. And while we were checking out the scenery, sipping on our drinks, I felt a tap on the shoulder. I looked to my left.

"Hey, cutie." It was Vida, standing beside Stacy, shooting me a feral smile as if she wanted me to fuck her right there on the spot.

I smiled back, thinking she was standing a bit too close to me.

You see, Vida was the type of female who really didn't have to do much to enhance her beauty, even though she'd had plenty of those cosmetic surgeries done over the years.

And just like her friend Samara, Vida was sexy, too. She looked like someone who was pulled right out of one of those Straight Stuntin' magazines: She had that caramel, butter look. That whole Maliah Michel look that would make a nigga wanna suck her pussy out on the first date.

I'm not lying either.

She had the audacity to switch her voice up a bit, sounding like a cheap escort from the State of Virginia when she asked me, "Are you gonna perform tonight, or are you just gonna stand there, getting drunk?"

I kept my smile on her.

"Mmm!" Stacy thrummed, while sizing me up. "I see what you and Samara be talking about now."

I played if off as though I didn't hear that.

Stacy extended her hand to my chest and copped a feel. "Do you do private sessions?"

I laughed at her question, but just when I was about to respond back to Vida's sarcastic reply, Kevin cut me off: "It all depends on what y'all have in mind." He stepped in front of me, forcing Vida to take a step back.

"I don't believe we were talking to you."

"Girl, you needa stop trippin' and get over that bullshit." He took another step toward her. "You know you miss me."

"Don't flatter yourself, because I don't think so. You had your chance and you blew it. I'm moving on to bigger and better things in life. So you need to try and do the same thing, too." Then she changed her facial expression back to something more suitable and sweet, looking over his shoulder. "I'll see you later, Goldie Lox."

"All right." I nodded.

Then Vida and Stacy swaggered away, looking fine as hell.

Now, that's what I call bootylicious.

They both have teardrop-booties with deep swerves at the bottom, as if they were waving good-bye to me.

I kinda missed them already. So whether Vida and Stacy were serious or not, with all that flirting bullshit, I had to remind myself that they were Samara's friends and they were off limits. Because, for all I know, they were just probably playing around with me to perhaps tease Kevin for whatever reason. But then it hit me: Where in the hell was Samara at anyway?

"Ah, fuck that hoe!" Kevin said, cutting my inquiry to pieces. "That bitch ain't all that! She ain't nothing but a high price hoe!"

"Who?"

"That hoe Vida."

I was surprised. Although it was none of my business, I asked him, "What happened, I thought everything was cool with y'all?"

"Yeah, we were, up until a couple of days ago."

"Why? What'd happened?"

"Well, she had asked me the other week if I had a sexual fantasy that I wanted to fulfill. And I told her that I had one, but I didn't think she'd be down with it, though. Then she told me to try her; and I did. I had told that bitch I wanted to experience a threesome with her and any one of her friends."

"Nah."

"Yeah. But I was only joking with her though. However, the following week, this stupid-ass hoe popped up to my crib with Stacy."

"Nah!" I wanted to laugh.

"Hell, yeah, my nigga!" he added. "So we experienced our little ménage à trois together with Stacy. Just the three of us. And when that hoe Stacy was sucking me up, Vida wanted Stacy to stop what she was doing so I could hit her in the ass."

"Whose ass?"

"Vida's."

"Are you serious?"

"Yeah, my nigga. But let me finish, though. So when she asked me to do that for her, I told her to chill for a bit till Stacy gets through sucking me up first. But—"

I cut him off, laughing: "I know you didn't tell her that shit?"

"Shit me, if I didn't! My nigga, that hoe Stacy was sucking a nigga up like the world was about to end within minutes and she wanted to go out with a blast. So why would I stop her? That shit was feeling too good. So right after she got finished doing her thing on me, I looked up and saw Vida standing there with her arms crossed over her fake-ass titties, like if she was mad at me and shit."

"So what happened?" I felt somebody brush their hand over my dick, but I ignored it.

Kevin went on to say, "Nothing happened. She just started talking shit about how she couldn't wait until her man gets out of prison, and all that bullshit!"

"Who's her man?"

"I don't really know. But from what I've heard so far, he's some fuck-nigga from Brooklyn, New York, who used to hustle up there in VA by the name of Burt."

"Oh."

"But the word on the street is that this snitching-ass nigga came home already; in which, there are a few dudes who wanna catch up with him for telling on their homeys and shit! So I really don't know why that bitch is telling me about that fuck-nigga for!"

I felt lost here. "But I still don't see why she would be trippin' with you about that, if she was the one who initiated that whole thing and brought Stacy over at your crib for the threesome?"

"Oh, I forgot to tell you about this too," he said. "I got a little carried away with my story. But check it, though: when Vida was going off at the mouth at me, she sorta got mad and left the crib."

"Damn, for real?"

"Yeah, and that stupid-ass hoe left that bitch Stacy in the house with me. In my bed. So what you think I did?" Since I kept quiet, he answered his own question: "So I dicked that hoe down instead; for the whole night, too!" He paused for a second. Then added: "Just to think about it. I even called you that night and left a message to see if you wanted to come over and run a train on Stacy. But you never called me back."

"When?"

"I think it was last week Wednesday, around three in the morning."

Oh, shit! I remembered that night.

"But," he went on to say, "now Vida doesn't wanna holla at me anymore because Stacy ended up telling her how I ate her pussy out that night when she left...."

That night? I wondered, as if there were other nights as well?

"But I still don't know why that hoe would be trippin' for over some bullshit like that anyway!" he added. "It ain't like I told her the truth, that her friend suck dick better than her."

I laughed.

"I know one thing for sure, though."

"What's that?"

"A hoe is a hoe! She'll be back. I know she will. They always do."

I immediately thought about Tamara, some fast-ass-hoe I used to fuck with back in the day.

"Hold up, my nigga!" Kevin was suddenly sidetracked by a bunch of females who were flagging him over to their table. "I have to go to work. I'll holla at you later." He strode away.

As I stood there scanning the club, a chubby-faced Spanish broad who looks to be in her mid-fifties with a few small ridges over her lip approached me, wearing an old-fashioned dress. And just like every other female in this spot, she was getting her freak on by rubbing her hands across my chest, as if she was checking out the merchandise before she decided to use my services. And of course, she was loving every second of her thorough inspection, especially when she grabbed my dick.

"¿Tu hablas espanol?"

"No espanol."

"Okay, no problem, papi," she said in a broken English. "You dance for me … I pay."

"You want me to dance for you?" I twirled my hips in a circular motion, pointing my finger at her, then at me.

"Si. Yes."

I grabbed her hand and started leading her to a private cubicle in the back of the club. "Just you and me," I said to her. "Okay?"

"Si, papi, si." She wore a perverted smile.

As I approached the entranceway of an empty cubicle, Stacy staggered into me; she sounded drunk as hell when she said, "I have been looking for the ladies' room for the past fifteen minutes. And if I don't find the restroom soon, I might as well forget about it and go home to change my clothes instead."

"It's over there, in the back corner." I pointed her in the right direction.

"Thank you, hon." She blundered forward and wove through the crowd.

And I couldn't help but wonder where in the hell was Samara because—

This Spanish broad, whose name was Monica, had broken my chain of thoughts when she pulled me into a private cubicle with her. And once inside, I pulled the curtain shut to make the scenery look taboo like. And it looked nice, too. The room gave out a dim but secluded dark-atmosphere look. It made customers feel cozy, if not naughty.

Monica threw herself on the leather sofa with a lewd look in her eyes. "¿Cuanto, papi?" she asked, then started taking money out of her purse.

"No, no, no. I can't do that." I tried to take control of the situation when I saw her, pulling her Fruit of the Loom down. "Only dancing, ma."

She froze, looking a little disappointed with her panties down to her ankles.

I immediately started grinding in front of her, hoping that might ease the tension down some.

It did.

She leaned back on the sofa, smiling.

When she started caressing her things, stroking them up and down, I almost laughed at her. She was making funny faces, while mumbling something under her native tongue that I didn't have a clue about.

With a sexual intent, she reached out and brushed her hand over my manhood. Her eyes widened, admiring my flaccid muscle. I smiled. Then she brushed her hand over it again. And again.

Goliath started to wake up.

Her mouth agape. Then a horny smile slapped across her face, while exposing her coffee-stained teeth.

It couldn't get any better than this. She looked at me, then went back to my rising nature. I snatched my chaps off and started twisting my body in a circular motion.

Yeah, I knew I had her now when I placed her hand back on my dick.

She stretched a bigger smile across her face this time.

I started pumping in front of her. She got excited and threw two fingers between her legs.

I laughed, but kept it under control. I stayed with a steady dance pace, twirling and popping my hips for her.

She started making those funny "Ohhs" and "Ahhs" sounds, gnawing on her bottom lip while keeping her eyes on my pouch, softly squeezing on it with her hands.

So to spice the atmosphere up a bit, I pulled my dick out for her.

Meet Goliath: my fat-headed souljah.

And her mouth gaped.

I gave into temptation and told her, "Go ahead and kiss it."

She looked at me, then at my dick again.

"Go ahead." I tapped the head of my dick on her lips, then pulled it away, tantalizing her with it. Then I tapped it on her lips again.

She tried to catch my dick in her mouth on the next tap but I quickly pulled it away from her. I waited, then went for it again. She caught my dick on the third tap when she opened her mouth wider, taking the whole thing inside her mouth.

I felt the blood rush to my brain when she bobbed her head once, then twice, over me. Then she did it again and again, with a slight pull.

I felt loved.

Within seconds I heard the curtain pull open. I looked behind me while Monica was inching further down on my dick, each time she bowed her head.

It was Rita. She stepped inside the cubicle with us and pulled the curtain shut.

I twisted back around and watched Monica do her thing on me. Give or take, about two seconds later I felt Rita kiss my back.

Kevin had a white chick bent over a table, pretending he was actually fucking her from the back.

Three of her friends cheered him on.

"You go, boy!"

His performance lasted about half an hour straight before I realized he couldn't drain them for any more money. He pranced to the next table over, hoping to earn some cash from other females. There were four of them in total.

"So why don't you come over here," one of the females said, extending her hand out, waving a twenty-dollar bill at him. "And let me see how you work that."

He smiled and hopped his way over there like a rabbit. Her eyes lit up in ecstasy. But before she tried to get slick on him, he snatched the money out of her hand and stuck it in his speedo underwear. A naughty look appeared on her face. He rested his hands on her shoulders and started grinding his manly tool in front of her.

She was loving it. She snatched out another twenty dollar bill before someone else tries to steal him away from her. But it was too late: Kevin saw one of her friends pulled out a fifty dollar bill, the one who was sitting at the far end of their section in the blue cardigan sweater.

Sold! To the lady in blue.

A greedy smile shot across his face. As he tried to work his way over there to the lady in the blue cardigan sweater, that other chick, the one who he initially danced for a short moment ago, grabbed his wrist. Here, he literally had to slap her hands off of him to break free from her grip. Her smile disappeared. He didn't care. He hopped toward her friend, but then he hesitated a bit when he saw a ten dollar bill lying on the floor about two feet away from her. He thought about it: if he didn't drop it, she did. But whichever way he looked at it, he wanted it. It was free money. He froze right in front of her, then gyrated his body as if he were about to twist around. But then he froze again—with his hands in the air, with his back facing her. About a second later, if that, he shook his ass like a wobbly bowl of Jell-O.

She pulled out a few more bills.

Then Kevin went into another motion: he squatted a bit, twirling his hips—as if he was grinding inside a good piece of pussy—while keeping his eyes on that ten dollar bill in front of him. To which that broad in the blue cardigan sweater got excited and rested both of her hands on his buttocks, following his spiral motion. He bent over just a little more, pretending like he was about to touch his toes, then reached for the money. He got it!

WHOP-POW!!!

"What the fuck?!" He quickly twisted around once he felt a heavy slap across his ass. "I don't get down like that!" He froze right there. His eyes widened; his face was painted with fear. He actually felt his heart skip a beat and drop somewhere inside his chest. No, it fell somewhere inside his stomach. "Oh, hell nah!" he murmured under his breath.

"So, come on! Whatchu waiting on, sonny?!" Ms. Ginsberg asked him. "Back that ass up and show me that trick again!"

Kevin stood up and tried to make a run for it, but Ms. Ginsberg grabbed hold of his underwear, yanking him back to her.

"Just hold the fuck up for a second!" He checked his underwear as thought to make sure it hadn't torn. He then scanned the area for an escape route. But, there wasn't any. He felt trapped. He had no other choice, but come up with a quick excuse: "I don't think the manager allow" —he did a quick head count around him— "five people at a table together. So to be on the safe side, I'm just gonna leave before he catches me over here. This is the only job I have right now, and I'm not trying to lose it either." He reached for his belongings. "I'm sorry ladies, but I have to go."

And just when he was about to walk away, Ms. Ginsberg slapped a harridan smile on her face which puzzled him. He froze again.

Perhaps that had a lot to do with the doodle of money she pulled out of her bra, fanning it before him.

His eyes followed her motion: He saw nothing but twenties and fifties.

Then Ms. Ginsberg said, "Well, I don't think your manager would mind if you accommodated a few close relatives of mine: Mr. Jackson and Sir Grant...."

A presidential smile grew on his face. "Oh, my...," he whispered to no one in general, feeling a bit hypnotized; then spoke up: "Why didn't you say that from the beginning? ... Mr. Jackson and Grant are good friends of mine."

She smiled back.

He snatched the cocktail drink from the lady in the blue cardigan sweater and guzzled her drink down his throat in one shot.

"Now, get over here and show me that trick again."

"Yes, ma'am."

I made about $1300 thus far and my night wasn't even over yet. So, technically speaking, I couldn't complain. I even made a buck-fifty entertaining two bisexual females without going all the way with them. And they were cute, too.

They both had that wifee type look about them. I'm dead serious.

One of them was a plus size, who was sorta built like Queen Latifah—and I'm talking about the whole work: ass, tits, and all—while the other one was kinda petite with cute lips and hazel eyes. But check it, though: in the middle of my performance, they wanted me to whip my dick out and provide a little service for the both of them. I declined their offer because I was kinda worn: Rita and that Spanish broad Monica had drained me dry. They got three nuts out of me. But that didn't stop those two bisexual chicks from providing sexual services on each other, though: because, right after I told them No, that thick broad immediately stuck her head between that slim chick's legs, giving her the time of her life.

"So … alrighty then." When I stepped out of the cubicle, I was immediately swarmed by some more females.

"What about a little privacy with the four of us?" one of them asked me in a business-like manner. "And we'll pay you for your services."

"Sure." I smiled at them. "I can do that for y'all."

"What about in there?" they all chimed in unison.

"Nah. Not in that one." I wanted to laugh. "That room is quite occupied for the moment." Then I immediately became distracted when I saw Stacy a short distance away, in some sort of heated argument, with a few females inside the club. "Hey! Y'all have to excuse me for a second." I stepped away and strode over to Stacy's rescue.

"If you know what's best for you," a short, ghetto-ass chick was saying in front of Stacy, with her finger in her face, "you better just get the hell away from us!"

"Why don't you make me?"

"Damn girl!" I said, throwing my arm around Stacy's neck. "It's about time I found you." I cupped her breast by accident. "I've been looking all over for you." I removed my hand, then turned to her foes. "Ladies, let me borrow her for a second."

"Yeah, you better take that bitch outta our faces before we fuck her up," some other broad said from out of the group.

"Y'all ain't gonna do shit to me!" Stacy sounded intoxicated. "And yo' mama's a bitch! Bitch!"

I snatched Stacy back when I saw not one, but two fists swung directly at her face. A few people stepped in and helped me break up the confrontation. I walked Stacy away and we strolled through the club until we found Vida sitting in a section where a bunch of females were celebrating a chick's bachelorette party.

And get this: Vida tried to play it off when she said, "I was looking for y'all. Where y'all been at?"

"Hmm!" Stacy didn't believe her; neither did I. "Oh, sure you were."

"For real, boo!" Vida seemed sincere. "But I gave up because I thought you were—" she paused with an impish smile on her face, looking at the both of us; then continued with "getting your thing off."

"Well" —I felt dumbfounded by her remark— "since the both of y'all are together again, I'm just gonna head back to work now."

"If you're gonna head back to work," Stacy began to ask me with a freakish look in her eyes, "why don't you dance for us then?"

"I'd told you already, I can't do that for y'all. Y'all are Samara's friends."

"So?!" they both said. Then Stacy continued on her own: "I mean, it's only dancing. It ain't like we're fucking and shit." She then dropped her voice down a bit, almost to a whisper: "Something I wouldn't mind doing with you...."

I pretended like I didn't hear that, playing it off. "Now, how's that gonna look like if I dance for y'all, knowing that both of y'all are Samara's friends? But where's she at anyway? I thought—"

"She's doing her own th—" Stacy started to say, but cut it short.

"She's doing her own, what?" I was curious to know. "Her own thing?" I paused. Then asked, "Is she out there with someone else?"

Stacy panicked: "Don't tell her that we told—"

Vida nudged her in the ribs. "Girl, shut up! You're drunk." She then turned back to me. "Don't pay her any mind, she's—"

"Hey," it was my turn to cut her off. "I know y'all Samara's friends, and y'all gonna look out for her. Believe me, I understand. Y'all supposed to. My homeys and I be doing the same shit too, looking out for each other. So to make y'all feel at ease, what I just heard from y'all is gonna be our own little secret. I'm not gonna even mention it to her. Alright?"

Stacy was cool with that because she immediately said, "Since it's like that then, why don't you dance for us and let that be our own little secret too?"

I laughed. She got me there. "C'mon," I said, leading them to an empty section in the club. "Let's go in that cubicle over there in the corner."

"Hell, yeah!" Stacy and Vida led the way.

Minutes later, I was dancing for them. It kinda felt a bit unusual to be dancing for Samara's friends. I swear it did. But then again I did it anyway. However, I took my dancing routine down a notch because the more I popped and shook my hips, the more excited they were getting. I could honestly say that Vida was happy. Now Stacy on the other hand was acting totally out of line. She had her hands all over my body. And I do mean all over my body literally. To which her eyes concentrated in one area, and one area only: that bulged print in front of my G-string pouch.

Vida played her part, too. She was softly dragging her nails over my back.

But I guess Stacy couldn't hold back any longer when she snatched my G-string down and demanded, "Gimme some of that dick!"

I pulled my underwear back up.

She snapped again: "You needa stop fuckin' teasing me like a little faggot, and just give it to me!"

"Girl, you're wild as hell!" I tried to play it off, holding on to her wrists.

"Nigga, please! You haven't seen wild yet!"

It was about that same time that I felt a few taps on my shoulder; I looked to my left, sort of behind me.

It was Kevin. "My nigga, after you get finished here, come holla at me in the dressing room."

"Alright."

He walked away.

Something musta happened to him, I thought. Because, besides him looking troubled about something, he didn't even try to persuade Vida to give him another chance. He just gave her that regular head nod before he stepped off.

"Hey!" I told Stacy and Vida. "Let me holla at y'all later. I wanna find out what's going on with Kevin."

"But why you have to leave so early?" Stacy got upset. "Fuck that busta and just chill out with us!"

"I would love to but I can't right now. I think something happened to him and I wanna go find out if everything is alright. I'm gonna get back with y'all on a later day."

Vida cut in. "But what if we—." she started to say, then looked at Stacy, then back to me.

"But what if we, what?" I asked her, then looked at Stacy, then back to her.

Vida's eyes locked onto mine as if she were searching for the right words to use when she asked me, "Have you ever had a fantasy that you've always wanted to fulfill but you haven't fulfilled it yet?"

I considered her question for a short moment, then I remembered about the conversation that Kevin had shared with me a few hours ago regarding that ménage à trois that he experienced with Vida and Stacy at his house.

"Nah. I don't think I have a fantasy that I would like to fulfill at this time," I told her with a slight laugh, lying through my teeth. "But when I do have one, you'll be the first one to know about it, though. Alright? But on a real note, I have to catch up with y'all later."

"Well" —Vida shot me an inviting smile— "we just gotta see about that."

Most definitely, I liked the sound of that. I smiled back. "So, lemme ask you a question then?"

"Sure." She slid her hand inside my underwear. "What you wanna know?"

I just kept quiet and took a seat on the sofa, resting my hand on the back of her head when she put my dick in her mouth. I reached over and kissed Stacy.

She welcomed it, then softly whispered my name, "DaShawn."

"Huh."

She broke loose from my mouth, tantalizing me with the tip of her tongue, brushing it against my lips. "You wanna fuck this pussy?" She lapped my mouth again.

"Uh-huh." I really did. I have always wanted to fuck her ever since that day I mysteriously found that stack of photos of her on my car windshield window.

"Well," she paused to kiss me again. Then said, "You have to eat it first."

But before I could tell her, Okay, just lay on her back, she started doing that already.

I stuck my hands underneath her skirt and pulled her panties off; she helped. I tossed them to the side. I smelled the sweet aroma, and I couldn't wait to dine.

"Go ahead, baby. Don't be shy."

I smiled and went in.

I stepped into the dressing room nearly an hour later than Kevin had expected me to; he rolled his eyes at me.

"Yeah, whatever." I looked at my wristwatch. It wasn't even one o'clock yet, and this sucker looked like he wanted to leave already.

He looked at me again, throwing his shirt on with a wounded look on his face.

"What the fuck happened to you?" I asked. "Have you pulled a muscle or something?"

"Nah. It's nothing. I'm alright."

Several guys in the room started laughing.

I looked at them, then turned back to Kevin.

But before I could inquire about it, he cut in: "My nigga" —he started flipping through his money roll— "how much money you made tonight?"

"I don't know. Probably enough to be satisfied with. But who in the hell did you come across with? Oprah?"

One of the guys in the room announced, "Nah. Not quite. But she does have a powerful hand like her though."

I looked at my homeboy, Hot Sauce, from the other side of the room. Then it dawned on me as to what he said. "Man!" –I immediately twisted back to Kevin. "I know you didn't dance for Ms. Ginsberg?" I tried to spin him around, jokingly. "Let me see it!"

"Hold the fuck up! This shit is killing me." Kevin slowly pulled his pants down a bit and showed me the finger welts. "So does it look bad?"

A few guys in the room gathered around me to get a look at it too. Then some of guys breathed a slow, "Damnnnnnn," in one accord.

"Nah, it's alright," I lied to Kevin, pushing the fellows away from him. "You can barely see it."

"Well, it sure doesn't feel alright. This shit is killing me right now." He gently pulled his pants back up. "I just needa go home and run some cold water on it."

"Yeah, that would be your best bet."

Then somebody shouted: "And file a criminal complaint against that old bitch!"

Everybody in the dressing room started laughing—including myself.

After Kevin was finished dressing, we headed out of the club so he could take me home. He barely spoke the whole way there.

"Is everything alright?" I asked him once we pulled up in front of my driveway.

"Yeah, I'm alright. But I was just wondering if I fuck'd up by giving that crazy hoe my cell number."

"Who?"

He looked at me. "Ms. Ginsberg."

I decided not to comment on that. "So, alright then." I opened the SUV door and got out. "Just give me a call if you need anything."

"Shit! I almost forgot about it. Whatchu doing on Saturday night?"

"Why?"

"I need your help again for another bachelorette party." He turned the radio volume down. All the way down. "Don't let me down on this one. I need you. Actually, they asked for you anyway."

"Yeah, I'm cool with that. I got you." I shut the passenger door. "Just come by and pick me up."

"Alright."

As soon as I walked in the house, I checked my phone messages. There were a few messages, but only one of them stood out from the rest. It was from Naomi. She called because she had noticed there were several missed calls from my home phone number were on her caller ID. It was probably Destini who made those calls, I mulled, because they sure weren't made from me. However, I couldn't help but notice how Naomi's message was precise and straight to the point, with a simple hello. It was obvious she wanted to keep any sort of friendship at a distance.

Which that was perfectly fine with me.

After checking up on Destini and taking a shower, I stretched over my bed, feeling emotionally and physically worn out. I swear, it felt like my days weren't the same anymore since the whole concept of fatherhood popped up in my life. I was actually enjoying my life, burden-free without any responsibilities over my head. But now … how could I say this … I have to watch my awesome lifestyle vaporize before my eyes. Something I dreaded.

"You came back home."

I turned toward the doorway.

It was Destini, with Abu in her hand. "I can't sleep."

I set it off on Saturday evening.

No lie.

I cooked up a nice oxtail meal for all of us with a side dish of white rice. It was a little something my mom used to make me back in the day. And believe me, I hooked it up the same way: I marinated the oxtail in some seasoned lima beans for a few hours before I cooked them together. And—let me put it like this—the oxtail must have tasted really great judging from how Destini, Carlton, and Uncle James were eating it, because they were sucking the gravy out of the bones. I wanted to laugh, but I just kinda shook my head at them instead.

When Carlton saw Uncle James sucking on his fingertips, he clowned on him: "You happy-ass-gump, you needa go find a room on South Beach and get your freak on."

"Go to hell, you faggot!" Uncle James got up from the table and left the kitchen when he heard the doorbell.

I got up, too; then suddenly came up with a nice strategy. I prepared Destini a small bowl of chocolate chip ice cream without her asking for one. "Here you go, boo."

She looked astonished.

I rested the bowl in front of her, hoping that would loosen her up a bit before I headed out to work tonight. And everything was running quite fine until she finished her ice cream and ran into the family room with Carlton: Uncle James had one of his drinking buddies, a man by the name of Alfred, over by the house visiting since Mr. Yin didn't want anyone hanging out in front of his liquor store anymore.

"Hey there," Alfred tried to coax up a conversation with Destini when she took a seat on the couch. "How are you doing?"

She ignored him, trying to enjoy BET Comic View with Carlton. Alfred repeated himself.

No comment.

He kept his eyes on her.

And that did it: she turned to him, giving him a distained stare.

So Alfred asked her in a playful manner: "whatchu looking at, Miss I-can't-talk-to-you?"

"You, ugly! Who else you think I'm looking at?"

Carlton laughed.

Alfred quickly looked to the left side of him. "James, you sure were right about this one. She does have a filthy mouth. But it's nothing a good bar of soap couldn't fix."

Destini turned back to the TV.

"Oh, hell no!" Alfred piped out. "How dare you roll your eyes at me? I oughta take you to my neighborhood and let them little gals over there teach you a thing or two—"

The doorbell rang, cutting in on him.

Destini leaped from the couch and ran to the front door.

It was Kevin. "What's up, little mama?"

"Oh, it's you."

"Who else you thought it was?"

She walked away without answering him.

He shut the door and made his presence known as he entered the family room, saying "What's happening fools?"

Except for Destini, they all greeted back.

After a quick admiring look, Alfred lunged from his seat, tooting, "Whew-weeee! Now, that's what I'm talking about." He walked over to Kevin with a flunky smile on his face and said, "I remember when I was about your age, I used to dress just like that back in my early years. I probably got that same linen outfit in my closet right now, as we speak. I just gotta dig it up and show them to you."

Uncle James jumped in: "You needa stop lying to him. Because you know damn-well you grew up under a Jehovah Witness' household, and your mammy and pappy didn't allow you to wear that type of stuff."

"Uh, mind your own business!" Alfred snapped, heading back to his seat.

When I walked to the doorway of the family room, my presence immediately made itself known without me saying a word. I guess it was the Bay Rum cologne I was wearing that did the trick. Everybody's eyes were on me.

"It's about time, my nigga!" Kevin got up from his seat. "And why you always be trying to out dress me for? We're only going to a bachelorette party."

"Man, stop crying and let's get outta here."

Destini ran up to me. "So you leaving again?"

"Yeah, I have to go to work tonight."

"Okay then, have fun," she said, then extended her arms out to me, taking me by surprise.

I was stunned. I reached down and gave her a hug. A nice, tight one. "All right, sweetie," I told her, peeling her off of me. "I'll see you later once I get back. So be good while I'm gone. Okay?"

"Okay."

I headed out of the house with Kevin.

"We needa hurry up over there to that hoe's bachelorette party," Kevin said, while walking to his SUV. "Her friends gonna pay us really good if we can lighten up this chick whose supposed to get married tomorrow afternoon."

"Yeah?"

"Fuck, yeah!"

"How much they're gonna pay us?"

"Six fifty each," he said, then slapped me upside my head.

I swung at his muthafucking' ass, but I missed him: He leaped out of the way and ran to the other side of his ride.

I stopped chasing him. "Why the fuck you hit me for?! You stupid asshole!"

"Because you said so."

"When the hell I told you to hit me?"

Kevin hesitated at first, then slowly walked back to me and said, "Turn around." Then, he snatched a note off the back of my shirt and gave it to me.

It read: Hit me.

I immediately thought about Destini. I glanced over at Kevin when he popped his SUV doors open, then back at the house with a huge smile on my face. "Yeah, you got me," I whispered, taking the passenger seat.

"Who?"

I turned to him, realizing what he had just asked me. "I'm talking about Destini," I said in a delighted tone. Then changed the subject: "So, where's the party at?"

"In Fort Lick-a-dale, my nigga.... Ohh, yeah!" He reached into his pocket and pulled out a pack of condoms. "Huhn!" He tossed it to me. "You gonna need them for those hoes over there in Broward."

I doubted it. But I placed it inside my duffel bag anyway. "Thanks."

It took us just under half an hour to drive to Ft. Lauderdale and an additional ten minutes to find the house where the bachelorette party was located. And when we arrived at our destination, there wasn't an available parking space in front of the house. We parked three houses up the block.

"Hold up, my nigga!" Kevin pulled out his cell phone. "I'm supposed to call some hoe by the name of Joyce first. She supposed to sneak us inside the house."

"Cool." I grabbed a stick of Juicy Fruit chewing gum from his dashboard.

Within a minute or two, a lady who looked to be in her mid or late forties came from around the house wearing a house dress.

She must be Joyce, I thought. She was brown-skinned. Kinda dark brown.

She seemed to be in a good shape for her age. Heavy up top, but thin at the bottom. She looked like someone that a typical guy might be interested in. But not me, though. I liked my females thick and chunky. Anything over size 40 below the waist. Nothing but ass and hips. A plus size female. A body frame sorta build like Jill Scott. Yeah, a perfect A-frame. But in this chick's case, it was totally the opposite. She had big boobs, with no junk in her trunk. I'm not lying: she had no ass at all. It was just flat back there. And her legs … Oh, man … Her legs were about the size of a baseball bat. I swear. Her face on the hand was a bit cute, though. And so was that four-karat diamond wedding ring she wore on her finger.

I was impressed.

"I'm the one who called for y'all," she said. "My name is Laura, a friend of Joyce."

Ohhh…. So, I was wrong.

She shook our hands and we introduced ourselves to her.

"Okay, y'all just follow me," she instructed us, while weaving around garbage cans and two bicycles on the side of the house. "You know, my other friend Pamela, the one who's getting married tomorrow, is in the living room with the rest of our friends. I want y'all to show her a good time tonight."

"Sure."

We all strode to the back door and saw three other females who were waiting on our arrival.

"Mmm! Chocolate and caramel swirl," one of the females said. "This gonna be good."

Laura cut back in, as we entered the foyer, and whispered to us, "I would like the both of you to come out with your dancing routine immediately after you see the living room lights cut off and on. Okay?"

We both nodded.

"Is there any type of music that y'all prefer?"

"Oh, yeah, I'd almost forgot," Kevin whispered back, then reached into his duffel bag and pulled out an old Uncle Al mix CD. "Play this."

Laura grabbed the CD and ran into the living room with her three friends before their friend Pamela got suspicious.

I rested my duffel bag right beside Kevin's and started stripping down to my underwear.

"It's on tonight, my nigga." Kevin seemed excited when he handed me the baby oil. "Did you see how that chocolate bunny was checking me out?"

I kept quiet, folding and placing my clothes into my duffel bag.

Then he sort of laughed. "We're definitely gonna get some pussy tonight."

We?

Again, I doubted that. I rubbed my body down with the oil. And without any question, speaking for both of us, we looked fabulous. We threw on our costumes. I wore my police officer's uniform while Kevin wore his thuggish, bad-boy strip off outfit. One of our favorite melodramas: cop and robber.

I reached for my hat.

"What the two of you doing in here?"

Kevin and I twisted around.

"**What about a** little music?" Laura recommended, then stuck Kevin's CD into the entertainment system. "It's something that a friend of mine gave me at work today."

"Who?" asked one of her friends, because she worked beside her.

Laura pressed the PLAY button on the CD player and gave Margaret a cold stare. "I do have other friends at work, you know," she said, then walked over to the light switch on the wall and clicked it off, then switched it back on; then off again, repeatedly. "Does the LIGHT in here look dim to y'all or is it just me? Because—"

"Good God! What are you trying to do?! Blind us with your foolishness?"

Laura turned toward an older lady sitting on the couch. "I'm sorry, Aunt Hellen."

"Go! That's our cue!" I pushed Kevin off some light-skinned chick who walked up on us earlier.

He bolted into the living room like a thief; I ran after him and tackled him from behind. By the look of things, it seemed like we had frightened everybody in the room. Even Laura, too. All of them had curled up in a semi-fetal position to protect themselves. There were about twelve of them in total.

I pulled Kevin to his feet and told them, "Don't worry about this criminal, ladies. Everything is under control here…. I just caught him running inside this house after a police chase."

"Why?" a nosy broad asked me. "What did he do?"

"He just pulled off a heist from a jewelry shop downtown and got away with a bag of diamonds."

"LOCK HIS ASS UP!" somebody else shouted.

I answered, "That's exactly what I'm gonna do after I give him a full body search." Then I snatched Kevin's outfit off from the back, with a good yank, and immediately he was stripped down to his G-string.

I let him go.

"Good, God!" somebody yelled from the corner of the room. "Leave him alone!"

Kevin started dancing for them.

Laura turned the music up a few more notches.

"Waita second!" I said, scanning the crowd for the bachelorette. "I believe he has an accomplice in here with him and I'm gonna find her." I looked at Laura when she sat back down for some help, and she discreetly pointed Pamela out for me.

Pamela was sitting in the love seat, wide-eyes, with excitement painted all over her face. Her lips were luscious-looking. She definitely had that cute yet home wrecking look: twenty percent innocent, eighty percent Alicia Keys.

I strolled over to her. "How long did you think you could hide from the authorities?" I asked. But before she could say anything I snatched my shirt off.

Pamela's smile widened a little heavier than before, as she watched me snatch my pants off next. I stripped all the way down, leaving only my G-string and police hat on. I felt like I had an easy connection with everybody in the room, especially with her. I was having a ball: I was twisting and grinding my body to the sound of the tempo. And everybody was loving it.

When I twisted around—and was just about to pop, lock, and drop it, and toss my hat off to the side—I panicked. I kept still and kept my hat on. I had to. My heart took a gigantic leap when I saw Sister Mary, Ms. Betty's best friend, run into the room. I immediately twisted around to help conceal my identity from her.

I couldn't believe this shit!

Her presence alone frightened not only me, but everybody else in the room. When she came running in, a few females sat back down.

And I'll be damned! She took a seat beside some other older lady to keep her distance and watched us.

Be cool, I told myself over and over again. But I knew good enough to recognize trouble close up.

"Pssst!" I got Kevin's attention. Then I beckoned my head toward Sister Mary who was eyeballing the both of us, separately.

He seemed clueless. "What's up with you?"

Laura cut in before I could respond to him: "Is everything all right?" She was just being nosy.

"Yeah," I nodded, "everything is alright. But I just needa second with my homey." I grabbed Kevin's arm.

"Sure, take your time."

"Thanks." Once we stepped out in the hall, I explained everything to him.

"Nah, for real?!" He peeked around the corner of the doorway to see Sister Mary for himself. "Oh, shit! That's her for real, my nigga!"

"Yo, we have to get out of here."

"Hold up." He took another look at her, then back to me. "My nigga, don't even worry about this hoe. I got this one for you."

"You got this one for me?" I asked, not quite understanding that bullshit!

"Yeah."

"Are you fucking stupid?!"

"Nah, but trust me on this."

"Trust you?"

"Yeah."

But before I could respond, he ran back into the living room leaving me out in the hallway by myself. I swear, I don't even know why I fuck with this idiot! I needed a plan. A good one. Think. I peeked back inside the living room.

When Kevin initially ran back inside the room, hopping from one leg to the other like an Indian, all the females (beside Sister Mary and that other elder lady) started clapping and acting a fool, cheering him on. He was working them. That was one of his specialties—entertaining a crowd of females.

Laura's eyes started scanning the doorway. I dropped to the floor so she wouldn't be able to see me peeping in on them.

Then she asked Kevin, "Where's your friend?"

"Huh?" he hesitated a bit.

"Where's your friend, Goldie Lox?"

"Oh, he'll be back. He went to the bathroom." Kevin then went over to her, popping his hips, hoping to keep her distracted.

Then my worst fear began to unfold before me: Sister Mary got up from her seat and headed toward the doorway. I immediately got off the floor and ran straight to the bathroom, slamming the door behind me. A few seconds later I heard a knock; I panicked.

Sister Mary asked, "Are you alright in there?"

"Yeah," I lied to her. "I'm alright! I just need a few minutes!"

"Take your time. I'll be right here waiting."

You have to be kidding me. I dropped flat on my stomach and peeked underneath the door. "Damn!" I accidently muttered under my breath when I saw her feet on the other side of the door, literally waiting on me to come out. "I knew I should have never come here."

"Did you say something in there?"

"Uhhh ... I said my stomach is acting up on me in here."

"Well, take your time. I can wait my turn."

Kevin shook his ass, jiggled it for a hot second, and then started twisting his hips in a gyrating motion as if he was playing with an invisible hula-hoop.

Round and round he went.

Pamela and the rest of the females were enjoying themselves.

It was a great party.

When Kevin took another look behind him to keep his eyes on Sister Mary, he didn't see her anymore. She was gone. He became hysterical; he ran over the doorway, hoping to locate her.

And WHAM!

She was right there in the hallway, facing the bathroom door with her arms folded across her heavy breasts.

"There you go!" He thought of a quick strategy and went along with it to make his presence known to her. "You-big-sexy-thing-you!" He started performing one of those—whatchamacallit?—limbo dance moves, a short distance away, with his back leaned back a bit as he approached her. "The party's in here, so whatchu doing out here by yourself? Are you hiding from me?" He began to dance close to her. Just inches away.

She ignored him, concentrating more on the bathroom door.

Then Kevin extended his hands out to her and broke her arms free from her breasts. "C'mon—."

"Don't you dare!" She snatched her hands away from him. "Don't you ever put your filthy hands on my again! You dirty heathen!"

"But you're missing all the funnnnn," he dragged while moving his body in a provocative way.

"This damned heathen's party doesn't amuse me at all!" She then folded her arms over her breasts again, cutting her eyes from him. "I have an important issue at hand. So you just run along and do your father's work and poison this world with your evil deeds. Because I know exactly who y'all are." She kept her eyes on the door.

"Okay, you asked for it." Kevin spun her around like a circus ballerina and ground against her buttock.

She broke loose from him. Her eyebrows rose and her lips formed an embarrassed "O" when she faced him. "How dare you?" she whined, feeling outrageously violated. "I'm old enough to be your mother, young man!"

"Yeah, probably so." He continued to move his body in a sexual way in front of her. "But you're not!"

"How dare you?!" She fended off his sexual pumps. "You just stop it! Stop it!" She rested her hands against her chest. "Just stop it right there, young man!"

He ignored her. He didn't even give her any eye contact: his eyes were penetrating on her coochy area instead, while his hips kept pumping back and forth.

Sister Mary stepped back because he was getting a little too close to her. But the more she moved away from him, the more he pursued after her with a stronger pump. "Good heavens...."

Several females who were in the living room stuck their heads out through the entranceway, looking up the hall.

Sister Mary finally escaped from Kevin, heading back to the living room, screaming hysterically, "Oh, JESUS, help me!", as Kevin was directly behind her, slapping her on the ass-cheeks.

And once they stepped inside the room, Kevin gave Sister Mary a solid pump on her amusing badonkadonk, knocking her phat ass— meaning her ass was nice, chunky, and beautiful looking—on the sofa.

"Please!" she practically begged. "Get this possessed man away from me!"

Laura, Pamela, and the other females were stunned at first by the way Kevin was acting on Sister Mary until they saw him jump on the sofa with his legs overlapping her thick thighs—while standing on the sofa's cushion—grinding his G-string pouch directly in front of her face.

"Oh, my...." Sister Mary looked as though she were about to faint. She kept herself conscious by throwing one hand over her eyes and the other hands between her and Kevin, trying to push his pouch away from her face. But it didn't work because his nuts were close to her chin. She tried to inflict some sort of pain on him by squeezing his dick, but it backfired.

Kevin laughed and held her hand on it.

"Oh, my god!" She tried to break her hand loose from his hands now, but she couldn't. He was too strong for her.

In the meantime, it seemed like everybody else in the room was enjoying themselves, almost doubled up with laughter.

Everybody, but Sister Mary.

"Oh, God!" she yelled out again. "It's getting hard in my hand!" She tried to shake her hand away. "Get it off of me! Please, young man, let your hand loose…. Oh, my! It's hard!"

Kevin ignored her plea.

Pamela laughed aloud. "This is my best party ever!" She kept a smile on her face. "Thanks, Laura!"

"Anything for a friend."

Pamela got up from her seat. "I'll be right back. I'm gonna put something more comfortable on."

"Okay, just hurry back before you miss out on all the fun."

As she was walking away Kevin palmed her little ass. She quickly ran out of the room like a nun who finally realized that life has so much more to offer than to sit around a bunch of horny priests who are only after little usher boys.

"**Oh, I'm sorry,**" Pamela said, after she accidentally ran into me.

"Nah, that was my fault." I felt like she was the one who deserved an apology. Because, in all truth, I was peeking around the corner in that blind spot where she was unable to see me at.

"Don't be foolish, silly. I bumped into—"

"Excuse me," one of Pamela's friends just appeared out of the blue and staggered right past us—drunk—straight into the bathroom.

Pamela smiled at me. "I think she had a little too much to drink. Just give me whatever she had."

I would have laughed at her banter at any other time, but right now my mind was concentrating on Sister Mary, fearing that she would escape into the hallway and catch me.

"Is everything all right with you?" Pamela asked.

"Yea-yeah.... Why?"

"Oh, it's just that, uh.... Never mind. Well, excuse me for a moment. I would like to go change into something a little more cozier so I can join you all out there."

"All right then. I'll be waiting on you."

Her face began to glow. "Well, you really don't have to wait that long, if you don't want to." She then turned from me and started swaggering toward a room as if she were giving me an open invitation.

Yeah, right! Just imagine that bullshit!

She needed about fifty more pounds on that ass if she wanted me to entertain that thought.

I felt relieved when she walked away. One problem was solved. But the worst one still remained: Sister Mary.

I took another peek into the living room to keep a close eye on her. But to my surprise I saw her walking in my direction.

Shit!

The first thing that came to mind was to run. And I did just that. I tried to run back into the bathroom, but it was occupied with that drunk lady who had just staggered past Pamela and me a short moment ago, while we were talking in the hallway. And get this: when I pushed the door open on her, she was sitting on the toilet stool stiff as a statue, as if she were holding her breath. Only her eyelids blinked. I'm dead serious. I wasn't sure if she was pissing or doo-dooing because, when our eyes collided, I got the hell out of there before she started screaming on me. I ran down the hall and busted open the first available door on my right.

It was a close call. Sister Mary missed me by an eighth of a second, if that.

"And I'll be damned!" Just when I thought my troubles were all over with, everything turned for the worse. "I'm sorry!" I piped, twisting my head back around.

Out of all the rooms in the house, my silly-ass ran into Pamela's bedroom while she was changing into something different. And I would like to emphasize the word changing here, because she was semi-dressed, throwing on a lingerie.

I went for the door again and pulled it open. But when I saw Sister Mary heading my way, I immediately shut the door back. I looked at Pamela.

When she told me she was going to put something cozier on, I swear, the last thing I expected her to be talking about was something small and transparent. And I was absolutely sure of it that she wasn't wearing anything under her lingerie. Because, in addition to those two pretty, dark areolae around her nipples, she had the same shade all over her body. I couldn't help but check her out. She had a nice set of titties. And they were huge, too: I think 38-DD, if I judged correctly.

No doubt, a nice playpen for some bedroom action.

She threw a smile on her face—as if she knew what was on my mind—and strode to the stereo. She went straight for the radio dial, tuning in for an easy listening at first. Then she changed the radio station to something more wild: Power 96. She settled in with deejay Lucy Lopez, a Spanish cutie.

I felt trapped.

Pamela got all seductive-like, walking up to me while gnawing her bottom lip. And just when she was about to say something, Sister Mary knocked on the door, then tried to push it open on us. I slammed the door back and applied pressure against it, preventing her from entering. She tried to shoulder her way in. I fought back, then pinned my foot at the bottom of the door; it worked.

"Pam!" Sister Mary shouted instead. "Are you okay in there?"

I quickly nodded my head, hoping Pamela would follow my lead.

"Yeah!" she answered Sister Mary back through the door. "I'm alright! Why? Is there a problem out there?"

"No. Not really. I was just checking on you since you haven't returned back to your party."

"Ohhh," she gasped. "No, I'm all right. But I'll be with you all shortly. There's a few things I have to do first." She took a step closer to the door and palmed my dick like a pitcher grabbing hold of a baseball.

I didn't flinch. I couldn't. I just allowed her hand to stay there.

"Okay," Sister Mary said. "I'll see you in a bit then."

"Uh-huh," Pamela whispered back, paying Sister Mary no mind at all, concentrating more on the flaccid muscle in her hand. She looked me in the eyes, as though she wanted to kiss me.

"But one more thing before I go," Sister Mary added.

"Uh-huh."

"Have you seen that high-yellow boy who was dressed in the police uniform? Because I can't find him anywhere around here."

Pamela followed my lead again and said, "No. I haven't seen him. But when I do, I can't wait to see what he has to offer me on the last night before I jump the broomstick tomorrow."

"Huh?"

Pamela giggled quietly. She never answered back.

Sister Mary walked away from the door.

I breathed a sigh of relief to Pamela. "Thanks."

But she couldn't wait to get down to the naughty stuff again, grabbing me by the underwear toward the bed.

"Ho-hold up!" I held her hand. "Let me perform a little something for you first."

"What?" She paused for a short moment. Then added: "Why don't I just perform for you first?"

I sorta laughed at her: "You wanna dance for me first?"

"Yeah. Why not?" She sat me at the edge of the bed, then ran over to the stereo again. But this time she turned the radio volume up a little because Missy Elliot's "Lose Control" was playing. "You know," she went on to add, "when I was in college, I almost became a dancer too."

"Oh, for real?" I didn't believe a word she had just said.

"Yeah." She began to wiggle her body like a crippled snake. "Can't you see I have what it takes?"

"Oh, yeah, you look like a professional," I lied with a straight face, then leaned back a little with both of my hands resting behind me—like two kickstands—to prop myself up. "You certainly have all the moves."

"Now" —she smiled proudly— "watch me back this ass up for you."

I hid a laugh from her. It wasn't the fact that she was offbeat that had me cracking up on the inside, but rather because of the fact that she had no ass back there to back up for me. Her booty was flat like a Papa John's pizza box. She didn't even have an ounce of fat back there to keep a brother satisfied. Believe me, I have seen better looking asses on white chicks. Far better; especially in Georgia. Not to mention South Carolina too. So really ... who was she gulling, I wondered. But one thing I knew for certain, though: she was popping her hips, in and out, giving all she had, moving closer to me as if she were preparing to give me a lap dance. And who knows where this might lead to, I thought. I swallowed hard. I mean like really, really hard.

Fuck this shit!

I glanced over to my duffel bag. I needed a condom just in case. You should never underestimate situations like this. I extended a leg out, hoping to draw a bag over to me without getting off the bed. Her twat was right there in front of me, pumping back and forth, just inches away from my dick. And I needed to suit up.

The moment called for it.

The only difference between Pamela's bedroom and King of Diamond nightclub in Miami was that we were the only ones inside the room, secluded from everyone else. And just when the scene was getting heated, Pamela tried to pop her ass a little better for me before she ground my lap. But something went wrong: Her body jerked a bit.

"Ow!" She held onto her lower back. "I think I broke something."

I leaped up and got in front of her. "Throw your arms over my shoulders." I wrapped my arms around her waist and slowly started raising her body upward until she stood straight up again. "So how does it feel now?"

"Ahh," she exhaled, wrapping her arms around me. "I feel a little better now, but I still feel a sharp pain."

"Where, right here?" I asked, with my arms still around her back.

"Oh, yes.... But a little lower."

"Right here?"

"No.... Just a little lower."

I smiled because I had a funny feeling she was going to say something like that to me. I walked over to the bed and asked her to lie on her stomach.

"Why?"

"Because I have a perfect remedy for you."

She smiled back. When she laid on the bed, she slowly cracked her legs open for me to steal a peek at her chocolate chip cookie.

I was impressed: She had a Brazilian bikini wax. I felt tempted.

The radio was playing a bit too loud, though: it was like killing the vibes inside the room. So I turned the volume down a little. But just before I returned to the bed I scanned her body. It was workable, I thought, then reached for my duffel bag.

Kevin had his hands full for the moment. He was still entertaining the females in the living room.

Sister Mary was in there too, but she kept her distance—in the corner of the room—observing their sinful activities. "How disgusting," she murmured, watching everybody else fondling Kevin's body like they were sexual nymphos. "You all make me sick to my stomach."

About ten minutes later, one of the females by the name of Cathy brought things to a stop when she got upset. "Joyce!" she snapped. "Why you have to be so darn greedy?" She paused. Then immediately added, "We would like to touch on his dick too!"

Joyce didn't pay her any mind, she was making naughty, wry facial expressions at Kevin with her perverted "Whews" and "Ahhhs".

Cathy snatched her purse off the floor and grabbed a business card out of there. "I would like it if you could call me when you have some time" —she extended her hand to Kevin— "so we can continue this on a later day. Because my money is just as good; if not, better!"

Kevin quickly took her info, and she left.

Sister Mary looked at the clock on the wall. "Now, where is this gal?" she whispered, speaking to no one in particular. "It's nearly one in the morning, so what can possibly be keeping her from her own party?" She snuck out of the living room to investigate Pamela's whereabouts before Kevin caught her trying to leave again.

She strolled down the hall and knocked on Pamela's bedroom door a few times, but there was no answer.

That's weird, she thought.

Then she tried to open the door but it was locked. "Pam musta fallen asleep," she mumbled to herself. "She has a big day tomorrow...," her words faded somewhere around here when she heard some sort of sighing sound coming from the other side of the door.

She stood still, then edged her ear against the door to eavesdrop on Pamela. Then she heard a clarion, moaning cry from the other side of the door: "Ohhh, ohh, ohh yes. Oh yes.... Ohhh.... That's it! Please don't stop! Don't stop! Oh, yes, right there. Oh, yes! That's the spot. Oh, yes, rights there. Work it, baby. Work it out for me. Uh, Uh, ohhh, yes—"

Sister Mary couldn't take it any longer. Perhaps that was the reason why she started pounding on the door like a Nazi soldier looking for a hiding Jew. "Pam!" She kept rapping on the door. "Pam I know you're in there! Don't do this to yourself! You're getting married tomorrow!"

Pamela shouted back: "Not right now! Not right now, Aunt Mary! Uh! Uh, yes! ... Not right now-ooooow!"

Sister Mary was shocked.

"Now, what did I tell you about sneaking away from me?"

But before Sister Mary could twist around to see who that was, it was too late: Kevin had already snuck up behind her like a thief in the night and ground his dick between her meaty buttocks.

"Oh, Jesus!" Sister Mary gaped her mouth, wondering if that was a hard crucifix or his—

Kevin ground on her again. But this time he stabbed his dick directly on her booty-hole. Yeah, that spot: On her backdoor.

She collapsed in his arms.

He knew she hadn't passed out because when she looked up at him, she spoke in a feeble tone of voice: "Can you take me to my room.... I feel kinda light-headed."

"Oh, hell yeah!" He threw her arm over his shoulder, heading toward the back room. "What about in there."

"... Sure."

Pamela was stretched out on the bed, lying on her stomach with baby oil on her back.

"Oh, thank you," she said after I got finished massaging her back. "I haven't felt so relaxed and invigorated in such a long time. Thanks."

"Uh, that was nothing." I swear, even though she wasn't wearing any panties, my intention was strictly on easing the tension out of her back. "So accept that as my wedding gift, from me to you."

She laughed a little, propping her back against the headboard, folding her legs over one another like a Navajo Indian. Her titties were huge: it consisted of two watermelon jugs and raisin size nipples. The California kinds. No kidding. I felt the urge to reach over there and start sucking on either one of them. They were plumpy looking—just craving to be sucked on—especially that right one. It looked a little bit bigger than the other one.

"You're such a sweetheart," she said, shooting me an expensive smile while patting me on the leg. "We have to try to do this more often. I feel so renewed."

"Well" —I smiled back, trying my hardest not to look below her chin— "at least you can say that."

"Why do you say that?"

"It's nothing. I'm just blabbing off at the mouth. That's all."

"Please, I insist. Tell me."

"Woman," I tried to joke with her. "I barely know you. How will it look if I shared my problems with you?"

"But you wouldn't be sharing your problems with me. I only want to know what's bothering you."

"But I barely know you."

"So ... that makes it even more convenient for you to tell me because now you can speak freely without holding anything back." She paused for a short moment. Then added: "Just think of it this way ... it would be like we're just thinking out loud."

"Damn, you're good." I sorta laughed. "You sound like one of those shrinks who be trying to get up in people's minds and shit."

She raised one of her eyebrows higher than the other one, then relaxed them.

"Oh, hell nah!" I was taken by surprise. "You're kidding me, right?" I paused, only for a few seconds. Then asked another question: "You're a psychologist, for real?"

She nodded with a little smirk. "For the past eleven years."

"Nah, you're pulling my leg."

"Why do you say that?"

I looked at her breasts, then back to her eyes. "Because you sure don't—. Well, please don't take this in the wrong way, but you sure don't look like a psychologist."

"Believe me, I have heard that many times before." She smiled with appreciation, as if she wanted to laugh with me. "But I can assure you, us doctors come in all different shapes, sizes, and colors."

"I see that now." I looked at her breasts again.

She laughed. "Remember," she tried to get back to our main topic, "telling someone about your problem is just one of the keys to unlocking your dilemma." She paused for a second. Then continued with, "Some people let their dilemma out by speaking to others, and there are those who like to write it out. Because either way you look at it, it'll set your mind free. We all encounter these obstacles in life. It's a learning process to allow us to grow. As a matter of fact, I have an issue that I'm battling with right now, as we speak."

"You?" I said in disbelief. "But you're supposed to be the doctor here?"

"Of course I am. But I'm also a human being, like everyone else, who has feelings and choices to make in life."

My smile started fading away. "So what are your issues then?"

She hesitated for a moment before she came out with it. She began telling me how she was supposed to marry a man, by the named of David Shall, a psychologist like her, who really loved her.

And from what she said, her fiancé was willing to accept anything to secure her happiness. But still, she wasn't absolutely sure about marrying him because she believed she has some sort of complication with her ovaries: She just couldn't produce any children for him. Although she said she loved him too, she didn't want to deprive him of raising a family of his own. But according to her, David didn't care about that. He had unconditional love for her, ever since their high school days. He knew about—get this—their complications, and still he didn't care. He had even spoken to her about adopting a child. But in spite of everything, she knew it wouldn't be the same.

I tried my best to be open-minded about all of this, and when she finished telling me about her ordeal, I told her, "We have to remember one thing though."

"And what's that?"

"We don't choose the fate that lays before us," I began to say. "It's fate that chooses our destinies: She knows what's best for us. Yeah, we all could agree to disagree that all of us have some crazy notion about why we are put on earth and for what supposed purpose. But for many, it's for some unexplainable reason beyond our imagination. To some we are here to experience and enjoy the five senses: touch, taste, feel, smell, and see. But only he, she, or even some people might even say they. I'm talking about those supposed supernatural beings in the sky. The gods, as they like to call them. Only they can explain it to us. And that's only if it's true when our time is up down here on earth. Even then, we'll probably be surprised to learn who we really are and what actually created us.

"So whether we were created due to a natural disaster in space by some kind of explosion from one of the suns or by some sort of alien beings out there. Only at the end of time can that be revealed to us.... No books. No priest, rabbi, or imam can choose our fates for us. Because our fates lie deep within us, not in some mythological belief system in some religious text that we're constantly killing each other over. You see, as human beings, we fail to remember our number one gift of all."

"And what's that?"

"Joy," I told her. "Which all of us have. We should never forget about that gift. It's right there within our soul. In which all we have to do when we're feeling down and sad is activate it because it's right there in front of us. It will help us find a way out of our miseries and misfortune."

"You just lost me there," she said. "But you just said—. Uh, never mind. Your point is?"

"My point is this," I went on to say. "We are all faced with obstacles in our lives that we must go through so that we can perhaps learn from them.... And if it's fate that placed your fiancé in your path for you to be happy, to make you feel complete, then it's fate that put y'all destiny together. So you should be joyful, boo. What I'm saying is just follow your soul, it's your best mentor—"

"But don't you mean, I should follow my heart?"

"Nah. You should never follow your heart. Your heart can easily deceive you. It blinds you from the truth. Because most of the time, we try to follow our desires based on what our hearts hope for, but rather what's best for us."

There was a brief moment of silence.

Then she finally said, "All of these years in this complex field, I can honestly say that was the most intriguing things I have ever heard before." She then leaned forward and kissed me on the cheek. "Okay, it's your turn now."

I gave her a long, youthful smile. "Actually, I believe I have just solved it myself. With your help, of course."

"You're such a sweetheart. Perhaps it was our fate that allowed us to meet on this day. Because I certainly feel good right now. What about you?"

"Yeah" —I sorta nodded my head— "I feel good too."

"But I know another way to make you feel even better."

"Yeah? How?"

Without words, she made an unmistakable gesture, looking down to my private area.

"Girl!" I grabbed a pillow from beside her and slapped her with it. "You're getting married tomorrow."

"So!"

I got off the bed.

She then leaped on my back. "That's tomorrow. A day that isn't promised to anyone. But today is today; a day of its own. So let's make use of it and have some fun."

I tried to shake her off my back, but she had a good grip around me. We both fell on the bed together. My back against her soft breasts.

"Okay, okay," she said. "If you're scared and you don't wanna have sex with me, just tittie-fuck me then."

"Just a tittie-fuck, and no sex?"

"Yeah."

I thought it over for a few seconds. "Uhh, what the hell! I'm cool with that. But that's it. Understood?"

Without a response, she let go of me. She then slid over and positioned herself on the bed. She propped herself up a bit, laying on her back with her titties standing up at attention, hanging freely. I smiled; she smiled back. Then she pressed her titties upward from the side, applying pressure to them so they could stay firm and close together.

They looked beautiful.

I pulled my G-string off and started yanking on my flaccid muscle to get it right. And it did after about the fifteenth pull. It sorta got hard, but not all the way there yet.

She licked her lips. I smiled again and climbed on top of her, resting my rod between her breasts. She started giggling, then stopped.

Within seconds, she made me look down at her when she started making all those "Mmms" and "Ahhhs" sounds while smothering my dick between her warm skin. And it felt good and tight.

I got into my rhythm and leaned toward her, resting my hands against the headboard, sliding my manhood back and forth between her melons.

"Mmmmm," she dragged again with a sweet sound to my ears. Then said, "Work these titties for me, baby."

Oh, yeah.... My mind musta blanked out for a moment because I started taking better strokes as if I were really up in some pussy. My dick grew stronger.

"That's it," she barely whispered. "Fuck these titties for me, baby…. Mmmmmmm, that's it. Fuck them for me. They're yours."

I started taking curvy strokes now. Those long curvy strokes, with all back motion. I closed my eyes and thought about Whoopi Goldberg, because Pamela sorta sounded like her.

"Yeahhh, that's what I'm talking about. Fuck these titties, baby."

"Oh, yeahhh," I whispered back, sliding my dick back and forth, repeating my rhythm with a steady pace because it was feeling too good to be true. "Just go ahead and squeeze them a little tighter for me, Whoopi."

And Pamela did.

Then immediately afterward, I felt her lips brushed against and head of my dick. And then again. Even after my next pump as well. I wanted to stop, but I couldn't. Better yet, let the truth be told, I didn't want to. It probably had a lot to do with me opening my eyes and seeing what Pamela was doing down there. She was perking her lips out, kissing the head of my dick, with her mouth slightly opened.

I have to start watching The View more often.

Then I watched Pamela stick her tongue out, acting like she wanted to get a taste of me. Then she did, with a little help from me that is, on that following pump. Her tongue felt soft and wet. I loved how it felt. I wanted to feel her tongue again, so I pushed a little closer toward her mouth. Then she did the unthinkable: she swiped her tongue underneath the shaft of my rod, as if she wanted my dick inside her mouth. I almost fainted. I wanted to stop now. I swear I did, but my hips wouldn't allow me to. I kept going, watching her stretching her tongue out a little further, tempting me, daring me, and double daring me.

And then, Oh, my goodness, Pamela blanketed her lips over the head of my dick with a light suction kiss when I took another pump. I swallowed hard. I kept pumping. I couldn't stop. Or at least, that's what I wanted to believe, because I wanted her to do it again. And I'll be damned! She did. Then she opened her mouth for me and my dick slid inside there.

I closed my eyes and imagined Whoopi Goldberg was down there, working wonders on me.

Now, that was good!

I pulled my dick out of Pamela and barely sat at the edge of the bed. I was sorta out of breath. I reached over and grabbed my underwear off the floor. I turned back to her, feeling satisfied. I couldn't believe it. She was sensationally great. And just a short while ago, I had the audacity to rate her a 7, on a scale of 1 to 10, when in fact she deserved an 8 with that tight pussy of hers. But, however, if she was willing to do a threesome with me and Kevin—I swear—I wouldn't mind bumping her up to a 9, or even a 10, if she allowed me to hit her on her ... never mind. I might be pushing it.

But, from the look of things, she seemed like she wouldn't mind me hitting her in the ass either. She had a naughty smile on her face. So I stayed on the bed with her, for about two hours straight, talking about everything that came to mind: from the finger nail scratches she left on my back to me busting a nut inside her when the condom busted.

"So, what we do from here?" she asked, then reached over to give me a kiss. "Because I know I wouldn't mind staying in contact with you."

"Me, too."

We both saw a car light flashed across the window.

She looked at the alarm clock beside her. "It's getting late."

It was 5:20 in the morning.

We finally ended our conversation with a warm kiss and promised to meet up again. Perhaps at her office.

Of course, I didn't mind.

She got off the bed and threw on a T-shirt. After I got dressed, she walked me back into the living room to meet up with Kevin. But he was nowhere in sight.

"I think he musta left," I told her. "So, I guess I have to catch a cab home."

"No. You don't have to. I can take you home if that's the case."

"Thanks." I tried not to scan the room but I couldn't help it. Several of her friends were all scattered about the place, stripped down to their bras and panties. I even noticed that someone had tossed their panties up on the chandelier. "And I'd be damned. That's my homey's bag over there."

"So most likely he's still in the house."

"I guess so."

We left the room and went down the hall to go search for Kevin.

About five minutes later, we finally found him sleeping inside one of the bedrooms, curled up beside a female who was covered from head to toe. I smiled because I knew I wasn't the only one who got some pussy last night.

I squeezed his nostrils to wake him up. It worked.

He wobbled his head to break my fingers loose; he seemed frightened at first until he saw me at the bedside. "What the fuck are you trying to do, my nigga? Kill me or something?"

"C'mon," I whispered back. "Let's go."

"What time is it?"

"A little after five."

He slid from under the bed sheet, naked, then scanned the floor for something.

"Oh, my...."

We both looked toward the doorway.

It was Pamela, and she seemed like she was enjoying the view.

"There it is." Kevin found his underwear near the window and slid them on. And as we were about to sneak out of the room, he stopped when he saw a pen on top of the chest dresser. "Just gimme a second." He grabbed the pen and started jotting something down on the back of the receipt. "I'm gonna leave her my info."

"Oh, yeah? I can't believe this." I headed back toward the bed. "I have to see what you were working with last night." And just when I was about to pull the bed sheet off her face, he stopped me.

"Nah, let her sleep, my nigga." He shoved my hand away from the sheet. "You're gonna wake her up."

"Man, stop tripping. I wanna see what she looks like."

"She looks alright. That's all you needa know. Let's go."

That wasn't good enough for me because I wanted to see her for myself. I went for the bed sheet and tried to pull it off her face again, but that creep shoved my hand away once more.

Oh, hell nah!

I pushed him back and went for the sheet again. He grabbed me. I resisted. I tried to shake his hands off my wrists, but he wouldn't give in. He wanted to protect her identity at all cost. But it wasn't like I wanted to fuck her or something behind his back. I just wanted to see what she looked like. That's all. But it didn't make a difference, though, because our horse playing beside the bed did the trick anyway. She rolled over just before the bed sheet slid off her face.

And I couldn't believe this shit!

How could this stupid muthafucker sleep with this bitch!

Sister Mary opened one eye, and then the other one.

I dove to the floor. I had to. I didn't have enough time to run out of the room. She would have caught me. And I guess Pamela couldn't believe it either. Because when I looked her way, she dipped from the doorway. Then seconds later, I heard a door slam, somewhere down the hall.

But Kevin stood at Sister Mary's bedside. "Ms. Sleepy-head," he played it off to her, perfectly. "I didn't mean to wake you."

"You didn't," she lied, sounding a bit hoarse. "But whatchu doing out of bed?"

"I have to go. It's getting late and I have to head out. But here." He extended his hand out to her. "Take this.... It's my info, so give me a call whenever you have time."

"Well, I have the time for you now, if you wanna go for another round."

I nearly gagged.

Kevin kicked me in the ribs, and told her, "Not right now, you-little-animal-you." She purred like a little feral cat; to which he continued with, "Maybe another day."

"Sure" —Sister Mary started blushing— "we can do that." She paused. Then added: "Lemme put my teefisses back in my mouth."

That did it.

As she reached for her dentures off the nightstand, she must have heard me making that puking sound because, immediately afterward, she asked Kevin, "Did you say something, baby?"

"Nah, that was my stomach." He then kicked me again. "I'm kinda hungry."

"So lemme get up and make you something to eat."

"No-no-no." He kinda panicked, holding his hand out to her so she couldn't get out of the bed. "You don't have to. I'm just gonna go home and eat."

"Are you sure?"

"Yeah. Just go back to sleep and call me when you get a chance."

She agreed.

Within minutes, Kevin and I were outside just before the sunrise. As we jumped inside his SUV, I didn't want to talk to him. Or better yet, I didn't even want to look his fucking way! He fucked up! And I'm dead serious about that, too. He shouldn't have slept with that bitch! I could only imagine what she going to tell Ms. Betty now.

"What's up with all this silent treatment, my nigga?"

"Don't take this shit in the wrong way, or lightly. But what the fuck possessed you to fuck the caseworker's friend?"

"Didn't I tell you that I had your back and not to worry about her?"

"Yeah, but—"

"But nothing! As long as I got her, we got her. And besides, in a way, you kinda got off on her last night too."

I swear, I wanted to punch him in his muthafucking face, but I didn't. Rather, I just asked him, "How the fuck I kinda slept with her last night?"

"How?" He kept his eyes on the road.

"Yeah, how?!"

He looked at me, then back to the road. Then said, "Because when she told me that she knew who we were last night, when I helped her to that room that you had found us in, she started saying some bullshit like, she was gonna tell her friend on us."

"Damn." I turned to the passenger window again.

"Yeah, but don't worry about that though. After she said that shit to me, I was like fuck it then. Because, if that be the case, I wanted her to tell her friend something else too. So I stuck my hand in her muthafucking panties and started pumping my fingers in her as if I was sending a Morse code to China."

I spun back around to him. I really had to look at this sick bastard! I couldn't believe what he had just told me.

And he went on to say, "She's a freak, my nigga. For real. Because when she put up that little fight with me when I then slid my dick inside her, she started mumbling that same shit outta her mouth about she was still gonna tell on us, so I tried to cover her mouth with my hand and that hoe started licking on my fingers and shit! And the first thing I thought about was Oprah. No lie. So to make her feel better, I stuck two fingers inside her mouth and told her to pretend like if she were sucking on your dick. And that bitch—"

"Whose dick?"

He turned to me and said, "Yours." Then he turned his head back to the windshield. "And my nigga, she was sucking the fuck outta my fingers too, telling me to talk dirty to her while I was dicking her down."

"Nah." I wiped the frown off my face.

"Hell, yeah!"

"What'd you say to her?"

"Suck my homeboy's dick, Oprah. Suck his dick," he said almost in laughter. "And that shit was feeling so good, my nigga, I told her okay, it's my turn now. And you won't believe it?"

"What?"

"She got some fire-head. One of the best heads that I've ever had before."

I laughed.

"What's so funny?"

"Man, you're sick!" I kept laughing at him. "I don't know what could have possibly possessed you to fuck that old-ass broad? Suppose you would have caught ringworm from her?"

"Shiiiit, if that hoe has ringworms, it'll be worth the risk then. Because her pussy felt good and tight. And that cracka, Mikey wasn't lying about older chicks either." He paused and looked at me. Then: "Hey, you wanna get some of that?"

"Some of what?"

"Some of that hoe's pussy."

"Are you fucking crazy!"

"Oh, because if you wanted some pussy from her, you probably had to end up giving her—" he started to say, but cut it short right there.

So I pursued after it because I wanted to know: "End up giving her what?"

He ignored me.

I'm not going to lie, I was clueless as to what he was talking about at first. But when Kevin kept quiet and accidentally licked his lips, a crazy notion came to mind: "Yo, I know you didn't eat that bitch's pussy last night?"

He kept his eyes on the road.

"Man, as long as you visit my crib," I said between a light laugh, "don't even think about drinking out of my glasses anymore."

He barely jerked his head to the side and said, "So."

I punched him.

Having a job was one thing, but working one's fingers to the bone to maintain a job is another thing. It's a totally different thing. But what if you were your own boss, and worked according to your own schedule?

It would be exceptional.

And that's the sort of lifestyle Naomi has, as a small business entrepreneur. The true definition of an independent woman. She owned and operated a small architectural enterprise from her home. Yet she still found time to take breaks, here and there, and keep up on her work assignments. She knew serenity was a good thing, and she was enjoying every bit of it by relaxing at her desk without any stress or worries. A pencil in one hand; the phone in the other. What more could she ask out of life?

Not a damn thing!

So why in the hell Ciara was bugging Naomi about an appointment that she had scheduled for an old friend of hers about two weeks ago, as if it were important to Naomi now? It wasn't. At least not in this lifetime. So instead of losing her composure, Naomi pulled the phone away from her ear and slowly shook her head in disbelief.

"Hello!" Ciara's voice echoed from the phone receiver. "Naomi, are you listening to me?"

Naomi placed the phone back to her ear. "Yeah, I'm listening to you," she said. "I'll give him a call to remind him about his appointment."

"Good! Because I put my neck on the line for you this time."

Naomi laughed. "You shouldn't have."

"What?"

"I'm only joking. I'll give him a call right now, because I'm sorta busy working on another project."

"Okay! I'll speak to you later then."

When Naomi cleared the phone line with Ciara, she hesitated a bit before she dialed a seven digit number in her phone. But then she had second thoughts.

She hung up.

"It's about time you responded to my messages."

No comment.

Then I gave it another try: "I thought you would never call me back."

"Do you know who you are speaking to?"

"Yeah. This is Sonja, right?"

"No! This—"

I cut her off: "I do have a caller ID, Naomi."

There was a short pause. Then she broke the silence with a little sarcasm: "I see you're full of games. But I should have expected something like that from you. The unexpected."

"Don't even go there." I got serious but in a friendly way. "Let's put that behind us, because if I could take back my yesterdays, our today would be much better than what it is right now. But that's something we can fix, right?"

"You must be retarded."

I laughed.

"Who you think I am? One of those trashy females that you are used to? Well excuse me, I'm not one of them!"

"I know."

There was another pause, a little longer than the first one. Then she asked: "Do you remember my friend Ciara from Decorous' Fashion World?"

"Yeah."

"Well, she gave me a call a moment ago and asked me to give you a call just to remind you of your two o'clock appointment."

"Yeah, tomorrow, right?"

"No, it's for today."

"Today?"

"Of course, today. I told you last week. Did you forget about it?"

"Nah, I remembered." I lied to her. "I just got my days mixed up a bit."

"Oh."

"Well, I have to see if I can reach Carlton to babysit Destini for me. Or, unless you don't mind watching her for me until I get back."

"... I would love to, but I can't right now. I have this project I'm working on." She took a quick pause. Then continued: "But from what I know about Decorous', you can take her along with you. They have a kids' room connected to the lounge area. I think Destini would enjoy it."

"All right then. Let me get ready and head out of here before I be late."

"Okay."

"I'll let you know how everything went. If you don't mind?"

"Sure. You can do that."

"Take care."

"You too."

Immediately after she hung up, I ran into the family room. "Destini, hurry up! Get dressed. We're running late!"

Destini's face broke out with two ridges between her eyebrows. I guess she got upset that I shut the video game off while she was playing on it. But who cares? She got up and went to her room to change anyway.

Within half an hour later, I was ready. Well-groomed with a splash of Cool-Water on my neck. If anything, I wanted to give the executives at Decorous' a good impression about me, so I wore my custom-made suit that I designed myself. I took a quick look at my wristwatch: I was an hour away from my scheduled appointment. An hour eighteen minutes away, if I had to be precise about it.

"DESTINI! HURRY UP! YOU'RE GONNA MAKE ME LATE!"

About two seconds later she came running in the hall.

"What the hell happened to you?" I looked at my wristwatch again, then back at the same dingy shirt she was wearing just a moment ago. "I thought I told you to get dressed."

"I am dressed."

"No, you're not. Who're you trying to kid?"

"But I am dressed."

"No, you're not! You can't wear those."

"Why?"

"Because I said so, that's why. So go back in there and put something else on. Something more decent and not so sleazy looking!"

"But all my clothes look like this."

"What are you talking about? What about the outfit I made for you last week?"

"It's in my room."

"So why don't you wear that one?"

"Because you told me not to."

"I didn't tell you not to—." I started, then decided to cut it short right there to rub my temples instead: she was giving me a fucking head-rush. Think. "Okay" —I looked at her again— "you can wear it now. So please, hurry up and go change for me. I'm in a rush. And while you're in there, don't put those ugly-ass sneakers back on either! Wear the ones I bought you the other day."

She turned away from me, then mumbled something under her breath as she headed back to her room.

And that's when it hit me: "What the hell you just called me?!"

By the time I arrived at Decorous' Fashion World, I had about twenty minutes to kick back and get my lines together before my scheduled meeting.

"Go grab two seats for us," I told Destini, pointing toward the back row. "The ones over there."

"Okay."

I walked to the receptionist's desk and told her who I was.

"Okay, Mr. Powell, you can have a seat and I will call for you once they ask to see you."

"Thanks." I walked to where Destini was sitting.

To be truthful, I didn't feel a bit worried about the upcoming interview. I didn't. Really. I guess I was concentrating more on what their rejection would be this time: "Uhh, that's a little too old-fashioned for us, Mr. Powell," or "Your work is not what we're looking for, Mr. Powell." Or better yet, "I'm sorry, Mr. Powell, but we're looking for something different at this time."

I just shook my head because I was kind of used to all the denials that were thrown at me in the past.

I rested my portfolio on my lap, then on the floor, then on my lap again. I had second thoughts. I crouched over a bit, pressing my elbows down against the leather casing. I stared at my folded hands, as if I was praying for a miracle to occur, while tapping my foot against the marble floor.

Then it dawned on me: I was friggin' nervous when I felt butterflies in my stomach.

I twisted to my right when I heard a few people laughing.

From a short distance away, near the corner of the room, over there beside the small artificial palm tree, there was a good size cubicle for children to play in. It was neither too small nor too big. It was just right. A decent size. And from the look of it, there were five kids playing in there. They were running inside the cubicle, like the Little Rascal gang: they were loud. You could actually hear them from anywhere inside the waiting area. And of course, there was this one little freckle-faced kid among them whose name was Sammy. He was the loudest out of all of them; he had control over the other four rug-rats.

"Okay, I had enough of this," he said. "I don't wanna play cops and robbers anymore." He turned to his two buddies, winked at them, then twisted back to those other two smaller kids in the cubicle with him. "I wanna play football now," he told them, hoping to get more physical. Even though the two other kids who had picked to be on his team had the advantage already, he needed an extra person to be on the other team to balance it out for him.

They all looked out the cubicle entrance; Sammy smiled.

Destini looked at me. She acted as if she wanted to say something, but she just looked away.

Then, out of the blue, I heard Destini's belly give out a slight growl. I looked at her; she looked back at me with a weird expression on her face.

"Are you hungry?"

She hesitated, then said, "Uh-huh. A little."

"Give me a second." I got up and walked over to the vending machines on the other side of the room and purchased two cans of orange soda, two packs of powdered doughnuts, and a few bags of chips. "Huhn, eat these for now. And once we get finished here, we can go out to grab us something else to eat. Okay?"

"Okay." She burst open a bag of barbecue corn chips.

"Is there a specific place where you'd like to go eat at?"

She looked up with a smile. "Burger King."

I agreed.

Then somebody threw a piece of paper, hitting Destini on the side of the face. She immediately twisted toward the cubicle, looking upset. I looked, too. And the only ones who stood out there, among the five kids, were two little youngsters. A little girl and a four-eyed, geeky-looking kid; they motioned their hands to her.

"Don't even think about it," I told Destini. "You're not going over there."

It was at that precise moment that an angry Black woman stormed out from a doorway near the receptionist's desk, going off at the mouth about the interview she just had with a few executives. She stormed right past us, straight into the play room and snatched that little four-eyed kid by his hand.

"C'mon, we're leaving!" she told him, nearly dragging him along the way. Then she suddenly stopped when she reached the center of the room as she realized that all eyes were on her. Yes, even mine, too. Then, she informed us: "These people don't know a damn thing about the fashion industry! They're nothing but a bunch of filthy voyeur, pigs, who only want to pollute our Black inner cities with" — she threw both of her hands above her ears, twiddling two fingers on each side of her head to indicate quotation marks— "with something more revealing or skimpy-looking that can draw the younger, hip-hop generation to our retailers' markets—"

"Ms. McMiller!" a security guard cut in, while stretching his hand toward the exit, "would you please leave the premises. You're causing a disturbance in this place of business."

She shot him a poisonous stare and said, "You can kiss my black ass! And how do you like that for a disturbance?" She then left the building with her geeky kid dragging at her side.

Within seconds, everything was back to normal again, as if nothing had ever happened a short moment ago. Now, that was a damn shame! Ms. McMiller's statement was swept under the carpet and nobody in the room had the heart to discuss it among themselves. Speaking for myself, I wasn't afraid. But then again, I thought it would be in my best interest to mind my own damned business! Hey, I didn't know her. And besides, even if I did, I didn't want to piss these people off before I could get my foot in the door.

"Mr. Powell!"

I looked straight ahead.

Fuck! It was the receptionist. She was looking directly at me.

I literally felt my heart skip a beat. Maybe two beats. Then I raised from my seat and said, "Yes," with my hand in the air as if I were back in grammar school.

"They would like to see you now."

"Thank you." I turned to Destini and said, "Stay right here until I get back. And be good."

She nodded. "Okay."

Immediately after I disappeared through the double doors that led to the hallway, Naomi's friend, Ciara, was waiting for me. She led the way.

Meanwhile back in the lobby, Destini was sitting peacefully by herself until Sammy and three other rug-rats sat beside her.

Now, what do they want? Destini probably wondered, looking to her left side, and then to her right.

Sammy and his gang wore impish looks on their faces as they were clogging up her territory.

"Hey!" Destini grabbed the powdered doughnut from Sammy's hand. "That's not yours! That's mine!"

Ciara stopped me a few feet from the conference room. "Loosen up," she recommended while straightening the wrinkles from my shirt. "When they ask you questions, make sure your reply is short and simple."

"Okay."

"You'll do fine."

"Thanks, I needed that."

"Believe me," she tried to reassure me again when she saw my facial expression, "you'll do fine."

Yeah, that was easy for her to say, I thought. I approached the conference room doorway and stopped. All eyes were on me, coming from six people. Two males, four females. I smiled to hide my jitters from them and walked inside.

The conference room was large enough to hold about thirty people. But like I said, there were six of them. However, they were sitting around a long oak wood table that was located directly in the center of the room.

Ciara walked to the table, gave a quick introduction as to who I was, then took a seat.

The head man in charge was Eric Dorsey, a medium-built guy with a dark Wesley Snipes skin complexion, who was casually dressed in expensive clothes and who also had the appearance of a wanna-be pimp, although he looked like somebody's grandpa who retired from the street life a long time ago.

"Please, have a seat," he said, waving his hand across the table, indicating that I could sit anywhere I wanted.

"Thank you." I decided to sit a short distance away from him, down by the other end of the table. But mysteriously, a chair slid out from under the table and blocked my path. I looked across the table, where the chair had slid out from, and there were two plus-size females with at least a pound of makeup on their faces. They smiled at me.

What the hell! I smiled back and sat in front of them.

We chatted for about two minutes before Eric interrupted us with: "We needa get down to business here. I don't wanna hold you up any longer than I have to, Mr. Powell." He looked at his colleagues with a hollow stare; then back to me. "So, can you show us what you have to offer so we can make a decision? And I do apologize if that sounds a bit rude, but we're all working on a tight schedule here and our time is very valuable."

"Yes, but of course. I'm sorry for that. So let me show you what I have here." I placed my portfolio on the table. It seemed like everybody in the room raised their eyebrows. "Right here," I said, displaying one of my drawings, "you all can see that this art design is quite different from other sketches you might have come across before. Actually, this is one of my favorites. Not only do I love the violet color for this turtleneck sweater, but I love the casual look about it."

Eric shot me a sarcastic smirk. "This isn't particularly different from other designs we've seen before," he claimed. "So what makes this drawing superior to the others?"

"Good question. Well, what makes this drawing special is this…. What if we took the northern winter wears and converted the material into something lighter for the weather down here—"

"You're losing me," he said, then cut his eyes from me to his secretary, quietly belittling my explanation. Then he looked back at me.

To which I continued: "With this design, what I'm trying to explain is we can change the sweater material from something thick into something much thinner to fit our weather down here in the south. The similarities will remain the same. I believe it will bring a new look for those who enjoy that northern-style, but who prefer to live down here in the south with us. Do you understand me now?"

"No, not really. I can't grasp what you're trying to convey here. Just move right along."

"Sure." I displayed another drawing. "In this illustration, you can see a silk dashiki. But unlike that deep split down the middle, I redesigned it, as you can see ... I lifted the collar up a bit here to fit perfectly about the chest area."

Eric wasn't impressed. He cut his eyes from my work and pressed the button on the intercom, that was located on the table right in front of him.

"Yes, Mr. Dorsey!" a female's voice came through the speaker.

"Sharon, can you tell me how many more interviews we have scheduled for today?"

"Two more, sir."

"Okay. I think I'm finished here. So you can send in—"

I cut him off: "But I'm not finished yet! I have a few more drawings that I would like to show you."

"I'm sorry. But I thought you had something worth my time."

Worth your time? That's a new one for my collection.

"But," I still contested, "you haven't given me a chance to show you all my drawings yet."

"I'm sorry, Mr. Powell," he had the audacity to say, while getting up from his seat. "But we're looking for something different. And I know I'm not just speaking for myself here when I say this ... I'm sorry."

I looked around the table, which everybody else had that impassive look on their faces. Absolutely empty. I turned back to him and wanted to tell this country-ass nigga to Speak for yourself. You punk-ass bitch!

The meeting was over: Just like that.

I tried my hardest to convince him, but he wasn't going for it. He just walked me to the front part of the office, over by the receptionist's desk. But before I could tell him to Go fuck off, we both heard a slight commotion—over by the seated area—which drew our attention there.

It was Destini; she was arguing with a little youngster, toe to toe. "Give me my daddy's soda back!" she demanded.

"It's mine!"

"Is not! You're lying!" Destini extended her hands out and grabbed onto the soda can. "Give it here!"

"No!"

I tried to rush over there because they started tugging for the can. And just as I approached them, the little boy released the soda can and said, "You can have it then," giving her full control of it.

SPLASH!

The soda spattered all over Destini's face and clothes.

"No! Don't!" I caught Destini's hand just in time before she threw the soda can at the little boy. "Let me have that."

She let go of the can and tried to break loose from me.

I wrapped my arms around her. "Did he hurt you?"

"Let go of me!" she started crying. "It's not my fault! He came over here, messing with meeeee...."

"I know it wasn't your fault."

Eric strode up beside us. "Is everything okay over here?"

"Yeah, she's all right. She just got some soda thrown on her by that little youngsta over there."

"Hush-hush now," Eric said to Destini, trying to get her attention. "You shouldn't be crying like this in front of those little kids over there. Because you'll only give them something to laugh about."

"I don't care! That ugly boy threw my daddy's soda on me."

"Who did that to you? Which one of them?"

"That one right there! He did it!"

Eric looked over to Sharon, the receptionist, and told her to find out who the little kid belongs to.

"That's your brother-in-law's kid."

"Whose, Winston's?

"I'm afraid so."

He smiled. "That just give me a good enough reason to get rid of him now. Tell him that he's fired! And make sure that he clears his desk out by four o'clock." He turned back to Destini. "Does that make you feel better now?"

"Nooo," she dragged. "I wanna beat him up because he tried to mess my outfit up that my daddy made for me."

"What outfit?"

"The one I'm wearing."

"But I don't see anything wrong with it."

"Yeah, because it fell off already. You're late. But it was on a second ago." She glanced down on her shirt and noticed a few drops of soda that were still clinging to her. "See! There it goes!"

Eric saw the soda drops, then he also saw them roll off her too, straight to the floor, leaving no soda stains on her shirt. I guess he couldn't believe it because he looked surprised when he turned to me. "Did you design this outfit for her?"

"Yeah, about two weeks ago."

He looked at his assistants and they seemed to be impressed by the quality of the design too. They all surrounded Destini, as if she was a living mannequin inside a department store.

Eric turned back to me. "Do you have other drawings similar to this one?"

"Of course," I lied to him. "Actually I have a few drawings, right here in my portfolio."

"Well, I don't mean to bother you, but do you mind stepping back into the conference room with me to discuss those drawings in private."

"Of course I don't mind."

He cut to the secretary's desk. "I need you to cancel all my appointments and if anyone should ask for me, tell them that I've stepped out of the office."

"Sure thing, Mr. Dorsey."

As we were walking back to the meeting, Destini ran up beside me.

And just when I was about to tell her to wait in the lobby for me, Eric cut me off: "She might as well come along with us too. Because if it weren't for her, we probably wouldn't be having this second meeting right now.

He had a point there. So, on that note, I held Destini's hand as we walked up the hallway together.

Back inside the conference room, we all sat around the same table, with Destini at my side. I started to display my sketches again.

"So," Erick cut in and asked Destini, "Which one of these drawings do you like?"

"All of them?"

A few people laughed, including Eric.

"Well," he went on to say to her, "seriously, if you had to pick just one of them, which one would it be?"

She looked puzzled. Confused. Lost. Then she looked at me.

"So," Eric asked again, "which one?"

"Which one?" she whispered, cutting back to him. "... Only one?"

"Yeah."

She hesitated a little more, then said, "None of them right there."

Oh, my goodness! I couldn't believe it: She had betrayed me.

"But I thought you said that you liked all of them?" Eric asked her.

Yeah, me too, you little traitor.

"I do like all of them. But...."

"But, what?" he asked her.

Yeah, but what, Destini? I would like to hear this shit, too!

Destini sighed. Then, she stuck her hand inside her pocket and pulled out a folded sheet of paper, and said, "It's because I like this one better: he made it for me."

My face showed a sign of relief. I could breathe again.

Eric asked, "May I see it?"

She handed the drawing to him.

He unfolded the sheet of paper, then mumbled to himself, "No more worries about messy clothes.... How am I gonna present this new concept to the company?"

I looked at Ciara with a smile. She smiled back. I cut back to Eric. He seemed to be lost in his thoughts. Then, all of a sudden, we heard a slight grumbling sound.

Eric broke his concentration, looking at me. Then, all of us looked at Destini because the sound came from her direction.

"Why y'all looking at me for?" she asked them, pretending to be innocent. Then she looked at me: "It wasn't me, I heard it too."

Everybody in the room laughed quietly to themselves.

"I'm sorry for that," I said to them. "But I promised her earlier that I would take her out to get something to eat after our interview."

"I see." Then Eric pressed the button on the intercom and advised Sharon to place a food order at the local deli shop, the one that stood directly across the street, for everybody in the conference room. He looked at Destini. "What kind of sandwich would you like to have?"

"I dunno."

Eric spoke back into the intercom. "Yeah, Sharon! Just have somebody run over to McDonald's and order a kid's meal for the little one in here. No! Just make that a number one. A big Mac, large fries, and a coke."

"I don't want any Coca Cola!"

"Hold on for a second, Sharon," he said, then turned to Destini. "So what would you like to drink with your meal?"

She smiled. "I want a chocolate milkshake."

He relayed the information back to Sharon and we got down to business.

About half an hour later when I finished giving my presentation, I could tell that they were astonished by my work. I had given them an exceptional performance. I know I had, because they all said so. Eric seemed to be so much into my presentation that he kept bobbing his head the whole time, while munching on his ham and cheese sandwich.

Scanning everybody's face around the table, I couldn't help but remember what had happened a little earlier when Eric had told me that he was looking for something different for his Decorous' establishment. But now—just looking at this—with those same designs inside my portfolio, he was saying that I could be part of his team.

His team?

What the hell! I liked the idea.

After the meeting, Eric and I walked to the front lobby while Destini stood a few steps in front of us, slurping on her chocolate milkshake.

"You know," he reassured me again, "I really meant what I said to you in there. If you could give that same presentation, the same one you have just given me in there, but to my senior partners next week for our upcoming board meeting on Monday, I can see a beautiful future here for you at Decorous'. You would be working directly beside me. It's all up to you now. All I can tell you is this, you just make sure that you don't let me down next week. I'm gonna pull a lot of strings to invite some of the higher executives to the meeting as well."

"I think I can do that for you."

"Just make sure you do that. And in the meantime, I need you to get plenty of rest this weekend, because you'll need it on Monday. I have a good feeling we're gonna knock them out with our drawings."

Our drawings?

Hell, I liked the sound of that, too.

"Sure thing." I have heard similar promises before, but none of them sounded as half true as this one. I just couldn't believe my dream was finally about to be fulfilled. I was going to be a marketable fashion designer.

I started cogitating on this upcoming Monday meeting, determined that no matter what these next few days called for, I wouldn't be distracted by anything. No clubbing. No partying. And no to just about anything else that might pop up in the meantime. My mind was made up. I would dedicate my time to nothing other than preparing for my make-or-break presentation. I have to. Not only would I be at that nine o'clock meeting on time, but I would beat them there.

When Destini saw me shaking Eric's hand at the exit, she looked relieved. Within seconds, Destini and I were out in the parking lot. I wanted to leap for joy and click both of my heels together—like a happy leprechaun—but I kept my composure down. I didn't want to expose my puerile nature out there in the parking lot. I had ample time to celebrate later.

As soon as I cranked the car engine, I saw a guy in my rearview mirror, carrying a small box in his hands, with a young child walking alongside of him.

"Eh, Destini. Isn't that that same little kid who threw that drink on you earlier?"

"Where?" She grabbed the door latch. "Where's he at?"

Carlton took another pull of his indo-weed, then stretched his arm around his Cuban shawty's shoulders who was sitting beside him on the couch. "This some good shit right here," he said to her while exhaling smoke from his mouth and nose. "I bet you Castro doesn't have shit like this over there in Cuba." He took another pull of his weed again and showed it to her. "Uh-uh. Only in America, ma." He slowly blew smoke out again.

Carlton's shawty was a cutie, for sure. She had a milky-white skin complexion with long, curly red hair that nearly reached down to the middle of her back. Although she was heavy boned—a plus size to some—she was pleasantly plump in all the right places. 42-28-52. She was nice and phat, with thick hips. Her thighs were humongous, and Carlton took pleasure in caressing them, inching his hand under her miniskirt, working his way between her legs.

She tensed up.

"Huhn!" He took another pull of his weed, then passed it to her. "This should loosen you up a bit." He watched her; he smiled. "Yeah, that's what I'm talking about, Angela," he encouraged her, trying to boost her ego. "Go ahead and take another hit of that shit!"

She looked at him with a smile; he smiled back. She giggled and accidently coughed up smoke. She seemed to be new at this. She smiled again and took another pull of the weed, but it was a stronger pull this time.

The top of the weed bud lit up bright, very bright, and then immediately started racing down to the other end of the joint.

"Hey! What the fuck are you doing?!" He snatched the weed from her. "You're killing my shit! This shit cost money.... ¡Mucho damned dinero!" She nodded; and then his eyes began to scan the room. He reached for the malt liquor off the cocktail table and shoved the bottle at her. "Huhn!" Take a swig of this instead, if you wanna hit something. It's more on your level anyway."

Then suddenly, they both looked toward the entranceway when they heard somebody rattling a key into the front door.

Carlton got spooked; he immediately reached for the air freshener beside the sofa and sprayed it around them.

Angela slid her miniskirt down a little to look appropriate.

"Fix your shirt too," he told her, as he pulled his zipper up. "Your tittie is nearly hanging out."

Destini ran in the family room and suddenly stopped! She eased her way out of there and accidently bumped into me.

"Where you going?"

"He has a visitor in there."

"Who?"

Carlton twisted around and saw me. "What's up, cuz?" he said. "This Angela, my little Spanish mami I was telling you about last week."

Of course that was a lie: he never mentioned her or that name to me before. But then again, I played along with him and greeted her anyway. Then I cut back to him. "Let me holla at you for a second."

He stepped out in the hallway, acting weird. And before I could say anything to him, he said, "Before you start trippin' and shit, lemme tell you—"

"Yo!" I cut him off. "They loved my designs!"

"Huh?"

"They loved my art designs!"

"Yeah, for real?" His facial expression changed.

"Yeah."

"It's about fucking time. I knew you were gonna get your chance one day."

"I have to call Naomi and let her know about it, too. I'm going out to celebrate."

"Oh, alright then."

Just when I was about to walk away to make that call to Naomi, a reek smell hit me. "Were you smoking in the house?"

"Who, me?"

"Of course you, who else could I be talking to? You're the only one standing in the hall with me."

"Oh, nah dawg. I wasn't smoking. I was trying to get something to smoke a little earlier though, but I couldn't find anything. Why, do you smell anything?"

Do I smell anything? "As a matter of fact, I do."

There was a pause.

"Oh, nah! You know what you probably smell?"

I was all ears.

"... That probably be that weed-smell that Angela had on her. Damn, how could I let that one slip my mind? She smoked something just before she came over here." He then tried to play me as a fool, lifting his shirt to his nose, smelling it. "Oh, yeah, I can smell it now. It musta got on me when she was all over me."

"Tell that shit to somebody else." I stepped away from him and headed to my bedroom to make that call to Naomi.

I threw my favorite blue jeans on the bed, then reached for the phone. I dialed Naomi's number and the answering machine cut in on the second ring. At first, I wanted to hang up but then I decided not to.

"Yeah, hello, Naomi," I started to leave a message after the beep. "This is, uhhh.... This me, DaShawn. And I just wanted to let you know that everything went fine at Decorous' Fashion World today. They liked my designs, which there's a strong possibility that I could be working with them soon. Perhaps sometime next week if everything goes as planned. As you know already, this was something I was looking forward to. And I have to admit it, none of this would have been possible if it weren't for your help. So, thanks." I paused for a second, hoping to find something better or even something more appreciative to say. But I couldn't find the right words to use. I had a mental freeze. Then I went on anyway: "Well, I'm about to go out to Boomers with Destini to celebrate this special occasion with her, and it would be nice if you could meet us out there. Because like I said—"

"Yeah, Naomi!" a voice suddenly came over the phone line. "Pleaseeeee. Pretty pleaseeeee, Naomi. Come out with us too!"

I cut back in with a "Hello?"

"... Hello."

"Destini?"

"... Huh?"

"Girl, get off the damned phone and hang up!"

"Okay." Destini hung up, but she only left me a few seconds to leave a message to Naomi before the machine cut me off.

When I changed my clothes into something more comfortable to wear, I headed to the family room to get Destini and head out to Boomers, but she was nowhere in sight.

Now, where could she possibly be at? I thought. I felt lost. And where's Carlton at, too?

I stood there senselessly for a short moment, then gave up: "Yo, DESTINI!"

Nothing.

I waited a second or two before I started walking toward her bedroom. And just when I was about to yell out her name again, the front door swung open.

It was Carlton. He ran into the family room—only for a hot second—then headed toward the front door again.

"Yo, CARLTON!"

He stopped just before he exited the house.

"Have you seen Destini?"

"Yeah, she's out there in the car waiting on us."

Waiting on us?

"But I thought you were with your girl?"

"Yeah, I am. But she's gonna wait for me in my room till we get back."

"Till we get back?" I started walking toward him. "So you're not gonna stay here with her?"

"Hell, nah. She will be alright by herself till we get back. Because I would be damned if I miss out on this celebration. Destini said that y'all were going out to Boomers."

"But what if your girl snoops around and go through my shit while we're not here?"

"Nah, you don't have to worry about that. I took care of that already."

"How?"

"I told her to stay inside my room till I get back, because we have a psychopathic uncle who just got released from state prison for rape. So I told her to be careful while she's in here because if our uncle catches her out in the hall—"

"Who? Uncle James?"

"Man, don't try to get me caught up in that he said, she said, bullshit! I never gave her his name. But yeah, it could be him, though."

You have to be kidding me. "And she believed that shit?"

"Oh, hell yeah! She has no choice over that. I'm her man."

I refused to say anything else on this topic. I led the way out of the house.

Destini was in the passenger's seat of my car, waiting for us. And one thing I knew for sure: she was excited. She had a huge smile stretched across her face, wobbling her head, while waving her hand from side to side. I sorta laughed at her.

As I was walking toward the car, I cut my eyes from Destini and started scanning the old block where I lived practically my whole life, aside from those six years I lived with Aunt Enid on the other side of town. And to be honest, it seemed like nothing much had changed around here since. It was like the same old bullshit! The people. The houses. The wanna-bes. The hood-rats. Even—

Amanda, the neighborhood hoe from across the street, waved hello.

I waved back and popped the car door open. I took the driver's seat, waiting on Carlton to get in.

Destini was blabbing off at the mouth about something. I ignored her. I guess my mind was elsewhere. Waaay out there: Somewhere. Actually, I was locked on a few kids up the block who were playing around in their yard, while some of their parents—mainly all mothers of course—sitting on the front porches, watching their little young ones acting a fool out there.

Carlton got inside the car, taking the front passenger seat.

"See, I told you," Destini said to me, while jumping over the seat. "You weren't listening to me!" Then she hit me with Abu and took a seat back there.

"I heard everything that you said to me, you little knuckle-head."

"So what did I say then?"

"I ain't telling you now."

"Why?"

"Because."

"Because of what?"

"Because you hit me with that ugly-ass monkey of yours."

"You're lying!" She shot me a scorching stare. "You weren't listening to me. Because if you did, you would have heard me telling you to pull off before he got in the car with us."

Carlton twisted around to her. "Oh, yeah, that's for us now?"

She ignored him. "And just to let you know something," she started to tell me, with a growing smile on her face, "this ugly monkey supposed to be you, remember? So if Abu is ugly, what that makes you?"

"Stop playing, Destini!" I cut onto 183rd Street. "And get that—! Get that cute monkey outta my face before you make me crash."

She ignored me, while dangling Abu in front of my face. "Say, pleaseeeeee...."

I slammed on the brakes when I almost busted a red light.

Destini ran from me. Then, within seconds, she came back with a huge smile on her face. "Hurry!" She stuck her hand out toward me. "Hurry! Gimme some quarters! Hurryyyy!"

But before I could give her a few of them, she snatched a whole roll of quarters out of my hand and took off running again.

"No! Stop!" I yelled to her, but that became pointless when she hit that first corner over by those huge video games; she disappeared within the crowd.

I quickly strode in the same direction, damn near fretting. Then I felt relieved. I found her. She was a short distance away from where she bent that corner, on the left side, playing some type of martial arts video game—one very similar to Mortal Combat, but different— with aliens and the human races fighting among each other. A battle for the universe, I guess.

Carlton popped her upside the head.

"What's that for?" she asked, looking up at him.

"Because" —he raised his hand as if he were about to pop her again, but he didn't— "you ran off like you don't have any damned sense. You coulda waited for me so I can play against you."

"But I did wait for you."

"Stop lying and move over. I'm about to smash your ass for that shit now!"

Now, that was a shame: I could have sworn Carlton was going to put her in check for running off from us like that. But instead, this fool wasn't acting any different from her. He stood next to her, gripping the joystick and battling her in their little grudge match, acting like two little kids going at each other.

Although I had grown out of that stage of playing childish video games many years ago, I must admit watching the two of them go at it took me back to those younger years of mine when I used to run down to the corner store with Kevin every day after school. We would play Street Fighters, competing against each other, just like Destini and Carlton were doing right now. I couldn't help but smile at them. After all, the stubborn little girl that stood before me had the same traits I had back in the day. Always ready for a challenge. She must be secretly carrying on the legacy of my bloodline without even knowing about it. So I did precisely what any other father would have done under these same circumstances: I cheered her on.

"Watch out!" I told her, while trying to encourage her to do better. "You can't let him grab you like that. He's gonna kill you.... Stay away from him.... Yeah, there you go." Her combatant figure started getting the crap kicked out of him by Carlton's fighter.

"See what you made me do?" she told me, looking bothered. "You messed me up!"

I was shocked. "I didn't mess you up. You messed up on your own. I didn't have anything to do with that." I had to put her back in her place. "You were playing like you didn't know what the hell you were doing. And you got exactly what you deserve for not listening to me."

She gave me a cold stare, then looked at Carlton. She tilted her head to the side as if she was a part of some Mafioso crime family, giving him the indication that she wanted to ice me out on her own.

He smiled and stepped aside.

"Oh, yeah?" I accepted her challenge. "You think you can beat me?"

She remained silent, grabbed two quarters out of her pocket and slid then in the video game.

"Oh, it's on now!" I stepped up and popped my quarters inside the machine, too. "I see I have to teach you a little lesson."

The battle began, and Destini smashed my sorry-ass fighter in about nine seconds. I looked at the joystick, then shook it a little. "I think this shit isn't working right!"

Carlton laughed at me and so did Destini.

"Oh, hell nah!" I stuck two more quarters in the machine and told Destini, "I bet you can't do it again."

As soon as the second match began, I started hitting on the wrong button and she took full advantage of my poor video game skills. I didn't have a chance against her. I had no other choice but go to plan B: a little backup plan that I didn't expect to use against her. But hey! Like I said, she left me with no other choice.

I leaned my body weight against hers, making her lose her balance. She tried to withstand my weight, but she couldn't. I was too heavy for her.

"He's cheating! He's cheating!" she protested to Carlton, still trying to hold her position. "You can't do that!" she told me, attempting to push me back with her hip. But I didn't budge a bit. Not even a little bit.

What a joke, I thought. She felt like a little cat brushing its tail against my leg.

But since she wanted to play like that, I bumped her back and she nearly went flying. She caught her balance by gripping the joystick. But the game was over in a matter of seconds. I had vanquished her combatant figure. And I could honestly say I felt proud of it too.

She shot me a mischievous smile and started bobbing her head. She then reached into her pocket again and snatched out two more quarters.

Are you serious? I thought. I wanted to laugh at her.

We went at it again. We were acting like two little toy poodles playing out in the front of the house, pumping and pushing one another, trying to see who was in control. It had nothing to do with the video game anymore. That became obvious. It was more like proving a point. Our pushing and shoving lasted for about two strong minutes before I gave in when she kicked me.

"Hey!" I let go of the joystick to rub my leg. "You can't be doing that!"

She burst out laughing.

So, I snatched her up, directly above my head. "Oh, it's funny, huh?" I told her, shaking her playfully like a little piggy-bank, as if I wanted my two quarters back.

"You started it!" she said between broken giggles.

"No, I didn't."

"Did too."

When I looked into her eyes, it was at that very same moment that I discovered something different about the whole concept of being a father. It was captivating; something that I will never forget. That little girl that I held in the air was me. My very own image.

As people walked by they couldn't help but stare at us. It probably looked fake to them. Perhaps like one of those TV episodes where a father loses his daughter at the beginning of the show but finally finds her at the end of the show. A perfect reunion.

"C'mon." I put her back down. "I know a game you can't beat me at." I led the way—with Carlton following us—to several video games from my younger days: Donkey Kong, Pac-Man, Mario Brothers, and some other older games as well.

We played against each other for about an hour straight, flip-flopping without choice of video games—one after another—while enjoying our time together.

"Hey! You wanna take some pictures over there?" I asked her.

She quickly nodded her head with a smile.

Our interaction must have surprised the hell out of Carlton because he started acting strange for some reason. When Destini and I stepped into the photo booth, that numbskull pulled the curtains open and tried to jump inside with us.

Destini tried to stiff-arm him out, but unfortunately, it didn't work: She wasn't strong enough. "You messed our picture up, Ugly!"

"Yeah, so you think. But if you don't get your hand off my face, I'm gonna make you look ugly too."

I jumped in and told Destini, "Don't worry about it, we can take another one." I then told Carlton to step out.

He did.

But just when everything seemed to be going fine for another photo shoot, Carlton stuck his hand into the booth and jiggled it around, hoping to ruin our photos again.

But I guess two could play at the game because Destini grabbed his arm, as if she were Hannibal Lector, and sank her teeth into his forearm.

Good! He yelled and pulled his arm back out of the booth. Right after that, the atmosphere grew cheerful and warm.

However, I knew there was going to be a problem when Destini yanked my hand and said, "I gotta use the bathroom."

"Right now?" I asked, while we were walking toward the go-carts. "Can't you hold it until we get finished with this?"

"Ooooowww," she moaned, then began twitching her legs from side to side. "I have to go! I have to gooooo.... Ooooh, I can't hold it."

When I saw her doing all that twirling stuff with her legs, I rushed her toward the ladies' room and immediately stopped at the doorway. I stood there with her for a moment, contemplating what I should do from there. Because there's one thing that we all knew for sure, I wasn't going in the rest room with her. She tried to pull away; I yanked her arm back.

"Eh! What are you doing?" she kinda snapped. "I gotta use the bathroom."

"Okay, but listen first." I tried to give her some quick parental advice. "Just make sure you place toilet paper on the toilet seat before you sit on it. Okay?"

She nodded.

"And don't be talking to anybody while you're in there. And I mean, nobody!"

"Okay."

"And make sure that you wash your hands after you're finished in there, too. Okay?"

"You gonna make me use the bathroom on myself!" She started twirling her legs again.

Carlton cut in: "Girl, go use the damned bathroom before you piss on yourself!"

Since he put it like that, I released her wrist and she dashed into the restroom. I guess I was acting a little over-protective about her when—

"I kinda like the little kid. What about you?"

"Huh?" I took my eyes off the restroom door, then quickly turned back to Carlton. I was zoned out: he brought me back to reality.

"I said I like the little kid."

Oh! I smiled. "Yeah, me too," I told him, then took a short pause. Then added: "You wanna hear something crazy?"

"What?"

"I never thought I would live to see a day like this."

"Why you say that?"

"You know when Jessica skipped town, I thought I would never see my child again. But now—"

"Oh!" he started chuckling, "so you're admitting that she's yours now?"

"Man," I nodded with confidence, "I have always known that she was mine, all the time." I paused for a second before I continued: "She looks just like me, act like me, and she damn near speaks like me too. It would be impossible if she wasn't my daughter. It's just that this whole fatherhood shit hit me all too fast and I didn't want anything to do with it. I just didn't have the slightest clue about being a father."

"Word?"

"Yeah. So you already know, the best thing for me to do at that time was to deny her as much as I could. But" —smiling heavier— "I'm gonna have to learn now because I have a daughter to raise and look after. And you wanna know something?" I paused again. Carlton nodded, and I went on to say: "This whole parenting thing isn't really hard at all. It's like running in a relay race with a baton in my hand, and then when it's time for me to pass the baton off, I have to pass it off to somebody who is capable of carrying it on for me.... So who else can I depend on?"

Carlton nodded his head again, wanting me to continue.

And I did by saying, "Nobody else but someone who I can trust. And since I'm her father, I have to start acting like one and get her ready for this long race in front of her." I smiled again, but this time with pride. "She's my daughter. It's me who she'll be representing out there in this crazy-ass world."

"That's fucked up, my nigga!"

"About what?"

"My nigga, I have Angela and all those other bitches around the neighborhood believing that Destini is my daughter. And you can believe it or not, but that's how I've been getting all those hoes lately. But now you gonna fuck it up for me because those hoes be feeling sorry for me and shit, saying how they wish they could find a nigga like me."

"Nah."

"Fuck yeah!" he said. "But now, you're gonna mess it up for me."

I started laughing at him. "I was wondering why all those broads were coming over to the house a lot—" I paused when my eyes caught two females over Carlton's shoulders. "Whatever you do, don't turn around: There are two shawties behind you starting us down over there."

"Where?" he turned around to look, scanning the area. "Where they at?"

"Why did you do that?" I felt embarrassed. "Shit! I think they're coming over here now."

"Who? Them right there?"

I turned back to the ladies' room, pretending I hadn't notice those two chicks heading our way.

But Carlton on the other hand stood there with a self-confident smile on his face. He eyeballed them as they were approaching us. And I guess he already knew which female he wanted because he whispered over to me: "Check out the shawty on my left. The one in the purple hip-huggers. That hoe looks thick as hell, my nigga! You better not mess it up for me."

"Hello, fellas," **one** of the females said behind my back, greeting Carlton first. "My name is Yvette and this here is my cousin Joy from New Jersey."

"Hey, what's happening?" Carlton said, trying to sound cool.

I turned around and shot them a head nod, then we introduced ourselves to them.

"So," Carlton asked the light-skinned chick in the purple hip-huggers, "where in New Jersey you're from?"

"Oh, do you know about Jersey?"

"Nah, not really. But I've been up in the northern States a few times before."

"Oh, so have you heard of Paterson, New Jersey?"

Of course he has, I mulled. Who hasn't heard of Paterson, New Jersey before? That spot was, and still remains, one of the Government's most profitable, ghettoest cities in America—where they housed minorities at, sorta like what the Nazis did to the Jews back in the day for their concentration camps—which is filled with hood-rats and wanna-be thugs for the Government's future investment to breed and house these type of people for their prisons on taxpayers expense. And get this: a vast majority of the people who lived in that infested city, like many other Black cities in America where drugs are strongly promoted, either use heroin or sniff cocaine on the regular basis without any hope of direction. So give thanks to Brown v. Broad of Education for the lack of Government funding for public education for Blacks and Hispanics in the inner city ghettos. Because it's no longer segregated schools, but rather segregated school zones to keep Blacks away from proper education.

"Nah. I don't think I've ever heard of that place before," he told her.

I twisted to the side to look at this liar.

"But I know," he continued with, "I can count on someone like you to tell me all about it, though."

"Most certainly. I can do that."

"So what about tonight?"

She hesitated a bit, but when she was about to answer him, Yvette cut her off. "What about you?" she asked me, probably hoping that we could go out on a double date or something. "Are you gonna hangout too?"

I smiled. "Yeah, I can, if there's no obstacles involved."

Yvette read between the lines and took a step closer to me. "Why, should there be any?"

I liked that about a woman who could throw that feminine shit out the window and go for what she wants, without worrying about what other people might say or think.

The scene was definitely getting heated now. And by the look of things, I knew these broads were down for whatever. And the W in whatever was not silent. Yvette and Joy had that look about them; and they weren't ugly either. Actually, they both looked doable to me. This chick Yvette sorta looked like Gabrielle Union, but with a little more ass than hers, while her cousin Joy looked identical to Tyra Banks. A tall Amazon broad with thick-ass hips. They both looked like they could fuck and suck a nigga up all night long, if one had the strength for it. And I would be an idiot to pass up on an opportunity like this.

As the conversation was getting interestingly hot and tempting, things cooled down considerably fast when I felt someone pat-drying their hands on my pants. I looked down and saw Destini there. I twisted back to Yvette.

"I think I'm gonna have to take that back."

"Take what back?"

"I'm not gonna be able to hangout tonight. I had already promised my daughter here that I was gonna spend the rest of the week with her. But we can always link something up for another day."

"Oh, that's your daughter?" Yvette asked. "She's such a cutie."

I looked down at my side. "Yeah, this little cutie here is my daughter." I turned back to Yvette. "Her name is Destini."

Yvette looked at her. "Is everything okay with you?" she asked Destini, bringing all eyes on her.

Destini's bottom lip began to quiver. Her eyes were wide with shock; they became watery for a reason.

I placed my hand on her chin and tilted her face upward toward mine. "Are you all right? Did somebody mess with you while you were in the restroom?"

She slowly shook her head and a teardrop rolled down her face.

Yvette asked her: "Why are you crying then?"

Destini gave her an evil stare, then cut her eyes away from her to me. "Daddy, can we go now? I'm hungry."

I wasn't sure if I wanted to smile or shed a tear too. But I could tell you this, though, I was happy: She called me Daddy, and it felt real.

"Sure, I can get you something to eat. But just give me a second here first." I turned back to Yvette. "So let me have your info so we can continue this on another day."

"Sure." She stuck her hand inside her purse to grab a pen.

Then Destini started coughing as if something got caught in her throat.

"What's the matter?" I started patting her on the back. "Do you need something to drink?"

She removed her hand from her mouth and nodded. "Uh-huh. I need some soda."

I turned back to Yvette. "Would you excuse me for a second? I need to go get her something to drink."

"Okay."

Carlton stayed behind with them.

As I led Destini to the water fountain, she looked back at Yvette and shot her a disdain stare.

"Just go ahead and drink up," I told her. "And stop looking at people like that."

"Like what? I'm not doing anything wrong."

"Girl" —I almost laughed— "just go ahead and drink some water before you start coughing again." I waited. She took a sip of water. "Oh, hell nah! I know that's not all the water you're gonna drink?"

She nodded.

"The hell you are!" I joked. "You're not finished yet! You needa go ahead and drink some more of that."

She gave me an infuriated look. "Like I told you before, I need some soda, not water."

I looked at my little mini-me and laughed. "C'mon." It would be pointless to challenge her there when in fact she was right. "I might as well get you something to eat too, before you pull another fast one on me again."

By the time we reached the customer's line, Carlton approached us and gave me Yvette's info written down on a napkin.

"Good looking out." I read it. Then looked back at him. "Did she say anything when I stepped off?"

But before Carlton could answer my question, a female's voice cut in, and said, "It all depends on who was she?"

Carlton and I turned to confront our nosy spectator.

"Naomi!" I nearly fainted.

"Who else have you invited?"

Destini twisted around in a flash. "Naomi!" She seemed happy, wrapping her arms around Naomi's hips. "You came!"

"Of course I did, hon," she said, then looked at the napkin in my hand and slightly motioned her head at it like a golden retriever. "What's that?"

"This?" I looked at the napkin, then balled it up. "Oh, it's nothing. It's just a dirty napkin." I then tossed Yvette's info in the trash can.

"Uh-uhh!" Destini said. "That was that ugly lady's telephone number over there." She then pointed toward the corner.

We all looked in the same direction where the little snitch was pointing at. But Yvette and Joy had already stepped off and disappeared within the crowd. That was good. I felt safe. I turned back to Destini and tried to play it off as if she was joking around. Naomi had no other choice but believe me on that unless she wanted to stick her hand into the trash can to find out the truth.

Okay, then ... it wasn't worth it.

When we reached the cashier's counter, I ordered us a large pepperoni pizza pie with soft drinks. Four Fruit Punches. Then minutes later we were seated at a table—in the far corner of the diner section—enjoying our pizza and conversing about my day at Decorous'.

"I can't believe that," Naomi told me, unconsciously shaking her head. "And then he asked you to step back in the conference room?"

"Yeah. It's funny, isn't it?"

"Of course. I'm just happy that everything worked out for the best."

"Yeah, me too." I nodded slowly and accidentally allowed myself to drift off in my thoughts.

But Destini immediately brought me back to reality when she tapped me on the shoulder. "Right, Daddy, didn't they say I was your little angel too?"

"They certainly did."

"See Naomi, I told you they said I was an angel."

"Of course you are, hon." Naomi smiled. "Everybody knows that already."

Carlton muttered out: "Yeah, probably so" —while looking at his slightly bruised forearm— "the dark angel of immorality."

His remark was one thing, but that facial expression that he wore on his face made Naomi and me burst out laughing. And for the rest of the evening we all laughed and joked with one another as the clock wound down. It was like one of those good soap operas—once you are drawn to it—it's hard to turn away. And that's exactly what happened to me. I spent the rest of my evening at Boomers', observing Naomi. She was a woman who didn't do anything to disguise her true self. Everything about her was real. Her smile. Her openness. And even that goofy cackle of hers made my spirit laugh right along with her. She had the sweetest personality that most people wish they had: that gentle kindness.

And for myself, like any other man with a good head on his shoulders, I knew I had a prize-winner at the table with me. I felt a bit infatuated with her, and I wasn't sure whether I was just moonstruck by her glossy lips or simply enthralled by her charm. Either way I look at it, she seemed unaware of the effect she has bestowed upon me.

I kept a smile on my face.

"Oh, my!" Naomi looked at her wristwatch, then grabbed her purse. "It's past ten o'clock already. It's getting late, and I need to head back to the house."

"Perhaps we could set another date?" I suggested.

"Perhaps." She got up from the table and threw her purse strap over her shoulder.

Destini cut in. "But we didn't even go on the go-carts yet!" she declared, probably hoping that Naomi would change her mind and stay a little while longer.

But Naomi told her, "Not today, hon, perhaps at another time. I have a few things I need to attend to." Then she slowly started stepping away from the table.

"Well," I started to suggest, "allow me to walk you out."

"No, you don't have to. I don't wanna spoil y'all fun."

"But I insist." I grabbed my drink and got up from the table. "That's the least I can do for you. And besides, it's getting kinda late out here for Destini anyway."

"No, it's not!" Destini tried to make a stand.

"Sweetie, don't worry about it, we can come back here on another day."

Neither Destini nor Carlton looked like they were ready to leave yet. But then again, they didn't have a choice in the matter. I was the one with the ride.

When we all left the building, Destini and I walked Naomi to her car. She had parked a short distance away from my car, just four cars down. Then a short moment later we were saying our good-byes.

"It's about fucking time," Carlton muttered loud enough so I could hear him when Naomi slipped inside her car.

Destini ran over to him and waited for me to catch up. Or at least, until I unlocked the doors for them with the little gizmo from my key chain. But I didn't. They would just have to wait on me till I get there. Within a matter of seconds, Naomi drove up and stopped directly behind my car; she rolled down her passenger side window.

"Is everything alright?" she asked.

That simple question struck me senseless for a few seconds. I should have been able to answer her back easily. But, for some reason, I couldn't. I just stood there.

So she added, "Have you lost your keys?"

Of course. That's it! I began to pat my pants pockets. "I musta lost them somewhere in there." I looked over at Boomers' front entrance.

"Do you need me to help you find them?"

"Nah," I turned back around to her. "You don't have to do that. And besides, I doubt it if I could find my keys in there right now, especially if nobody has reported them yet."

"So why don't you go find out then?" she recommended. "You never know—somebody may have already turned them in."

"Yeah, I think you have a point there." I walked back to Boomers and disappeared through the glass doors. They all stayed behind.

When I came back out of Boomer's, no more than about two minutes later, Carlton asked me, "Have you found them?"

"Nah."

"So," Naomi began to ask me, "what happened?"

"Nobody has seen them or turned them in yet," I told her. Then twisted to Carlton and Destini. "Most likely, we're gonna have to catch a cab home and have a tow truck drop my car off at the crib."

"Well, you don't have to catch a cab," Naomi said, grabbing my attention. "I can drive y'all home and you can save the money."

"But I don't want you to go outta your way. You did say you had something important that you're working on."

"Don't be silly. I won't be going out of my way."

"But I have to call a tow truck to come out here" —I looked at Carlton, hoping that he could assist me without me directly asking for his help— "to pick up my car first."

"Nah, you don't have to worry about that," he said. "I got you. You and Destini head on out home and I'll stay here to wait on the tow truck. But in the meantime I'm gonna go back inside Boomer's to see if I can find your keys myself."

"Are you sure?"

"Yeah," he assured me. "You better leave before I change my mind."

I guess he was right. I told Destini to get inside Naomi's car while I strode over to the front passenger's door. I paused. I felt guilty. I shouldn't do that to Carlton. I walked over to him, sticking my hand in my pocket, then pulled out a twenty dollar bill, balled up and folded. "Here you go." I passed it to him. "Pay for the tow truck and tell him to keep the change."

"With twenty fucking dollars! What kinda change—" he paused when he realized that the money was wrapped around something; he suspiciously studied it. A smile grew on his face as he caught on. "Playa-playa," he praised me in a sort of whisper form. "I swear to God, I knew your ass was up to something—"

"Shhh, keep it down," I whispered back. "Give me about half an hour before you decide to leave."

"I got you."

I walked back to Naomi's car and slid in. She looked at me with one of those smirks on her face, perhaps sensing something. But nah, I doubt it, though. I know a female's intuition is good, but it can't be that good. Then she smiled at me, putting me in doubt. I felt bewildered. But just before I could question her about that smile she was wearing, she looked in her rearview mirror and adjusted it. Not so much to look out the back window, but rather to look at Destini who appeared to be upset that we have left earlier than what she had expected from us.

"Sweetie, put your seat belt on for me," Naomi told her.

Destini did. However, she pouted a bit as she folded her arms across her chest, watching Carlton through the side window walking back inside Boomers. "That's not fair," she muttered.

As Naomi drove out of the parking lot, I had something on my mind that I want to ask her. So I started out with a polite word of thanks to coax up a general conversation during out ride home.

"Don't mention it."

"Well, thanks anyway. But if you don't mind, may I ask you a question?"

I guess there was something in my tone that made her cut her eyes from me, with that please-don't-ask-me-what-I-think-you're-gonna-ask-me look, because she barely shook her head before she said, "Sure, what is it?"

About an hour later, Naomi pulled up in front of my crib.

And I'm like … damn! The time flew by so quickly that I wasn't even finished interrogating her yet. But I couldn't help but feel sorry for all that she had shared with me already. I swear, I found her story to be extremely profound and heartfelt due to the pain her ex, some punk-ass coward, had subjected her to.

But when she turned toward me and looked me in the eyes—I'm not gonna exaggerate this shit right here—I felt crushed. I got a little peek through her painful windows. I wanted to say something to her, but she pulled the curtains shut and turned away from me. I immediately fell into a trance, if you wanna call it that. It became silent inside the car as we kept our thoughts to ourselves. I felt like I was supposed to say something encouraging to her. She deserved it. Something. Anything. But I just kept my mouth shut because I didn't want to say the wrong thing to her.

After a slight hesitation she said, "It's getting late…."

"Yeah, you're right." I went with the flow. "C'mon, Destini, say bye to—" I began, twisting around to the back seat, but immediately cut it short when I noticed that Destini had fallen asleep already.

Naomi looked to the back seat, too.

"She's knocked out."

"Don't wake her. Let me get the door for you."

"Thanks." We both got out of the car.

As Naomi opened the back passenger door, I gently picked Destini up without waking her. Naomi led the way to the front doorway of the house, turned, and gave me that questioning look.

I tilted my head to the side. "Underneath the mailbox."

"That's right." She reached for the spare key, and made her way inside the house.

I trailed behind her, straight to the back bedroom. I laid Destini down on the bed just before my arm was about to give way. I eased over to the doorway and watched Naomi tuck Destini in bed, then afterward we both walked out of the room together.

We went down the hall and chatted for a while before Naomi started insisting that she had to leave again. But there really wasn't much for us to talk about anymore since we had basically touched on everything already.

When she came back to her senses again, she eased for the door. "Well, it's getting late."

"Let me get that for you." I tried to beat her to the doorknob, so I could at least be gentleman-like, by opening the door for her. But something else happened instead: our hands collided. My hand over hers.

She stopped and looked at me.

I was suddenly overwhelmed with some sort of magnetic force. I drew my mouth closer to hers, wanting to kiss. And I went for it. It was nothing hard, just the regular stuff: some "Gone with the Wind" type of thing. Then, I released my mouth from hers before she went hysterical on me. But she didn't. She just stood there against the wall with her eyes closed, then exhaled deeply. I accepted that as a slight invitation to continue. And I did. I went for another round, with no-holds-barred this time, going all the way. I threw my tongue back in her mouth. She wrapped her arms around my neck and kissed me back. It was on now. We shared a strong, passionate kiss with each other as if there weren't going to be another day tomorrow. And yes ... within seconds, my dick got hard.

Rock hard!

I lifted her up a little, just high enough to rest her legs around my waist as our tongues fought against each other. I glided her back down the hall toward my bedroom.

"Nooo," she moaned, periodically breaking kisses from my lips and mouth. "Let's not do this.... It's too early."

That was the last thing I wanted to hear. I went for the door anyway. "It's never too early," I told her between our kissing, closing the door behind us. I laid her on the bed and began to remove her blouse. She wore a peach-colored bra. I think Victoria's Secret. I just couldn't wait to suck on her swollen nipples. And just when I was about to unlatch her bra, she stopped me.

Fuck!

"Please don't get upset," she said. "But I don't think we should be doing this."

"Why? Don't you want to?"

She hesitated at first. "Yes, of course," she admitted. "But I...."

"But what?"

"I just don't wanna rush into something and have you to think less of me."

I gently raised her head back up. "I will never think less of you." I then rested my lips against hers and started kissing her again. I slid my hand down into her pants and then inside her panties, then between her legs. She spread her legs apart and allowed me to caress her love-spot. It felt soft and juicy down there; my mouth watered.

But before I knew it, she stopped me again, saying, "Nooo.... Let's stop."

I couldn't believe it.

She prevented me from going any further by propping her hands against my chest.

"Okay." I pulled my hand out from her panties, trying to be a gentleman about it. I swear, if she weren't watching me, I would have sucked the juice off my fingers but I couldn't play myself like that. "Whatever you want."

Then, she asked me: "Do you have a condom?"

A condom?

I looked over by the closet to my duffel bag. I wanted to smile. I knew I had a pack of Trojans in there. The ultra-thin kind. I leaped out of the bed before she had a change of mind. I had experienced a lot of those in my lifetime. And while I was out of the bed, I unplugged the house phone—to be on the safe side—so we wouldn't be interrupted.

By the time I came back to bed, Naomi was looking innocent, just hugging herself to hide her breasts from me. So to ease any insecurity on her part, I told her the truth: "You look beautiful."

She didn't say anything back. She just kept her eyes on me.

I allowed her to watch me strip down to my boxer shorts before I got back in the bed with her. We embraced with warm kisses at first, but then the scenery immediately became intense again. I pulled my boxers off and undressed her. She had a Kelly Rowland look: Dark and sweet.

Wow!

She looked unbelievable.

I rolled a condom on and spread her legs apart so I could slide my dick inside her. It felt soft and wet. She tensed up, feeling my manhood pushing her pussy lips aside. Her face showed some sorta mixture of pain and pleasure as I entered her. Her pussy felt tight, and I didn't even have it in all the way. I pulled back—only a little— then slowly pushed my fat sausage in her again.

She leaned her head back while gnawing on her bottom lip.

I tried to keep my eyes closed, but I couldn't. This pussy of hers was feeling too good to be true. I guess I didn't want to miss anything. Who could blame me? It was a Kodak moment: a memory worth keeping forever. But then, I saw a teardrop running down the side of her face.

"What's the matter?" I stopped moving. "Do you want me to stop?"

It seemed like she thought about my question before she said, "No," as tears began to roll down her face. "You don't have to, if you don't want to...."

"Are you sure?"

"... Yeah."

Thank goodness! I started working on her pink paradise again. She loosened up a bit and started getting in the groove. In the background, Chapter 8's song began to play from my satellite radio: "I Just Wanna Be Your Girl."

Perfect timing. It sounded pleasant; right for the moment.

"DaShawn...," Naomi softly moaned in my ear.

"... Uh-huh?" I kept grinding my dick in her, trying to work my way deep in her.

"Do you remember," she stammered a bit, "when ... I told you inside the car about my ex?"

Oh yeah, this pussy is most definitely the bomb. "Uh-huh," I said, while feeling her back wall now.

"Ummmmm," she sighed. Then managed to say: "That was two years ago. That was the last time I had been with a man…. So please-please, make this night special for me."

Whoa!

I stopped again. Two years ago, I thought. "Don't worry," I told her. "I'm gonna make this night special for the both of us." I slowly eased my man tool out of her. I wanted to start over from scratch.

The whole thing, from the beginning.

I tilted my head to the side and began to run my tongue along the side of her neck. She tasted sweet like a pack of Starburst candy, and I felt a compelling urge to proceed further with my lick-athon to find my favorite flavor: Cherry.

I slowly went down to her cleavage with my tongue, then eased on over to the other side, directly above her heart. I wanted to leave a sentimental impact there. I had to. I allowed my tongue to travel to her nipple now. Chocolate covered raisin. I nibbled on it a bit. Her nipples grew strong.

"Ohhh, yesssss…," she moaned. "Please don't stop."

In response, I started sucking on her nipples with a little force, pulling on them—one at a time. She was loving it. I started circulating my tongue all around them for a moment, then worked my way down to her belly-button.

"Ummmmmm," her breathing became heavy. "Please don't stop, DaShawn. It feels so good." She slowly dragged her nails over my back. "Please don't stop."

I managed to tell her, "I won't," as my tongue worked wonders across her thigh; then her inner thighs.

And if she thought that was something, she hasn't felt anything yet. I positioned myself between her legs, parted them carefully and rested them on my shoulders. My fingers gently parted her labia lips, pulling them away from each other to get a better view of her pinkness.

She was soaked down there.

I couldn't take it any longer. I lapped her once, then twice, then buried my face between her legs. I started licking along the line of her pussy lips at first, then stuck my tongue deep inside of her. I tried to go a deep as I could. And there it goes: That same cherry flavor that I was looking for. It was sweet.

I nibbled on her clit for a moment before she threw her hands on the back of my head. I held my position and shivered my tongue against her clitoris bud. I started out in slow motion at first but then picked up my speed when she started grinding her pussy in my face. I shivered my tongue faster and faster. I quickly stuck my middle finger inside her, directly on top of her G-spot and shook my finger against it. She got excited. I relaxed my tongue, just applying pressure against her clit. I stayed still. She started pumping her pussy in my face with a little force, rocking it back and forth. And on her fifth pump I cranked my tongue back up and started working on her clit again. Faster and faster. She gripped onto my ears and shoved her pussy in my mouth. "Oh, yes...."

A naughty thought ran across my mind; I went for it.

I declined my head just a little and swept my tongue across her booty-hole. Only twice. Then, I went back to eating her pussy again.

But get this: When I lapped my tongue across her backdoor, her whole body went stiff, especially her legs. She nearly ripped my fucking ears off my head when she howled, "Uh-uhhh!"

I wanted to laugh but I was enjoying the taste of her pussy in my mouth.

"Oh, yes! Please don't stop," she kept repeating. "Please don't stop." Then, within seconds, she was at the peak of her climax. I picked up my speed a little more and she shouted: "Uhhh...! Uhhh...! Uhhh-Uhhhhh! Oh, no! I'm about to cum! I'm about to cum! Oh, my God!" She grabbed a tighter hold of my head, shoving it into her pussy. "I'm about to cummmmmm...."

And she did: all in my mouth. I swallowed her juice. She slowly relaxed. When her legs stopped quivering, she released the pressure from my head. And before she knew it, I climbed back on top of her, in a kitty-position, with her knees facing the ceiling. It was only right for me to get my share of the pie now. I slid my fat sausage back inside her. She had no other choice but close her eyes this time.

After about nine slow pumps inside her, she opened her eyes again; and at this point, they were agleam with tears. I didn't know if it was from pain or some emotional enjoyment that she was experiencing from me. However, I kissed her on the lips anyway to ease whatever morale thought that she might be going through right now. Because, for one, I would be damned if I was going to stop what I was doing to ask her What's the matter. But, as it turned out, my kiss paid off. She kissed me back, wrapping both of her arms around me while I was slowly grinding my lubricated muscle deep inside her.

"Ohhh, Naomi," I whispered in her ear. "You feel good...."

She began to rock her hips in a gyrating motion, causing her pussy to slide all over my pole. It felt good. Really good. Her pussy muscles clamped tight around me. Something like a socket wrench. And before I knew it, my back arched on its own. I kept pumping in her and it didn't take long before I busted a monster load inside her. I collapsed right there on top of her. Although I wished I could have lasted a little bit longer, I was still satisfied with the few minutes she had given me. There will always be another day, I thought. So, from right there, I made up my mind, if she didn't have a problem with it: I wanted her to be my girl. And I was dead serious about that too. Only if she allows me to be.

And it didn't have anything to do with the sex either. It was just her whole persona of being a lady; not to mention, single like me.

I looked deeply into her eyes for moment—only for a few seconds—then eased my muscle out of her. I looked up to the ceiling, wondering how I was going to approach her about my thoughts.

But before I could rationalize my feelings about her, she rolled over and rested her head on my shoulder. Then asked, "Is something wrong?"

My mind was bewildered. I waited a second—okay, maybe about two seconds—to get my thoughts together before I turned toward her.

Uncle James stuck his key into the keyhole to unlock the front door, but he didn't enter the house as usual. At least not yet. He waited for a short moment; understandably, he suspected some sort of foul play.

He ajar the door just far enough to stick his handkerchief through the gap. Then yelled: "This means that I give up! ... Do you hear me?!" He waited a few more seconds before he stick his head through the opening and added, "I said, I give up, Destini! Did you hear that?!" He paused. Then added some more: "I said I give up!"

There was no response from her. Not even a peep. She must be playing her silly video game, he thought. When he finally stepped inside the house and scanned the room, the coast was clear.

Good!

He shut the door behind him, then out of the blue, Destini leaped from behind the couch—like a militia who is ready to take out one of the high executives from Wall Street—with that high power water rifle in her hand, pointing it toward Uncle James' face.

He immediately held his chest. It felt like his spirit tried to run away without him.

"What a coward!" Destini said while packing up her combat supplies: two water balloons and some old boots. She mocked him as she began to walk away, "I give up! I give up, Destini... Did you hear that?" She stopped and twisted around. Then said, "Just to let you know something" —she reached for her water pistol behind her, which was tucked in her pants— "I found this underneath your pillow. Don't let it happen again, because you ain't gonna like the outcome of it." She headed for the hallway again.

Uncle James let go of his chest and went for his belt. "You little—"

Destini quickly twisted around, displaying her water gun. "What?" she asked him, with her finger on the trigger. "You little, what?"

"I didn't say a damn thing!" He stood there in disbelief. "And if I did, I wasn't even talking to you anyway."

"Oh." She walked away.

"You little damned devil!" Uncle James murmured to himself when she bent the corner. "She just better be glad that I have this damned headache right now. Because if I didn't, I'd whoop her little ass."

"Did you say something?" Destini asked, appearing from the corner wall.

"No. I didn't say anything. I told you that already. You must be hearing things."

She gave him a suspicious stare before she walked away again.

"Enough of this bullshit! I can't even speak in this damned house anymore!" Uncle James pulled the belt from around his waist about the same time he unlatched it. "Who in the hell does she think she is? I'm a grown-ass man!" He took a step toward her direction, heading for the room down the hall. "I'm gonna settle this shit once-and-for-all and whoop her ass!"

"I CAN HEAR YOU IN THERE!" Destini's voice echoed from the family room.

Uncle James froze right there. He didn't dare go after her now. She probably had some sort of booby-trap waiting on him, he believed.

After a moment's thought, his mind was convinced. "She's the devil's daughter, not my niece," he whispered, then looked toward the ceiling for some sort of spiritual uplifting. "Lord, if I didn't follow your instructions before, I damn sure follow them now! So if you can hear me, save me from this little devil. And if you could do that for me" —he crossed two fingers behind his back— "I'll stop drinking. I swear."

Meanwhile, back in the family room, Destini was watching her favorite cartoon show—Road Runner—when Carlton stepped into the room a little hot-headed.

"You don't hear me talking to you?" he snapped at her. "I wanna know if you can still hear me from inside there?"

"I said, I can hear you already! Dag!"

"You better watch how you talk to me before I punch you in the face." He tried to intimidate her before he stepped back out of the room. "Let me know if you can hear me or not, because I have a funny feeling that you're lying to me."

"But I'm not lying to you! I did hear you last night."

"I'm gonna find out; and you better not be lying to me either." He stepped away and went back to his bedroom.

Destini knew Carlton wouldn't hit her, but she played right along with it anyway, just as long as she could use that same tactic on Uncle James.

There went her cue.

"I TOLD YOU ALREADY! ... I CAN HEAR YOU IN THERE!" she yelled out to Carlton.

From the other room, down the hall, Uncle James' eyes lit up.

This shit wasn't making any sense to me!

I found myself twisting and turning in bed, and it wasn't because I was having a fucking nightmare either! I just couldn't sleep with Carlton and Destini shouting through the hall.

I threw a pillow over my head, hoping to block them out, but it didn't work. Then, all of a sudden, it became quiet out there.

Finally!

I sorta dozed back off, but that didn't last long: The telephone started ringing in my ears.

You son-of-a-bitch!

I could have sworn I had unplugged that phone last night. But, by the look of it, I musta unplugged the answering machine instead. I rolled over to my side and snatched the phone up on the fifth ring.

It was Naomi. "I didn't wake you, did I?"

"Nah, not really. I was just laying here, thinking...."

"Oh."

"But hey, whatever happened to you last night?" I was curious to know. "Because when I woke up this morning, you were nowhere in sight."

There was a pause. Not a long one, but it wasn't a short one either. Then she said, "Honestly?"

"Yeah...."

"I was afraid."

"Afraid of what?"

After another brief pause, she admitted, "Because you were scaring me with all those things you were telling me just before you went to sleep. You have to remember something: I have been hurt before and I'm not trying to rush back into another relationship and get my feelings hurt all over again. Marcus really hurt me."

"But that wasn't me. Marcus musta been a damned fool, because I know I wouldn't have done anything like that to you."

She giggled.

"What's so funny?"

"It's like every time a guy wanna get with a female, he'll use those exact lines, as if y'all rehearsed it from some sort of playbook." She laughed. Then mockingly added: "But that wasn't me. I would never do anything like that to you—"

I cut in: "You know, you're an asshole, right?"

She burst out laughing; I laughed right along with her.

"Okay then." I stopped laughing. "Let's start this over from the beginning, just as if we were only friends here.... And wherever that leads us, we'll go from there. Does that sound fair to you?"

"Yeah, sure. Why not?"

"Okay then, since we've established that, I wanna take you out to eat. Only as your friend, and maybe a movie afterwards."

"Sure."

I smiled. "Okay then, I'll see you this evening around five o'clock, so we can get an early start."

"This evening?"

"Yeah."

She paused with a slight hesitation, then asked, "Can Destini come along with us?"

"Well ... actually I was planning on asking you if it was okay with you if Destini can come along with us, too." I straight out lied to her. "But since you asked me first. No, I don't mind."

She giggled again. "You are such a big liar. But you were cute about it though."

I joked, "Just tell me about it."

We spoke for a few more minutes and decided to change out dating arrangement for three o'clock instead. We both wanted to see an early movie. It's much cheaper than the later ones. And besides, I wanted to break the bad habit of allowing Destini to stay up late at night. I had a new role to play.

A daddy's role.

When I got off the phone, I headed toward the bathroom to wash up but I became sidetracked by a hissing sound. At first I thought nothing of it until I heard it again.

I looked to my right.

"Psst! Over here."

I twisted around. It was Uncle James hiding in the closet, with a Miami Dolphins' helmet on.

"What the hell are you doing in there?

He didn't answer me. Instead, he stuck his head out from the closet and scanned the hall. "Where is she?" he asked me after a few seconds.

"Who?"

"That little devil: Lucifer's daughter. Who else you think I'm talking about? Destini, you damned idiot!"

"Are you alright?"

"Hell, nah! How could I be alright when I got that little devil attacking me every-goddamn-time I step foot inside the house. I can't even think in here anymore without her reading my thoughts."

"Are you losing your fucking mind?"

"Am I losing my mind?" he tried to mock me. "Hell, nah! God told me she was a devil."

"God?"

"Yeah, God!" He stood his ground. "He told me that just a while ago."

On that note, I didn't want to stay there and listen to that bullshit! I just walked away, of course, hearing him going off at the mouth on me now, for ignoring him.

"Whatever."

After my shower, I walked into the family room and saw Destini and Carlton going at it over a game of Mortal Combat. Just like two little kids, as usual.

"Destini, I'm about to cook breakfast. What would you like to eat, pancakes or waffles?"

She looked at me, then quickly twisted back to the TV, and said, "I ate already!"

"Oh, you did?"

"Uh-huh! Some Cap'n Crunch—Oww!" She suddenly looked at Carlton, and then at her arm. "You jerk!"

"What were you saying?" I asked.

There was a pause.

"Sweetie—"

She cut back in: "Well ... I'm still hungry."

"So what would you like to eat?"

There was another pause.

"Sweetie!"

Then she finally said, "I wanna have some sunny-side-up with a little dash of salt and pepper on it. And ... ummmm, some bacon and toast ... slightly buttered. And ummm, a cup of toffee."

"Did you say toffee?"

After another short pause she looked at me and shouted, "Not toffee, silly! I said coffee." She smiled, then looked at Carlton.

"Coffee, huh?" I didn't give her enough time to respond before I added, "Are you sure about that, sweetie?"

"Uh-huh, I'm sure."

I played right along. "So how would you like your coffee?"

She had the nerve to place her finger on her lip this time as if she were pondering that question. "Uhhh, make it—"

"With five spoonful of sugar with no milk, right?"

"Yeah. How did you know?" She looked at Carlton, then back to me.

"Just put it like this, tell your lazy-ass uncle beside you to get up and make his own breakfast."

Carlton slouched down in the couch.

Then I added: "And after you get finished playing with your video game, sweetie, come in the kitchen and give me a hand."

Just before she could say anything back to me, Carlton's shawty, Angela, walked up beside me, and said, "¡Eh, yo, papi!" to Carlton. He twisted around. Then she told him, "I have to leave right now. I'm running late for work."

"Alright then, ma. Just gimme a call when you get off tonight. Okay?"

"Okay. I'll see you later." Within seconds she found her way out of the house, with ease.

I shot back to Carlton. "I know she didn't stay here all night, waiting up for you to come back?"

"If I tell you the truth, you probably won't believe me."

Destini cut in and told me, "He beat her up last night!"

"Stop lying!" Carlton said to her. "And I don't even know why you keep saying that for?"

"Because I heard her crying last night, telling you to stop hitting on her, and you didn't. You kept beating her up."

"Stop lying because I didn't hit her."

"Did too. I heard her saying, Uh, uh, stop, stop for a second, not so hard. It hurts. Not so hard, baby, uh, uh—"

"Eh-eh-hey, enough about that!" I cut her short right there because it wasn't Carlton's girl that she heard. "Just don't worry about what you heard last night. You just make sure a guy doesn't put his hands on you like that. Okay?"

She showed me her little fist. "He won't."

I smiled. "Okay, that's good to know. But in the meantime, that's enough with the video games. You might as well come in the kitchen and help me out in there."

"But I'm not even—"

"Destini!"

She hushed up.

Carlton shot me a suspicious stare but before he could say anything, I cut in again and told him, "I got you on this one. But don't try to make a habit out of this either."

He kept quiet.

As soon as Destini and I entered the kitchen, the phone on the wall started ringing. We both looked at each other.

"I don't know about you," I began to say to her, "but I'm about to prepare us some breakfast. So I don't have the time to be answering any phone calls right now."

Destini smiled, then took a long, thoughtful look at the phone too. She shrugged her thin shoulders, then came over to me and had the audacity to ask, "Can we have some chocolate milk for breakfast instead?"

Ms. Betty could have been doing anything else other than working overtime on the weekend; especially on Saturday morning since she'd rather spend her day preparing for bingo tonight. She won a hundred twenty dollars last week. But today, it was quite different, though: Being that it was hot and humid, she had a score to settle.

She leaned over her desk and hung up the telephone on the fifth ring. She sat in silence, mulling over her thoughts for a moment, twirling an ink pen between her fingers before she reached another decision. She picked up the receiver again and dialed another number.

A man answered the phone on the second ring.

"Arthur, is this you?" she asked.

"Yeah, it's me," he said in a slow southern tone. "Who is this, Sister Betty?"

"Uh-huh." She leaned back in her chair, feeling relieved. "It's nice to know you're in today."

"Yeah, I'm putting in a little overtime: I need the extra bucks."

"Oh, I know what you mean. But how are you doing anyway? I haven't seen you in church lately. Is everything alright with you and Sister Ellen?"

"Oh, of course, we can't complain. We're doing fine. We drove up to Georgia last week to visit somma our kin folks.... We were having such a good ol' time up there, until those bad nephews of mine showed up."

"I'm sorry to hear that."

"Oh, it ain't your fault." He took a short pause. Then asked, "So, what made you give me a call at this hour of the day?"

"I need your assistance again. Nothing outta the norm. Just the basic stuff."

"When?"

"Today. As soon as possible. I wanna be back in time for bingo."

"All righty then. I'll send somebody to your office in a few."

"Oh, thank you."

"Uh, I'd do anything for you, Sister Betty. I'll see you at church tomorrow."

Ms. Betty chiseled a smile on her face. She thanked him again, put the phone back into the cradle and began straightening out some paper on her desk. "Oh," she muttered to herself, while reaching for her brass knuckles in her bottom desk drawer. "I'll be needing this."

"Y'all must think I'm stupid or something," I said, while cleaning up the kitchen by myself since Destini and Carlton were taking their time slowly eating brunch at the table.

Destini glanced at me and giggled.

Her little bad ass!

And just when I had finished washing the skillet, Uncle James walked into the kitchen and placed a dirty plate in the sink.

"What the hell happened to your hands?" I acted concerned.

"What's the matter with my hands?" He started flip-flopping his hands over on both sides to get a good look at them himself. "Boy, are you losing your damned mind? It ain't anything wrong with my hands."

"Exactly! That's my point! You needa wash your own damned plate then!"

Destini started laughing at him.

"You little turd!" Uncle James snapped on her. "What are you laughing at? Because if anything, you needa go wash your dirty face and find some manners for your elder!"

I looked at Destini. "And that reminds me," I began to tell her, "I need you to go take a shower and change into something more suitable—"

"But I showered already."

"When?" Carlton and I both asked her about the same time.

"Earlier!" she told Carlton. Then looked at me. "When I got up this morning, when y'all were sleeping."

"So, you showered already?" I asked, while walking over toward her.

"Uh-huh."

Before she knew it, I snatched her arm up: high enough to take a good whiff of her underarm pit. "Oh, hell nah!" I scooped her little lying-ass up and threw her over my shoulder, carrying her straight to the bathroom. Uncle James laughed at her—all the way there. I then placed Destini in the bathtub, fully dressed, and turned the shower faucet on her.

She kicked and waved her arms at me. But at this point, I didn't care. She acted as if she was getting swept under a huge tsunami.

Yeah, I saved her alright.

I grabbed her arm. "Stay still!" I told her, then reached for the shampoo bottle. "Huhn! Let me put some of this in your hair!"

"It burns!" She tried to put up a fight. "It's burning my eyes! You gonna make me blind!"

"Stop moving!" I scrubbed the shampoo in her hair until it became foamy; I waited about a minute or two before I rinsed it out. "You can open your eyes now."

She did, looking at her arms first and then at mine. Strands of hair covered her face like a prehistoric cavewoman who got caught out in the rain.

Uncle James was finding that amusing. He kept laughing at her. I looked at the soap dish. She probably knew what was next because she tried to jump out of the bathtub.

I grabbed her.

"Yeah!" Uncle James began to cheer me on. "Wash her! Wash her dirty little ass!" he shouted by the doorway. "And while you're at it, DaShawn, see if you can wash her filthy mouth out too!"

I grabbed the soap and went straight for her underarm. I really didn't care whether she was dressed or not. I was determined—one way or the other—to bathe her.

"Let me shower myself!" she shouted. "I'm not a baby!"

"Are you sure?" I lowered her arm.

She quickly nodded her head without saying a word.

"Okay. But you better not be lying to me either. Because if you are, I will come back in here and finish washing you myself."

"I'm not lying." She seemed serious. "I swear on my mommy."

"You don't have to swear; especially on your mom. I'll believe you if—"

Uncle James cut in: "She's lying! She's lying! Don't believe her! She's Lucifer's daughter, I tell you! It's in her nature to lie to you!"

"No, I'M NOT!" she shouted back at him. "GET OUT!" She then threw a soapy sponge at him, hitting him upside his head when he tried to make a run from the doorway.

"God dammit!" He left.

So I told her, "Just go ahead and finish your shower. And, in the meantime, I'm gonna set your clothes on the bed for you. Okay?"

She nodded.

I walked out of the bathroom and went straight to her room. I laid a pink Baby Phat's kid outfit on the bed and pulled out a new pair of white tennis shoes from underneath a pile of clothes in the closet.

About five minutes later she stepped into the room—soaked and wet, with the same clothes on. She had a large towel wrapped around her body.

"Damn, that was quick." I finished making up the bed for her. She didn't respond. Rather, her teeth were steady clinging against each other.

"Well" —I headed for the door— "go ahead and get dressed. I'll be in the den if you need me for anything. Okay?"

She kept quiet, nodding her head.

"Alright." I shut the door behind me when I left her room.

Meanwhile, across town, Naomi stood in front of the mirror, searching for a flow in her reflection, but there wasn't any.

At least nothing to criticize herself on.

She knew she didn't look like one of those BET's video vixens, perhaps to some. But what she did know, she had something that those video chicks didn't have: she had character. Class. Nice personality. Beauty in the inside. She knew she was an average-looking cutie, and the mirror knew that too. She stood strong like Sojourner Truth.

Ain't she a Woman?

She wore a regular smile at first, then, slowly but surely, a mischievous smile began to take over. She squirted a splash of

Mmm perfume by Paris on both sides of her neck and headed for the door; when she opened it, she stood there for a moment, contemplating whether she should go on this date or not.

She took a deep breath. A really deep one. This would be a new beginning for her. She hadn't been on a date in a long time. And like every beginning, it has an end. Would this beginning have a happy ending for her, she wondered. It was a question that hammered her curiosity.

She closed her eyes and took another deep breath. She kicked one leg outside the door. The first step of moving forward and no turning back. She opened her eyes and stepped outside of the house with her other leg.

She locked the door, then proceeded down the driveway toward her car.

She felt rejuvenated, refreshed, restored.

"I think I'm just gonna go with this stack right here," I told Carlton, as I gathered up my favorite drawings into a small pile for my upcoming appointment at Decorous' Fashion World. "I'm sure I will use the rest of them some time down the road. What do you think?"

He shrugged. "That's on you to decide. I wouldn't know the difference, my nigga. All of that shit looks the same to me. It's nothing but a bunch of drawings."

"They're not just drawings. It's call art. Apparently you don't know what that means."

"Yeah, whatever. But hey! Does your hoe have a sister or a friend for me?"

"Who?"

"Your hoe Naomi."

"Nah, she doesn't have one."

"How you know that she doesn't have one for me?"

"Because she isn't like that. She's different: she's not a hoe."

"My nigga, don't let me find out that you're breaking weak for a bitch already."

"Nah, never that. I'm a playa for life. But for real though, I would appreciate if you don't call her a bitch anymore either." I gave him a guilty smile. "I'm thinking about making shawty my ol' lady."

"You joking, right?"

"Nah."

"My nigga, you're stupid!" He laughed at me. "And I mean like really stupid, too."

"Yeah, whatever you say." I placed a few more sketches inside my portfolio, blocking out his sarcasm. I had other things on my mind: like the possibility that I might become a fashion designer soon. Yeah, like really soon. And it couldn't get better than that. So perhaps, all that bosh about Destini being my lucky charm was actually true. The real deal. In a way, I started to believe that mess too, because my life has taken a sudden change for the better ever since she stepped into my life.

"I don't think I like pink."

I looked toward the doorway. I felt spellbound. I didn't know how to respond to Destini's remark.

But Carlton did when he dragged, "God damn, girl!" He stared in disbelief. "You needa start taking more showers if you're gonna be looking like this around here."

She scrunched up her face as if she didn't like his comment.

I got up from my desk. "I'll be right back," I told her just before I ran out of the room. She stood there, watching me dash up the hallway. About a minute later I came back inside the room with a comb and brush in my hand.

Destini looked terrified.

"C'mon, let's go over there." I guided her to a nearby chair. "I'm gonna hook you up."

She hesitated before she sat in the chair in which I tried to give her some candy curls at first, but after a few unsuccessful attempts, I changed my mind and gave her twisted-plaits instead. Twelve big ones. She looked incredibly beautiful with them.

I mean that. And I'm not just saying that because she's my daughter.

I stood there in silence, admiring her appearance. I felt like a proud father. I'm dead serious. I can see it now: family picnics and trips together. So I went straight forward and asked her, "Have you ever been to Disney World before?"

She slowly shook her head at first, but then gradually caught on to my question. She smiled. "No. But I was supposed to go when my mommy got better."

It was at that precise moment when the doorbell rang.

I looked at my watch. It was a quarter to three. Just a little earlier than I had expected. "I think that's Naomi at the door."

And that's all Destini had to hear before she ran out the room.

The doorbell rang again. Destini picked up speed, arriving at the front door in a matter of seconds. She sprung the door open and to her surprise, it wasn't Naomi.

It was Ms. Betty. She wasn't alone. She was with a deputy sheriff.

"Hello, dear," she said to Destini in a soft but rugged tone. "Is DaShawn here; inside the house with you?"

"Yeah," Destini hesitated for a short moment, "he's here."

Ms. Betty then turned to the deputy and gave him a confident smile. She didn't even bother to follow up with another question before she tried to enter the house.

But Destini said, "Waita second! I'll be back!" She then slammed the door in Ms. Betty's face, and then ran down the hall.

"Slow down, Destini," I told her when she stormed back into my study. "Now who was that at the door?"

She ignored my question, retorting back from where we originally left off: "What were you saying about Disney World?"

But before I could even give her a reply, the doorbell ran again for the third time. "I thought you went to answer the door?" I asked, while getting up from my seat. "It's probably Naomi out there."

"No, it's not!" she said. "It's not her. It's that ugly lady that be coming over here all the time"

"Who?"

She shrugged. "I don't know her name. She's that lady who always be asking all those questions about me."

The doorbell rang for the fourth time.

I knew exactly who Destini was talking about now. I headed off to the front door, leaving her and Carlton behind. In a way, I was kinda glad that it was Ms. Betty, since this would save me a trip from driving down to Family Services—after my Monday morning meeting at Decorous'—requesting the release forms regarding Destini. At this point, I'm like fuck it! I don't need a paternity test anymore to tell me something that I knew already. And besides, I couldn't wait to see this bitch's facial expression when I tell her about my plans. I would finally get her off my back.

When I opened the door that deranged bitch had the audacity to give me an evil stare and pressed the fucking doorbell—a few more times—out of spite, as if she didn't see me.

"Jesus Christ! I'm standing right here in front of you!"

"I know you are!" she snapped back. "I'm not blind. I thought perhaps you were going deaf!"

It would be pointless to even argue with this bitch! She would be out of here soon. Out of sight, out of mind, I thought.

"Where's Destini?"

I was confused. "Is there a problem?" I cut my eyes from her to the deputy, then back to her.

"No, there's not a problem that I can't handle myself," she tried to be sarcastic, as if I was some punk-ass nigga, then slapped a white envelope on my chest. She then stepped inside the house with the deputy beside her.

"What is this about?" I looked at her, then cut back to the envelope.

"Open it and read it for yourself," she sounded upset. "I've left you several messages on your answering machine regarding it." After a short pause, she added: "You do review your messages, don't you?"

I didn't even waste my breath responding to that: I was concentrating on this damned envelope in my hand. I opened it up and pulled out a three-page legal document. I only read the first page and was confused already.

Hold the fuck up!

I looked at Ms. Betty, then to the document again. I unconsciously scratched the top of my head. This shit wasn't making any sense. So I allowed my words to come out simple enough for this bitch to understand me.

"What the fuck is this?

I felt my stomach literally tied itself into a knot.

I couldn't say anything but focus my eyes on the first page of the Family Court's Order. This has to be a mistake!

Ms. Betty acted as if she were thrilled to see me looking crushed. And out of the blue, some sort of unearthly energy forced me to spin to my right side. It probably had a lot to do with me hearing Destini and Carlton laughing as they dashed into the family room. Ms. Betty focus on Destini, too, and began to head in that same direction.

"Hold up for a second!" I blocked the entranceway with my arm stretched out in front of her, trying to gather up my thoughts. "Is this correct?"

"It most certainly is. One hundred percent accurate. Just read it for yourself."

I tried not to show it but I shook my head because I couldn't believe it. I had always heard of ESP, the telepathic capability to communicate with another person, but today I definitely became a true believer. When I looked at Destini while she was playing with the video game, she must have felt my heart because she twisted her head toward me and smiled. It seemed like she was trying to lift my spirits. You gotta believe me. She didn't usually do things like that, but today she did. And since it was like that, I tried to channel back into her mind and tell her to run.

But she didn't. She just sat there.

C'mon, Destini. I tried it again: Get up and run!

But Destini didn't do anything. Not even a budge. Rather, she just turned back around and continued playing her stupid grudge match against Carlton. Then, it seemed like everything went in slow motion once she gave me that heart-crushing smile before turning back to her game.

I snapped.

I threw the Court's Order at the deputy, slamming it against his chest. Like I said, I snapped. I didn't care at this point. The deputy extended his arms out to me, probably to apprehend me, for an assault on a law official, but Ms. Betty stopped him. She reminded him of their main objective, the reason why they had come to my house. So, to avoid any obstacle, Ms. Betty and the deputy strode right past me and walked into the family room. I just stood there at that doorway looking lost and confused.

"Destini," Ms. Betty called out for her, standing a short distance away.

"Huh?" Destini's eyes were focused on the TV.

"You needa gather up your belongings so I can take you to your new home. You can't stay here anymore."

Carlton instantly stopped playing the video game and nudged Destini in her side to get her attention.

And it worked. "What you did that for?!" She gave him a menacing look. "I'm telling my daddy that you hit me!"

He didn't pay her any mind to that, but tilted his head to the side—in the same direction where Ms. Betty was standing—urging her to turn and look up.

She did.

When Ms. Betty repeated herself to Destini, she went on to say, "Mr. DaShawn Powell isn't your biological father. Therefore, you can't stay here with him anymore."

Destini immediately brushed aside what Ms. Betty said to her and gave Carlton a sarcastic giggle. "You're right, she is crazy."

Ms. Betty looked at Carlton as if she wanted to make a comment to that. But since he quickly twisted back to the TV, she held her tongue and went back to Destini. "Get up! And gather your belongings! You are leaving with me, now!"

Something in Ms. Betty's tone made the room feel cold. Destini looked at me, then back to Carlton. It wasn't a laughing matter anymore. She saw our faces. It was serious. Then it hit Destini: She acted like she couldn't breathe. She watched Ms. Betty with horror. Then Destini got up and ran to me.

"What's she talking about?" she asked. "Why I have to go with her?" She paused, only for a split second. Then followed up with another question: "Why? You don't want me here anymore?"

I stood there like a dummy, trying to get my thoughts together. I wanted to tell her the truth, but I couldn't. My mind went haywire on me. I couldn't believe it, they'd had me on the assumption that Destini was my child for the past three months. And the saddest part about it, I really believed them. I felt tricked.... Bamboozled.... Hoodwinked.... Led astray. In other words, I was straight out played like a gullible sucker!

Those dirty bastards!

"Why don't you say something?" Destini asked me in a shrill, broken cry.

Nothing. Not even a smile to reassure her that everything was going to be all right. Just nada. I stood there shaking my head, not believing this bullshit!

"But I thought y'all said that she was his, though?" Carlton directed his question at Ms. Betty.

But before she could say anything, Destini ran over to him to find some sort of support, pleading, "Please don't let them take me away!" She cried. "I wanna stay here with y'all! She's lying! I know she is, because y'all the only family I have!

Carlton probably felt more touched than dazed, because he quickly snatched Destini by her arm as if he wanted to run out the door with her. But he didn't. Perhaps he thought about the consequences of that action when he let go of her arm. That was kidnapping. We all knew that. He looked at me, then at Destini, and then at Ms. Betty. Without toning his emotion down, Carlton's words burst out in vain: "Who in the hell can say that your testing was accurate anyway?"

Nope! That didn't work. Not even a bit. If anything, Carlton's question at Ms. Betty had pissed her off! She cocked her neck back like a merciless cobra, willing to strike and put him in his place, but she turned to Destini instead. "C'mon! You're coming with me, young lady!" She then snatched Destini by the wrist and yanked her.

"Noooo...." Destini tried to break loose from Ms. Betty's grip by falling to the floor, even trying to pull her arm away from her. But that didn't help much.

"You have to come with me, one way or the other." Ms. Betty tried to pick her up.

"Noooo!" Destini panicked and cried out to me. "Stop her! Stop her, Daddy! Tell her to leave me alone! Please, Daddy, tell her!" Destini cried. "STOP HER!" Then Destini slipped from Ms. Betty's grip, and hit the floor again. She even kicked her legs after Ms. Betty, hoping to get Ms. Betty away from her. But it didn't work either.

When Ms. Betty squatted downward, she wrapped both of her arms round Destini's waist and snatched her off the floor like a bag of groceries.

All Destini could do was cry, scream, and kick. She extended her arms out to me, hoping that I could hold onto her. But I didn't. I just stood there, paralyzed, as she cried in front of me.

I didn't like that shit at all! I swear I didn't.

Uncle James came running into the family room, probably awakened by all the shouting he heard from his bedroom. And when he saw Ms. Betty holding onto Destini, he ran back out of the room.

"Please, stop her!" Destini cried out.

Within seconds Uncle James came back in the room and stood in front of Destini; then shouted: "In the name of Jesus! I rebuke you, Satan!" He then threw some sort of liquid substance in her face. Then added: "Now, leave from your daughter—"

Ms. Betty cut in. "You fool!" she shouted at him, smelling her arm. "That's alcohol, not holy water!"

"It's all the same damn thing! And who do you think you're calling a fool? Fool!"

She didn't even bother to entertain that comment. Rather, she thrust herself out of the family room, with Destini in her arms. The deputy led the way.

Destini screamed out to Uncle James. "Please help me!" she shouted between whimpering cries. "Please help me! Help meee.... They wanna take me away!"

"Don't worry yourself. It's only the devil trying to leave outta your body. Just relax yourself!" Uncle James turned to me, perhaps looking for some sort of confirmation on that crap. But since my eyes were hollow-looking, he cut to Carlton. Then asked: "What the hell's going on in here?"

And that's when Carlton gave him a quick synopsis of what was taking place, as Ms. Betty dragged Destini through the hall.

"But that's nonsense!" Uncle James said. "Anybody can easily see that Destini is a spitting image to DaShawn."

I twisted to my right to get a good look at this idiot for saying that.

Meanwhile, Destini started screaming out loud as she held onto the front door frame. "Please, don't let 'em take me away!" She cried. "Please Uncle James, help me! Please help me! I swear on my mommy, I won't be bad anymore! Please HELP meeeee...."

Uncle James looked shocked, then turned to Carlton. "Boy, did you hear that?"

Of course he did.

Uncle James' eyes instantly became watery just before he shouted at Ms. Betty: "You just waita darn second there!" He strode toward her. "This ain't gonna be another one of those damned Elian Gonzalez cases here! You just can't be marching your raggy-ass inside this house and take her like that.... So, get your damned hands off my niece, god dammit!"

Ms. Betty sucked her teeth and thought that situation out before it escalated to the next level. So, on that same token, she tucked Destini beneath her arm, and stuck the other hand inside her purse. "And whatchu gonna do if I don't?" she asked Uncle James, while sliding on her brass knuckles.

"Uhh, I never thought about that one."

"So you'd better get outta my way, because if you were to put your damned hands on me, I'll knock your punk-ass out!" Then she snatched Destini's hand off the door frame with a strong pull.

Uncle James stood there like a coward while several people in the neighborhood were gathering around the house being nosy, watching Ms. Betty having a little trouble putting Destini in the back seat of the deputy's car. But after a little push here and there, she finally got Destini in the car without any injuries.

I stood nearby, watching the whole episode that was going down. Destini's face was painted with grief and pain. And I knew for sure, she was hurt.

When Ms. Betty was finished, she brushed her dress downward and walked over to me. "I'm sorry for the misunderstanding," she had the audacity to say. "But things like this occur at times...."

Her so-called apology didn't even penetrate my mind. How can I say this? I was standing there physically, but mentally, I wasn't.

I was locked on Destini—the whole time—while she was crying inside the deputy's car.

Carlton came out of the house with two suitcases in his hands. "Huhn!" He handed them to Ms. Betty. "These belong to Destini."

"Oh, thank you. These will save the State any expenses of purchasing clothes for her. The State took a terrible hit after Scott took office. So, these will do just fine."

I looked at her as if she were speaking to Carlton in an unknown language.

The deputy popped the car trunk open and helped Ms. Betty with the suitcases.

Ms. Betty apologized again as if she really gave a damn, then moved toward the passenger side door, up front, and got in. She stayed there for a few seconds, jotting something down in some sort of log book.

When I looked toward the back seat of the car, I saw Destini pounding her hands against the window, as tears ran down her face. It crushed me. Then our eyes locked on with each other. She paused. She gave me a helpless, tearful look that ripped my heart apart. I nearly collapsed, wanting to hold my chest. Destini seemed like she wanted me to help her out, but how could I? I was neither her father nor next of kin. Basically there was nothing that I could do for her.

When the deputy buzzed his siren for a quick second, a small crowd of people stepped away from the vehicle, allowing the deputy to drive away with Destini and Ms. Betty.

I stood there and watched them disappear three blocks up the street when they made a left turn. My eyes watered.

Destini was gone.

No more laughter. No more jokes. And no more of the energy that she brought to the house. I knew that. They knew that. We all knew that: she was gone.

Carlton stood beside me for a moment while Uncle James walked back to the house, mumbling off at the mouth and cursing, "These sons of bitches! How could they do this to us? ... She called me Uncle." He stepped inside the house and slammed the door behind him.

I stared up in the sky, looking for the answers, since I had plenty of questions that I wanted to ask that damned mystery god up there. But I doubt if the bastard really existed. So I looked to the ground instead, hoping to rationalize my own situation out by myself. Because, if I had to be technical about it, I had long ago come to the conclusion that this invisible god, as they called it, was only created by the Egyptian top thinkers who wanted to feel superior over the uneducated. Whereas, they took advantage of the opportunity to manipulate their citizens into believing in their ideology belief system of hope, faith, and fear in their make-believe invisible god. By which these same top thinkers went a little further to manipulate their slaves into doing what the High Priests of Ancient Egypt asked them to do; without any question asked; obeying their dictatorship no matter what; or how heavy the burden might be, because prosperity would be given to them. And the grand prize—if they served their oppressors well in their lifetime—they would earn the blessings, not on earth but rather in some nonexistent heaven with this make-believe god of theirs.

What a fucking hoax!

A belief system that was later stolen by the Greeks after their invasion in Africa—because Alexander, the- not-so- Great, was scared to die, wanting to live by the Egyptians' fairytale—in which it was later watered down into my adopted belief system under the Christian doctrines of a non-existent god, who doesn't hear a fucking prayer.

I felt like an idiot.

I knew I hadn't done anything so horrible in my life to deserve this adversity that was bestowed upon me.

I felt betrayed. Fate had stabbed me in the back. The saddest thing about that was, I had trusted my fate, not only with my life but the point of allowing her to introduce me to this supposed daughter of mine. A daughter who wasn't mine by a long shot. Let the truth be told, I had really believed she was mine from the start. And I had, had the audacity to try to mold myself into something I wasn't.

A damned father!

How stupid was I? I was played like a fool!

Those motherfuckers!

Perhaps Kevin was right all along about these trifling-ass hoes around here, claiming particular dudes as their babies' fathers, because of certain credentials in their background.

What a dirty bitch!

"I heard that he was abusing that poor child in there," one of the neighbors' voices cut through my train of thoughts. "That's why they kicked his door in and took her away from him—"

I immediately twisted around, hoping to identify the one who made that remark, but I was thrown off when I saw everybody's goggling-eyes looking at me. So I allowed my tone to come out razor-sharp.

"What?!" I threw my hands up a bit, begging one of them for a fight. "What the fuck y'all looking at?!"

Nobody answered. Instead, they kept their eyes on me for a hot moment until I started to approach them.

Carlton grabbed my arm. "It's not worth it."

I looked at him, then at those nosy-ass bitches again. Now, that was more like it: they began to break off and go their own separate directions, murmuring off at the mouth about me.

It was at that time when I saw Naomi pulling up in front of the house, looking for a parking spot. I made eye contact with her. She smiled at me, but I didn't have the energy to smile back.

I just walked away and went inside the house.

Naomi finally found an available parking spot across the street, next to Amanda's house. By the time she grabbed her purse and opened the car door, Carlton approached her.

"What's up, ma?"

"Hey." She greeted him, while scanning the block. "This is the first time I've seen a residential street this crowded. It's as if they're about to have a block party."

"Nah, not exactly. But check it out, though: I don't think this would be a good time to see my cuz...."

"Why? Is he upset with me?"

"Nah, it ain't like that." Carlton shook his head and tried to explain everything to her the best he could. "So it's up to you if you still wanna see him."

Then, as she was considering her options, they heard a loud sound of shattering glass. They both looked across the street, and then immediately ran to the house to investigate what it was.

I fucking snapped in my study!

I bent over to pick up my Nefertiti's head sculpture off the floor. Thank goodness it didn't break. I just wish I could say the same thing for a few other items inside the room. I guess I lost it—emotionally.

The whole room looked as if it got hit by a category-four hurricane: everything was turned upside down.

"Are you alright, Shawn?"

I turned around.

It was Naomi.

Carlton stepped up to the entranceway about a second later, standing beside her.

Naomi cut her eyes to the broken window. She turned back to me and saw the frustration on my face. She acted as if she wanted to say something, but she closed her mouth back.

I cut to Carlton and barely jolted my head to the side.

He caught on and walked away.

Then I told Naomi, "Destini's gone," as I reached down to pick up a chair.

"So I have been told. Carlton had just informed me about what had happened a moment ago. But are you going to be all right?"

"Yeah." I think I nodded my head before I changed the topic. "So, I see that you made it."

She tried to play along with me, wearing only a half-smile. "If I said I was coming, you can bet your life on it, I'll be here...."

"I can finish this up later." I left everything where it was, even though I'd rather be left alone. "Let me go get ready."

"No, you don't have to.... We don't have to go out this evening. We can put it off for another time."

"Nah. I can't do that." I gave a quick look at her attire, then back at her. "I don't wanna spoil your plans since you got prepared for our date already."

"Don't be silly, this old strapless dress? I had it buried in my closet for years. It's nothing, believe me."

I kept quiet.

So she suggested, "You know, we can stay here and watch a movie?"

"Are you sure?"

But before she could respond, we heard a loud shout across from us: "What the fuck's going on in here?!"

We looked to the window.

It was Ricky, the neighborhood crack-head, holding up an electric pencil sharpener in his hand. "Dammmmm," he dragged. Then: "It looks like the feds were up in here, tearing your crib up!"

"What the hell's your problem?!" I asked him with a little bass in my voice because he had frightened Naomi. "And what are you doing at my window?"

"I was walking by and saw your broken window," he began, then started looking around the window frame, "and I just stopped by because I was wondering if, uhhh...," he paused; then looked at me. "Hey, you wanna buy a pencil sharpener? I'm selling it really cheap." He showed it to me. "I know you probably need one, so how much money—"

"Did you lose your fucking mind? That's mine!"

"No, it ain't!"

"Yeah it is." I strode toward the window to get a better look at it, but he took a step back.

"No, it ain't," he said again. Then added: "So how did I get it, if it's yours? I didn't break in your crib and take it outta there."

"If you don't gimme my shit back, I'm gonna come out there and beat the shit outta you!"

"Oh, you wanna try me like I'm some soft-ass nigga. I'll KNOCK your red-ass out, right in front of your girl; then take her from your pussy-ass!"

I swear, my first impulse was to jump straight out the window to punch him in the mouth, but I twisted around and tried to make a run out the doorway instead.

Naomi grabbed me. "Don't listen to him, sweetie. He doesn't know any better. And besides, unless you can run really fast, I don't think you'll be able to catch him." She looked out the window.

I did too; I saw Ricky running up the block.

"See. I told you so."

I guess she was right. A smile appeared on my face. "C'mon" —I wrapped my arm over her shoulders— "let's go see what kinda movies Carlton has in there." I led her up the hallway toward the family room; then playfully suggested: "What about My Baby Got Back, volumes thirteen and fourteen? I've heard that shawty Monique got buck wild in there."

"I bet you did. But we're not gonna watch any sex tapes."

"I was only joking."

"Oh, sure you were," she mocked, as we entered into the family room.

"So, what about Nine and a Half Weeks instead?"

Now, this was the life to live.

I had my head resting on Naomi's lap, releasing my frustration about Destini's situation. After about twenty minutes of me divulging my deepest thoughts to Naomi about it, I felt better. Burden-free. Although I had built up resentment for all I had been through, I also had plenty of sympathy for Destini, too. I think Naomi knew that in a way from my facial expression alone.

I was hurt and disappointed.

After spilling everything out of my heart to Naomi, it seemed like she could somewhat relate to my issues. Or at least she understood what I was talking about. Based on my calculations alone, of Destini's birthday and going back nine months beforehand to when I was with Jessica, I had convinced myself that Destini was my daughter for sure. One-hundred percent sure of this. And I couldn't even imagine in a million years that Jessica could have slept around with another guy while I was with her.

But the facts proved otherwise: she did.

I'm not stupid!

When I had put all the cards on the table, and thought it out thoroughly, the facts showed that Jessica had another ace card up her sleeve during our game of poker to run a full house on me. There's no question about it. She cheated. And now when I thought of all the guys who could possibly have gotten her pregnant and brought forth this innocent child in this world, all I could do is ask myself, Why me? Out of all the guys who Jessica had been with, Why me? I wanted to know. I needed to know. But nothing came to mind. So I guess it was a desperate move on her part, a fruitless hope to accuse somebody. And that sick bitch chose me.

What a trifling hoe!

"But I can't understand why I didn't notice something from the beginning," I began to ask Naomi, "when Jessica just got up and left me?"

Naomi shrugged while massaging her fingernails through what little hair I had on my head. "She probably left you because of that."

"Because of what?" I looked up at her.

"Because she probably didn't know how to face you with the truth."

"Do you really believe it was that, for real?"

"Sure, that could be possible. And if it wasn't that, it must have been your sloppy kisses then." She laughed a little. I looked up at her again. Then she added: "Because you don't know how to kiss, even if your life was depending on it. So I can only imagine what y'all relationship went through."

Oh, hell nah! I grabbed one of the sofa pillows and hit her with it. "It's not like you can kiss any better."

"Hmm! I know I can kiss better than you," she said between giggles; then she playfully shoved my head off her lap, knocking me to the floor.

I immediately got back up and cornered her with both of my arms, trapping her on the sofa so she couldn't run. "So you wanna play, huh?" I felt the urge to kiss her right there, right then, right now, to prove I was a better kisser than she. So I did. I started off with something soft, nothing sloppy or wet. Just a warm peck at first before I took it up a notch. She positioned her head and kissed me back. I leaned in closer. And just when my flaccid muscle started to get hard—right against and between her legs—Carlton walked in the room with the phone to his ear.

"Okay, here he is," he said into the receiver, then handed the phone to me. "It's Aunt Enid."

I got off Naomi and took the call when Carlton left the room. "Hello?"

"Yeah, this me, baby," Aunt Enid said. "Are you alright?"

"Yeah, I'm all right. What about yourself?"

"Just fine," she said. Then added: "Carlton told me about everything. It's unbelievable. I'm sorry that you had to go through that. But are you sure you're alright, because Carlton told me you tore your place apart."

"Nah. It wasn't like that." I was forced to lie to her because I didn't want her to worry about it. "It's just that my study needed a little makeover, so I was rearranging a few things around, that's all. But other than that, I'm doing alright over here." I smiled at Naomi. "And you can believe me on that." I blew a silent kiss at Naomi.

She blew one back.

"Ohhh," Aunt Enid said, then hissed right after that. Then added, "I don't know about that boy anymore."

"Who?"

"Carlton!" she nearly yelled in my ear. "He called here, telling me all this mess about you, and nearly gave me a heart attack."

"Don't worry yourself, it wasn't anything like that."

"Thank God!"

There was a pause.

Then I broke the short silence. "Auntie, if you don't mind, can I ask you a question?"

"Sure, just as long it ain't like one of those stupid questions that boy just asked me."

"Who, Carlton?"

"Yeah, who else you think I'm talking about?" she said. "That boy called here asking me if he kidnapped Destini from those folks, can they stay at my house until everything cools down."

I wanted to laugh, because I knew Carlton had gotten strongly attached to Destini, but instead, I approached it differently. "So what you think is gonna happen to Destini now?"

"The usual," she said. "Family Services usually has a court hearing, and from there, they'll decide on what they're gonna do with her. Basically the court will determine whether to send her back to Tallahassee where she come from, or allow her stay down here." She paused. "But I can make a few calls to see what's gonna happen to her if you would like me to."

"Yeah, can you do that for me? Because in reality, she didn't ask to go through this mess." I felt a slight vibration in my pocket. "Hold on for a second, Auntie." I reached for my cell phone and answered it. "Yeah, what's up? Make it quick."

It was Kevin: "Nigga, stop acting stupid."

"Man, what you want?"

"Are you busy right now?"

"Yeah. Why?"

"Because I wanna know if you wanna chill for a little and ride out to some hoes' house over there in Carol City with me?"

"Whose house?"

"That hoe, Sharon's?"

I looked at Naomi. "Nah, I'm alright. But hey, let me call you back in a few."

"Why?"

"Because I said so, that why—"

Aunt Enid interrupted me through the other phone. "Baby!"

"Hold on for a second, Kev." I jumped back to the other phone. "Yeah, Auntie."

"I'm gonna make those calls for you and see what's going on with Destini. Okay?"

"Oh, all right then."

"I love you."

"I love you too."

She hung up.

I looked back at Naomi because she had her eyes on me, watching my every move. I raised my index finger, indicating that I needed another second. She smiled. I smiled back, then jumped back on the cell phone and changed my voice up a bit.

And Kevin kinda flipped on me, shouting in my ear: "What the fuck's the matter with you?!"

"Nothing."

"So why are you trippin' then?"

"I'm not. It's just that I'm having a bad day. That's all."

"Why? What happened? You caught the syphilis or something?"

"Nah, it ain't anything like that."

"Yeah, it is! I can hear it in your voice," he laughed. "Who burnt you?"

Ah, fuck it! I decided to tell him about Destini's ordeal.

"Nah...," he seemed to be in disbelief. "You gotta be lying to me?"

"Nah, I'm dead serious."

"Dammmmmm…. That's some fuck-shit, my nigga! But now you see why I don't be believing half of the shit these hoes be saying about me around here. See, I told you! They ain't anything but a bunch of lying-ass tricks…, trying my dawg like that."

"But it's nothing, though. I'm over that shit already."

"That's good, that's good," his voice faded. Then picked back up. "So are you still going to work tonight?"

Tonight?

"Nah, I have to pass on that," I told him while looking at Naomi, smiling. "I'm gonna stay home and chill for the night; take a hot bath with some of that sweet smelling bath oil that I purchased last week from outta the mall. And perhaps throw on a Kenny Lattimore's CD and—"

Kevin cut me off: "What the fuck are you talking about? That's nonsense! If you're not gonna go to work, I'm not going either. I'm just gonna come over there and chill out with you for a bit; and bring a few homeys with me."

"Nah. You don't have to do that."

"Don't be stupid, my nigga. I know how you feel. I'll be right over in a little."

But before I could say anything to him, he hung up on me.

Damn!

I looked at the receiver as if I were expecting him to jump out of there. But he didn't. I looked back at Naomi. And she didn't need to be a rocket scientist to know that something was disturbing me, so I told her the truth: "That was Kevin…. He said he was coming over."

She sat up. "So let's straighten your den before he gets here."

I stood there, silently, knowing that it would probably take Kevin about a half an hour to drive over to the house. Meaning, I had plenty of time to get my groove on with Naomi before he got here. I looked at my wristwatch. It was a little after seven o'clock. And sure enough, I could give Naomi the best twenty-nine minutes of her life. I looked back at her.

"Don't even think about it," she said with a light chuckle while getting up from the sofa. "You nasty freak."

"What are you talking about?"

She laughed as she headed for the doorway. "You know exactly what I'm talking about," she said between giggles as she stepped in the hallway. "C'mon and let's get this room cleaned before he gets here, you freak!"

I stood my ground. "I swear, I don't even know what you're talking about." I headed out of the room, walking directly behind her. "I swear to god, I don't."

She twisted around to look at me. "And you swore to God on that?"

"Yeah, because I'm not lying. I swear."

"You're gonna burn in hell for that." She laughed just as she entered the den.

"So you might as well let me get a little sum-sumthing from you so I take the memories of you along with me down there."

She twisted to face me.

I **straightened up** the furniture in my study, then afterwards I covered the window with a plastic bag to prevent the AC from escaping out of the house.

I also kept a close eye on Naomi because she was doing a little more than just helping me out: She was reorganizing the top of my desk, even though it didn't need it. Its reasons like this as to why I don't allow anyone to touch anything in here. Or better yet, to even step foot inside this room when I'm not—

"Hey-hey-hey!" I called out to her when she went for the desk drawer. "Do you mind if I show you something?"

"Sure." She stopped, then pushed the drawer back where she found it: Close. "What would like to show me?"

"Perhaps," I went with the first thing that came to mind, "you can give me your input on something." I stepped down from the chair.

"On what?"

"On my art designs. I'm gonna need your advice on which drawings you think I should go with first."

"Sure."

I grabbed my portfolio and laid it on a nearby table to get her away from the desk. And it worked. I opened my portfolio and started displaying one drawing after another. I started with my most moderate children's designs, then proceeded to the exceptional wears.

I guess she adored my work, she threw a smile on her face. "You have to give me this," she said, raising a thin strip of paper toward her face to get a better look at it.

"What's that?"

She twisted it around and showed it to me. It was a four snapped-shot picture that Destini and I took together from a photo booth. I wanted to tell her to keep them, but I couldn't. I didn't want to seem cold-hearted just because I'd found out that Destini wasn't my child.

So I settled with something different. "How did that get in there?" I asked, as if her guess would have been better than mine. "We took those yesterday night at Boomers."

Then the phone rang.

"Yeah," I answered it. "What's up?"

"It's me, baby," Aunt Enid said. "I got off the phone with those folks down there at the juvenile center in Overtown, and they have informed me that Destini is housed there, as of right now."

"Oh, for real?"

"Uh-huh. In which they also said that she's scheduled for an eight-thirty court appearance on Monday morning."

"Oh, on Monday?"

"Uh-huh, but hear this—"

I cut her off: "Did you say Monday? This upcoming Monday morning at eight-thirty?"

"Yeah. Why? Is there a problem?"

"Nah-nah. It's nothing," I said. But honestly I had actually thought about going to court on Destini's behalf to show her support. But eight-thirty, Monday morning?

No way.

I had a meeting with a few executives at Decorous' Fashion World that Monday. Yes, the same Monday of Destini's court hearing. So most likely, Destini would understand the conflict. And besides, she needs to learn how to deal with her own issues so she can go through certain obstacles in life by herself—I know I did—in order to grow strong mentally and emotionally.

"But...," Aunt Enid started, then stopped.

"But, what?"

After a short pause, she said, "But there isn't much you can do since you're not her biological father."

Well, there you have it. You heard it for yourself: It wouldn't make a difference if I showed up or not, because like what Aunt Enid just said, it wouldn't change the situation. I wasn't Destini's biological father.

Then it hit me.

It felt like Jodi Arias had just stabbed me in my chest with a rusty kitchen knife. I forced myself to breathe, which my words came out dry but soft. "So, what's going to happen to her from here?"

"Basically the same thing I predicted earlier," she said. "She'll be going back to the district from which she has come from, up there in Tallahassee. And if they can't find any close relatives of hers within a month or two, there's a possibility that she might get adopted by some married couple who probably can't have children." There was a short pause. Then she went on a little further to inform me about the rules and regulations regarding adoption mess.

"Ohhh...."

And she went on.

I became speechless. I had my own personal theory on everything she was telling me. I had heard of other young children in similar situations. Just do the math. That poor girl would probably be shuffled through HRS, from one household to another until she ended up in some fucking pedophile's house. And just the thought of that made me sick!

"Alright then," I cut her off. "Thanks for looking into that for me.... I would have to call you back later on this because I have company over here right now."

"Oh, okay. I'll speak to you later."

"Okay."

She hung up.

I put the receiver back on the cradle. I stood there in silence, trying my hardest to be strong. But the more I tried, the more I was being drawn back into the memories of Destini. Memories of some great moments that were worth being treasured for the rest of my life. I thought about that time when she came into my bedroom with her eyes filled with tears and spoke to me for the very first time when she quoted that engraved message on the back of that gold medallion that I gave her mother back in the day. I remembered that day vividly, as if it was yesterday, because I was stunned that Destini could actually speak. That memory by itself forced a smile on my face. Then I remembered a different time when laughter was shared. And based on that chain of memories, I missed the little rascal even more—

"DaShawn!" Naomi said, breaking up my reveries and bringing me back to reality. "Are you okay?"

"Yeah-yeah, I'm alright. I was just thinking about what my auntie had just told me about Destini."

"What did she say?"

I filled Naomi in the best I could regarding Destini, from the beginning to the end. Then I further told her about the conflict of Destini's court date with the upcoming meeting at Decorous' Fashion World on Monday morning.

The room grew quiet.

"You know," Naomi broke the silence with a great suggestion: "I can go to Destini's court appearance and see about her while you're at your business meeting. I could just fill you in on everything when I speak to you thereafter."

"That's all right. You don't have to go outta your way for me," I said, while hoping that she would insist on going. "You have done too much for us already."

"Don't be silly. Destini is a friend of mine, too. So technically, I won't be going too out of my way."

That's exactly what I wanted to hear.

And she went on to say, "Actually, I was planning on going out to the courthouse anyway."

"Are you sure?"

"Of course I am."

"You're such a lifesaver." I reached over and gave her a kiss on the lips. "Thanks."

"Thanks nothing! You're going to owe me on this one."

I smiled back, then looked over at the clock on the wall. I could pay you now, I thought. It was only 8:27 and Kevin still hasn't gotten here yet. But check it: when I twisted back around to her she acted as if she knew exactly what my intentions were. She had an awkward look in her eyes.

So I played it off, throwing a monkey wrench in her equation before she got me first. "You pervert," I joked, while heading for the doorway. "You needa get those dirty thoughts outta your head. We're about to have friends come over."

"Yeah, right," she made it clear that she didn't believe me when I walked past her. "Whatever."

We headed for the kitchen.

"What you think Destini's doing right now?" I asked.

"I don't know. But whatever it is, it can't be all that great. I can't even imagine how she could cope with the pain of finding out that virtually everyone who played a role in her life has lied to her."

Damn, I'd never thought about it like that. "So" —I was curious to know— "do you think I kinda played in some sorta role in her life too? As someone who misled her?"

She hesitated before she stopped pouring us drinks to look at me.

Don't be surprised, a temporary confinement can be pure hell for some.

When people think of a juvenile detention center, they probably don't know what to expect. Maybe some type of bright building with children's drawings all around the premises; a revolving glass-door or some sort of automatic door that slides open when someone or they stand in front of it. And most likely, when they entered inside the building, they might even imagine to be greeted by some elderly lady in a blue uniform, or perhaps by a Catholic nun with a crucifix hanging from her neck.

But not in this case, because the Juvenile Detention Center that is located on the corner of 27th Avenue is totally the opposite from what you would imagine. The building had a dull gray color that gave it the appearance of a penitentiary. In fact, there was even barbed wire surrounding the facility to prevent the children from escaping. And if you think that's something, just check this out: The barbed wire was purposely set up on the gates to rip the children's skin apart if they attempted to escape from this hellhole. The only thing was missing were gun towers.

Now, if that wasn't enough to frighten the life out of a child, just imagine when you step inside to get a better look at what they are up against: Because the inside of the building wasn't any different from the outside. Once you passed the entrance to the children's section, you could actually feel the abandonment of being alone—that cold, Orphan Annie feeling—as you passed through several electric doors down the hall. There was a long stretch hallway with about twenty-six cell doors, split up on both sides of the walkway, facing each other. They were no different from the dog cages that you would find at your local animal shelter. All the cells were small, and the children were forced to call them their living quarters.

Just picture that...

Destini was lying on the mat, in a fetal position, on the floor, whimpering and crying with what might once have been a white bed sheet but now it had a rust color to it with the brownish spots, covering her body.

Then someone shouted, "Lights out!" from down the hall. And in a matter of seconds, all the light inside the cells were shut off.

It became pitch black in Destini's cell at first, but slowly a gleam of light from outside in the hallway started lurking in from underneath the door. Her cell mates—one Cuban and the other, she guessed, was either Haitian or Jamaican—rolled over and went to sleep.

Destini wanted to go to sleep too, in order to force this day to blow by, but she couldn't. She opened her eyes for a moment but immediately shut them back. Not only her eyes were burning all day from crying, but the thought of being back in the same frightening environment—like the one in Tallahassee—gave her the creeps.

She was afraid; and who could blame her? She knew she hadn't done anything to deserve this. Her mother had died and left her all alone. And the thought of that made her cry even more.

A dream that she once had not so very long ago, a yearning of having a family all over again, had mysteriously and unexpectedly begun to come true while she was living under the roof with three grown men, but then ...

POOF!

It was like a magic trick.

The family Destini thought was hers had vanished before her eyes. She cried: The man her mother claimed was her father, wasn't her father after all. She felt betrayed.

She cried some more until she was able to fall asleep.

Somehow I knew this was going to happen.

As soon as Naomi started loosening up a bit, our conversation got interrupted by the doorbell.

Damn!

"Let me go get that." I got up on the fifth ring. "It's probably Kevin." I went to answer the door. And I called good money.

It was him. "What's up, fool?"

"Don't be coming up in here with that bullshit!" I blocked him from entering inside the house. He was standing beside Fabulous, Mikey, and some other dude that I had never seen before carrying a box of Papa John's Pizza in his hand. I cut back to Kevin. "Why the fuck you don't be answering your cell phone?"

"I got caught up on something," Kevin said then shoved me aside with his forearm, stepping inside the house. "That hoe Vida wanted to see me for a second. And, oh, yeah!" He stopped, then beckoned his head toward the back. "Before I forget: this the new guy who's gonna be a part of our team. His name is Cinnamon Toast."

"What's happening?" I acknowledged him, as they entered my home. I followed them to the family room.

Naomi rose from her seat. "It's getting late," she told me, then grabbed her purse. "Can you walk me out?"

"Yeah, I can do that. But you know, you don't have to leave, if you don't want to?"

"No, I have to. It's getting a little too late for me to be hanging out."

I walked her to her car.

"Thanks."

When she opened the car door, I placed my hand on her arm to prevent her from going any further. "Why don't you stay a little while longer?" I practically begged her. Then added: "I swear, I'll get rid of them right now if you give me the word. Just say it."

"No," she sorta laughed a bit, "you don't have to do that. I really have to go anyway. Just go and bond with your friends for today. We'll make it up on another day."

"Tomorrow?"

"I don't know about that," she said with a smile. "But you never know, there could always be a possibility of that." She stuck one leg inside the car, then paused. I moved in close to her, and did exactly what she probably hoped for: I gave her a nice, long kiss, and afterwards, we both exhaled deeply as we eased away from each other. She smiled, then got inside the car. She didn't say anything else. She didn't have to. A smile grew on my face. I ran back in the house once she drove away.

"Is your hoe gone yet?" Kevin asked me, while eating on a slice of pizza.

"She ain't a hoe. But yeah, my shawty left already." I sat across from him. "So let me give you the whole story on what happened today." Little by little, I told him everything that went down, while Mikey and that new dude Cinnamon were playing on the video game.

"That's fucked up, my nigga," Kevin said when I finished telling him everything.

"I know, just tell me about it."

His eyes wandered off until they reached the coffee table—directly in front of him—and locked onto Destini's photos.

I guess Naomi had left them there by accident.

Kevin picked them up. "You gotta admit it, she was a little wild one, though." He kept his eyes on the photo.

"Yeah, she was." I leaned across the table to get a better look at the photo in his hand.

Then, that dude, Cinnamon, got a hit on his cell phone. "It's her," he told Fabulous and Mikey, then answered it, stepping away from the TV.

Fabulous and Mikey followed him because, supposedly, from what I heard him telling them, he had just recently met a female at the club last night who was a nympho. And Fabulous and Mikey wanted to know if she had any friends for them.

"So what's up?" Mikey asked.

"Yeah, she has some friends. But she only had one of them over there with her right now."

Fabulous jumped in to ask: "What she looks like?"

"She ain't a skank, if that's what you're wondering about. She looks alright," Cinnamon assured him. "I saw her already." He then spoke back into the receiver for a few more seconds before he hung up.

"So what'd she say?" Mikey followed up to ask. "She gonna get another friend or what?"

"Nah, it's only her and her girl chilling out tonight." Cinnamon headed back toward the couch. "But she did say I could bring somebody over with me, about an hour from now."

Fabulous and Mikey looked at each other, probably about to play a game of Rock, Paper, Scissors to see who was going to go along with him.

"My man!" I got Cinnamon's attention. "Where you say you were from?"

"I never did. But I'm from Overtown."

"Oh, word?" I admired his style. "It's just that I haven't seen you around before."

"Nah. You haven't. It's because I just got finished doing a twelve year bid with the feds."

"Word?"

He nodded.

"Get the fuck outta here! Twelve years?"

"No lie," he said, without even a trace of a smile. "They hit me with a drug conspiracy charge because I hung around a few brothers from my neighborhood." He paused for a second. Then went on to say, "And just because I wouldn't tell on them, the prosecutor flipped the script and said that I'd also played a major role in the drug conspiracy. The prosecution in my case got so desperate that they gathered up a few Black brothers from federal prisons to make statements against me, claiming that I had sold them drugs back in the day."

We all kept our mouths closed, so he could continue.

And he did: "When I went through my court proceedings, I swear on everything I love, I didn't even know those niggas."

"So why would they lie on you?" I asked.

"Because the prosecutors promised to cut their prison sentence in half if they cooperated with them, what else?" he said. "And the saddest thing about that is, the prosecutors be knowing their cooperating witnesses be lying and shit! But they didn't give a fuck just as long as they can get another Black conviction under their belts while throwing us in prison, whether smashing us in trial with these lying-ass niggas or forcing us to plead guilty to avoid a life sentence in prison because we don't know what the prosecutors gonna make up against us in trial…. Dawg, those crackas are vicious!" He then turned to Mikey. "No disrespect, homey."

"Man, I'm not on that type of time. Go ahead and speak your mind."

Cinnamon turned back to me. "Dawg, have you ever heard of the word, 'Gulag' before?"

"Nah. I don't believe I have."

"Well," he went on to say, "you can find that word in the encyclopedia and it explains how this guy by the name of Archipelago Solzhenitsyn published a few books called 'The Gulag Archipelago' back in nineteen-seventy-three about the Soviet Union's prison system. I even read two of his first books, which he exposed the Soviet Union on how they were building and scattering those concentration prison camps throughout their country, locking up as many people they could get their hands on. People who were like ordinary criminals, without the financial backing to defend themselves in court. Mainly, those who were either poor or uneducated.

"The Stain's Administration was even locking up those who were in their opposition's political parties, and those who were from all different ethnic backgrounds: Jew, Germans, Polish, Russians. I mean like everybody who they felt was a threat to them, just locking them up, making them into slave laborers and even using some of them in government experiments by exposing them to certain poisonous toxins to see how the toxin would work against their prisoners.

"And believe it or not, these prisoners went through a legal court system over there. Just like the federal court system that we have over here in the United States. But going back to the Soviet Union, the Stalin's Administration incarcerated millions of their own people during the nineteen-twenties through the fifties, giving those people long sentences in the Gulag prison system, forcing them to be slaves to the State and working them for little or nothing, just to survive."

"Yeah?" I guess that's where Hitler's regime got their concept from when they did the same thing to the Jews in the Auschwitz's prison camp in Poland, I thought. But what the hell is he giving us a lecture on world history for? "I'm just happy that I'm in the twenty-first century then."

"Yeah?" he said in a way to mock me.

"Yeah." I stood my grounds.

"Well," he started, then gave it to me raw, "these crackas stole the Soviet Union's blueprints and brought that same concept over here in the United States, locking up as many Blacks and Hispanics they could get their hands on. They are even locking up some of those white Americans, too. And just like the Soviet Union and Hitler's regime back then, the United States government is constantly building federal prisons all over this country, as I speak, making slaves laboring factories that they call 'UNICOR' and scattering them all about the place; having their own citizens working for about twenty to fifty cent an hour, making products for the government and military.

"Then, in turn, the government turns right back around and ask the masquerade Congress, whom most of them have foreign last names, for billions of America's taxpayers dollars for the Military Spending Bill for their unnecessary wars overseas that they love so much. And as a repercussion of all this, we as American citizens get fucked with their high taxes; when in fact, inmates are working in the prison factories for pennies, making everything the government needs for the military. And it's quite funny because people in society have the audacity to wonder why the unemployment rates in America is sky high, when all they have to do is look into the prison industries: that's where some of their factories went to. And I can guarantee you this, too: inmates won't lose their jobs in these factories to overseas countries. I can put my life on that.

"Inmates work as cheap laborers like the Chinese overseas, and make about everything the government wants them to make. And I mean like, everything. I know it may be hard to believe, but the federal prison system is a part of a big-ass corporation with private investors and stockholders that includes judges, lawyers, prosecutors, and even some Congressmen and women. They all get piece of the action, off the taxpayer money, sending people of color to jail for a long period of time for some bullshit, if their fraternity brothers, the police officers that is, aren't killing Blacks on the streets. You can see it for yourself on the news; I'm not lying

"Just like what the Soviet Union and Hitler's regime did back in the day; and do your own study about it. I swear, you'll find the same comparison with the United States government right now. But this shit goes even deeper than that, if I break down the whole new concept of their eugenic sterilization of Blacks, not only by the poison that is to Blacks while in prison, but rather, how they are throwing Blacks in prison with long harsh sentences, to prevent them from producing any offspring that could possibly be a threat to white America in making them the minority here in two thousand fifteen. Or better yet, how the United States government is locking up as many people who they could get their hands on to obtain our DNA, finger prints, and voice recognition for their NSA database.

"But do y'all wanna know the saddest part about this prison shit, besides the time when the Clinton Administration signed that bill to build thirty-seven more federal prisons to lock our asses up for some bullshit?"

I nodded my head a bit so he could continue.

"These crackas are making the United States into a police state right underneath our noses. We are just too blind to see that shit, because we're caught up in all the manipulation in the news that they throw out there in the media, whether by TV or newspapers for their galvanization for the public reaction. Sorta like what they did with the Nine-Eleven drama and that fake Osama bin Laden hunt…. Yo, that shit doesn't seem fishy to you that the government claims to have captured and murdered Osama bin Laden, but then they also go on to allegedly buried him out there in the middle of the ocean. Out in the ocean, of all places. Now there's no way for anyone to find his burial place to verify that shit! I swear, I don't believe a word these people say anymore. And just to support what I'm talking about overall, they had passed the Terrorist Bill just—"

Fabulous cut in: "Yeah, to go after those terrorists over there in the Middle East!"

"So you think," he said. "That same Terrorist Bill is going after us too: anybody who stands in their way from obtaining their New World Order. And if you think that's hard to swallow, wait until you get a load of this: They are even going after our children too, under some shit they supplemented under that same bill they called The Gang Act." Cinnamon took his eyes off of Fabulous, cutting back to me. "Then they had that puppet Obama up there in the White House, on national TV, telling Moammer Gadhafi to allow Libyans to freely protest over there. But when the Occupiers of Wall Street tried to do the same shit over here and protest peacefully, this same government here flipped the script on them and started locking their asses up!" He paused for a hot second.

I thought he made a strong point there.

Then he went back to that prison mess again: "You see, these crackas have the whole game on lock. They are achieving their whole plan against us to keep us divided. They know that if they lock away our fathers for many of years, shipping them from prison to prison, far away from home, that will eventually break our family bonds with each other. This government is just using the same blueprint that they used during the slavery days, hoping to destroy any sorta family bond that Blacks have for each other.

"And just like back then, during the slavery era in this country when Black fathers were sent from plantation to plantation in hope to break their family bond with each other; now our same fathers of today who are sent to jail will eventually lose their respect over their households and family because of their absence. Their wives or significant others will eventually leave them to find someone new, jumping from one relationship to another, hoping to find a decent replacement for their hubby's absence. And if this Black man has a son, the chances are that same son will look to the streets for that missing father figure. Which statistics shows, this same child of his will end up dead or in prison like his father. All of which, that's the government's ultimate goal to destroy us as a race.

"Just look at it.... It's our younger generation who's joining these gangs at an early age. Sometimes ten years old, or even younger. But for what? For protection, because their pops in some federal prison for x-amount of years. Now, that's some crazy shit! And if this father has a daughter, I'm sorry to say this but, if she doesn't become a stripper, she'll become a hoe. Just look at the image they display about our Black sisters on BET in those rap videos." He paused a moment. Then added: "That's why I don't even watch BET anymore. That fuck-nigga Johnson sold us out for a bitch-ass basketball team! Basically, he's telling us that we have no place in white corporate America, but rather be their athletes and rappers, for their Sambo entertainment. But now our generation has to be lost because we were stripped away with the only Black news station that can enlighten us on the truth so we don't have to allow our families to go through this modern day slavery within these federal prisons."

Damn, I thought about Destini as to what the future held for her.

Kevin looked at me, then went back to Cinnamon.

I looked back at Cinnamon, too. "Hey dawg, no disrespect. But I don't wanna hear about this right now."

"I respect that. I just wanted to keep it real."

"I feel you. But I think you oughta write a book about that."

"Yeah, I thought about it. But if I do decide to write one and end up dead somewhere, fall ill to some type of illness, or even have a heart attack, y'all be the first ones to know that these crackas had me murdered."

The room grew quiet.

I then thought about Jessica's father. She never really got to know him because her stupid-ass mom pulled Jessica away from him at a young age when he went to prison. Which, of course, he eventually gave up on himself and became a victim of the penal system in which he later died in there, I think—if I remember correctly—of AIDS.

Cinnamon pulled his keys out from his pants. "Yo," he began to ask the fellows, "which one of y'all wanna go along with me to my shawty's crib?" He looked at Fabulous first, but since Fabulous gave him the indication that he was straight, he turned to Mikey. "What about you?"

"Hell, yeah, I wanna go!" Mikey said, while getting up from the sofa. "I might as well get all the fun I can get right now before those crackas come after me too." He laughed, stretching his pants outward, looking down at his manhood. "Because, not only when they find out, but when all of you muthafuckers find out what this Jewish cracka is working with, all of y'all gonna be afraid of me too."

We burst out laughing.

Then Fabulous told Mikey between laughs, "You're a sick cracka, my nigga!"

"Yeah, I might be sick alright," he said, while getting serious. "But I'm just sick and tired of all this racism shit! We hate because we choose to hate, not because we have to."

"That's some real shit, dawg." Cinnamon gave Mikey a brotherly handshake, with a half hug. "Let's get up outta here before those shawties bounce on us."

"Sure thing."

Cinnamon turned to us. "Alright then, we gonna holla at y'all later," he advised us. "And if nothing comes through for us, we'll meet up with y'all at the club later on tonight."

Fabulous and Kevin nodded their heads, while I just kept my eyes on him.

Directly after Cinnamon and Mikey left the house, I asked Kevin, "Where in the hell did y'all find that nigga from?"

He sorta laughed, then got serious. "I ran into him in the mall the other day when he came outta a job interview. He said no one would hire him because of his past criminal record."

"Word?"

"Yeah, so I picked him up and showed him the game before he turned to the street for support."

"That's good." The government is going to have hell on this ass, if homey writes that book about the new era of modern day slavery.

We all chat for a little while longer, just shooting the breeze about this and that before Kevin and Fabulous decided to head out to the nightclub and make themselves some money. Yeah, I contemplated the idea of going along with them, but I decided to stay home for the night and get an early start on tomorrow morning. I had to get prepared for that presentation on Monday.

After Kevin and Fabulous left, I headed for my bedroom but suddenly stopped in front of Destini's bedroom. I could have sworn I heard some sort of giggling sound coming from out of there. I scanned the room, where life and energy once ran free. But now, there was nothing there. It looked and felt like Jesus' tomb.

Nothing but a bunch of old rags left behind.

I shook my head, not because there was a strong possibility that I was losing my mind, but rather, because I kinda missed the little nagging girl who wouldn't go to sleep until someone read her a bedtime story or sung her a lullaby.

I stepped away and went to my bedroom. I was definitely calling it a night. But I couldn't fall asleep for reason. I found myself tossing and turning in bed, trying to find that good sleeping position. But I couldn't find one. I gave up after the hundredth roll. I just reached for the phone and dialed Naomi's number instead.

She picked up on the eighth ring.

"Hey, what's up?" I tried to play it off as if I weren't worried about anything.

There was a pause. A long one. Then she asked me, "Is everything all right?"

"… No…. I can't sleep." My eyes got watery: I thought about Destini.

Something was wrong with this scene.

Uncle James was about to sneak inside the house early Sunday morning, hoping to avoid any mischievous action from Destini. But then he remembered something: She wasn't there anymore. He smiled. There's no doubt about that. He stepped inside the house with a 1973 pimp swagger. He leaned to the side, with his right arm swinging back and forth, feeling free without any worry of being attacked by some young assassin with a high powered water gun in her hand. He shut the door behind him with a back kick.

Now, that's what Uncle James was talking about: Freedom.

He found peace and quiet inside the house. He couldn't have asked for anything better. He strode down to the family room and there wasn't a soul in sight. Just how he liked it. Now he could have a little private time for himself. To set the mood off right, he zoomed in on a sex video by Zane's Entertainment—the Chocolate Covered Cherry Popper, volume 2, with that sexy chick Brandy doing her thing in it—lying beside the TV.

A light clicked in his head.

And lotion was the first thing that came to his mind. He smiled hard. But before he got down to the nitty-gritty, he wanted to check the house out, just to be on the safe side, to make sure that nobody was in the house with him. He strolled down the hall to the back end of the house, and damn! His eyebrows tightened up with frustration.

Just when it seemed too good to be true.

I dropped the newspaper, just below my eyes, to look by the doorway to see who asked me that stupid-ass question.

Oh....

Without saying a word back to Uncle James, I continued scanning the business section.

"So," he began to ask me again, "whatchu doing here at this time of the day?"

"Can't you see I'm reading the fucking newspaper?!"

"Hey! I'm not the one who took Destini away from you. So you needa chill out some: I'm not your enemy here."

"Yo" —I dropped my arms on top of the desk to get a better view of him— "just leave me the fuck alone! I don't wanna be bothered right now."

It seemed like he wanted to say something, but I guess he changed his mind when I started reading the paper again.

He walked away from the doorway.

The phone rang.

I shouted loud enough for him to hear me: "If it's for me! I'm not here!"

A majority of the young girls at the Juvenile Detention Center were either braiding each other's hair or watching some sort of soap opera on TV, while some of the younger girls were playing 'Duck-Duck-Goose: A silly childhood game where a bunch of kids sit on the floor, forming a circle, while the main participant walks around the sitting circle, patting the other participants' heads, calling them ducks until she decides to call one of the participants a goose and runs away from her. And the object of the game is for the person who is called a goose must chase the main participant around the circle in order to tag her back before she takes her seat within the circle.

In this case, it was a little Haitian girl, who was no older than six years old. To which she accidentally ran into Destini while chasing after that little Cuban girl who had just called her a "Goose" a few seconds ago.

"I'm sorry," the little Haitian girl said to Destini while trying to catch her breath. "I didn't mean to hit you."

Destini didn't say anything back to her.

"Do you wanna play with us?"

Destini shook her head.

The little girl shrugged her skinny shoulders and said, "Okay then. You can't say I never asked you," before she continued her pursuit.

Destini twisted back around and looked out the thick window to avoid the feeling of being helplessly trapped in this environment.

Later on that evening after a light dinner—a regular T-bone steak and a baked potato smothered in garlic butter—I was in the middle of cleaning up when the phone started to ring. I would have answered it on the fifth ring but it seemed like someone else in the other room had picked it up already.

So I kept cleaning.

Then, within seconds, I heard Carlton from the family room cursing a broad out over the phone. He was raising hell in whatever kind of language he was using on her.

And he sounded pissed off too! Very much so.

All I heard from where I was standing at was "Fuck hoe" this and "Fuck hoe" that. It was probably LaTonya, I assumed, or one of them fast hooches that he always be messing with.

Although it wasn't any of my business, my curiosity wanted to know who he was cursing out like that. So I quietly picked up the phone to eavesdrop on his heated altercation. And that's exactly what it was: Heated, with a capital H.

Ouch!

They were having a shouting match, then Carlton's voice got even a little stronger over the phone line: "You fuck-ass bitch! Why the fuck you told her some shit like that for?! She's only a little girl—"

"Well! She should have never fucking called me a fucking hoe first!"

This can't be, I thought.

I felt ashamed.

"BITCH!" Carlton cut back in. "That was my little niece you told that to!"

"She's not even your niece, you stupid-muthafucker! And who the fuck you think you're calling a bitch?!"

"YOU, BITCH!"

"NO! YO'MAMA a BITCH! You faggot, punk muthafucker!"

I couldn't believe my own ears. The female's voice I heard over the phone line belongs to none other than Samara's. To hell with the name calling: That's a childish argument whose mother was what. But to me, Carlton was right. That little girl that they were talking about was my little … I mean, was little Destini.

Yeah, we all knew that Destini could be a little bug-a-boo at times. But still, she was young, something this bitch should have considered when Destini was my daughter for the past three months—up until yesterday.

When Destini had told me about Samara called her mother a two-dollar-cum-drinking-hoe, Why didn't I believe her? The signs were all there that morning when Destini had that sudden outburst before me.

Damn!

I let Destini down when she needed me.

"You stupid bitch!" Carlton snapped on Samara, breaking my train of thought. "If I ever catch you anywhere in my path, I'm—"

"You faggot muthafucker, you ain't gonna do a muthafucking thing to me!"

"You just better watch your ass around here, bitch, because—"

I decided to cut in: "Carlton! Chill out for a second. She didn't call here to speak to you. She called here for me. So lemme holla at her from here."

The phone grew silent for a few seconds until Samara broke back in: "Boo, I don't know what the fuck his problem is, but you better tell him something because he doesn't know who he's fucking with. I could get him fucked up at any time I want—"

"Bitch!" Carlton snapped again. "You can get anybody you wanna get, Hoe! You know where the fuck I live at!"

"Yo, Carlton!" I tried to take control of the situation. "I said to chill the fuck out already! And Samara, you needa chill out too!" I paused for a second. Then said: "Yo Carlton, lemme get a minute

with her." I wanted for him to hang up, but I continued anyway:
"Samara!"

"Yeah, boo!"

"All that threatening shit on my cousin isn't even called for. But let me tell you something though."

"What?"

"Check this out: as long as you live, and I mean this literally, don't ever call my crib again."

"What are you talking about? He started it first."

"Nah, Samara, it's bigger than what you think. Because that same little girl who you disrespected by calling her mom some foul name like that … just take my word on this, her mom wasn't what you painted against her. However, not only Destini you disrespected, but you had disrespected me as well when you crossed that line about her mother to her."

"But that bitch got pregnant from someone else and dumped you!"

"You don't understand: she had her reasons for leaving. But check it, just do me that favor: Don't call here anymore."

"Well, fuck you too then!" she shouted in my ear before she hung up on me.

Right after that I heard a second click before I placed the phone back into the cradle. I guess that was Carlton. I stood there for a moment, lost in my thoughts before I headed back to the sink to finish washing the dishes.

Everything went back to normal: a quiet home.

And about an hour later, while I was in the study hovering over my art designs, Carlton strolled up to the doorway looking dandy, like a fresh pressed hundred dollar bill.

"Hey," he started, while slapping a gold watch around his wrist, "you wanna go out on a double date with me and my hoe Tonya?"

"Nah, I'm all right."

"Are you sure?"

"Yeah, and besides, it's a little too late for me to be calling my shawty's crib, asking her to go out tonight on a short notice."

"Nah, my girl gotta friend who's coming along with us. And she has a phat ass too! You should come along and check her out, so you can release some of that shit off your chest."

I smiled while flipping through my art designs. "I'm alright, dawg." I looked at him again. "But good looking out though. It's just that I have a lotta work I'm trying to get straight for this presentation for tomorrow morning."

"That's on you, my nigga." He walked away and left the house.

After a while I neatly placed my drawings back in the portfolio. I was satisfied with the order I was going along with. I hit the light switch and went straight to my bedroom. Just when I was about to jump in the sack, the phone began to ring I looked at the alarm clock on the night table. It was a little after ten o'clock. Believe me, I could have allowed the telephone to keep ringing in my ears but that little voice in my head told me to do something different.

I snatched the phone up on the fourth ring.

Oh, it was Naomi.

Naomi stepped out of the bathroom, fixing her hair into a ponytail, walking up to the bedside. "Honey," she said while buttoning up her blouse. "You needa start getting up or you'll be late for your job presentation."

Just when I thought I could sleep in a state of delusion, I had to wake back up in the world of confusion.

My body felt paralyzed and my eyelids seemed glued together. But my smile—oh, my goodness—it was living the life somewhere in cloud nine. And I wasn't a bit bothered by Naomi disturbing it either. She had blessed me with a wonderful time last night. I had gone three full rounds with her, doing just about everything, from 69-position to me even popping her in the ass.

"Good morning, sweetie," my voice sounded a bit scratchy. "What time is it?"

"It's going on eight o'clock, and I have to start heading out to the courthouse before I hit traffic on my way there."

"Oh, shit! I almost forgot!" I leaped out of bed and ran to the bathroom to freshen up; by the time I got out from there, Naomi had already left the house.

I strode over to the closet and grabbed my black slacks and cream colored dress shirt by Steve Harvey. It fitted just right. I slid on my crocodile shoes and tossed my money-green tie around my neck.

Cross over; up; under; through; and pull. My tie hung just right. I smiled when I saw my reflection in the mirror.

I felt ready.

Meanwhile, across town, the employees at Decorous' Fashion World were marching through the hallways getting in their zones, like a bunch of army ants at work. And just like the queen ant, it was uncommon for the regular workers to see the CEO of the company unless something big was going down. Nevertheless, that was the case here when they stepped inside the conference room and saw Mr. Stephen Goldberg, the owner and CEO of Decorous' Fashion World. He was the head man in charge. The shot-caller. He made all the final decisions for Decorous'. And basically, the only reason he had decided to come to this presentation this morning, other than it being an emergency board meeting called by someone who worked on the second floor, there was a lot of hype regarding this new collection of children's clothing that could elevate his company to the next level over his competitors. And Mr. Goldberg couldn't wait to see the art designs himself: he was interested in the new ideas.

But for a fashion design company, it seemed like the employees there wore just about anything he or she could get their hands on when they woke this morning; especially that secretary who just walked inside the conference room with that two-piece wrinkle dress suit on. She looked a little like Rosie O'Donnell, with heavy bags under her eyes.

If there was something in this world that could hold back the hands of time when a person is in a rush, the deputy officer at the Juvenile Detention Center would have used it to stop the clock for at least fifteen minutes so he could make it to the Family Courthouse on time. He had a few children scheduled for court this morning.

But don't get it twisted, though: the courthouse was on the same complex with the juvenile's hall. It was just a hop and a skip away, leaving no excuses. However, he was still running late. Experience wasn't required. He was Black! So thank goodness for Affirmative Action.

Enough said.

This officer was overweight and out of shape. He stood at six three and weighed every bit of 342 pounds. He was huge. Really huge. He had a wide chest, large shoulders, and wore a butt-naked face to go along with his bald head. He had a look that would make you ponder for a moment about which zoo he had escaped from: the Bronx or Miami Metro? And by the look of the loose skin around his neck, this officer looked to be in his late fifties; and he had a name that fit his outside appearance, Clifford L. Robinson.

Well, at least, that's what his tame tag read.

He stood in the hallway with Mrs. Thompson, the caseworker for the detention center, while lining up a few children against the wall in alphabetical order, for their 8:30 court appearance. Destini was one of the seven children. While a few of the kids were acting obnoxious, talking loud and making rude remarks to one another, that wasn't the case for that one particular youngster by the name of Lewis Brady, who seemed to be up to something. And that was the main reason why Mrs. Thompson gave Officer Robinson one of those stares, while making a gesture towards Lewis, because Lewis kept looking over his shoulders, acting suspicious. She wanted Officer Robinson to pay close attention to him.

So, to be on the safe side, Officer Robinson had Lewis to stand at the end of the line, directly in front of him, as he allowed Mrs. Thompson to lead the group, starting with the girls up front. That was a regular routine for them, putting the more severe juvenile delinquency at the end of the line.

And on they went, like Snow White and the seven colored dwarfs.

Mrs. Thompson opened up the side door and led them into a long straightaway hallway that would take them through several other halls, and an elevator ride upstairs, and a short path straight to the court's bull pen until their names were called by the judge.

According to Mrs. Thompson's estimation, it would take them about five minutes to get there.

Officer Robinson shouted: "Get back in line!"

I walked out of the house with a cup of coffee in one hand and my art work in the other. I popped the car door open, tossed my portfolio to the back seat, hopped in, and sped off.

What can I say? I was in a rush.

I was driving at a regular pace at first until I saw the digital clock on the dashboard that read 8:23 a.m. I panicked. I had less than twenty minutes to make it to my scheduled appointment at Decorous' Fashion World. I floored it, of course. I had to.

I was dipping and cutting through traffic like an experienced Indy 500 race car driver. A Honda Accord cut in front of me. I wove around it, and then stuck my middle finger at the old punk as I sped pass him. I'm not lying. I made it to my destination in fifteen minutes. Unbelievable. Now all I had to do was to find a decent parking spot.

The head honcho and the executives at Decorous' were gathering inside the conference room. They all looked anxious: They couldn't wait to see what all the excitement was about.

Eric Dorsey has been drawing a lot of attention to this upcoming presentation ever since last week Friday. You see, Eric had something to prove to the executives upstairs, and after today, he would be looking for that upstairs office that overlooked parts of downtown. He had a good feeling about this presentation.

A really good feeling.

He looked at his wristwatch. It was a quarter to nine. Then he looked at the twenty-plus impatient people who were gathering around the table with him. He cut to Ciara and muttered, "Where in the hell is this damned fool at?"

It was about time!

I finally found a parking spot. It was a block up the street from Decorous'. I jumped out of the car and tried to make a dash for it.

Shit!

I forgot my portfolio!

I twisted back around and popped the back door open to retrieve my art designs. But when I extended my hand inside the car to grab my art work, my eyes caught a glimpse of something furry-looking underneath the driver's seat. I immediately leaped back because I didn't know what it was.

A cat? A rat? A goddamn gremlin? I didn't know. I was just clueless.

I quickly zoomed in on the little critter and took a better look at it.

Oh!

I felt stupid.

It was Abu: Destini's toy monkey.

"Whatchu doing down there?" I reached for him, feeling a bit embarrassed when two men in business suits walked pass, eyeing me.

Then something happened. I caught a mesmerizing moment that flashed through my mind. I thought about that time when Kevin and I went to Dade Land Mall with Destini; and then, within a matter of minutes, she wandered off. Just like that. I could never forget that day. I was terrified and worried sick about her.

But after a quick search, I finally found my little rascal inside of K.B's Toy store, kneeling beside Naomi who later became her friend, my friend, our friend, and later my girlfriend. And it was Naomi who bought that same monkey for Destini, along with some other cool stuff. And I could honestly say this: Destini hardly left Abu's side from that day. She had him everywhere she went. At the dinner table; in the family room; just about everywhere around the house—Abu was there with her.

I can't even imagine what that poor child is going through right now, I thought, because she accidently left him behind. My eyes cut away from Abu and looked up the street toward Decorous' Fashion Building. I felt stuck, and somehow I remembered what Eric had told me about Destini last week when he said, "She might as well come along with us too, because if it weren't for her, we probably wouldn't be having this second meeting right now. And besides, she seems to be a little angel. You're lucky little angel."

On that last part, Eric was right: Destini was indeed my little angel. But the truth of the matter she couldn't be here for my presentation because I was not her legal guardian. But then, all of a sudden, my recollection switched to something different: A reminder of a brief conversation that I had with Carlton at Boomers.

"So, you're admitting that she's yours now?"

"Man, I have always known she was mine, all the time," I remembered telling him that day. "She looks just like me; act like me…, and damn near speaks like me too. It would be impossible if she wasn't my daughter. It's just that this whole fatherhood shit hit me all too fast, and I didn't want anything to do with it. I just didn't have the slightest clue about being a father…. So you already know, the best thing for me to do at that time was to deny her as much as I could. But I'm gonna have to learn now because I have a daughter to raise and look after—" My mind froze right there for a short moment and a small reminder echoed inside my head: "I have a daughter to raise and look after." And it kept repeating itself over and over again until I was able to shake that refrain out of my head.

Which I did, only after I tossed Abu back inside the car. I snatched the driver's door open and got in. I sped off like a New York cabbie, leaving tire marks about ten yards out on the street pavement.

At this point, I didn't give a fuck! I had a daughter to save from being trapped up in this—whatchamacallit system?—let's just call it the genocidal legal system for our Black youth of today.

The courtroom floor was carpeted from one side of the room to the other, with decorated polished oak wood furniture throughout; and thus half filled with people.

The court's attendant shouted, "All rise for the family court judge, the Honorable Ronald J. Spencer!"

And everybody in the courtroom stood up as the judge entered the room, an O.J. Simpson look alike, and only sat back down when the judge had done so. However, the court's bailiff stood the whole time near the corner of the judge's bench.

Judge Spencer cleared his throat and took a sip of water from the drinking glass that was sitting in front of him. His bench was set high. High enough to look over the whole courtroom as if he were some sort of mythological god, looking down upon the so-called infidel without craning his neck.

Rumors had it that Judge Spencer was the type of person not to be fucked with! He was a black man, and he had an Uncle Tom's inferiority complex about his skin complexion. He hated it. So, to be a part of the secret society that he joined many years ago, he followed after those evil folks in the Reagan's Administration who put him in power to commit genocide against his own race so it wouldn't look suspicious to others.

Hey! What do you expect? It was just a new form of a William Lynch's syndrome, of a Black on Black crime. But in this case, it was a nigga with a little authority under his belt, sorta like Clarence "Sell Out" Thomas who had no rights to replace Honorable Thurgood Marshall, while being contrary to the Talent Tenth that W.E.B. DuBois had spoken about.

And there's no question about that either.

So step aside Joe Clark, because Judge Spencer is the new head nigga in charge. Not with a bat, but rather with a black lynch robe and a wooden gavel to prove it.

Ms. Betty and a few other social workers were in the courtroom preparing for their cases to be heard, while Naomi and several others were sitting behind a wooden railing. There wasn't any particular placement they were assigned to sit at, they just sat wherever they found an available seat in the courtroom until their cases were called.

The first child who was summoned out of the holding tank—which was located directly behind the courtroom—to stand before Judge Spencer was a little light skinned kid, Lewis Brady. A court officer quickly secured the doors as Lewis approached the oak wood table. Then the clerk read out the case number as the room grew quiet and still.

Lewis sat at his assigned seat at the table, on the left hand side, facing the judge's bench.

Judge Spencer gave him a quick, annoyed glare, not because of the nasty cup of coffee he had early this morning, but rather because this was the second time he had seen Lewis in his courtroom this year alone.

Somebody coughed.

Judge Spencer looked into the sitting crowd, daring whoever it was to cough again.

Nothing.

That was more like it.

Judge Spencer looked back at the folder in front of him and started flipping through a few pages from Lewis' case file. Then he broke his silence with an angry tone: "Son, I'm coming to the realization that it's hard for you to understand my intolerance regarding your truancy from school. So what seems to be the problem here?"

You could have heard a pin dropped from across the room.

Lewis kept quiet, not knowing where to start. Should he explain that he was getting picked on by his peers in school; and even on his way to and from school. Or should he start off by saying he wishes so much for his father to get out of jail to protect him. Or better yet, he was being pressured to join the Blood's because the local gang, who claimed to be Crip's, was bullying him around. Or—

"I'm starting to think you need a little vacation," the judge broke Lewis' train of thought, while writing something down on a piece of paper, "in a boys' home for young delinquents like yourself until you get your mind together to know what you want outta life." There was a slight pause. Then he did one of those things with his eyebrows—while his head was still tilting downward—to look across at Lewis' table to shoot him that I-don't-care-anything-about-you stare. Judge Spencer's eyeglass almost slipped off his nose. He pushed them back up. Then he spoke in a shattering tone that sent chills throughout the courtroom: "Do you wish to go to jail?"

Obviously, that was something Lewis didn't want. His eyes painted with fear because he knew most of the young guys who come out of Juvenile Hall either claimed some sort of gang affiliation or, even worse, to become a Sunni Muslim. He quickly shook his head.

"Okay, I'll accept your head motion as a no, son," Judge Spencer said. "And based on that, I'm not gonna send you to the Juvenile Correctional Department at this time. But however, I'm going to send you back to the detention center for thirty more days so you can have some more time to think about what you wanna do with your life. And after these thirty days are up, it is then that I will make my decision regarding your status."

Lewis's bottom lip started trembling, and eventually, tears started running down his face.

Judge Spencer dismissed Lewis' case right there by ordering the court officer to escort Lewis back to the bull pen.

And he did.

When Naomi stepped out of the courtroom for a short breather, she immediately saw the officer—the same one who escorted Lewis through the side door inside the courtroom—standing a few feet from an open door. She walked over to him and politely asked, "Do you have a young girl by the name of Destini Powell listed in there?"

"Uhhh ... I believe we do."

"Do you think it's possible that I might see her before she goes into the courtroom?"

"I'm sorry. But I can't do that for you. This is a restricted area. However, you can see her once she's inside—"

And it was at that precise moment a female court attendant walked up behind him, from inside the restricted room, and said, "Hey, Frank, they're waiting on the young gal: Destini Powell. Send her on in. She's in cell three."

The officer turned back to Naomi. "Excuse me, but she's being requested at this moment." He then went back into the bull pen, shutting the door behind him.

Naomi went back into the courtroom and took a front row seat. About a minute later, Destini walked into the room and her face immediately lit up like a California wildfire when she saw Naomi there. She cried, allowing tears to run down her face. She tried to run toward Naomi. But the court officer grabbed her arm; then led her to the execution table where Lewis Brady was once sitting. It was a sad but a beautiful moment. There was no doubt about it, Destini was happy to see someone she knew.

Naomi tried to hold a smile on her face, but after seeing Destini's watery eyes, she shed some tears herself.

Ms. Betty approached the other table directly beside Destini's and gave her full name and job title to the court. Then she explained the case to the judge.

Judge Spencer gave Destini one of those hopeless stares: It wasn't looking good for her.

But Destini didn't know what was going on. This was all new to her. She turned to Naomi for some sort of answer, but Naomi didn't do anything. There was no expression on her face. Not even a little sign of hope to encourage Destini to be strong. There was nothing there. Absolutely nothing! Naomi just sat there motionless. Destini felt abandoned, even though Naomi was in the courtroom with her. A teardrop slipped out from the corner of her eye, not because she didn't understand what was going on anymore, but rather because of the question that continually haunted her: Why won't God hear my pleas?

Another teardrop followed.

Destini only wished that her mother was still here with her so she wouldn't be going through this ordeal. Or at least somebody else who understood the pain of losing a mom at a young age. Like, perhaps, the man who she thought was her father.

Another teardrop fell from her eye. Then she let go of her guard and cried in front of everybody. She cried.

I was about a few minutes from the courthouse.

I was driving as fast as I could. I swear, I was. I was cutting and weaving through late morning traffic like a New Jersey car-jacker. I even busted through traffic lights—a few of them—because I was determined to reach the Family Courthouse in time before Destini's case was flushed down the drain.

So I floored it, pushing the pedal to the metal. I saw traffic ahead. I made a sharp left turn, then a quick right turn, and drove a long straightway.

I finally arrived at the courthouse. I made it there a lot quicker than I expected. I had no time to lose. I parked in the No Parking Zone in front of the court building. I jumped out and tried to run inside the building but I was immediately stopped by two officers who told me to slow down.

"I'm sorry," I told them. "But I needa find Judge Spanker's courtroom!"

"Whose?" one of them asked.

"Judge Spanker's courtroom."

Both of the officers seemed to be confused for a moment, then the one on my right asked me, "Do you mean, Judge Spencer?"

"Yeah, I believe so. It was something like that."

"Well, Judge Spencer's courtroom is down the hall," he said, pointing his finger to the left. "About forty yards down when you hit that corner on the right. His courtroom is on the left hand side: Courtroom one-oh-nine."

I quickly walked without thanking them, and as soon as I hit the first corner, I saw Naomi walking straight toward me. I ran up to her. "Where's Destini at? Did she arrive yet?"

"Yeah," she said, barely nodding her head while she blotted her eyes with tissues.

"What happened?"

"She will be going back to Tallahassee to the original district she come from."

It felt like I had just got kicked in the nuts by Hillary Clinton. "Where's she at?"

Naomi pointed her hand in the direction behind her.

As I ran down the hall, I began screaming out: "DESTINI! ... DESTINI! ... WHERE ARE YOU? ... AY, DESTINI!"

Anywhere but here.

Destini was in the holding tank, crying to herself. She sat forlorn in the corner, waiting to be sent back to the Juvenile hellhole; pending a transfer back to Tallahassee's district. After a while one of the little kids across from Destini got her attention.

"Why are you messing with me for?" she asked him in a quivering broken cry. "Just leave me alone! I'm not bothering you!"

"But I think somebody's calling your name out there."

That got Destini's attention. She edged her ear closer to the bars, wanting to know if somebody was actually calling for her out there. She heard something, but she wasn't sure. Then she leaped from the floor, pressing her ear even closer to the bars this time. Her eyes wouldn't blink, although she wanted to. After a second or two, she definitely heard the screaming of her name beyond the brick walls.

She couldn't believe it.

She shouted back: "I'M IN HERE!" She couldn't hold back her tears. "DADDY! I'M IN HERE! ... IN HERE!" she cried. "I'M IN HERE!"

The three little youngsters in the cell across from her started shouting too, "She's in here! She's in here!"

I **stopped just** inches away from some doorway where a court officer was posted up at. I could have sworn I'd heard Destini's voice somewhere around there, trying to reach out to me. So I yelled back: "DESTINI! WHERE? WHERE YOU AT?!"

"Hey, hey, hey!" the officer said to me. "You have to keep it down out here! The courts are in session."

Like I gave a fuck! "I think you have my daughter in there."

"Who's your daughter?"

"Destini Powell!" I told him, then tried to walk inside the room where he was standing at. "I've come to pick her up."

The officer stopped me by stiffening his elbow into my chest, preventing me from going in the restricted area. "You can't come in here!" He gave me a direct order. "And besides, she's already been in court. She has to go back to the detention center—"

"Which court?" I cut him off. "Where's the judge at?"

"He's in the courtroom over there," the officer said, tilting his head to the right.

Naomi cut in: "He's in that courtroom" —she pointed her finger in the same direction— "right there."

I took off running again. It was only a real short distance away. And when I got to the double doors, I snatched them both open. The hell with everybody else in the courtroom, the first person my eyes focused on was Ms. Betty.

"You bitch!" I ran up to her with my finger in her face, while she was standing before the judge with another case. "I want my daughter back!"

Ms. Betty seemed frightened at first, but when she realized it was me, she snapped back. "You lowlife bastard! She's not your child! And who in the hell you think you're talking to like that?"

Judge Spencer nearly flipped out, shouting, "Order in my court!" He then began to bang his gavel against a small wooden base board. "I want order in my court!"

"I'm sorry, Your Honor," I told him. "But this woman right here took my daughter from me, for no apparent reason at all!"

Ms. Betty cut in: "She's not your daughter! That's why I took her away from you!"

Judge Spencer asked, "What's going on in here?"

"I'm sorry, Your Honor," Ms. Betty began to explain, "but this boy right here is under the assumption that he can claim a child that isn't his. And it would be a waste of this court's time to even entertain such nonsense."

"What's the child's name?"

"Destini Powell!", we said together.

"Who?" Judge Spencer looked at me and gave me an evil stare. "I'm not talking to you, young man." He cut his eyes from me. "Ms. Betty Brady."

"Thank you, Your Honor," she said. "We were talking about Destini Powell."

"The young girl from Tallahassee who I have just seen a short moment ago?"

"Yes."

"Okay, then. Why don't you run everything by me again because I'm a little confused here."

And she did. She told him everything all over again as if he had forgotten about Destini's story already.

Judge Spencer looked at me and said, "So far, from what I'm understanding, you don't have any legal rights in this matter, young man." He dug into a file before him. "As the paternity test shows, you're not the biological father of this child." He started rumbling through some paper again. "For this child, Destini Powell."

"And that's the problem that I'm talking about, Your Honor."

"What problem?"

I ran into a dead end. I was stuck.

He cut back in: "What seems to be the problem here?"

What the hell, I went for the first thing off my mind. "This woman is going by some saliva test that I know isn't accurate," I declared, making the only argument I could think of. "Because I know this child is mine."

Ms. Betty contested: "No, she's not!"

Judge Spencer cut back in, talking to me, "But young man, how do you know this child is yours? Do you have anything to support your claim?"

"Of course I do!"

"Well, what is it?"

What is it?

I became speechless for a few seconds. I kinda felt trapped. At this point, I was like what-the-hell again because I had nothing to lose. "Well, I'll tell you exactly how I can support my claims, Your Honor." I got bold and pretended as if I were a fake-ass Freemason like him, trying to give him a sign. "From the day my daughter came home to me, this woman here has been after me, nagging and complaining about how I was an unfit parent to raise my daughter—"

"That's all irrelevant here," Judge Spencer said when he cut me off. "Where are your facts to support such a claim?"

Where are my facts?

"That's what the hell I'm trying to explain to you!" I accidently snapped at him. "You see, Your Honor, this bitc—. I mean this woman right here told me a while back she was gonna make sure that she would take Destini away from me, by any means necessary." I don't know why, but I felt like quoting Malcolm X there. Then went on to say, "And I know she did something to fabricate the paternity test to take Destini away from me."

"How dare you say that about me?!"

Oh, hell, nah! I twisted to Ms. Betty and demanded: "Shut the hell up! And lemme speak!"

"No, you shut the hell up!"

"You nagging old—"

Judge Spencer started hammering his gavel against the wooden base board while shouting, "Order! Order! Order in my courtroom! I want order in my courtroom!"

I bolted my lips together; so did Ms. Betty. The room grew quiet.

"The both of y'all approach my bench!" he barked. "Now!"

As we approached the bench, I gave that bitch a quick poisonous stare, hoping she could read my mind. You better watch your back.

She looked at me.

And I couldn't believe it: she shot me back with that same icy look in her eyes.

Oh, it's on now! If I ever get the chance, I'm gonna gut this bitch out like a pig!

Judge Spencer broke up our huffing: "Ms. Betty, did you make those remarks to him?"

"Of course not!" She turned back to me; her facial expression was furious, then she twisted back to Judge Spencer. "I might have told him that he was an unfit person to be a father, but I certainly didn't say it like he's trying to paint it before this court."

"See," I cut in. "I told you so."

Judge Spencer cut his eyes to me. "Young man, I have no tolerance at all when somebody's trying to make a mockery out of my courtroom. And for that reason, if I find out that you're running a game here, I will hold you in contempt."

"But I'm not lying, Your Honor! She just admitted it to you herself."

He gave me a penetrating stare.

Well, I wasn't afraid of him either. He could get it too. I had a sharp knife in the car.

After a brief, frustrated moment, Judge Spencer slid some sort of scheduling notebook in front of him and read something to himself. He paused. Then told us, "I will have to postpone this case until a little later because I have other cases that I would like to address first." He looked at me, then back to Ms. Betty. "So what about two o'clock this afternoon?"

I answered that without any hesitation. "That's fine with me."

"Ms. Betty Brady?"

She looked up at him and said, "No, Your Honor. I don't have a problem with that."

"Okay," he said. "I'll see the both of y'all here in my courtroom at two o'clock."

"Cool." I smiled.

Ms. Betty turned to me and gave me an ugly look.

Whatever, bitch!

Once I exited the courtroom, Naomi suggested that I call Aunt Enid for some advice, although I was planning on doing that already. I pulled my cell phone out and dialed her number; she answered the phone on the second ring with a friendly hello.

I didn't waste any time. I went straight to the point. "Are you busy right now? Because I'm gonna need your help."

"Thank you for coming"

"Don't mention it."

I filled Aunt Enid in on everything after I introduced Naomi to her. Then, as we started walking up the corridor, I saw Ms. Betty a short distance from Judge Spencer's courtroom.

"There she goes right there," I said to Aunt Enid. "The caseworker who's trying to send Destini back to Tallahassee."

"Which one?"

"The one over there in that dull green dress...."

"Her right there?"

"Yeah."

Aunt Enid didn't respond, merely shifting her purse from her left hand to her right, then strolled over there to Ms. Betty.

Naomi and I stayed back, keeping our distance.

"Excuse me, Ms. Betty Brady?"

Ms. Betty twisted towards Aunt Enid. "Yes, how can I help you?"

"My name is Ms. Wimberly, and I'm DaShawn Powell's aunt."

Ms. Betty shot her with an icy, scrutinizing stare. "Well, what can I do for you? Because I'm on a tight schedule here."

So Aunt Enid went into one of those violin speeches. The one where a person is supposed to feel some sorta compassion for another person.

Yeah, that one.

But in this case, the violin wasn't working here because Ms. Betty just didn't care about anybody's up-brining, being raised without both parents. The paternity test had raised a crucial question regarding the status of the biological father in which she was sticking with it.

"Well, can't you recommend another paternity test? At lease for a second confirmation?"

"No. I won't do that. Do you know the odds of a test coming back inaccurately?"

"No. Not quite."

"Slim to none. In fact, I haven't heard of a single case where an inaccurate result has been reported. The father's saliva is always tested several times before a final decision is made."

"Well, you know," Aunt Enid then tried a different approach, "I run a foster home myself. And I was wondering if there's a possibility that you can recommend that Destini stay with me until this whole misunderstanding is resolved?"

"What misunderstanding?"

"You know, all of this...."

"All of what? I don't have a slightest clue as to what you're talking about." Ms. Betty fell silent when she saw several individuals entering into Judge Spencer's courtroom. She twisted back to Aunt Enid. "I'm terribly sorry, but I have another court appearance that I must attend to. Excuse me."

Naomi and I started walking up behind Aunt Enid when Ms. Betty strode away from her.

"And this moody bitch claims to be a Christian," Aunt Enid murmured under her breath, unaware of our presence. "How dare you use that blessed name in vain?"

I burst out laughing.

She turned around and noticed us standing behind her. "Well," she tried to hide her embarrassment with a giggle. "Jesus knows I'm not lying about her."

Yeah, you got that right.

After a short moment, Aunt Enid started telling me that my custody battle for Destini was a no-win situation. With all things considered, I had to agree with her on that. I needed a miracle, if anything.

Then she came up with a resolution: "Let's go inside and push our luck anyway."

"Yeah, we can do that. But my court hearing isn't until two o'clock." I said, then looked at my wristwatch. "We have another fifteen minutes before I have to go back inside there. But y'all can go ahead and wait for me though. I'm gonna wait out here a little longer for Kevin to get here: I called him right after I spoke to you, and he said he was gonna show up because he had a plan."

"What kinda plan?"

"He didn't say."

"Okay then. I'll see you once you get inside," she told me. "I need to go rest my legs."

"All right."

Naomi cut in: "I'm going to go inside with her too, so I can grab us some good seats in the meantime. Okay?"

"Yeah, all right." I gave her a kiss.

Naomi stepped away and followed Aunt Enid.

I watched them disappear into the courtroom. Then for the next ten minutes straight, I paced up and down the hallway, waiting for Kevin. And still, there wasn't any sign of him anywhere. I called his home phone again, but he didn't answer it. I tried his cell phone.

Nothing.

I gave up: he wasn't going to show up, I thought.

I went back into the courtroom and sat beside Naomi. She looked at me and extended her hand out to mine, giving me her unconditional support. I needed that. I looked at Ms. Betty and watched her for a moment, fumbling with something inside her handbag. Then a silly notion came to mind: She probably has one of those voodoo dolls in there.

And just as my suspicion rose as to what she was playing with inside her bag, the bailiff shouted, "All rise for the Honorable Judge J. Spencer.... His court is now in session!"

Ouch! I felt something painful in my rib. I looked back at Ms. Betty, thinking, "That bitch just stick me with a needle!"

I tried to play it off when I stood up with a phony smile, but when the judge's clerk announced, "Human Rehabilitation Service of Children Division versus Mr. DaShawn Powell," my heart took a terrible fall into my stomach. My smile vanished.

When I saw Ms. Betty spring from her seat and approach the table with that intimidating smirk on her face, I felt my whole world started tumbling down before my eyes. She had a look on her face as if she knew what the outcome was going to be already.

Just another victory under her belt.

You see, I can recognize that same damned smirk from anywhere. It was a hypocritical smile that officials—prosecutors, politicians, and court's representatives—give the court when a decision has already been rigged up from the beginning. And I felt it in my heart that this shit was rigged up like a stage show.

Just look back at Saddam Hussein's trial.

"Ms. Betty Brady," Judge Spencer said, while twisting his chair to the left side. "I will hear from you first."

"Your Honor, I object to that!" I leaped from my seat. "She's lying! That's some bullshit! I'm telling you she's lying to you!"

"You can hold your objections till later, son. You'll have your turn to speak. And I will advise you to restrain yourself from using indecent words in this courtroom." Judge Spencer then looked at Ms. Betty with a pleasant smile. "Please, continue."

"Thank you, Your Honor," she said, then turned to me with that disgusted look on her face. "As I was saying, before I was rudely interrupted." She turned back to Judge Spencer. "The only reason why I told Mr. Powell that I would do my best to prevent him from obtaining legal custody over this child was because I find this young boy unfit to be a parent." She paused for a second or two, combing through her paperwork. Then continued: "I can run down a list of things that he did to put this young child's life in jeopardy."

I blurted out: "How?!"

She shot me with another ugly stare.

I swear, I wanted to go to her table and slap that look off her fucking face. But I controlled myself when Judge Spencer shot me with the same look.

Ms. Betty cut her eyes from me and continued: "And just to name a few, Your Honor, I'd like to let this court know that this man right here exposed that young girl to booty-shaking clubs, where they serve liquor at."

"Excuse me!" Judge Spencer interrupted her this time. "But exposing her to what sort of environment? Did you say, booty-shaking clubs?"

"Yes, I did. That's what I said." She looked at me again, and emphasized: "Booty-shaking clubs!" She then twisted back to Judge Spencer.

"For the record," he began to ask, "what type of clubs are those?"

"You know," she said. "The devil's dens, where he sends all his children like him" —she pointed her finger at me— "to go about certain nightclubs to seduce helpless, innocent females by dancing in a very provocative manner to take away their hard-earn money."

"Oh, I see." Judge Spencer acted as if this was all new to him.

What a fucking character.

To hell with this! I cut back in: "But, Your Honor! What she's telling you right now is irrelevant to the issue that I raised against her. I don't even see what this has to do with the paternity test being inaccurate."

"Mr. Powell, I already told you that you'll have your chance to tell your side of the story.... On your turn."

"But—"

Judge Spencer cut me off again, "You have to wait your turn, Mr. Powell!"

I got in my feelings and murmured something harsh under my breath, hoping that a few spectators could see the shadiness that was going on in here.

"Excuse me, son?" Judge Spencer asked me. "Did you say something?"

"No, Your Honor." I had a second thought about that, shaking my head. "I didn't say anything."

"Oh, yes he did!" Ms. Betty snitched on me. "He said that this was a bunch of bullshit!"

"Oh, did he, huh?"

I felt like I was being double teamed. Like I told you before: This was a no-win situation that I was in. For real, I wanted to say something else but I decided to keep my mouth shut before I made matters worse than they were already.

Judge Spencer didn't pay me any mind: instead, he instructed Ms. Betty to continue. And she did, explaining her case for about ten minutes straight without me interrupting her.

"So, where is this young girl now?" Judge Spencer asked once she had finished.

Ms. Betty shrugged her heavy shoulders. "I don't know, Your Honor. But my best bet, I believe she was sent back to the detention center."

"Excuse me, Your Honorable Spencer," a courtroom's officer cut in. "If it pleases the court, I must say that we have that young child, Miss Destini Powell, in our holding cells."

Judge Spencer nodded. "Can you fetch her for me?"

"Sure thing." The officer walked out of the room.

Suddenly I heard somebody hissing.

"Back here."

I twisted around.

It was Kevin with a smile on his face, giving me the thumbs-up.

"Damn, what took you so long to get here?" I asked.

"I hadda take care of something first," he said, then winked his eye at me. "You gonna owe me on this one, my nigga."

I didn't know what he meant by that. But just when I was about to inquire about it, I heard the side door open up. I immediately turned back around and saw my little princess with swollen eyes as if she had been crying all night. Although it felt like Ms. Betty had stuck a needle in that voodoo doll again, it still didn't stop me from stretching a smile across my face. And I guess everybody in the courtroom knew that too when my eyes became watery.

Destini ran to me and we both embraced for a long moment. She was the first one to pull away. Without any hesitation, she slapped me across the face.

"What took you so long to come get me?" she asked, smiling. "What am I gonna do with you?"

I kept quiet. Perhaps I deserved that. I couldn't stop the flow of my tears. I never thought I would be able to see my Destini again.

"Hey, sweetie!" Naomi managed to say to Destini, wiping her own tears away.

Destini acknowledged her back with a flaunt wave, and then twisted back to me. "Get yourself together," she cautiously whispered to me. "I have a plan."

"What plan?" I wiped my eyes.

"A plan that I put together," she said. "And it will work if you listen—"

Judge Spencer intervened, banging his wooden gavel against the base board, demanding order in his court.

Destini turned around to look at him, giving him an ugly stare. She ignored him and turned back to me. "Daddy, my plan will work. I know it will."

"Young lady! I demanded order in the courtroom! And that means I want ORDER!"

Destini shouted back at him: "You needa five minute break MISTER! I'm talking to my daddy, so you needa learn your manners! Before he beat you up!"

A few spectators in the courtroom burst out laughing and I guess Judge Spencer felt embarrassed because he started banging his gavel on his desk again, demanding order. At this time, everybody quieted down.

But it was wasted on Destini because she twisted back around and tried to explain her strategy to me.

I cut her off: "Sweetie, you can't talk to the judge like that. He—"

"Okay, okay!" She brushed me off. "But listen to my plan first."

I gave in, hoping that she would hurry up and get it over with.

"I'm gonna tell that old man over there that I have to use the bathroom—." she paused because I started shaking my head to her. Then she asked, "What's the matter with you?"

I had a change of mind. I shook my head a little faster, in a discreet way, praying that she would seal her lips shut.

"Why you keep saying no for? I'm not even finished telling you my plan yet. It'll work. I know it will."

Okay, I stopped. I had to play my cards right.

She started back up again: "I'm gonna wait about five more minutes and ask that ugly man over there can I use the bathroom." She threw a smile on her face. "And when he says yeah, I'm gonna meet you outside by your car. Okay?"

I cleared my throat. "Kids nowadays," I tried to joke, looking over her shoulder. "With all these crazy movies out here, they have quite an imaginary mindset. It's unbelievable." I smiled, but it was a phony one. The moment called for it.

"Oh, really? The voice came over Destini's back. Then asked, "So when are you planning on asking that ugly man to use the bathroom?"

"Not right now," Destini started to say, while turning her head in the direction the question had come from. "I'm gonna wait until—" she froze right there when she realized Judge Spencer was standing directly behind her.

"Oh, sure you will, young lady." He then extended his hand to her. "But in the meantime, I need you to have a seat over here in the witness box for me. I have a few questions that I need you to answer first."

As he started leading Destini to the witness stand, she looked back at me. "Look, Daddy!" she tried to whisper, while pointing her finger at Judge Spencer's gown, tittering, "He's wearing a dress."

A few people inside the courtroom started laughing again.

Judge Spencer twisted around with a furious look in his eyes, while giving an intimidating stare at the crowd. The laughing ceased. He then turned back to Destini and said, "Young lady, have a seat right here!"

She did.

Judge Spencer walked around his bench and took a seat. After he settled in, he advised Destini, "Young lady, I'll be asking you a few questions and I want you to answer them to the best of your ability, with all honesty. Do you understand that?"

Destini kept her mouth shut but she did nod her head, I guess, to let Judge Spencer know that she understood him.

"Please state your full name for the record."

She kept quiet, shooting him an angry stare.

"Young lady, that means ... what's your first and last name?"

She broke her silence. "I know what you meant."

"So if you knew what that meant, why didn't you answer my question when I asked you?"

"Because...."

"Because of what?"

"Because my daddy told me not to speak to strangers."

Somebody in the courtroom blurted out a loud chuckle but when Judge Spencer looked in that direction, the laughing stopped.

"The next time I hear another outburst in my courtroom, so help me God, I'm gonna hold that son-of-a—," he cut it short right there, then correct himself, "I would hold that person in contempt." He then turned back to Destini with a different approach. "So where is your father?"

Destini sighed heavily, then pointed at me. "He's right there! Are you blind?!"

Judge Spencer snapped. "Young lady, look! I've had it up to here" —he raised his hand above his head— "with your smart remarks! And I will be damned if I'll tolerate any behavior like that, especially in my courtroom! Do you understand me?"

Destini nodded.

That was more like it. Judge Spencer added, "So when I ask you a question, you just make sure that you answer it. Do you understand that too?"

Destini nodded again.

"Okay, again," Judge Spencer looked relieved. "For the record, please state your full name for the court."

Nothing.

"Young lady, I don't like to repeat myself!"

"Well, don't then. Because I don't like to repeat myself either!" She then folded her arms across her chest.

Judge Spencer's eyebrows shifted ominously and just when he was about to open his mouth, I intervened: "Your Honor! Do you mind if I speak to her for a second?"

He hit me with a perplexed look, then closed his mouth back. After a slight hesitation, he motioned his hand at me. "Go ahead and do whatever."

I immediately approached the witness stand and told Destini, "You have to chill out and answer his questions."

"Why?"

"Because I need you to."

She thought about it for a few seconds. Then told me, "Only one condition."

"On what condition?"

"If I answer his questions, you have to take me to Dairy Queen and buy me some chocolate ice cream...."

"Okay, I'll do that for you, if everything works out for us." I gave Judge Spencer a slight nod to indicate that he was free to proceed with his questioning.

He acknowledged me back with a casual nod, then looked at Destini.

I headed back to my seat.

Then Judge Spencer asked Destini, "For the third time, young lady, will you please state your full name for the record?"

"Destini … Powell-ooo-ooo," she purposely dragged, while howling like a wolf.

Judge Spencer sighed angrily, then composed herself. "For the record," he began to say, feeling a bit satisfied, "she said her name is Destini Powell." Then he went on to ask a few more questions in support of Ms. Betty's defense. "And it was also said that you slept on the couch when you were temporarily housed at Mr. Powell's house," he paused for a short moment. "Is that true?"

"Uh-huh, sometimes."

"Waita second, I'm confused here. Did you, or didn't you have a bed to sleep on?"

"Yeah, I had a bed to sleep on."

"Oh, so you did have a bed," he mumbled under his breath, while jotting something down on his note pad. His glasses started sliding off to the tip of his nose; he pushed them back up.

Then just when he was about to proceed with the next question, Destini shouted: "I have to go to the bathroom!"

Judge Spencer looked at her; and immediately an ugly look was painted on his face. He probably remembered that plot he overheard from Destini when he walked up behind her a few minutes ago.

"I don't know what you think," he began to snap at her with a shout, "but I have had enough of your games. I won't tolerate your behavior in my courtroom!"

"But I really have to use the bathroom. I'm not lying to you."

"Well, if you have to use the potty, you just gotta use it right there in your shorts then!"

A slight commotion erupted amongst several spectators in the courtroom who probably thought the judge was out of line for denying Destini the right to use the restroom.

Judge Spencer looked toward the crowd, he opened his mouth, then shut it. He cut his eyes away from them and looked directly at me, then at Ms. Betty. "I would like to see the both of y'all in my chambers!" He got up from his chair. "I will continue this in chambers."

"Excuse me, Your Honor!" Aunt Enid stood up, rising one finger in the air.

"Yeah, what do you want?"

"Do you mind if I be allowed to enter your chambers?"

"And who are you?"

"I'm DaShawn Powell's aunt. My name is Ms. Enid Wimberly. I'm a caregiver for a foster home here in Miami and I'm deeply concerned about this child, Destini Powell."

He hunched his shoulders a bit. "That's on you: I just wanna end this case and get it over with. You may join us." He stepped away from the bench and pushed open a nearby door that led straight into his chambers. Ms. Betty, Aunt Enid, and I followed right behind him.

Once we stepped inside the judge's chambers, my eyes took hold of the room. It was nothing like what I had expected it to look like. I had watched plenty of TV shows that sorta represented the legal system. Like, one of them off the top of my head, Law and Order. But my favorite, Suits.

Besides me being totally infatuated with that character Jessica, it was a great show.

But even in that show, I had seen a few judges' chambers decorated with some type of icon mounted up on the walls: Like a photograph of themselves taken with the current or former President of the United States, two or three law books propped open on the desk, an American flag in the corner of the room near the window, and perhaps a family portrait sitting on top of the desk.

But with Judge Spencer's chambers, it wasn't so. It was quite different. Way different. It was kind of dull-looking, decorated with old-fashioned furniture.

My eyes scanned his unused bookshelf, then his desk. I noticed a Bunny Ranch's brochure sitting directly on top of his desk, halfway buried underneath several legal documents.

Judge Spencer caught me looking at the brochure and immediately covered it up, giving me that you-nosy-bastard look. Then he swayed his hand across from us before he sat. "Please have a seat."

"Thank you."

We all sat in chairs directly across from him.

And Ms. Betty didn't waste any time going straight for the kill. "Your Honor!" she began to say, "this case shouldn't have gone this far. Because as the record shows, Mr. Powell here" —she turned to the side and gave me an evil stare, then went back to the judge— "is not the biological father for this child Destini Powell. And the paternity test proves that. Therefore, I believe it's in the best interest of the State not to proceed any further with this case."

Judge Spencer bobbed his head. "I think I have to agree with you on that," he told her, then looked at me. Then added: "Son, Ms. Brady has a valid point here. And it certainly seems to me that you have a good heart for this child. However, the truth of the matter still remains, you don't have any legal rights over this child; and I don't have the authority to release her over to you. I am bound by the law to send this child back to the original district that she came from."

The room grew silent.

At this point, I didn't know what to say or do. My mind was deadlocked on Saving Private Destini: my little souljah.

I tried to think of every possible way to have Destini back under my roof, but I couldn't come up with a good scheme. Then, all of a sudden something clicked inside my head. "But what about my auntie's foster home, right here in Miami?" I said, throwing it up for proposal. "Why can't Destini stay over there?"

"What are you talking about?" Judge Spencer asked.

"I'm talking about my auntie right here." I held my hand out toward Aunt Enid. Then added, "She has a foster home here in Miami; where Destini can stay so she doesn't have to go back to Tallahassee."

"Oh, really?" He thought about my suggestion for a few seconds, knowing he had the authority to release Destini into a foster home, as long as the HRS approved it. He looked at Ms. Betty.

But before he could ask her anything, she was already shaking her head. "No," she said. "I think that would be a bad idea because our department head already has a full case load that we're barely keeping up with now. And to add another child to our district would be an unnecessary burden for us. It would be absurd."

The room grew silent again.

"Well, I think you're right about that," Judge Spencer agreed with her. "Because I myself have been loaded with cases over the past few months." He paused, then looked at me. "Son, I'm sorry it has to come down to this, but my hands are tied behind my back under these circumstances. So, based on the facts presented here today, I must stick with my original order and send this child back to Tallahassee."

Ms. Betty grabbed her cell phone and read a text message from it.

I had definitely had enough of this bullshit! Arguing with the judge was pointless. I had no other choice but give up. And I did. I felt my body sink into the chair—like I gotten caught in some yucky quicksand—as I looked to my left and watch this old nagging bitch enjoy the pleasure of seeing the judge snatching my joy away from me.

I swear, I felt like jumping up and punching that bitch in her face when she cut her eyes from me, looking back at her cell phone. But I kept my cool: vengeance has its right time and place. And I know when I'm gonna get mine.

I got up from my seat.

We were all taken by surprise.

When we entered back into the courtroom, the first thing that caught our attention was Destini's horseplaying: She was up at the bench, sitting in Judge Spencer's chair, acting a fool with his gavel in her hand.

"Order in my court!" she mocked Judge Spencer, while banging the gavel against the base board, entertaining the small crowd beyond the wooden railing. "I want order in my court!" She then pointed at a few people, starting with a Hispanic lady first, while shouting, "I sentenced you to thirty years in prison! You, ten years! You, life! You—"

"Young LADY!" Judge Spencer snapped, looking at the court officer who was trying to get Destini out of the chair. "What the hell's going on in here?!"

"I'm sorry, Your Honor." The officer finally got Destini out of the judge's chair, walking her back to the table.

Everybody in the courtroom grew quiet.

As Judge Spencer took his seat, Ms. Betty went back to her assigned table and Aunt Enid sat back where she was sitting originally.

I went back to my assigned table, sitting beside Destini. She tried to get my attention, poking her fingers into my arm, but I wouldn't look at her. I just couldn't. Not under these circumstances. I didn't have the courage to tell her the truth that we'd been defeated by those thoughtless bastards. She twisted around and looked at Aunt Enid, then Naomi. Destini noticed how Naomi was looking remorseful, with her hand over her mouth, after Aunt Enid had said something to her.

Something was wrong, Destini probably thought when she turned back around, focusing on the table in front of her as if she were pondering something.

Judge Spencer broke the silence in the courtroom when he went on blabbing off about some mess regarding how it was important that a child should be in a suitable family with a proper upbringing. "And this child, Destini Powell, needs just that—"

"Excuse me, Your Honor!" Ms. Betty interrupted him, with her hand in the air.

Destini was about to make a run for it; I stopped her. It wasn't worth it. Some pimp would probably find her at a bus station, promising her a bright future in Hollywood, walking up and down Sunset Boulevard.

"Yes, is there a problem, Ms. Brady?"

Of course there was. She seemed suddenly confused about something; she took another look at her cell phone before she turned back around.

"Ms. Brady, is there a problem?" he repeated again.

There was a brief moment of silence as they both looked at each other. Then she finally broke: "No, Your Honor, I don't have a problem. However, if it pleases the court, I would like to request that Destini Powell be transferred to Miami's district and be temporarily housed at Ms. Wimberly's foster home until we find a replacement home for her."

I couldn't believe my own ears! I took a double look at Ms. Betty to make sure it was her still.

"But I thought—." Judge Spencer started, but cut it short to proceed differently. "Are you sure about this Ms. Brady?"

She didn't answer him. Instead, she looked at her cell phone again before she took another look into the crowd.

So I took my eyes off of her and twisted towards the crowd too, because I wanted to know what the hell was distracting her back there.

It was her friend, Sister Mary, sitting beside Kevin. And then suddenly it all made perfect sense to me when Kevin shot his thumbs-up to me about forty-five minutes ago when he first stepped inside the courtroom, letting me know that everything was taken care of already. I became excited.

Ms. Betty gave Sister Mary an angry look. But Sister Mary ignored that by brushing her fingers—sorta as if her fingers were a sweeping broom—towards Ms. Betty, indicating to go on with it, showing her iPhone.

Ms. Betty twisted back around with fire in her eyes. "Yes, Your Honor," she said. "I'm sure about this. I can schedule a monthly visit at Ms. Wimberly's home and check up on Destini Powell's well-being."

Judge Spencer slowly shook his head, then cut his eyes away from her and looked at me. "Mr. Powell, I find this case very unusual. More unusual than any other case I've presided over before." He looked at Ms. Betty with a somewhat disgusted look in his eyes, then back to me. "And I can't find any reason why you shouldn't be allowed to visit this child at your aunt's home. But I must inform you that once the State finds a replacement home for this child, I cannot grant you any permission on visitation rights. That would be entirely up to her legal guardian. Do you understand that?"

I quickly nodded my head because I was too emotionally unbalanced to say a word. I got my ineffable joy back. I reached for Destini and snatched her up in the air. Although I tried to be strong, I cried when I embraced her.

Judge Spencer looked over his bench, shook his head, and mumbled something distasteful under his breath.

"Excuse me, James!" Ms. Betty had the boldness to call Judge Spencer by his middle name, because he said something about her. "Would you like to repeat that for me?"

Judge Spencer barely shook his head while holding back his anger. "It wasn't all that important," he said; then banged his gavel against the base board. After Ms. Betty walked away, he cut to this clerk and asked, "Do you have an ibuprofen with you? ... That bitch gave me a headache."

The case was over with.

When I carried Destini out of the courtroom, Naomi asked her, "Are you happy to be going home again?"

She shrugged with a smile. "Not really."

I had to laugh at that one. "What the hell you mean by not really?" I joked back. "Do you ever tell the truth?"

Destini shrugged again and said, "I dunno." Then immediately she wrapped her thin arm around my neck, squeezing it tight.

I guess she was happy to be back in my arms again; and so was I. I hugged her back.

As we were heading back toward the exit, I saw Kevin talking to Sister Mary a few feet from the doorway. "Hey! Let me have a word with Kev for a sec," I told Naomi and Aunt Enid, while allowing Destini to stand up on her own. "I'll catch up with y'all outside."

"All right."

They departed through the glass doors.

I walked toward Kevin while he was still conversing with Sister Mary; which I heard her telling him from a short distance away: "Remember y'all owe me one. So don't forget to mention it to him."

"I got you," he assured her.

"I bet you do," she said, then swaggered away when I approached them.

That shit left me puzzled. "What's that all about?" I asked Kevin, because when she stepped off she sized me up. But before he could respond, I went with something different: "And you have to tell me how the hell you pulled that one off?"

His eyes were still locked on Sister Mary. "Look how she's throwing that ass," he told me. "She still knows how to work that shit!"

"Man, I don't wanna hear about that."

He looked at me and said, "I don't know why? Because if anything, you better get used to it. We owe her a favor. A tune-up, with the both of us."

"What the hell are you talking about?" Then it dawned on me. I nearly shouted, with a disgusted look on my face: "Oh, hell, nah!"

"Oh, hell, yeah!" he mocked me back. "The both of us, next week. At her crib. Thanks to you."

I twisted around and tried to get another look at Sister Mary, but she had already left the building. I turned back to him. "You're sick!" I playfully bumped him with my shoulder. "Man, I'm not participating in that shit!"

"So you think."

I walked away, laughing.

He followed behind me, then caught up. "Hey, you wanna hear some crazy shit, my nigga?"

"Like what?"

"Like the fact that my hoe has some dirt on that caseworker in there."

"On who? Ms. Betty?"

"Yeah."

"For real?" I stopped walking.

"Yeah." He wore a TMZ reporter look: the information was concrete. "And you ain't gonna believe who she's fucking with?"

"Who?" I definitely wanted to make sure of this. "You're talking about Ms. Betty, right?"

"Yeah," he said. "She's fucking with that busta judge in there. They be going on some runaway trip together out there in Vegas like every other weekend, knowing that nigga is married to some other lady who they go to church with."

"Nah."

"Hell, yeah! But check it out, though: My hoe texted that bitch on her cell phone, telling her that if she didn't lighten up on you and give you what you wanted from her, she was gonna tell everybody in their church congregation about the sexual affair that Ms. Betty has with the judge in there."

I burst out laughing; he joined in, as we both started walking out of the courthouse.

"So, whatever happened with that meeting you had this morning?" he asked. "Did they like your—"

"Oh, shit!" I immediately reached for my cell phone and punched in a seven digit number.

The receptionist answered on the second ring with a polite voice: "Thank you for calling Decorous' Fashion World. How may I help you?"

"Mr. Powell," the receptionist said. "I'm sorry for holding you on the phone for so long. But Mr. Dorsey has instructed me, among other things, to let you know that he doesn't wish to speak to you."

"But, did you tell him that I was in court this morning?"

"Yes, I told him everything you advised me to tell him, sir. But unfortunately, he still doesn't wish to speak to you." She paused for a second. Then added, "But please, don't allow that to discourage you from pursuing after him. Just give Mr. Dorsey a few weeks and try him again. Hopefully, by then, he'll forget about the embarrassment that you have caused him."

"Yeah," I knew what she meant by that. "Okay then."

She hung up.

I managed to smile when I walked over to everyone in the courthouse parking lot, pretending like everything was hunky-dory.

And I had almost pulled it off, but I guess Naomi could recognize a fake smile from anywhere because she asked me, "Is everything all right?"

"Yeah, sort of," I said, hoping that she'd be able to read between the lines without me going into detail about it. "I just got off the phone with those people over there at Decorous', and everything didn't turn out as I wanted to."

Perhaps Destini didn't understand what I meant by that, but the rest of them did. They gave me that I'm-sorry-to-hear-about look. Then all of us fell into silence until Destini intervened.

"I want my ice cream now!" she said, while rocking my hand back and forth. "You promised me." I gave her a blank look. Then continued: "You promised me in there, if I be good, you were gonna take me to Dairy Queen and buy me some ice cream."

Okay, she made me smile on that one. I looked at Aunt Enid; then back at Destini. "I promised you that. Didn't I?"

"Uh-huh." She smiled back.

"So that means I have to stick to my word." I rested my hand on top of her head. "But before we go get your ice cream, I have to get you outta those smelly clothes first."

"I don't stink." She smelled herself: her left underarm pit. Then argued, "I showered at that place early this morning before I went to court."

We all laughed at her because, she had that distinct smell around her: That sour clothes hamper smell.

As we headed over to our vehicles, Aunt Enid told me that she couldn't go with us because other than that she had to make a stop at the Juvenile Detention Center to sign Destini's release forms and retrieve Destini's belongings, she had to head back home to attend to the other children in the house as well.

"Alright then."

"You just make sure you have her at my house at eight o'clock. I would like to go over a few things with her and introduce her to the other kids in the house."

"Alright, I got you." I gave her a kiss. "Thanks for everything."

By the time Aunt Enid walked away, Destini and I jumped inside my car; Naomi and Kevin inside their own rides. I drove up Biscayne Boulevard, playing my Sade CD. I turned the volume up a bit because when I glimpsed over at Destini, she was bobbing her head to the smooth rhythm of "Lovers Rock." She was enjoying herself, looking out the passenger window, smiling. I smiled right along with her; then it hit me. I suddenly remembered something.

I made a left turn on 79th Street, and Naomi and Kevin followed me. I drove a little farther up to 28th Avenue and pulled up in USA Flea Market.

"Stay right here till I get back," I told Destini, as I got out of the car. "And don't be touching anything either!"

I heard Kevin shout out from his SUV: "Where you going?"

"Give me a second! I needa grab a few things!"

About five minutes later, I came out of the flea market with a bag of kids' clothes. It was nothing expensive: just something clean and decent for Destini to wear while we went out.

A short time later, all of us were back on 79th Street. It took us about fifteen minutes to reach my crib. When I pulled up in the driveway and turned to Destini, she had a wide smile on her face. I kissed her on the forehead.

Welcome home, sweetie.

When we got out of the car, Kevin and Naomi finally pulled up in front of the house. I gave them that same smile Destini had on her face. That Chuck E. Cheese smile.

What can I say? I was happy too.

I stood there for a moment, scanning the neighborhood, waiting for Naomi and Kevin to catch up with us. And when I glanced over their shoulders, I noticed that big-tittie hoe, Amanda, from across the street, rinsing the suds off her car with a garden hose.

Her T-shirt was soaked and wet in which it smothered her breasts.

I smiled, trying not to be obvious about it, while sneaking a peek at those two shaded areas in front of her. But it was hard not to. She wore a thin white T-shirt, tied with a knot in the back. I'm not lying, she looked decent for a hood-rat.

So perhaps, if the opportunity presented itself again, I might give her another threesome with Kevin. Or I might even go over there next time by myself if she wore those same gray spandex shorts that she had on Thursday.

But for right now, I was straight. I have Naomi, my little chocolate bunny, at my side, fulfilling all my sexual needs from A to Z. I can't complain.

Amanda waved.

I'm not stupid, I waved back: Naomi was distracted, mingling with Destini, while tickling her.

Yeah, everything was back to normal again—just how I last remembered it.

Carlton stepped out of the house.

I could see Uncle James peeking through the crack of the door where the hinges were.

"It's about fucking time!" Carlton joked while looking at Destini. "What the hell took you so long to come back home? Do you know how long I was waiting for my damn rematch?"

I guess Destini didn't know whether she wanted to cry or smile, because she hesitated at first before she ran to him and settled for a hug instead. "I missed you."

"Yeah, I missed you too, you little crack-head."

She let go of him and they both ran into the house together.

It seemed like Naomi knew what was on my mind when she said, "Let me go in there to get her ready."

"Thanks." I extended the bag of clothes to her. She took them and went inside the house. I twisted to Kevin, hoping to start up a conversation with him in the meantime until Naomi got finished with Destini. But instead it seemed like he was already occupied, flicking his tongue at Amanda. "Man" —I playfully shoved him—chill the fuck out!"

"My nigga," he caught his balance, laughing, "don't hate because that hoe over there is feeling me. Do I have to remind you about what she said to me when I was hitting her from the back, while she was telling me, not to stop because she liked how my dick feels up inside her."

I kept quiet. I didn't find the need to explain myself to him because she had said that same thing to me when we ran a train on her, with me in the back of her too.

"Just look at her," he said. "Look how she's bending over for me, showing me that phat ass of hers! She wants me again. I can tell, my nigga." He paused. Then quickly got excited. "Look, look, look!"

"Godddammmmm...."

Kevin and I twisted around.

It was Carlton. "Just look at that!" he said while looking at Amanda. "That hoe is setting it out over there." He then stood beside Kevin, admiring the view. "My nigga, I'm willing to buy some of that pussy from her."

Buy?

I had to really look at this damn fool.

"Whew-weeeeee..." Uncle James stepped out of the house to get a better view at Amanda, too. "That sure looks tasty over there."

Kevin whistled to get her attention.

It worked. She turned her head toward us to look while leaning over the hood of the car, drying it off with a towel. From a nice angle, it looked as if someone invisible was taxing her ass from the back. She had her arms stretched out in front of her, using her shoulders, slightly fluctuating them back and forth in slow motion.

Kevin blew a kiss at her. She smiled. Then, he started doing that perverted thing with his fingers to indicate some sort of sexual intent. How can I put it? Well, for starters, he had formed a circle with the tip of his thumb to his index finger, connecting them together, then started penetrating it with his other finger, dipping it into the circle, back and forth.

Amanda laughed, then brushed him off with her hand. She then leaned a little further over the hood of the car, pretending like she wasn't paying us any mind. She displayed that beautiful backside of hers, while drying the car off.

Carlton was thrilled. "God is good!"

Kevin cut in: "All the time."

"And all the time?"

"God is good." Kevin gave Carlton a dap.

And I said, "Y'all some assholes!"

"Mm-mmm!" Kevin thrummed. "To hell with all that bullshit what you're talking about, my nigga! Because I swear to God, I would lick her asshole out just like that: bent over the car."

Carlton and I laughed at him.

But Uncle James took it out of context when he told Kevin: "You nasty-ass fool! Only God knows how many dicks she had up in there before. And now your stupid-ass wanna clean it out for her. You nasty bastard! That's why y'all young jitterbugs ranking the game for us elders. Y'all don't know a damn thing about pleasing a lady."

Carlton cut back in: "Hold-hold up!" He got our attention back on Amanda when she squatted to dry off the car tire. She was in a crouch position, undulating her ass up and down in slow motion. "Now, that's what the fuck I'm talking about!"

For the next twenty-plus minutes, we stood out there watching Amanda with her Daisy Duke shorts on wedged, all the way up in the crack of her ass until we heard a cough to get our attention. I was the first one to turn around.

It was Naomi.

And I'll be damned!

For the last eight years of my life, I could have never imagined this day would come. Ever since Jessica had placed that scar on my heart, I had somehow convinced my subconscious mind that love didn't exist, rather it was some sort of self-delusion, emotional imbalance that comes and goes whenever one breaks weak to loneliness.

But today, it was different: I realized my ideology about love was a crock of bullshit!

I had a different outlook about love now.

My distorted subconscious mind took a dramatic change for the better. I was in love again. My heart was reborn once more. Renewed. And this new love that I felt was nothing like what I had experienced for Jessica, or for any other female for that matter. It was much greater. But this time it wasn't just for some ordinary female either. It was for a young lady who I will always treasure in my heart.

It was Destini, the young lady who I would have the privilege to call my daughter. So to hell with that paternity test and what it alleged, because I felt it deep within my heart that Destini was mine. My daughter. My little angel. A gift that was given to me from the gods above. I was grateful to have her as part of my life.

With a shy face, Destini lowered her head and rested her chin on her chest. I kept my eyes on her. She seemed to be embarrassed for some reason. She probably didn't like how those candy curls looked on her. But to me, Naomi has done a magnificent job with Destini's hairdo because it brought her beauty out even more. The way those pink barrettes hung from Destini's hair illustrated the true essence of the word beautiful.

"I don't know about y'all," I began to tell them, "but after we go to Dairy Queen, me and my baby-girl are going out to Boomers afterwards."

Destini immediately picked her head up with a huge smile on her face. She didn't waste another second out there: She ran to my car, opened the passenger's door, and hopped inside.

"Uh-huh, girl!" Naomi said, while walking toward the car. "You know you have to sit in the back seat. So stop playing and get back there."

Destini leaped over.

I smiled and turned to Kevin. "C'mon, let's get outta here. And take them along with you in your ride."

About twenty minutes later, we were all sitting in the Dairy Queen on 163rd Street. We all ordered hamburgers and French fries, with a side order of banana boats to go along with our meal.

But Destini on the other hand went all the way out with her side order. She ordered a special chocolate deluxe: chocolate ice cream, chocolate fudge, chocolate sprinkles, and just about everything else that was chocolate that you could possibly think of.

I'm talking about the whole nine. Yeah, those Hershey's Kisses, too.

Some things never change.

Carlton and Kevin was clowning on each other with jokes, which Carlton shot him with a fake laugh, then tried to drag Uncle James into their little joke-athon. "You heard that weak shit!" he asked him. "That shit was so dry he could make the Sahara desert look like a rain forest."

"Yo, Carlton!" I jumped in. "Hold it down on the cuss words." I tilted my head toward Destini.

"Damn, my fault. I forgot." He looked back to Uncle James. "Did you hear that corny-shit what Kevin just said?"

I kept my eyes on this idiot.

Uncle James paused from eating his ice cream. "Boy, my name's not Uncle Bend-it, so don't put me in it."

Carlton didn't make a remark to that, he just shot Uncle James a sarcastic look instead.

"I don't know what the hell you're smiling about. Because I didn't say anything funny."

Carlton burst out laughing.

Uncle James turned to Kevin. "He gotta lot of nerve to be talking about your jokes," he launched his own attack against Carlton. "First of all, he needa worry about that little dry-headed girl he got coming over at the house. Because her head is so dry, she could make a cactus choke to death for...," his voice faded low. Then he picked his voice up: "Now, what the hell are you smiling about? I'm not even finished with my joke yet, you big dummy!"

And before he knew it, everybody, but Destini that is, was laughing at him.

"I see that they musta slipped something in y'all damned ice cream, because y'all acting like a bunch of crack heads."

Destini barely smiled, but not in a way as to make fun of him. She reached over the table to pass him a napkin, then indicated that he had something on his nose.

"Oh!" After Uncle James wiped the tutti-fruti off his face, he mumbled a "thanks" to her.

"You're welcome."

A smile slowly grew on his face.

She smiled back.

"I think I'm starting to like you, kid." He paused for a few seconds. Then added: "You know when that old sea-hag took you away from us, it just wasn't the same around the house anymore." He sorta paused again. Thought about something. Then said, "So, I guess I'm happy to see you're back."

"Thank you, Uncle James." She showed him a meaningful smile, something like the bright morning star. "I'm happy to see you again too."

Silence hovered around us.

I glanced at everyone around the table, then quickly shot back to Uncle James. His eyes were agleam with tears. I looked at Naomi, then back at him. I guess the uncle part did the job. A teardrop almost escaped from his eye but he wiped it away. He sniffled for a moment, then got himself together again. He managed to smile; and for the next thirty minutes straight, he was cracking jokes on all of us. And I do mean all of us—but Destini.

I just kept my eyes on her because she was having the time of her life. She seemed to be enjoying Uncle James' jokes, especially that one he threw at Naomi: "You ain't anything but a Kelly Rowland wanna-be, thinking your thang made outta gold, having my nephew over here acting like a damned fool for you. You black, blueberry, something!"

We all laughed.

I really didn't mind him joking on me, or my chocolate bunny for that matter, because I was concentrating more on making this moment last forever. But then again, I knew it couldn't because shortly thereafter when I looked at my wristwatch, I nearly panicked.

"Oh, shit! It's getting late!"

When I stepped out of Dairy Queen, I had a change of mind.

"For real, y'all," I started to tell Kevin and them, "it wouldn't make any sense for us to go out to Boomers right now since we only have about an hour to bring Destini to Auntie's house. I think it's best for us to put it off until a later time."

They all agreed, except Destini, of course.

"Perhaps this weekend?" Naomi suggested. "What about Saturday?"

We all agreed.

"But I'm not ready to go to Grandma's house."

I looked at Destini, then at Naomi. "You wanna go hang out on the beach for a while?"

"Sure."

Naomi and I decided to go to Sunny Isles Beach with Destini for the remainder of the time before we took her to Aunt Enid's house.

"But before y'all head out there…," Uncle James said, while gravitating toward Destini, "lemme give my pretty niece a hug first."

Perfect timing.

I guess that's exactly what Destini wanted from him, too. She immediately painted an invisible Santa Muerta smile on her face. Uncle James wrapped his arms around her; she did the same to him. They gave each other a warm embrace. A nice long one. The way how she held onto him, she acted as if she didn't want to let him go.

That probably made his day, knowing what it truly felt like to be an uncle. "I love you," he said, while trying to break free from her grip.

"Me, too." She finally let go of him after he overpowered her.

When he stood up and saw her innocent face, he smiled back. I did too. Knowing him, he probably erased all the bad memories he had about her: The water gun attacks, the back-talking, and all those little evil plots she set up against him. It was all over with now.

Water under the bridge.

For Destini and Uncle James, it was probably a new beginning for them. I was impressed. I allowed them to mingle for a moment longer before I headed to my car and got in. I was ready to get out of there. Seconds later, Destini and Naomi got in the car too.

"Ay, y'all!" I called out to Kevin and them, as I was about to pull out of the parking space. "I'm gonna holla at y'all later."

"Alright!"

As I was adjusting the rearview mirror, I noticed Destini quietly giggling and looking out the back window. "Ay, Destini." I got her attention as we cruised away. "Is everything alright?"

When she turned to me, her tee-hee facial expression faded away immediately.

And I do mean, immediately.

Something wasn't right here, I thought. I had a good hunch about that. My intuition forced me to look out the rearview window to see what had amused her so much; and my eyes set upon her frolicked act.

Uncle James looked pissed off about something. He was twisting his shirt around, trying to get a look at it, while Kevin and Carlton were laughing at him. And the first thing that came to my mind was Destini. She must have done something to Uncle James' shirt when she gave him that hug.

I could only imagine so.

And my assumption proved to be true when Uncle James twisted around and I saw a smeared chocolate fudge all over the back of his shirt. I looked at Destini. There was a hint of mischief written all over her face; then she cut her eyes away from me, probably trying to hide her guilt. It didn't make a bit of difference, though: her phony whistling gave her away.

"Destini" —I tried to play it off to see what she would say to me— "did you do something to Uncle James back there?"

She took her time before she looked up at me and said, "Huh?"

I parked the car at a fancy resort on Collins Avenue.

And as we walked along the sandy shore, Destini's eyes were locked on several people who were flying kites. You should have seen it for yourself. She seemed amazed how those kites were doing all sort of neat tricks in the sky. Naomi's eyes were transfixed on the kites, too.

"Hey!" I had an idea. "Give me a second!" I ran across the boulevard into a small beach shop, leaving them behind.

I saw, I liked, I purchased.

I came running out of the shop with a kite in my hand. Destini became excited and tried to help me unravel the package. "Waita second, sweetie!" I had to actually push her hands aside because they were in my way. "I'm gonna put it together for you first."

She relaxed and watched me.

That was more like it.

I put the kite together in three minutes flat. It was an image of a hawk. And it was huge too. To get things started, I ran a few yards out with a ball of string in one hand while the kite was resting on the sand. Then, when I advanced a few more yards forward, the kite suddenly took life. I guess the sea breeze from the ocean gave it the extra boost that it needed to climb into the atmosphere.

"Gimme, gimme!" Destini had her hands stretched out toward me, acting impatient.

"Waita second! I wanna get it right for you first."

She slapped a frown on her face.

After a few seconds, I told her, "Alright now" —I began to hand the kite over to her— "I'm not gonna let it go until you tell me that you got it first."

"I got it! I got it!"

Okay, I let it go. "Just make sure you hold onto it really tight, and don't let it go. Okay?"

"Uh-huh, uh-huh." She smiled.

Everything was going quite fine. Destini seemed like a professional kite-flyer. She acted as if flying kites wasn't anything to her. I joked that next she would probably like to try out one of those flying saucers that my ancestors came here on.

We both laughed.

Destini staggered forward, only a few feet in front of us, then to the side. She had a good grip on the kite. She wasn't going to let it go.

"Look at her," Naomi said to me. "She seems to be having a good time."

"Yeah, I know, right." I kept my eyes on Destini, then turned to her. "But what about yourself?"

"I'm doing all right. I'm just thinking."

"About what?"

There was a pause. Then she said with a slight hesitation, "About all of this."

I kept my eyes on her because I wanted her to explain it to me.

And she did. "About how I've seen another side of you," she said, "A side that I never thought existed in you: That sweet side of you."

"There's nothing sweet about me," I joked. "I'm one hundred percent man, not a bit of feminine in me. So if you're looking for someone who's sweet, you gotta better chance finding one of them up the road. Better yet, there go one right there."

"Stop!" she laughed, giving me a slap on the shoulder. "I'm serious, boo." I kept quiet, and she continued: "You really love her, don't you?"

I looked at Destini, and after a short pause, you might as well say that I whispered out, "Yeah, of course I do." I twisted back to Naomi. "But why do you ask me that?"

She ignored my question and proceeded with something else: "Do you think you could ever love someone else that much? Someone like a significant other, and maybe go the extra distance with her?"

Damn! She put me on the spot. I knew exactly where she was going with this now. I stumbled with, "I don't know.... Anything is possible."

Her expression gave me a sign that my reply was acceptable.

"But," I added, "what about yourself?"

"Yeah, I agree with you on that. Anything is possible. That's why I'm gonna start following my intuition, my gut feelings instead of my heart. Because I know my heart can easily deceive me with an illusion of hopes and dreams, if I'm not careful to face the reality that someone isn't good or compatible for me."

"Damn," I sorta laughed. "I feel the same way about relationships too."

"Well, my psychologist recently told me that."

"Huh?" My attention went on full alert.

"My psychologist," she repeated, "recently told me that." Then added: "I do have a psychologist. There's nothing wrong with that."

"Of course not." I took my eyes off of her. I wouldn't dare ask Naomi what was her psychologist's name—just out of curiosity. I fell into a deep thought, thinking about all of this.

Then, after a short moment, she broke the silence: "May I ask you a question?"

"Sure, go ahead."

"Let's assume we were in love with each other and—"

"What?!" I interrupted, turning back to her, playing.

"Hypothetically speaking, let's say that we fell in love with each other. Would you have the strength to respect me enough not to fantasize about another woman? Or even have the capability not to think about another woman in a sexual way?"

"Wow.... What a question that was. But anyway, yeah. I can respect you enough not to fantasize about another female."

"Okay, I'm not going to mention that incident outside of your house earlier today," she joked, but in a serious way. "However, based on what you just said, if were in love, would you ever stop loving me even if I became unattractive?"

"Nah. I won't stop loving you," I told her the truth. "Because if we were in love, you'll never become unattractive to me.... If you are beautiful to me now, you will always and forever will be beautiful to me."

She laughed. "Now you're pushing it, Casanova."

"I'm dead serious." I went on to explain my point to her. "If I were with you from day one, seeing your beauty, growing old with you until your beauty starts to fade away, as someone else might put it. Yes, I will still love you. Because we have to remember the importance here, it wouldn't be your beauty that hold us together: it would be the time we had spent together and what we have invested in our relationship that got us this far in life. It would be our love; not our looks."

She kept her eyes on me, not saying a word to that.

So I added, "You know what amazes me most?"

"What?"

"Have you ever looked in a Jet magazine, in the marriage section, with those cute elders at the end of the page who invested fifty, or sometime even sixty years in their relationship?"

She nodded.

"That is love," I admitted. "True love. They invested in their relationship; the history that they had built with each other from scratch. The good and the bad; in which their beauty never played a part in it. It was the years they have spent with each other that matters most to them. That's true love that can never be destroyed, but cherished."

"Oh, I see. You wanna play hardball. But what it I started looking old and wizen?"

"It wouldn't make a difference to me. Because the chances are I'll be growing old and wrinkled with you." I paused, stretching a smile across my face. "Even when your titties get all saggy and shit, reaching down to your lap, I'd still suck on them in hope to please you!"

"Eeuw!" She playfully shoved me. "You're nasty! Unless you're lying to me."

"I'm dead serious."

"So what you're telling me, you could love me forever?"

"Ho-ho-hold up now!" I joked. "Forever is a very long time. You know that, right?"

She shot me a sarcastic-look, like, No kidding, asshole.

So I added, "That's all that marriage stuff, where a reverend be pronouncing a couple to stay together until death do them part."

"Okay. That makes it even better then. What if we were married, can you love me forever?"

"Why are you asking me all these weird questions for?"

"Boy, just answer my question and stop being scared! I'm not asking you to marry me!"

"Well," if that's the case, "I really don't know right now. But whenever I marry a female, I'm gonna love her forever. And I'm not just saying that either, because forever is one of the main ingredients in a relationship that help hold the foundation of marriage together: As a lifetime commitment forever. To be with someone as your soul mate; somebody who you can spend eternity with, if possible."

"Even" —she smiled— "if my titties sag down to my thighs?"

"Of course!" I nodded with a smile. "Especially those little, dark nipples of yours. I would suck the milk outta them!"

She laughed. "But what if something should ever happen to me after we got married? What would you do then? Would you stop loving me?"

"I don't know. What do you mean, if something should happen to you?"

"I don't know.... Just say as if any mishaps should occur."

"Do you mean something like what had happened to that broad Terri Schiavo, or something like that?"

"Yes! Exactly!"

I laughed it off to myself and turned back around to check on Destini. I spotted her a little distance away, struggling with the kite in her hand.

Naomi nudged me in the ribs, probably thinking I was trying to evade her question. "Tell me!" She started pushing on me. "Why are you laughing?"

"Nope! I'm not telling you."

"Tell me! I wanna know."

"First of all," I gave in with a smile, "if we were to get married and something like that should happen to you: would I still love you?"

She nodded.

"Yeah, I would still love you."

"Would you, really?"

"Yeah, if we got married. Why not?"

"But would you allow them to pull the plug of my life support?"

"Your life support wouldn't rely on some plug ... it would rely on my heart." I touched my chest.

"So in other words, you would allow them to pull the plug on me?"

"After ten years of marriage?"

"Yeah."

I thought about that for a second, and it suddenly dawned on me what a wedding vow stood for: Until death do us part. So I told her the truth, "Nah. If I still loved you, I wouldn't do some crazy shit like that to you. Because if we both agreed to the terms of our marriage: through thick and thin; sickness and health; until death do us part, in which we both agreed upon that, yeah, I would love you forever because I would be bound by our agreement. And besides, if I have those folks to pull the plug on you, not only would I be breaking our contract, which is another form of a divorce to me, but I would be allowing those people to murder you as well. Because most likely, if I did something like that against you, by chance, I would have long stopped loving you a long time ago."

"Ahhh, that's the sweetest thing I have ever heard."

"And besides," I wanted to add, "there are benefits in it for me too, if you were hooked up to a plug."

"And what are they?"

I smiled. "Besides not having the benefits of you riding me, you would still be my in-house piece of pussy," I said with a slight laugh. "With your hospital gown on; along with that nice split straight down the middle from the back; with all that fucking ass you have back there; and with you having no panties on—." I paused for a second because she shot me an amused yet dubious stare. I laughed it off. Then continued: "I could hit your kitty-cat whenever I wanted to. Morning, noon, and night. From the back; from the side; from the top; and anyway I wanted it. Sheeeeit, I know you wouldn't mind, unless you wake up and tell me to stop. But knowing you, you'll wake up from your coma, begging me not to stop."

"You a sick freak!" She punched me on the arm and burst out laughing.

"Well, if you said that you loved me, you shouldn't mind if I get a few quickies on you." I paused, because she started playfully shoving on me again. "A minute here and there wouldn't hurt anybody. I would clean you up afterward, if some cum start leaking out of you. Because I'll be damned if I would have to beat my dick every night knowing I have pussy in the room with me, plugged up against the wall. And just to think about it, your kitty-cat would probably have that vibrating, bionic effect after being plugged up for so long. For all you know, you would probably enjoy that shit!"

She slowly shook her head, as if I were the only one sick here.

I shrugged my shoulders to express how I felt about it. "So now you know what to expect from me if we were ever to get married. And if you weren't unconscious, without being hooked up to a plug, just lying there in bed sleeping beside me, I'm still gonna try to get a piece of that kitty-cat from you."

"While I'm still sleeping?"

"Hell, yeah!" It's not like I'm fucking some other chick right now. Because if I were, I wouldn't be trying to sneak a piece of pussy from her while she's asleep. In my book, if a dude comes home and sees his girl sleeping in bed and he doesn't make a move on her, chances are, one, he already got some pussy where he had just come from. Or two, most likely, that nigga has gay tendencies. "Because the other morning while you were sleeping, I tried to get some from you but you woke up and gave it to me anyway."

She laughed and jumped on my back. "You're a nasty freak!" She tried to take me down to the sand, but I stood my ground.

Then, just when the mood seemed to be going right, we heard Destini scream out for help! The wind pulled the kite, and took her along for the ride. She held onto the kite, not wanting to let it go. But it seemed like the kite was getting the best of her in a game of tug-of-war. She blundered forward and lost control. Again, she immediately shouted for, "HELP!"

"I'm coming!" I shouted back, as Naomi and I ran toward her. But we were a few seconds too late.

Destini lost her balance and landed face first in the sand. It was only then that she let go of the kite, and it took off like a fighter's jet.

I picked Destini up. "Are you okay?"

"How can I be okay?" she began to ask with sand decorated her face, "when that ugly kite you gave me tried to kill me?"

I couldn't help it: I laughed at her. She looked funny.

Naomi laughed right along with me, too.

"So it's funny, huh?" Destini asked me in a sassy way.

"I'm sorry." I couldn't stop laughing at her.

She looked upset.

"Sweetie, don't be mad," I told her while trying to control my laughter. "I'm not making fun of you. I swear, I'm not. It's just that you have sand all over you face and it looks funny. That's all."

She started dusting sand off her shirt.

I looked at Naomi, then back to Destini. That's more like it, she was smiling now. I smiled back. Then within a blink of an eye while I was off guard, she rushed me like a defensive linebacker. I tried to make a run for it, but I tripped over my own leg when I tried to get away. And before I knew it, she knocked me over on my side. Yeah, it might seem a bit bizarre, but it's true. A second later, she was on top of me, rubbing sand all over my face.

I guess that's what I get for laughing at her.

After a few seconds of that, I gave in and joined in on her self-declared war. I grabbed a handful of sand and launched my counterattack back on her, determined to make her regret messing with me. But she was tough, though. She held her ground.

We stood toe-to-toe, with our faces turned in opposite directions, throwing sand at each other.

That lasted for about a hot minute until we heard Naomi laughing at us; she was basically getting her rocks off, watching us act a fool on each other.

So I asked, "Oh, it's funny, huh?", using the same words Destini used a short moment ago before she launched her attack on me.

Naomi didn't answer me. I guess she knew better not to: Destini and I were slowly moving toward her.

But it didn't make a difference now.

As Destini drew near to grab her, Naomi took off running like Saddam Hussein. So we chased after her slow ass.

"**What's the matter**, Tommy?" Aunt Enid asked the young child in her arms, because he was crying. "Hush now." She had a baby bottle in his mouth. But he spat it out and cried some more.

Then Aunt Enid saw the loneliness painted in his eyes. She tried to pick his spirits up with a smile, but that didn't work either. He kept crying. So she stood up with him, wrapped in her arms, and asked him with a motherly love, "What's the matter, hon?"

Nothing. He bawled out even louder.

She decided to pace the living room floor, going back and forth, while keeping a watch on the clock on the wall. It was twenty minutes to nine. She started to wonder how long it was going to take before he would fall asleep.

Only God knew the answer to that.

She started humming Tommy a soft melody from her church choir, hoping that would work.

It did: he stopped crying and gradually became tired.

"Thank you, Lord." Aunt Enid breathed a sigh of relief. Then, as she headed for the doorway to put Tommy to bed, the doorbell rang and woke him up. He started crying again.

Jesus Christ!

Just before Aunt Enid could reach the front door, it swung open on her. And to her surprise, it was the three stooges.

I tried to greet Aunt Enid with a kiss, but she shifted her head away from me. She had that irritated look on her face.

What's all that about, I wondered?

Naomi looked at me; I looked at her, then back at Aunt Enid.

"Whatever happened to eight o'clock?" Aunt Enid lashed out at me. "I see you still have problems following instructions."

Destini let go of my hand.

I wanted to respond to Aunt Enid, but I couldn't: she walked away, heading for the other room. I followed her, while Destini and Naomi lingered a few steps behind me.

When we entered the living room, Aunt Enid asked Destini, "Did you eat yet?"

Destini hesitated, then nodded.

I cut in: "We ate at Dairy Queen and ordered some hamburgers and fries.

"Oh."

"Actually," I went on to add, "that's what held us up from getting here on time."

A perfect excuse, if you ask me. It sounded reasonable.

"Well," Aunt Enid began, turning her attention back to Destini, "since it's late already, I just have to introduce you to the kids in—" She stopped what she was saying right there. Then asked, "Is that sand on the side of your face?" But before Destini could say anything to her, Aunt Enid cut back in: "It most certainly is. And it's in your hair too!"

Damn!

Aunt Enid immediately cut to me, probably wondering what my excuse was going to be this time.

I looked at Naomi.

Then Aunt Enid looked at her, too, and couldn't help but notice, "You have sand in your hair as well." She cut back at me.

And if you guess it by now, you're right: I decorated my face with a specious smile.

"And you really had me fooled for a minute there," Aunt Enid told me. "I see you're never gonna change." But before I could give her another excuse, she sucked her teeth and turned to Destini. "First, we have to get you in the shower and put some clean clothes on you."

Destini slid close to me. I looked down at her.

Aunt Enid told her, "Don't be afraid. There are other children in the house who you're gonna get along with. Actually, some of them are about your age too." She turned toward the doorway and yelled out, "Dominique!"

A few seconds later, a young girl came running into the room and asked, "Did you call for me, Grandma?"

"Yeah," Aunt Enid said. "This is the young lady I was telling you all about earlier. Can you show her where her belongings are so she can freshen up? Then, if we have enough time afterwards, we can have a quick family gathering in here."

"Okay." Dominique turned to Destini. "You wanna follow me so I can show you where your stuff's at?"

Destini didn't budge. In fact, she eased a little closer to me, grabbing hold of my pants leg.

It was obvious that she didn't want to follow her. So Naomi took over, reaching for Destini's hand, saying "C'mon, let's check this place out." Then she looked at Dominique. "Go ahead, sweetie. Lead the way. We're right behind you."

Dominique smiled at Naomi, and led the way for them.

Once they walked out of the room, I turned back at Aunt Enid and pretended to be relaxed. I tilted my head in the direction Destini had just walked out from. "She's such a beauty," I said to break the silence. "Isn't she?"

She agreed and sat on the couch with Tommy in her arms.

"So," I felt like it was a perfect time to ask my question, "do you think you could help me get custody over Destini?"

"I was afraid of you asking me that. I don't think it's possible because Family Services has been tough on their adoption criteria for the past few—"

"So, what are you trying to tell me?"

She looked at Tommy, then back at me.

Dominique led Destini straight to her bags, stopping along the way to introduce her and Naomi to several children in the house who didn't ask—but their eyes seemed curious to know—who were they.

They all shared some quick hellos, then went on their ways.

Destini unpacked her clothes, and Dominique led her and Naomi to the bathroom so Destini could freshen up.

"But it's colddd." Destini started complaining, even before stepping into the shower.

"Just wait a few seconds until the cold water runs out first." Naomi said, then stuck her fingers under the shower head. "Girl, this water temperature is fine."

"Oh, I thought it was cold."

"Oh, sure you did."

Destini took a quick shower—there was not doubt about that—and threw on her pink oriental pajamas, the ones that fit loose at the bottom.

It looked beautiful on her.

"Who's this?" Naomi asked, after she pulled a photo out of Destini's bag.

Destini drew near to look. "Oh, that's my uncle, Uncle Andrew. He died of the same disease like my mommy."

"But there has to be some other way around that, Auntie."

"There's no other way: that's the law."

"That's crazy. That doesn't make any—" I was saying before I got distracted by Destini when she ran up to me and grabbed my hand.

"What we doing tomorrow?" she asked. "Are we still going to Boomers? Remember, you promised me." She then turned to Naomi.

"Didn't he say that?" She twisted back to me, perhaps waiting for a response.

But I didn't give her one, even though we had all agreed to go to Boomers this upcoming weekend.

The room stood silent for a brief moment until Naomi said, "You know, I'm free tomorrow. What about dinner at my place?"

"I don't mind." I took a seat. It felt like my head was spinning in circles.

Destini turned back to Naomi. "So what you gonna cook?"

"I don't know. Probably some lasagna."

Destini twisted back to me, placing both of her hands on my cheeks; her eyes were painted with joy. "Did you hear that?" she asked, while smiling. "She said, *lasagna-aaaa…. Mmmmm.*" She licked her lips. "Our favorite."

Naomi suggested, "What about six o'clock?"

I finally broke my silence. "Yeah, that will be cool."

Destini immediately smiled at Naomi, then back at me.

Now, I had no other choice but smile back with her. It was a bogus one, though. I got up because I wasn't in the mood to sit around and talk anymore.

"Where are you going?" Destini asked. "You're leaving already?"

"Yeah, I'm gonna go. If I could stay, I would. But I have a few things I need to work on."

"But why you have to leave right now? You can stay a little more. She wouldn't mind." Destini looked at Aunt Enid. "Do you?"

But before Aunt Enid could respond to her, I cut in and told Destini, "I can't stay, sweetie. I have things to do."

She frowned.

"Uh, don't worry about it, boo." I tried to cheer her up. "There's always tomorrow."

"But I don't want you to leave. I want you to stay."

"Sweetie, I can't." I had no other choice but lie to her now. "I have another job appointment I need to go to tomorrow."

Naomi got excited. "That's wonderful. I didn't know you had an appointment set for tomorrow."

"Yeah," I had to play it off on her, too. "But I wanted it to be more of a surprise once I got my foot in the door this time before announcing anything to y'all. Because you never know what to expect from these people nowadays." I tried to pick my spirits up. "So now you know, I'm kinda superstitious about things like these."

"Oh."

Destini cut in: "So, are you gonna take me with you again? Because remember, I'm your lucky charm!"

Okay, she got me there: I smiled, this time for real. "Probably next time, sweetie."

Naomi jumped back in: "Well, if that's the case, I need to go home too. I have a lot to catch up on. I'm working on a project that I need to finish up." She turned to Destini, giving her a hug.

Destini broke loose from her and protested: "Y'all can't leave me yet!"

The room grew quiet.

"Why?" I asked.

"Because, you.... I mean" —she twisted to Naomi— "because Naomi promised me that she was gonna sing me a song first before I go to bed."

"I did?"

"Uh-huh. You did, earlier." Destini winked her eye at her. "You remember, right?"

"Huh?" Naomi missed her cue.

I cut back in: "But what about Auntie introducing you to the other kids in the house?"

All eyes turned to Aunt Enid.

"I can introduce her tomorrow morning, before breakfast."

Destini looked relieved. That sounded good to her.

As Naomi and Destini were heading out of the room, Destini twisted around and asked me, "You coming, right?"

"Yeah, I'll be there in a sec. I just needa discuss something with Auntie first."

"Okay." She walked out of the room.

I turned back to Aunt Enid. "I don't think I have the strength to tell Destini the truth: until I'm absolutely sure that I can't adopt her."

Aunt Enid didn't make a comment to that, but rather giving me that—*Oh, well, suit yourself*—look.

When Destini leaped into her bed, Naomi tucked her underneath a white-flowered bed sheet. The sheet looked a bit old fashioned, but still in good condition.

Naomi sat on the edge of the bed and scanned the room and couldn't but notice how enormous the bedroom looked to her. The bedroom was big enough that it held four other single-size mattresses in there, with Destini's bed positioned right in the middle. And there was still plenty of room to move around freely.

Then, out of the blue, a little girl who looked to be about five-years-old ran right past her and dived in the bed beside Destini's. On the left side. It seemed like the little girl was curious about the new lodger who would be bunking beside her, but she didn't show it until Naomi smiled at her.

She smiled back, showing her pearly whites, but with two front teeth missing.

Naomi then leaned close to Destini before she gave her a kiss on the forehead. Destini seemed like she wanted to treasure the moment. Her agleam eyes showed it. Then Naomi started to hum a soft melody before she began to sing one of Anita Baker's songs: *"Whatever It Takes"*.

I walked up to the doorway and noticed Naomi had started singing for Destini already.

Destini spotted me over Naomi's shoulder and smiled. I couldn't help it, I smiled back. I guess the moment called for—

"Excuse me!"

I looked down.

It was a little Spanish girl who wanted to enter the room, but I was standing in her way. I stepped aside and she ran past me to get closer to where Naomi was singing. This was probably magical to them.

Naomi took a quick peek over her shoulder and spotted me. She twisted back around, without breaking the flow of her song.

My smile stretched across my face as I leaned against the door frame, captivated by the moment. It was worth it. The whole shebang! I mean like everything. Then, in the next instant, it nearly crushed me because I thought about the hurdle that Aunt Enid had told me about Destini's adoption requirements.

I had already fixed up the back room at the house for her; I even hooked it up with a small computer and desk so she could do her schoolwork on. So that wasn't a problem. Finding stable employment wasn't a problem for me either—even if I had to work at a fast food restaurant like Micky Dee's, if that's what it took to adopt her.

But....

But how in the hell could I formulate a nuptial relat—.

To hell with this! I'm not going to entertain the thought that Aunt Enid put before me: because I'm nowhere near being on lockdown yet!

I felt miserable. Just the thought of that particular adoption criterion pissed me the fuck off!

I walked away.

Naomi's serenade was definitely working here. She was rocking Destini to sleep.

Yeah, Destini tried to fight it off, but her eyelids became a little too heavy for her. Naomi's voice took her further into the world of relaxation. And within seconds, Destini's eyelids dropped and never came back up.

She fell asleep.

When Naomi eased up from the bed, she noticed that Destini wasn't the only one who had fallen asleep in the room. All the other girls as well.

How cute, she thought just before she turned toward the doorway, only to realize that no one was there.

"But," I tried to keep my voice down to a whisper, "Auntie, can you at least look into that for me?"

"I told you already, there's nothing I can—"

"Keep it down a bit," I requested, trying to lead her a little further into the corner. "Somebody might hear you."

"Boy, have you lost your mind? Don't tell me how to speak in my own home. And get your hands off of me!"

Someone faked a cough to get our attention. I looked.

It was Naomi.

I felt like an idiot. I didn't know how much of our conversation she had heard, and I wasn't in the mood to ask her about it either. I just turned back to Aunt Enid and gave her a look that brought our conversation to an end. She silently agreed.

"Okay, then." I gave her a hug. "I'll see you tomorrow when I come over to pick Destini up for dinner. Alright?"

"Yeah. But what time you need me to get her ready?"

"I don't know. Probably a little after five o'clock." I turned to Naomi for some kind of confirmation, and she nodded. I twisted back to Aunt Enid. "Just get her ready about five o'clock for me."

Naomi cut in: "It was nice meeting you again." She extended her arms out to Aunt Enid for a friendly hug.

"Likewise."

And we left.

We sat in silence while I was driving Naomi to my house so she could pick up her car.

"I had a nice time today," she said, trying to coax up a conversation.

I looked at her, then back to the windshield.

She added: "And so did Destini."

"... Yeah, I've noticed."

The car grew quiet again.

"You know," she broke our silence once more with, "Destini really looked happy today when we showed up in court to support her. I'm just happy that everything worked out like this."

You gotta be kidding me. Worked out like *what?* I really had to look at her for saying that bullshit! "Yeah, if you say so." I twisted back to the windshield.

Damn, I shouldn't have said it like that. She turned to me, sorta like she was analyzing the side of my face. I'm not stupid, I kept my head straight ahead, pretending I didn't notice her eyeballing me.

But I guess it really didn't make a difference though, because she came straight out with it: "What's your problem?"

"What are you talking about?"

"You know exactly what I'm talking about."

"Nah. I don't. For real."

"What's going on?" she demanded to know. "Have I done anything?"

"No-no-no, of course not." I reached for her hand. "It's nothing like that. I swear. It's just that I have something bothering me right now. But it has nothing to do with you."

"Oh." She twisted toward the passenger's side window.

I drove for the next ten minutes without saying a word, still holding her hand. Naomi also kept quiet, focusing on the scenery outside the window.

When we finally arrived at the house, she asked me again, "Are you sure everything is all right?"

"Yeah, but of course." I raised her hand to my lips and kissed it. "Everything is fine." We quietly stared into each other's eyes for a brief moment until I opened the car door and got out before she did. And by the time she got out of the car, I was already there waiting on her. She grabbed her purse and shut the door behind her. Then I told her, "Thanks for giving me a wonderful time.... I really enjoyed your company today."

She looked at me as if I had said something wrong. And I guess I had because she said, "Oh, you're welcome", with a sarcastic smile on her face.

That kinda hurt.

I kept my eyes on her and watched her unlatch her car door. I felt really stupid. As she was about to get inside her car, I swear, I wanted to explain everything to her in regards to Destini's situation. But I just didn't have the strength to.

"Pardon me?" she asked with one leg inside her car. "Did you say something?"

Did I, I wondered. Something might have slipped out by mistake.

My voice dropped low, nearly apologetic. "So, I'm gonna see you tomorrow, right?"

"Yeah, around six o'clock. At my house."

There was another pause....

Then I finally said, "Alright, I'll see you tomorrow."

She didn't reply. She just stepped inside the car, shut the door, and rolled down the window.

"Tomorrow then." I stood there like a fool.

She looked up at me, and before she knew it, I stuck my head in the car and pressed my lips against hers. She closed her eyes and opened her mouth to welcome my tongue inside. Our tongues started dancing to a slow jam by Mary J. Blige in the background. I rested my hand on the back of Naomi's head. It always felt good to be in charge. It's that dominating feeling that drives me. But I guess she felt the same way to be in charge too, because within seconds, she cuffed her hands on the back of my neck.

Please stay, I tried to communicate with her mind. But apparently she didn't receive my message, because she suddenly stopped kissing me, leaving me in a twisted trance. I slowly opened my eyes, hoping that she would pop her car door open and walk in the house with me. But she didn't. She just stared at me. I slightly gnawed on my bottom lip, something I didn't mean to do in front of her because it showed the soft side of me.

There was another moment of silence between us.

Then she smiled, breaking my concentration. "Well, let me go before we end up doing something silly."

"Yeah, I think you're right."

She gave me a scrutinizing stare before she slowly pulled off.

I felt really stupid watching her drive away.

You see, I was told by an elder back in the day that ignorance has the tendency to follow after the tail end of intelligence by a very thin smoke cloud; whereas it could easily snag onto a person when he or she is not thinking straight. And, in this case, it was me who got caught up in the smoke cloud. I choked. I'd had an open invitation to do the naughty with Naomi, but I blew it. I missed my cue.

My body grew impossibly stiff in the middle of the street as I cursed myself for being such a dumb-ass! But then, while I was watching her drive up the block, I saw her car suddenly come to a stop.

Yes, a complete stop … and she wasn't anywhere near the stop sign at the corner.

I smiled when I saw her car making a U-turn.

Nearly two months have passed and I have kept what Aunt Enid had told me about my inability to adopt Destini as a secret.

I didn't want to spoil the atmosphere with the horrible news that I was unable to meet the criteria to adopt Destini as my own. So like I said, I kept it a secret. And besides, I didn't feel comfortable sharing that sorta information with anybody else. Because if it should leak out there—and Aunt Enid said it will eventually—Destini might find out about it in which it may crush her. But hopefully, things might change in due time; and perhaps, I would have Destini under my roof again. So for now, I visited her frequently on a daily basis, trying to fulfill that father-daughter relationship that we had begun to experience with each other.

But, all in all, nothing has changed much—other than that smack down that came across Samara's path in Dade Land Mall a while back. And to keep it real, she got her ass whooped out there. About three weeks ago—so I have been told—when Carlton was browsing through the mall with his Spanish shawty, Angela (yeah, the same red-headed chick from Hialeah), it so happened that he bumped into Samara out there. Apparently, Carlton hadn't forgotten about the heated conversation he had over the phone with her a couple months ago. He slapped a disgusted look on his face when he saw her; she swung back with that same ugly look and kept walking.

"Hey, ma!" Carlton immediately twisted to Angela. "Do you remember that time when you asked me how you could prove your love for me?"

"Uh-huh. I remember. Why?"

"Well, I will believe it if you fuck that hoe up right there." He pointed to Samara's direction. "That bitch in the blue hip-huggers."

"Her right there?"

"Yeah."

Then all of a sudden a mischievous smile stretched across Angela's face. "And if I *do* that for *you*," she began saying with a seductive look in her eyes, with a broken English, "*how* are you *gonna* prove to me that you love *me* too?"

"That's easy.... I'll do anything you want me to."

"Anything?"

"Yes, anything. And if you do that for me, I'll even lick that sweet tasting asshole of yours back there again."

Enough said.

At five six, a hundred sixty two pounds, with a thick body frame all the way around, 42-28-52, Angela stormed after her rival. *"Oye, mijita!"* she shouted toward Samara in her wild Spanish dialect, catching up to her within a matter of seconds. *"Ay! Ay, you!"*

Samara felt a tap on her shoulder and twisted around, being ticked off about it. She had the right to be upset. But before she could put Angela in check for tapping her shoulder like that, she saw a right hook heading straight for her face. Samara would have tried to avoid from being punched, but it was pointless. It was coming right after her.

She froze.

Samara didn't have enough time to either duck or cover up. However, she did the obvious: she closed her eyes. When that first punch landed on the side of her face, directly on top of her temple area, it dazed the hell out of her! She staggered, then her legs wobbled a bit. She tried to keep her balance when she saw a bright light. It didn't last long. It was short. Maybe a second or two. It was as if someone flashed a light in her eyes; after slapping her with a shovel over her head. It dazed the hell out of her. But when she got her sight back, she saw a follow-up punch from Angela's other fist.

Fuck!

Angela's knuckles landed on the other side of Samara's face, knocking the fight game out of her.

Samara tried to run for cover, but there was nowhere to go.

Angela was right there on top of her. Then Angela threw about eight or nine more punches at Samara, swinging her arms like overhand sledgehammers. One swing after another, hitting Samara over the head, back, and neck. Then, when Angela switched her style up a bit and hit Samara with a left uppercut underneath her chin—Samara didn't see a bright light this time, but rather the opposite—she fell into pure darkness. Basically, Samara got her ass knocked the fuck out! Her legs and arms were in an awkward sprawl position, stretched out like a big *X*.

Carlton then walked over to Samara, crouched over a bit, and mocked her back with similar words that she had used on him on the past: "Bitch, you just don't know who you're fucking with, because I could get you fucked up too! Just like that! But this one is not for me though, but for Destini, hoe!"

Other than that, Carlton was still being his thuggish-self. He was still selling his bootleg DVD movies and burning weed every chance he could get his hands on something to smoke.

But, waita second, let me back this shit up for a moment! Because, subsequently, just under a month after Destini's case went down in court—which I rather not go into that threesome I was forced to participate in, on two separate occasions, with Kevin and that dick-eater Sister Mary, over at her house—Ms. Betty made regular visits at Aunt Enid's home to check up on Destini, here and there, for the Family Services. But get this, though: Ms. Betty visited so frequently at the house that she somehow became a close friend of the family. And if you think that's something, you haven't heard the worst of it yet. There are some people in the house who started calling her Aunt Betty.

Now tell me if that ain't some bullshit!

I felt like whoever came up with that idea needed to get the crap kicked out of him. But to be honest, I actually thought the name Aunt Betty would be fickle and would eventually fade away after a while—like when the Bush Administration, along with those Democrats, who got away with their war crimes against those innocent people from over there in Iraq—but it didn't. Ms. Betty still holds the title of Aunt Betty with a few kids in the house. And stuff like this makes me wonder what the world is coming to.

It seemed like Ms. Betty had become a part of our family overnight. And since no one could teach this old dog new tricks, I continue to call her "Ms. Betty" for the time being.

But you know what: I truly believe she has a strong motive for playing the family close, though. Because a while back—no more than two weeks ago—when I headed out to this new nightclub on South Beach to work for a few hours, I suddenly realized I had forgotten my duffle bag at the house. So, for obvious reasons, I went back home to retrieve my bag because I needed my shit to go to work with, right? But check it: when I busted through the front door, Uncle James greeted me with, "What the hell are you doing back so soon?!"

At first I thought he was kidding around with me, generally speaking. "I forgot this!" I quickly said, as I snatched my duffel bag up from beside the couch and tried to get the hell out of there before he tried to hold a conversation with me. But just as I was about to head out of the room, I heard a female's voice echoing from down the hall.

"James, did you say something...? Well, if you did, I need another minute! I'm not ready yet!"

I froze. I looked at Uncle James, wondering who that was inside the house with us.

But before he could respond, she added, "Don't let the devil rush us! He has plenty of other people to taunt!"

I hesitated for a moment, looking down the hall now, mulling about whose voice was that.

Uncle James cautiously shouted back, with a symbolic message in between: "That wasn't me! That was my nephew, DASHAWN!"

"But I thought you said—." she started to yell back, but cut it short right there.

When I heard the door slam, I looked back to Uncle James. I kept my eyes on him, hoping he would tell me something about his new friend. But he didn't. He just kept his eyes on me.

The room grew quiet.

After about six seconds of tranquility, he finally broke the silence with: "Alright now. Don't you have somewhere to go? You gonna be late for work."

Yeah, I guess he was right. That was the only reason why I left the house. But while I was driving back to the nightclub, I replayed the whole episode back in my head. I mean like *everything* that had happened at my crib. Then it darned me. I became convinced as to who was that mystery female. At first her voice threw me off, but after a little consideration, I concluded that same voice that I heard belongs to none other than Aunt Bett—. *I mean,* Ms. Betty.

I laughed it off because I was absolutely sure it was her.

As for Destini, I kept my word with her. I have never missed a single day of visiting her since our time in court together. For the most part, we spend our days together hanging out at my house or going to various places like Miami Metro Zoo, Boomers, the malls, and yes of course, Destini's favorite place on earth: Dairy Queen.

She just loves their chocolate deluxe ice cream.

So I had made a promise to myself, the next time Destini and I go back to Dairy Queen, I was going to order the same thing she adores.

What can I say? I love her; I grew to love her more and more as the days went by. That was something I didn't anticipate doing: Loving her so much.

But hey! I guess that's how fate leads us all through life.

We never know what to expect out of life until fate plays her role out for us to see: After the dust settles down. So, I guess the moral of this short portion of my life story is this: Sometimes we are faced with something that might seem odd to us in the beginning, but if we allow fate to play her role in our lives, she'll do what's best for us toward the end. Believe me, I know from experience.

As it stands now, my philosophy is like this: What we love today may somehow, eventually or mysteriously, change our perception to dislike it for tomorrow. And that could go either way, too, *vice versa.*

I have found out that what I used to dislike about Destini at the very beginning, when all things are taken into consideration, are some of the very same things I love so much about her today. So be careful as to who you might hate or dislike today—whether that person be your in-law, neighbor, or someone who you are at odds with—because that person might be the same one who you will love tomorrow. Just look at my situation for example: although Destini wasn't my daughter on paper, I can't imagine myself not being her father.

By all means, you learned from me firsthand as to what I went through with Destini in the beginning when I didn't want to hold the responsibility as a father. But now, the thought of me not being able to adopt her is driving me crazy. I'm still not sure what fate has in store for us. But whatever it is, I just hope it's something good to be joyful about, you know? But for right now, I am grateful for what fate had done for me thus far by bringing Destini into my life.

That's a blessing in itself.

So, if you were expecting a more beautiful ending, I'm truly sorry for the disappointment, because we haven't gone that far yet to know what the outcome will be for us. In which, it would be premature for me to tell you the final outcome when I don't have a crystal ball. So if anything, I would ask you to have some patience and wait it out with me to see what fate has in store for us. And with that being said, just give me about six months, *at least*, before I can let you know how everything worked out for us.

But as for now, Destini and I are having the time of our lives. As a matter of fact, I made plans to spend some time with her today at Boomers once I got back from another job interview. I promised her I would give her a call in advance before I come by Aunt Enid's house to pick her up. But the truth behind me calling her in advance and making sure that she was ready before I get there was the least of my worries: I just didn't know how to face Aunt Enid anymore because she keeps telling me to inform Destini about her adoption status, as if that shit was easy for me to do.

Yeah, I know Aunt Enid is kinda right about wanting me to tell Destini the truth regarding the situation. There's no doubt about that. As they say, Honesty is the best policy. But this horrible news isn't easy for me to tell Destini either. How do I just come out and tell her the truth: *Sweetie, I don't think I'm gonna be able to adopt you. So I'm sorry about that. Okay?*

For goodness sake, she's only a little girl. That's something I just couldn't do. People do have feelings, you know. And besides, I strongly feel like I was doing the right thing here. I wanted to wait for that perfect moment to tell her the truth. And if that right moment so happen to come any day now—I swear—I would tell her.

The phone rang in Aunt Enid's living room.

Destini quickly snatched the receiver up. "Hello! Daddy?"

There was a slight chuckle on the other end of the phone. Then a man's voice said, "No-no, little missy. I'm not your father." He paused for a moment. Then proceeded: "But hello, my name is Dr. David Shall, and I'm wondering if I might speak to the lady of the house.... Ms. Enid Wimberly, please."

"She's outside right now!" Destini told him a lie, hoping he would catch the hint and hang up because he was tying up the phone line. "She's busy. You hafta call back a little later."

"Oh."

There was another pause.

"That's okay," he added to break the silence. "But perhaps you might be able to assist me with my inquiry about someone whom I have an interest in, if you don't mind. It's nothing really."

"What you said?"

"May I ask you a question, please?"

"What kinda question?"

"Nothing out of the ordinary, just a simple question about a particular person."

"Who?"

"A young lady by the name of Destini Powell. Does she still live there?"

Destini froze. Her heart began to beat fast. Then asked, "Why?"

"Because," he quietly laughed to himself, "I'm interested in adopting her."

Destini couldn't believe what she had just heard. She knew it wasn't a nightmare because she felt her heart skip a few beats. She took a deep breath and allowed her words to come out clearly enough for this guy David Shall to understand her.

"You can't adopt her!"

"Why?"

"Because, my father did that already! Go find somebody else to adopt!" Destini hung up on him before he could say anything back to her.

Her adrenaline raced.

She wasn't sure whether this guy David called back or not, because she went outside to wait on her ride.

I pulled up in front of Aunt Enid's house and saw Destini sitting on the front porch, probably waiting on my arrival. So I didn't waste any time—I didn't see Aunt Enid out there—I popped the passenger's side door open and told her to get in. But she just sat there, looking at me.

What's her problem, I thought as I looked at my wristwatch. It was 4:37. Okay, so I was a few minutes late. I still came, though.

She got up and kept her eyes on me. She seemed to be upset for some reason. Her face scrunched up with ridges between her eyebrows. She walked up to the car and gave me a scornful look.

There wasn't even a trace of gladness in her eyes to see me.

"What happened to you?" I asked.

But she didn't answer.

So I added, "What is it? Is it because I didn't call you in advance?"

She looked to the ground, then back at me. She grabbed the door handle, and just before she got in the car, she paused. She took another good look at me, then finally got in.

"Are you okay?" I asked. "What's the matter with—"

Whaw POW!

She slapped fire across my face.

That's a wrap!

Until next time. Be on the lookout for the sequel:

Ladies' Night Out

Author's Notes and Deepest Concerns

Look, I could go into a long story about what I would like to stress here in regard to my deepest concerns, but I would rather go straight to the point instead.

You see, there are plenty of children (like the character Destini in this fictional work) who are in foster homes, and who are in need of an adoptive parent, someone like yourself, to look after him or her as your own child in a loving environment. And I know if you search your heart and try to feel what those little children are going through right now, you would adopt one. Or even two for that matter. And please, don't make a poor excuse about the hard financial times right now or as to why you can't adopt a child when in fact you haven't even made the steps to inquire about one. So please, go to their website at **www.AdoptUsKids.org** or pick up your phone and call this toll free number 1-888-200-4005 and ask about a local adoption agency to see about a child who needs to be loved and cared for by you. You never know, you might even meet someone like Destini there, giving (okay, I'm smiling now) someone like Uncle James pure hell but giving you the greatest gift ever: a child who would love to call you "Mom" or "Dad".

So on that note, do what is right, go to your computer or pick up your phone and reach out to help a child who needs your guidance and protection.

And thanks….

Thanks for putting a smile in a child's heart when you ask about him or her. Or perhaps, even on their faces.

From your new found friend,

Acknowledgment

Jumping those hurdles and getting this novel published was a helluva joyride for me. There are plenty of people that I would like to curse out for holding me back—but I don't wanna waste my time bashing those pathetic losers. So instead, I'm just going to stay focused to acknowledge the following people because without them this book would not be in your possession.

First, a heap of gratitude goes out to my beloved ancestors for walking me through this era that I am now living in.

Thanks....

To the best parents who have been given to me in this lifetime. I love y'all: forever and always.

To my dearest friend Shawn Powell from Ft. Washington, Maryland, who illustrated the true essence of what a real friend is all about: a friend who would lay down his own life for another friend.

You are truly missed.

Ozzie B. Collins, Jr., one of the most distinguished gentlemen and scholars alive who inspired me for the impossible challenge of life and instilled the creative mindset that I have gained over the years, not only as a writer but an exploring-thinker as well. Thanks. I tip my hat to you, sir.

I would like to give a special thanks to some of my immediate family members, but I would like to also send out a special thanks to my grandma Ms. Maud and friends Robert "Rob" Barnes; Ryan "Bum" Joseph; Charles "June" Joseph Jr. and his wife Feroza; Anthony "Ant" Maldonado; Manuel "Manny-fresh" Palacio; Tracey (my proof reader); and all my people from the Dawg Pound (Paterson, New Jersey) to the Bottom in South Florida.

Now this one is very important to me: I would like to acknowledge a young man—possibly, if my assumption is correct—who was on MySpace under the alias name of Lewis Brady. And if I stand correctly, and you are who you are, get at me as soon as possible because I have a message for you from your father.

Now of course, I would like to also acknowledge a former friend of mine who was dear to me in the past and who I truly believed was my everything—my soul mate—but later shitt'd on me. And because of that, over the years, I have written 99 poems just about you. You know who you are, so I shouldn't have to reveal that openly because we both know the truth:

When you left me with these zombies—
You abandoned me for dead.
When I screamed out your name—
You had already fled.
Your words spoke of loyalty—
But your action showed betrayal.
As they ate from my skin—
Basically you helped them prepare their meals.

My paraphrase might not last a day—
But just in case, I have something to say:
FUCK YOU!
And let those awful words stay with you today.

I have always wanted your friendship—
Even though I am sad to say…
You have become this dirty trash to me, each and every way.
So FUCK YOU and FUCK YOU again—
Because I realize you were never my friend.
So when I close my eyes tonight and pray—
I will only wish that you could continue to stay away.

12/19/2001

Decorous' Books

Presents

Casanova

Casidy Zimmerman faced the most critical time
of his life that nearly destroyed him, completely,
until he stumbled upon the yellow brick road.

Turn this page for a sneak peak at

Casanova

Available in Spring of 2016

ACT 1

"**Can you sit** the fuck back so I could finish the friggin' story?" Joey started complaining the moment I leaned toward the front passenger seat while we were heading up I-95 to Ft. Lauderdale. "It's very annoying dude! To have a guy breathing down my friggin' neck!"

"Man, fuck you!" I hated when—

David pulled me back to my seat. "Casidy, let him finish the story. I would like to hear about it."

I guess David was right. I relaxed; then I quickly popped Joey upside his head before he saw it coming.

"You friggin' asshole!" He immediately twisted around and tried to attack me.

Ronald tried to stop him. But when the car swerved a bit, he took control of the steering wheel instead. "Can the both of y'all grow the fuck up?!"

"Alright! Alright!" I laughed at Joey while keeping my defenses up, balled up, blocking everything Joey was throwing at me. "All right, dude! I quit!"

After a few more slaps on my arms, he said, "So stop the shit then!"

"All right!" I eased up when he took his seat back.

Ronald said, "Just continue, dude. So what'd happened?"

"Well," Joey went right back into his gossip, "when Brad found out that he caught the herpes virus, he flipped! He almost—"

"Get the hell outta here!" David cut him off. "The herpes virus?"

"Yeah, dude. He almost losted it." Joey froze for a few seconds to let the suspense build. Then added: "Actually, Brad tried to beat the crap-shit out of his ex. He put her in the hospital with—"

"Who?" I was dying to know. "Monica?"

"No! Jenny!" he said, twisting around to me. "So let me correct that." He turned back around to Ronald, rotating his head back and forth to all of us. "His ex, ex-girlfriend Jenny."

"Get the fuck outta here." David looked lost.

"I kid you not, dude."

I asked Joey a silly question, knowing he just told us the answer to, "So, Brad is not with Monica anymore?"

"No. I had just told you that."

"She must've found out that he had the herpes virus."

"Did she?" Joey shot me a weird look, twisted back to Ronald. Then said, "This is where it gets ever better." He cut back to David and me now. "Do y'all remember when Brad was sentenced to do a year and a day in Broward County Jail: about a year ago? For that supposedly assault on that patron outside of a nightclub."

We both nodded our head.

"It wasn't just any ol' patron out there, it was his ex Jenny," he said, growing excited. "Brad was for certain it was her who gave him the virus, since he didn't fuck around on Monica. Y'all remember, right?"

We nodded again.

Then Joey went on to say, "So, to even the score with Jenny, he beat her up out there in front of everybody…. Completely lost it, dude. Jenny received thirty-three stitches and a fractured jaw bone."

"Nah." I couldn't believe it.

"Yeah. But the saddest thing about it when it came to light behind close doors, between his lawyer and the State's prosecutor, Jenny never had the herpes virus."

"Get outta here!" David looked stunned.

Before Joey could respond to that, he heard me say, "Monica," under my breath.

He turned to me and said, "Bingo!", while his smile disappeared. "But here's how he found out, though."

We all got quiet.

"Well," he went on to say, "when Brad was doing his jail sentence, he didn't know how to explain his genital herpes to Monica; not to mention the real reason why he had to sit in the fucking county jail for a whole year. So to play everything safe, he made up that bogus rumor about how he got into that fistfight with that patron outside of a nightclub that night. Remember?"

"I had fucking believed him!" David said.

"Me too." I did, really.

"So," Joey added, "to make a long story short. About two months later while he was doing his jail sentence, his then-girlfriend Monica was complaining about how she felt lonely ever since he was in there. Constantly bickering and complaining like a little friggin' whore."

"You got that right," Ronald finally broke his silence, exiting off the highway onto Sunrise Boulevard. "A sleazy whore at that."

"So," Joey laughed, "to ease the tension down some, Brad practically begged her not to cheat on him while he was in there. And if anything, if push comes to shove, just play with her dildo or something until he got out. Or even find a little girlfriend on the side, if she couldn't hold out for him until he got out of jail."

"Yeah?"

Joey looked at me and nodded. "Yeah. She supposedly liked the idea and agreed to give it a try, promising him that she wouldn't sleep around with another man." He paused for a few seconds. Then added, "So about two weeks later when she came back to the county jail to visit him again, she told him that she tried it out with an old friend of hers. A chick by the name of Laura who she knew from their college days …"

But I was confused as to what all this had to do with Brad catching the herpes virus, though. Because if anything, all this happened after he caught the virus.

Joey kept telling the story: "… and Brad was pleased about that. Monica spoke so highly of her friend Laura that he hooked it up somehow, and got both of them to visit him at the jailhouse together. And when he saw Laura and Monica walking through the door, he was spellbound by them, dude. To have two gorgeous babes to visit you at once, I can only imagine what he was thinking. But when that chick Laura sat in front of him, with a thick plexiglass between them, he noticed a fever blister on the corner of her lip, covered-up with a light shade of lipstick over it.

"He tried to be discreet about it, but within seconds, something registered in his mind: Something his lawyer inquired about, regarding that sudden case of herpes that he caught. His lawyer asked him back then whether he could have caught the virus from Monica, his then girlfriend, or from someone else who he might have encountered, who might have had a cold sore or a fever blister on the lips. Which Brad supposedly told him No. Not that he knew about. Or at least, that's what he thought at the time. Because, as his lawyer explained it to him, a fever blister could be transmitted from the lip area into a sexual organ when the blister is active or irritated; which then it could create what we all know as genital herpes."

"Get the fuck outta here!" David's face was painted with outrage, then confusion. "But even if she did something with that broad, it didn't happen until afterward."

"Exactly!" That was the same thing I was thinking.

Joey looked at Ronald, who had just made a left turn on University Drive. "I can't believe this. Are they both that fucking stupid or what?" he asked.

Then Ronald turned his head toward us. "That only means that slut was messing around with that tramp Laura long before she claimed she actually had." He twisted his head back around to watch how he was driving. "Long before Brad got locked up."

"Fuck!" I was shocked.

"What a slut!" David threw in. "Brad shoulda kicked her fucking ass too!"

To which Joey said, "Yeah, he wanted to do that at first but he was totally in love with her, dude. So he kept his suspicion to himself because—"

David cut back in: "What an asshole!"

Joey laughed. "But the story even gets better." He took a quick breather before he continued on: "With all that said, with everything he knew about what that slut did behind his back, he still loved her. So with everybody believing that he was supposed to come home after a year and a day, somehow he only did about ten and a half months in jail. If that, because of good behavior. And when this dumb-prick got out of jail, he wanted to surprise that whore by sneaking over by the house." Joey looked on the side of

Ronald's face, then back at us. "So when he took a cab home, he noticed her car parked out front. He snuck in the house to surprise her, but she was nowhere in sight. However, he knew she was there because the TV was still on. So this friggin' idiot creeped down the hallway to their back bedroom and found the door was shut. He musta heard some sort of moaning sounds coming from outta there. Probably Monica's and Laura's voice he heard in there, I can only assume, giving out some sort of porno sound in the background, because this prick took all his clothes off in the hall. Totally naked, dude. And when he opened the door, he saw Monica on her knees, bent over, viciously eating Laura's pussy out, and he froze right there."

Ronald pulled up in Joey's driveway and parked.

"Why?" David and I asked at the same time, dying to know with perverted smiles on our faces.

"Why?"

We both nodded our head.

"Because he saw a friggin' nigger, pulverizing his Monica from the back in a doggy-style, dude! Can y'all believe that shit?" Joey laughed. Then continued: "Well, she did say she would hold out for him until he got out of jail. So perhaps she knew he was getting out of jail that same day then." He laughed some more.

But it wasn't funny to me. Not at all. Not even a little bit. My smile disappeared.

"Get outta here!" David snapped. "She was getting fucked by a Black guy?"

"Yeah, dude!" Joey smiled with a razz nod as if he caught an orgasm from Brad's ordeal. "Out of all people: a nigger. She could have found a border jumper at least."

Silence hovered our surrounding.

My mind immediately drifted off. I thought about all those times when Brad used to boast about his relationship that he had with Monica, claiming that she was the one.

No, allow me correct that: She was the only one.

I remembered that clear as day. Especially all those times when he alleged how much she was in love with him and how he had her wrapped around his finger, because—get this—she couldn't go without him. But, all in all, we all knew that was a lie since Brad practically worshipped the ground she walked on. Because, besides the point he purchased her red Mercedes-Benz straight off the car lot just after a year of dating her, he slid a two-karat diamond ring on her finger, asking her to marry him.

So I could only imagine how Brad felt that day when he walked in on her. It must have crushed him, because I know he would have given the world to her, if—"

"I would have killed that fucking whore!" David shouted, breaking up my chain of thought. "Then I'd kill her mother, her father, her brother—"

Joey cut him off, laughing. "Her dad is dead already, dude!"

"So that make it even better for me then. All I have to do is go over to his cemetery plot, dig the bastard up and put two slugs in his fucking head for help making the slut daughter of his…. I'm dead serious! I swear to God, I am. Y'all know I'm fucking serious!"

The car grew quiet again.

Then Joey asked, "Can y'all imagine something like that ever happening to one of y'all?"

I looked at David for a split second before I turned to Ronald, because he said, "Nah. I don't have to worry about issues like that." He showed us his wedding band. Then quickly added: "I'm happily married."

"Well, I can tell y'all this then."

We all turned back to David.

"If something like that should ever happen to me, like that!" he barely shook his head. "Oh, man, I fucking swear on my mom, dude! I'm killing everybody: Her mother, her father, her brothers, sisters, grandparents. I mean like everybody! Her whole fucking family. Just about everybody Denise knows and loves. I swear, I mean like everybody!"

Joey and Ronald looked at me; so did David too.

After a brief moment, I shook my head and proudly said, "Rebecca and I are happily engaged. I'm like you, Ronald: I don't have to worry about things like that. Rebecca and I are happy together, so I don't have to entertain that thought."

Joey joked: "That's the same shit Brad used to tell us!" He looked at David. "Didn't he?"

"Of course that asshole did! He's fuckin' stupid!"

I snapped on Joey for wanting to jinx me. "You fucking asshole! Why don't you just get the hell out of here and go in your house to see what your ol' lady is doing in there! Because for all you know, she might be in there doing the same shit that Monica did to Brad!"

Joey got out of the car, looked towards the house, then back at me, smiling. "Well, with all that money that Melissa has, I wouldn't mind if she had Rebecca in there with her, waiting on me to pulverize her hot cunt from the back. Because you know how long—"

I immediately went for the door latch, jumping out of the truck, bounding to kick his ass out there! But he ran away from the truck and went inside the house, leaving me huffing and puffing, with my hand balled up into a fist.

"Casidy!" Ronald lowered the passenger window. "C'mon. I need to take you home so we can get ready for tonight."

I reached for the passenger door, looked back at the house, then got in the car a little hot-headed. "Watch!" I shut the door and the seatbelt automatically swung across my chest. "One day I'm gonna whoop his fucking ass! Watch! He gonna regret those same words he just said to me."

We drove in silence, nearly the whole ride to my apartment complex, until Ronald threw up in the air: "How in the hell did Joey gets to know all that crap about Brad anyway?" Then he looked at me.

As odd as it might seem, I had always been picked on. Not only for being Jewish, but for my name being Casidy Zimmerman that is. And no, if you are wondering, I share no relation with George Zimmerman, the trigger-happy-fellow in Sanford, Florida who shot and murdered that young boy, Trayvon Martin, for being Black and suspicious-looking in his neighborhood.

I'm Jewish, not Hispanic; my beautiful features speak for itself: I'm white.

But anyway, I used to live in Fairlawn, New Jersey eleven years ago in a small town on the outskirts of Paterson, New Jersey: a criminally infested city where Black and Hispanic folks lived dangerously, with no remorse for their journey in life. And being terrified by our surrounding area in New Jersey, my mom Lillian—may God rest her soul; who never got remarried after my pops got murdered outside of a convenience store across town—asked Mrs. Bauer, a close friend of the family, if I could stay in Florida with her for a year or two until she got a few things sorted out before I could come back home. Mrs. Bauer, of course, didn't mind.

That same week I took a flight down to Florida and moved in with Mrs. Bauer and her son Ronald in a pretty decent area in Ft. Lauderdale that is called Plantation Gardens.

A really nice community. Family orientated. And you could take my word on this: It was a different environment from where I had come from. Totally different. The people in South Florida were friendlier than the people from up north.

A big difference, they have that southern hospitality.

And since Ronald and I were living under the same roof together, we immediately clicked. We became more like brothers than friends. Although he was two years older than I was, sometimes I really felt like he truly believed he was my father from all the ass-kicking that he used to give me. But after a few months of me being his human punching bag, he eventually slowed down with the hits—which I guess had a lot to do with my mom passing away—after I started staying to myself.

I just wanted to be left alone.

Following that same year, we were off our summer break and forced to go back to school. Plantation High School. I could honestly admit that I truly admired Ronald's reputation in school that I actually joined the varsity football team to be like him. He played a linebacker; I was a defensive end. And it was about that same time when I was introduced to Brad, David, and Joey.

They were also a part of the team: The Colonels. But off the field, we were more like a clique, kinda looking out for each other.

You see, Brad was a charmer type of guy. The ladies' man, as they call it. He had a great sense of humor, educated, and very generous enough to give a female the shirt off his back—if he really believed that she deserved it. But don't get it twisted, though: he doesn't like it if someone would try to take advantage of his love.

He was a one lady's man, not a fool.

He valued the concept of a single relationship. No ménage à trios. No swapping; and to about anything else that wasn't involved with just him and his better half. And I guess that's why I had a high expectation on his relationship with Monica. I'm serious. I really believed she was the one...

Key word: was.

I thought she would be the one who would grow old with Brad and live out their lives together. To be honest, I actually thought that was something Brad and Monica had started with each other once he got out of jail, since he had just all of a sudden stopped hanging around us for some reason. But, as it was put out there on Front Street before us, it all made perfect sense to me now as to why he stayed away from us: he probably felt embarrassed, if not humiliated by the whole episode that went down with Monica's lewd, sexual behavior.

So, who would blame him?

I know I can't.

And when all things considered about David, let me just say this: He's a different case by himself. He's cool and all to hang out with, but honestly, that's about it. If you're in a good relationship with someone and you wanted to keep it that way, you wouldn't want David to hang around you very long. Just take my word on that.

During our years in high school, David was always the aggressive type of guy to hang out with. He was sorta the shit-starter; not only the shit-talker. We all saw him as the backbone of our defense team in football. He kept the hype and adrenaline flowing, even when we used to get our asses kicked by those colored kids who attended that historic high school, Dillard High: The school of the Panther.

And now at thirty-one years old, well after our high school days, David was still the same, having that delirium attitude about everything. And I do mean everything, literally. I guess it took a toll on him by allowing his vehemence to get the best of him over the years because he wasn't able to hold on to a decent relationship with a female no more than about five months—at best.

Pathetic to me, but he was content with his lifestyle. It was his life; not mine.

Now for Joey … uhhhhh … now where can I start with this character?

Well, for starters, he was someone I would have to describe as a goody-two-shoes. I really mean that. He felt like he had the upper hand over everybody in life—even us: his homeboys. So there's no doubt about it, he was arrogant, if not naïve. He wished to believe that he had all the sense in the world. Or, at least, that's how he acted in front of us.

I'm serious.

He even tries to portray like he had the perfect relationship in the world; and always in the mix of everything, wanting to be the center of attraction. Like, for instance, if any critical information would come across his path, he would thoroughly investigate it until he obtains everything he needs to know about it. From there he would be able to spread the tarnishing info like a virus within a Catholic church, trying to make himself appear to be better than the next person. But unfortunately, the only thing that Joey was missing the most— among other qualities that I'd rather not stress at this time— was his dignity as a man.

"He's a fucking asshole if you'd ask me!" David said, bringing the attention back to him. "I swear, if that prick ever dig up anything on me, to find something on me and my girl" —he slowly shook his head— "I swear, I'll kick his fucking ass!"

I cut my eyes to Ronald, laughing to myself as we listened to David going off in the background.

The usual.

"… then," as David continued, "I'll go over to his house and bang his wife on his own fucking bed! Because I know that rich bitch of his is a fucking whore! I swear, I'm not lying dude! Just let him fuck with me. He would be looking for a rude awakening. I swear to God!"

I didn't interrupt David: I just wanted him to vent it out. And before I knew it, Ronald pulled up in the parking lot of my apartment complex, off of Inverrary Boulevard. I smiled when I saw Rebecca's Toyota Corolla.

"All right." I got out of the truck. "I'll see y'all later."

"Hey, Casidy!" Ronald waited for me to spin around toward him before he continued. "Just try not to be late tonight. All right?"

"I got you."

David stepped out of the truck, then sat up front with Ronald.

I twisted back around and headed up to the apartment. And when I unlocked the door, for a reason, I thought about what had happened to Brad.

The apartment lights were off and I heard music in the background.

ACT 2

My breathing grew heavy when I stepped inside the apartment.

I saw Rebecca's shoes on the floor as if she kicked then off when she entered our crib. I shut the door and headed to the bedroom. I heard the shower faucet running from the bathroom. I felt relieved. I laid my keys on top of the chest cabinet and barely opened the bathroom door to get a peek inside.

"Casidy, is that you?!" she shouted from inside the shower.

"Yeah!" I saw a blurry image of her through the shower doors. "It's me."

"Oh, I'll be out in a second!"

"All right!" I started shutting the door back just before I added, "Take your time."

She said something back, but I couldn't make it out. I guess, besides her trying to communicate through a closed door, I was too busy taking my clothes off, stripping down to my boxer shorts. It wasn't enough. I needed to do something more. Think. I glanced to my left side, then to my right, then straight ahead. I smiled. I liked the idea. I ran over to the window and pulled the curtains shut; then I hit the light switch on the wall, making the room fall into pure darkness.

I couldn't ask for anything better.

I had two scented candles burning on both sides of the bed on each of the night tables. It made the atmosphere feel cozy, if not romantic, as my Tim McGraw CD played at a low volume. It felt like I was in some sorta dream world. Animated and creative. Something unreal. I laid in the center of the bed, naked, with one hand resting behind my head and the other hand holding onto my dick, yanking on it.

"That's it," I whispered, yanking on myself in slow motion. "Get up Hercules...."

Then within a split second the bathroom door opened from inside the bedroom and Rebecca stood there at the doorway with a yellow towel wrapped around her body. Her body looked half drenched. There were specks of shower water left around her neck and shoulders. And before I knew it, the towel dropped and landed at her feet.

Good heaven ... she's beautiful. My eyes explored.

You see, Rebecca was more than just my girlfriend, she was my fiancée: The other half of me that made me feel complete. In other words, she was my soul mate. My everything. Besides her being very attractive, she was smart, exciting, open-minded, just to name a few. Believe me, I could go on and on about her most favorable attributes, but it'll take days, if not years. But this is what I can say, though: she exercised frequently on a regular basis to stay in shape. Actually, her so-called job required it. She worked at Sally's gym as a fitness trainer in North Miami Beach.

And her body—Oh, god—her body was shaped like a classic Coca-Cola bottle. 36-25-37. I kid you not. She had an ass like Jessica Biel. But Rebecca's ass was a little chunkier and nice, with a pleasantly rounded shape to it. She did a lot of body squats to get it like that.

At five seven, Rebecca had a bright Alabama skin complexion, with cute freckles that decorated her nose and cheeks. No doubt, this red-headed beauty captivated my heart when I first laid eyes on her in our junior year in college—when we both attended Broward Community College together—eight years ago. She majored in Mass Media and Communication and I received my BA in Business Administration.

Although we had planned on getting married after our graduation, we kept putting it off till the following year. But if I had to be honest with myself, it was me who kept putting our marriage off. Because, truthfully, I wasn't financially established to uphold that status as a husband to her. My funds wasn't up to par. I was barely making ends meet.

However, for the past two years, it had been a little different: I was putting in overtime at Powell's Shutters as an installer, bringing in about seven hundred dollars per week.

Now, at the age of twenty-nine, I wanted to have Rebecca as my wife and live up to the promise I had made to her over the years. And besides, I wanted her to carry my last name as Mrs. Zimmerman.

I'm dead serious.

Yeah, of course, she would joke about it. Just like all the other years without me fulfilling my promise to her, showing me her naked ring finger with a playful sarcastic smirk on her face. But only if she knew: this was the year. My year. Her year. Our year.

I held my ground and kept stroking myself.

"I just hope I haven't kept you waiting," she said, while slowly walking to me with her seductive look in her eyes.

I kept quiet, slowly working myself.

"Oh, I see." She rested both of her hands at the bottom end of the bed, crawling her way up to me as if she were some sorta feral cat. "I guess you wanna play tough, huh? Well, let me just see about that." She suddenly stopped when she reached midway over my body.

My dick was rock hard. I kept stroking it.

"Well, well, look what we have here," she said, then pushed my hand off my swollen manhood, then grabbed hold of it herself. "Let me see if I can have Hercules to talk to me instead."

But before I could say anything to her, she ran her tongue from the bottom of my dick to the top. She shook her tongue over the head of my manhood to tease me a bit before she buried her mouth over it. She applied a little pressure against my rod with the help of her tongue this time.

My eyelids felt weak; they dropped. Her mouth felt relaxing. I kept my eyes shut, feeling her mouth sliding up and down over my candy stick.

"Yes," I finally broke my silence with a whisper, resting my hand on the back of her head. "Oh, that's it. That's what I'm talking about. Suck it. Suck it for me, sweetie."

She began to do just that, slobbering all over my dick as if it were a melting raspberry-flavored icicle. She started sucking and nibbling on it from the top, the side, and all those other parts her mouth wanted to explore. I swear, I enjoyed the softness of her tongue, working on my seven inch rod.

"That's it, baby." I started pumping my dick in her mouth. "Don't stop. Get it all."

Her slurping became loud, as she picked up her speed, flouncing her head up and down. Then she started pulling on my dick with a little tug, every time her head went up, with a little snag, giving a pleasant sound inside the room for about five minutes straight.

I felt my legs jerk, then immediately afterward I felt a twitch in my stomach. The feeling didn't last long. It only lasted for a second. Okay, maybe three seconds. Then, after I busted a nut in Rebecca's mouth, she eased away from my throbbing muscle, running her tongue over my stomach, working her way to my chest area.

I slowly opened my eyes and saw the flickering shadows from the candle lights on the top of her head and shoulders. It made the scenery look beautiful.

I helped her back up to me and, without any hesitation, I stuck my tongue in her mouth. She kissed me back—hard. I squeezed her ass cheeks. Both of them. Both at the same time. They were tough, yet soft. Just how I liked them. She gnawed on my bottom lip. I nibbled back on hers, then extended my hand beneath her to play along the coastal line of her pussy lips.

"Casidy...," she began to moan with my dick resting on her stomach, gyrating her hips, applying pressure. "I love you."

"I love you too." I said, nibbling back on her lip.

"I love you."

"I love you too," I repeated. Then immediately added: "Forever, if you'd allow me to."

"Yesss," she dragged, then grabbed my dick and wiggled it at her entranceway. "You know I will."

I tried to kiss her again but, when she stuck my man muscle inside her, she saddled up, resting her hands on my chest. I tried to give her eye contact, but her eyes were closed. She gnawed on her bottom lip, gyrating her hips in little circles, getting the feel of me deep inside her. Then, slowly but surely, her facial expressions began to change to something sweet. That Scarlett Johansson look. That bedroom, I-wanna-be-fucked look.

I rested my hands on her waist and slowly started working her. She reached in and kissed my forehead; then sat back up to ride me with an easy pace. Nice and slow. The moment had intensified a bit. Her titties hung firmly as they swayed back and forth. I was enthralled. Spellbound. I kept my eyes on them. She had the most beautiful set of raisin-size nipples that I have ever seen in my life. They were reddish and well-developed. Adorable-looking. I squeezed them both, applying a little pressure to them. And not long after she got in the groove and started pumping on me, sorta rocking back and forth. I shut my eyes, then opened them back. I guess I didn't want to miss anything.

"Casidy, tell me you love me," she requested, while picking up her pace, pouncing now. "Tell me you love me!"

I would have felt stupid if I didn't tell her: "I love you, sweetie." I rested my hands on her hips, trying to control her bounces. "I love you."

"So tell me!"

"I love you!"

"Again! Say it again!" She began to get aggressive with her rodeo-style bouncing. "Say it again!"

"Oh, yes! Yes! I love you!" I started pumping her back. "With all my heart! I swear I do! I love you!"

"Again!" She pumped harder.

"I love you! I love—"

She slapped me across the face, cutting me off. "Talk dirty to me, muthafucker!"

"I love—" I caught her hand this time before she slapped me again. Then I gave it to her raw: "Bitch! I love you!"

"More!"

"You filthy bitch!" I felt my dick beating her back wall. "I love you! I—"

"Squeeze my ass!" She rode me hard. "Hurry! Squeeze my ass!"

I did.

Within seconds she leaned toward me with her breasts in my face, flailing her body back and forth for a short moment before she let out a loud cry: "I'm about to cum. I'm about to cum.... Oh, Fuck! Keep going!" She bounced harder. "I'm about to cum. Don't stop!"

I didn't. I kept pumping in her, faster.

Then she pressed her body against mine and shouted, "Ahhhh, I'm cumming! Ah-fuck!" Her body trembled for about three seconds before she collapsed on top of me.

I felt her vagina muscle contracting. "I love you." I thought the moment called for such words. "You know that, right?"

"I know." She rested her face against my chest, breathing heavy.

I kissed her forehead, then slid out from underneath her.

As she laid on her stomach, I teased her with a light kiss on her shoulder, then back, then worked my way down to her ass. I parted her cheeks, making my way to her milky way.

She perked her rear up a little bit for me, and—of course, I couldn't resist the temptation—I lapped my tongue across her backdoor.

She gave out a slight moan, so I knew it was on now. I stood back up on my knees and positioned her into a doggy-style. That was one of her favorite positions, with me in the back. Her ass was poked up in the air, with her face lying flat on the bed.

I leaned over her back. "I don't know what I would do without you," I whispered in her ear, while rubbing my dick between her pussy lips. "That's why I want you as my wife."

She groaned, gyrating her hips in little circular motions.

I stuck my dick inside her. She stretched her arms out, gripping the bedspread, going with the motion. I drove in and out of her for about ten minutes straight before my words stumbled out.

"Fuck!" I started making ugly faces, working my way deep in her. "This pussy is good." I picked up speed, pounding her from the back, with everything I had.

She eased up, throwing her ass back on me. "Slap it!" she demanded. "Slap my ass!"

I did.

"Again!"

I did what I was told.

She perked her ass up a little bit higher so I could hit it right. "Fuck me!"

I slapped her ass again, hoping that she could shut the fuck up!

"Yes!" She started pumping her ass back and forth with a little force. "Fuck this pussy! Hard! Fuck me harder, Casidy! Harder!"

I reached the peak of my explosion.

"Harder!"

Shut the fuck up, I thought.

"Oh, yes! Fuck me, Harder! Harder!"

I tried to hold out the best I can from busting a nut, while enjoying the feeling. But I ended up throwing an arch in my back, banging the hell out of her. I went faster and stronger.

"Cum for me, Casidy!"

Not yet, I thought. I kept pumping in her pussy. I tried to think of something else to get my mind off her. I thought of work. Then my mind jumped to something different because I was working her pussy. The beach. No! Something else other than a beach due to bikinis and thongs be out there. Then, out of all things, I thought about fruits: Apples. Oranges. Bananas.

Fuck!

The thought about bananas forced me to look at my agleam dick, driving in and out of her fruit cocktail. "Ah, fuck!"

"Cum for me, Cassidy! Cum for me!"

No, not yet! Shut up! Not yet, I thought.

She squeezed her pussy muscles, trying to milk me already. "I want you to cum. Cum for me, baby!"

I closed my eyes, facing the ceiling, trying my damnedest not to cum for her. At least not right now. But that became pointless— even if I had a genie on my side, granting me a wish not to ejaculate—because within seconds I yelled out with an exciting, "Ahhhh!", just before I pulled my dick out of her—yanking it back and forth—to skeet a hot nut on her back.

She collapsed from exhaustion with her forehead on the bed, arching her back deep—with her ass poking toward me—gyrating her ass in little circles as if I were still inside of her. It was a beautiful sight to see. I kept stroking myself, trying to hold that sensational feeling for as long as I could. And then the opportunity presented itself: I rubbed my dick between her ass cheeks. Then, I tapped on her backdoor, playing on it with the head of my dick because a naughty thought came to mind. Then I went for it by rattling my skeleton key on her lock.

But all of a sudden she flipped over on her back, in a kitty-position, with her knees bent in the air. She cracked her legs open, displaying her pussy, while giving me an innocent but a guilty look.

I smiled.

"I want you to eat it for me," she whispered.

She didn't need to say anything more: I stuck my hands between her inner thighs, spreading her legs further apart. Just how I liked it, nothing but pure pinkness. I reached for the slice of kiwifruit and my glass of Martini. As my finger pulled her pussy lips apart, I went down and lapped against her opening to get a taste of her first. Then I rested a few slices of kiwifruit all around her pink paradise and poured Martini over it. Her body jolted. I guess the Martini was a little too cold for her. I smiled again and went down on her. I ate the first kiwifruit—slowly—while rubbing my chin along the coastal line of her pussy lips, teasing her before I put my tongue to work. Then I ate another kiwifruit.

She couldn't take it any longer: She grabbed the back of my head and thrummed, "Mmmmm-mmmm."

And that was when I went to work. I ate her pussy gently yet furiously for about twenty minutes straight, nonstop.

She just didn't have two or three orgasms: she had six of them in total.

We went to the bathroom afterward, bounding for the shower, the phone rang.

"I'll get it." I said, heading back to the room. "Because it might be Ronald again, wondering if we're still going to the movies with them tonight."

"Okay." She poured some Pantene shampoo in her hair. "And if it's him, let him know that we'll be there." She began scrubbing the shampoo through her hair. "And hurry on back because you know I don't like to be left alone" —she then wiggled her ass— "in the shower."

Well, on that demonstration, I ran out the bathroom and picked the phone up on the fifth ring. "Hello?"

There was a short pause. "Yes, hel-lo," a Hispanic male voice came across the phone line in broken English. "Is Rebecca in?"

"Yeah. Who's this, Juan?"

"Si. Yes."

"Oh, all right. Hold on for a sec." I tossed the phone on the bed and dashed back into the bathroom. "It's for you." I stepped in the shower behind her.

"Who is it?"

I tried to sound like a transgender, dragging, "Ya-wanda."

"Who?" she asked, twisting her upper body toward me.

I got serious and said, "It's your faggot manager from work: Juan."

With suds still in her hair, she leaped out of the shower, rushing out of the bathroom.

I watched that awesome sight of her behind, shifting up and down like an uncontrollable Slinky Toy. I grabbed my sponge and the Michael Jordan bath gel, feeling good to have a woman like Rebecca in my life.

Then I thought I heard something. A shout probably. I wasn't sure.

About three minutes later Rebecca came back in the bathroom, stepping in the shower, directly in front of me.

"What's the matter?" I asked her because she had a puzzling-look on her face.

After a slight hesitation, she said, "I'm not gonna be able to go out to the movie with y'all tonight."

"Why?"

"Because they need me to fill in for one of the trainers who's not gonna be able to show up for work tonight."

"But why that queer muthafucker just doesn't call somebody else to fill in for that spot? Or at least fire the nitwit and find someone else to take her position. Because it's like every other friggin' night that queer wants you to—"

"C'mon, baby." She twisted her head halfway around to look at me. "You know we can use the extra money." After a quick breather, she added: "Besides, you don't hear me bicker about it when you have to work overtime." She twisted back around.

Just like that.

I couldn't believe she had the audacity to throw that in my face. "Probably, because my ass is back in the house at seven o'clock! When you're just getting in!"

She kept quiet, just rinsing the shampoo suds out of her hair.

"To hell with this shit!"

"Where are you going?"

"And why the hell do you care?!" I grabbed my towel once I stepped out of the shower, twisting back to her. I wanted to know what her reply would be this time.

When she opened her mouth as if she were about to say something, she shut it back.

Just what I thought.

The telephone rang again.

If you would like to make suggestions, comments, or just wish to offer constructive criticism about my book, feel free to address it to either of the contacts below:

deezee364@gmail.com
deezee364@hotmail.com
deezee364@yahoo.com

Or hit me up at:

Facebook: @deezee
YouTube: @deezee
Instagram: @deezee
Skype:@deezee364
Tagged: @deezee364

THE BIG DEAL IS HERE!
Get Incredible saving on our most popular packages.
SELECT™ Package
$19.99 mo.
FOR 12 MOS.
PLUS ADD'L FEES.
BEST VALUE
REQ'S ENROLLMENT IN AUTO BILL PAY & 24- MONTH AGREEMENT.
OVER 145 CHANNELS
DIRECT SERVICES USA
1-888-408-3788
Call your authorized DIRECTV dealer for details.
Offers Extended through 1/27/16. New approvedp customers only (lease req'd). Other condition apply.
DIRECTV

About the Author

Dee Zee is a traveler who is seeking all the knowledge he can devour. When he is not writing and joking around, he enjoys spending his time combing through an encyclopedia and reading materials about prominent figures of his past; his ideal, Frederick Douglass.